THE CONFECTIONER'S TRUTH

CLAIRE LUANA

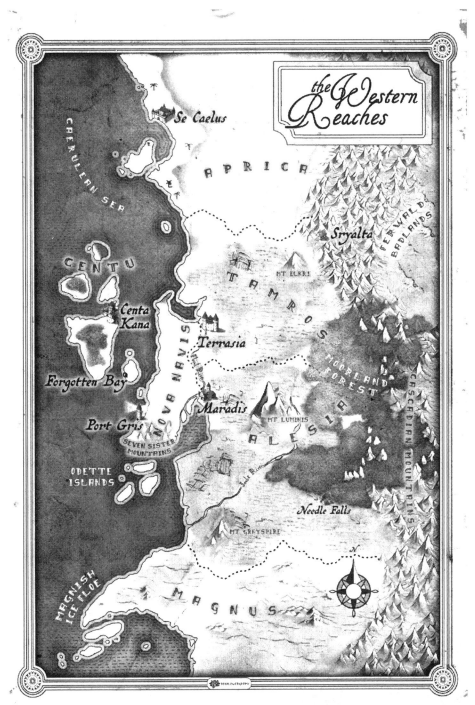

CHAPTER 1

It had been two weeks since the Imbris dynasty fell. Two weeks of gray, spitting skies, of blustery winds that swirled slick ochre leaves and thick woolen cloaks, finding the seams and burrowing in with icy fingers. The Maradis Morning newspaper had sworn that the skies cried for King Hadrian Imbris—that the heavens themselves mourned the passing of a monarch stolen from them at the height of his reign. A ruler who had been betrayed by one of Maradis's very own. At least that was what the newspaper had said on the first day. The second day, it had said nothing. And on the third day of the Aprican occupation of Maradis, the paper had welcomed Alesia's new rulers with praise and thanksgiving, encouraging the country's citizenry to do the same.

Wren thought that if the sky cried for anyone at all, it should cry for Virgil. And Queen Eloise. For Lucas, and the queen's other remaining children, fleeing for their lives. And for Sable, who they had buried in the Guild plot at the Holyhive Cemetery, with a swirl of ocean waves chipped into the mirrored rock of her headstone. And for Hale, who was well and truly lost to her. Who was worse than dead. But Wren knew that the gray Maradis clouds didn't weep for those she had lost. They wept because Maradis sat nestled against the windward side of the Cascadian Mountains, which locked in the damp marine air and storms from the west. The heavens cared little for the sorrows of mere mortals. It was just a matter of geography.

Wren stood in her room in the Confectioner's Guildhall, her forehead resting against the cool glass of her window, tracing a finger through the condensation that had formed there. In a way, she knew she should be grateful to be here and not the Block, Maradis's notorious prison, which was now under new ownership. After the Apricans had taken Maradis, Callidus had successfully petitioned the Aprican king for leniency for Wren and Thom—whose only crime, at least as far as the Apricans appeared to know, was escaping a holding cell in the Aprican camp. The bloody fight on the execution platform had left Hale as the only witness to her and Thom's efforts to free Lucas, Trick, and Ella. And apparently, Hale hadn't yet turned them in. Yet.

"Wren," came a voice from the door. It was Thom—she recognized the hint of apology in his tone. She had ignored his two prior knocks.

"Yes?" she asked, not moving her forehead from the glass.

"Why don't you come down to breakfast? You need to eat something. I haven't seen you eat anything in days."

"I've asked Olivia to send something up for me," Wren replied. "Thank you, though." It wasn't as bad as he'd suggested. She'd eaten some oatmeal with sweet cream yesterday. Or had that been the day before?

"No, you didn't," Olivia's voice said.

Wren turned to find them both standing there, Olivia with her arms crossed under her ample bosom.

Wren stifled a sigh. She tucked her robe around her, cinching it tighter.

"Come on. It'll do you good to interact with some real, live human beings," Olivia quipped. She wore a soft gray dress with a black belt, and her blonde curls were pulled into a ponytail. For Olivia, she looked remarkably subdued.

"I think I've had enough real, live human beings for a lifetime, thank you."

"Even us?" A pained look crossed Thom's handsome face. His narrow shoulders seemed to hunch over even farther.

Wren closed her eyes, chastised. "No, of course not you two. Fine. Just let me get dressed."

"How about a bath first?" Olivia crossed the room and picked up one of Wren's limp auburn curls.

"Okay, a bath too," Wren said. "I'll just meet you downstairs when I'm done. No need for you to sit here and wait."

Olivia plopped herself down in one of the chairs by Wren's window and Thom sat on the bed with a bounce. "We'll wait," they said in unison.

Wren did feel much improved when she emerged from her washroom thirty minutes later, clothed in a clean skirt and sweater, her damp hair braided over one shoulder. As she descended the Guild stairs like a grudging captive, the smells of coffee and bacon tickled her nostrils, rousing her appetite from its deep slumber.

"I guess some coffee would be nice," Wren said.

Olivia looked back with a roll of her blue eyes. "Coffee would be nice," she said, mocking Wren gently. "You're going to eat as much as Thom or you're not leaving that table."

Wren's eyes widened. "Thom eats like a starved ox."

"Better than pecking like a little wren," Thom shot back with a grin over his shoulder.

Wren's heart stuttered painfully. It was so much like the ridiculous little pet names Hale used to throw at her.

"Wren?" Thom turned, laying a hand on her shoulder. She had stopped walking. "Are you okay?"

She nodded quickly, closing her eyes for a moment to center herself. She could do this. It was just breakfast. "No bird jokes, okay?"

Thom nodded, his blue eyes softening. "Deal."

The dining hall was mostly empty, between the late hour and the loss of some of their Guild members. Wren looked for a stretch too long at the table where she and Hale and Sable used to sit—she could almost see their laughing faces, their quick fingers swiping berries off each other's plates. The table was empty today, the stretch of worn wood lonely and forlorn. She looked away, turning to the cornucopia of breakfast foods before her. The Aprican occupation hadn't seemed to trouble the Guild's cuisiniers or its storehouse. The food should have made her mouth water and her stomach rumble with insistence, but the thought of it turned her saliva to chalk in her mouth.

But knowing Olivia and Thom were watching her like two mother hawks, she filled her plate with a toasted bagel smeared with cream cheese and topped with smoked salmon and fresh dill, a shimmering poached egg, and a scoop of herb-roasted balsamic-glazed breakfast potatoes.

Thom and Olivia both nodded proudly as she set her plate down and went back for coffee and fresh-squeezed orange juice.

"Nice work," Thom said approvingly as she settled onto the bench. He himself had two plates—one piled high with waffles, berry compote, and whipped cream light as a cloud, the other with three king crab Benedicts smothered in mustard-yellow hollandaise sauce.

"Wait until she actually eats it," Olivia said, stealing a dollop of Thom's whipped cream to add to her coffee.

"It's not like I'm starving myself," Wren grumbled. "I just haven't had much of an appetite."

"Or much of a mind to do anything." Callidus, Guildmaster of the Confectioner's Guild, materialized at the head of their table like a dark shadow. "Nice to see you've rejoined the land of the living, Wren."

"It hasn't been that bad," Wren said into her coffee. By the Beekeeper, the stuff tasted delicious.

"Just weeks ago, I could hardly use the washroom without you and Imbris popping out of some keyhole you were lurking in. Now, I send you three summons to attend Guild meetings with me, and you won't even come out of your room."

Wren blanched at the mention of her boyfriend, Lucas Imbris. Lucas was heir to the Alesian throne, now that his parents and older siblings had been murdered in the Aprican coup. She hadn't heard a word from Lucas since he'd fled with his siblings Patrick and Ellarose, and she intended to keep it that way. She still didn't know if Lucas had recovered from the grievous wound he had received on the execution platform. He could be... Her heart stuttered over the thought. No. He wasn't dead. He was out there somewhere, free. Alive. And the less she knew about where, the better. She rubbed her fingertips across the face of the large ring she wore on a chain around her neck. It was Lucas's. Somehow, it was supposed to be a clue to where he hid. She hadn't the foggiest idea what it meant.

"Wren." Callidus snapped his fingers in front of her and she jumped. She'd been lost in her thoughts. She looked between Olivia and Thom—worry etched on their faces—to Callidus, who just looked angry, his thick brows joining above the scowl on his face. But behind the anger was something she thought she recognized, something written in the shadowed bags under his blue eyes. Something she herself had felt. Worry. Doubt. The pressure of leadership...of decisions...of being alone when it all went to hell.

"I'm sorry, Callidus," Wren said, a feeling of wretchedness surging through her. Callidus had almost died. She of all people should understand how that felt—should be there for him. She should be the person he could confide in now. Her mind stumbled over the thought. Now that Sable and Hale were gone. Now that the number of Gifted at the Confectioner's Guild was down to three. "The next time you summon me, I'll come. I swear."

"See that you do." His voice was soft. "I need my Guild members at one hundred percent. These are complicated times."

Wren nodded and Callidus whirled, his black coattails flapping in his wake.

"You blew off three summons from Callidus?" Thom's blue eyes were as big as saucers in his freckled face.

Wren held up a weary hand. "I'll do better." As much as she wanted to hide under her covers and never come out again, she couldn't do it if it meant letting down the few remaining people who cared about her. "Now...let me eat my lox. You two, tell me what I've missed."

Thom and Olivia looked at each other. "You mean beside the resistance fighters who managed to break into the Aprican munitions stores and are now bombing the hell out of the city?" Olivia said.

"Is that what those booms have been?" Wren asked weakly. She had heard something the last few nights.

Olivia pinched the bridge of her nose. "Yes, those are the booms."

"I hear that King Evander and his staff are meeting with people," Thom offered. "The military. The nobles' council. The Guilds. Making them swear loyalty."

Wren frowned. "What? Why? Have we talked to anyone from the other Aperative Guilds? Found out what these meetings are like?"

"Maybe that's something Callidus would have shared in one of the three meetings he summoned you to," Thom said around a huge bite of waffle.

Wren threw a piece of dill at him, and it floated down between them onto the table. "Not you too."

"There's talk that those who supported King Imbris were...taken care of," Olivia said in hushed tones, her blonde ponytail bunched in one hand. "We haven't seen Grandmaster Beckett since the coup."

"Marina hasn't heard from him?" Wren asked. Grandmaster Beckett was the traitorous grandmaster who had tried to seize the Guild from Callidus by turning him over for treason and execution. He sponsored Wren's friend Lennon and was father another of their members: the beautiful but cold Marina.

Olivia and Thom both shook their heads. "Not a word."

Wren frowned. "He did throw his lot behind King Imbris. Maybe he's cooling his heels in the Block."

"Or maybe he's at the bottom of the Cerulean Bay," Thom said. "I hear these Apricans like to make people disappear."

"That sounds like market gossip," Wren said. Part of her didn't want to hear about any of this. She was done with politics, with kings and plans and coups.

"I can't believe these are our lives now," Olivia said, pushing a raspberry around on her plate. "We're Apricans."

"No one will ever mistake us for Apricans," Wren said. "Well, you're blonde enough to be one, so maybe you could pass, but Thom and me? No way. Apricans are built like the Sower himself. Tall and muscular, and too handsome to be fair, especially for a bunch of invaders. Apricans look like..."

"Hale," Thom said.

Wren sighed. "Yeah, like Hale."

"No." Thom pointed behind her with a hiss of breath. "Hale."

Wren whirled on her bench, her elbow knocking into her coffee cup and splattering the dregs across the table. The slow-seeping liquid barely registered in her mind. It took all her energy to keep breathing, to keep moving the air into her lungs and out.

Hale stood in the doorway of the dining hall like a blond angel of destruction. An Aprican uniform of sky blue trimmed with gold stretched over his muscled form, the country's golden sunburst on his breast. His blond hair was pulled back in a ponytail, and his hand, the hand that had once stirred caramel and poured chocolate in the teaching kitchen with Wren, now rested on a sword hilt. But the worst change was his face. Gone was the easy grin, the playful crinkle in the corners of his turquoise eyes that told you that he was definitely, absolutely, up to something—something that you wanted to be a part of. It was replaced by a blank canvas, a wall of a man with nothing behind it. No light, no mirth.

Hale strode stiffly to their table and held out a letter sealed in gold wax. A bit of spilled coffee dripped onto Wren's skirt, but she couldn't move. She was frozen. She was stone.

"Wren, this is a summons for you, Thom, and Callidus. You're to meet with Emperor Evander's representative this afternoon."

Emperor? Thom mouthed to her. Wren was frozen to the spot.

Hale wagged the letter again, motioning for her to take it.

Thom finally reached out and retrieved it. "Thanks, Hale."

Hale nodded. "Okay then." He turned in his shiny black boots and walked from the room.

CHAPTER 2

*I*n. *Out. Breathe in. Breathe out.* Suddenly, Wren was gasping. She pushed up from the bench, her breakfast forgotten.

"Wren, are you all right?" Olivia put a steadying hand out, but Wren flinched away.

"I just need some air," she said.

"What are you going to do?" Thom called after her, but she was already out the door, into the hallway. Her feet pounded on the polished marble of the hallway, the plush carpet of the antechamber, and then she was out the front door, the October chill dousing her like a bucket of cold water. It shocked her senses and brought her back through the fog that had fallen over her. "Hale!" she called, wrapping her arms tightly against her chest and hurrying down the five Guild steps to where Hale was taking the reins of a chestnut horse from a groom.

He turned, his expression wary.

Wren pulled up short in front of him, tongue-tied now that she was faced with the reality of him. The last two weeks all she had wanted was to see him, to scream at him for what he had done—for betraying their entire country to the enemy, for stabbing Virgil, for turning Lucas into a fugitive she might never see again. But now that she was here...the words turned to ash in her mouth.

"Are you well?" was all she managed.

Hale let out a snort of a laugh. "Really?"

Wren nodded. Concern bled through her anger, mingling with it until she wasn't sure where one left off and the other began.

"I am as well as could be expected," he replied.

Wren shivered violently as an icy bit of wind swirled past them, cutting through the thin cotton of her skirt.

"Get inside before you catch a cold," he said gently.

There was more to say. Words, books, libraries worth of things to say. But at that moment, there was nothing but the silence of her lips, the pounding of her heart. So she turned to go, her movements wooden.

"Wren," Hale called.

She turned back.

"It's not like it was before. Sneaking around...playing at inspector or revolutionary. Don't cross Emperor Evander."

"Or what?" Wren's stubbornness kicked in. Her chin lifted in defiance. "You'll kill me like you killed Virgil?"

Wren was rewarded by a slight flinch of Hale's chiseled features. "I didn't tell them about you and Thom helping Lucas and his siblings, and I won't. But it's not a game we play here. It's war."

"And here I thought you'd already won." Wasn't that what it had all been about? Defeating King Imbris at whatever cost? Taking revenge on their former monarch for his part in Sable's death?

Hale shook his head, worlds passing behind those eyes. "You should have left when you had the chance."

"Some of us don't abandon our friends when they need us. If I had left, Callidus and Lucas would be dead."

"So what, you bought your prince another few weeks? They're going to find him. Maybe they already have."

Fear surged through her at Hale's words. Did he know something about Lucas's location? She struggled to keep her features calm and unreadable. "Maybe," she managed. "But maybe not."

"Just be careful. I can't protect you anymore."

She gave a fake little bow. "You have made that quite clear, Sim Firena," she said, referring to him by his formal Aprican name. Wren spun on her heel and marched up the steps and through the Guildhall's front door. As soon as she was through, she sagged against it. She felt weary to her bones. Perhaps it was time to go back to bed.

Hale set his jaw against the bite of the wind, trying to think of something, anything besides the haunted expression on Wren's face. She had looked gaunt, so painfully thin a stiff breeze might break her. But still, he'd have rather battled a dozen warriors than face the truth in her eyes. The truth of his betrayal. Of the man he used to be and the life he used to live.

He hadn't wanted to go to the Guildhall; the Aprican legionnaires could have sent any of a hundred soldiers to deliver the message. It had been his new commander Captain Ambrose's idea to send him. Just a bit of sport, the type of idle cruelty Apricans excelled at. It had been so many years since he'd lived in Se Caelus amongst people like Ambrose— he'd forgotten the politics and powerplays and backstabbing. He needed to remember quickly if he was to survive amongst his kinsmen. And survive he would. For this new life with its uniforms and cruelty and loneliness was the cost of the bargain he had struck, the price to be paid for Hale's revenge on King Hadrian Imbris. It had been his bet, but the stakes hadn't been his. Anger and despair had overtaken him after Sable's death, and in that moment all that had mattered was King Imbris's death. They would all pay the price for his moment of vengeance—the city and Guild who had taken him in, the people he had loved. The cost was nothing less than the freedom of a nation. That had been the bargain, and now he would live with it. Whatever suffering and horror came his way, he would embrace it, knowing it was only a fraction of what he had doomed the people of Alesia to. Maradis was a captive, and so he would be too. He didn't deserve the blessed relief of death.

Hale rode through the palace gates, his eyes sliding off the pale blue flag with its golden sunburst. He dismounted, handing his horse's reins to a groom, striding inside the walls of his new home. His new prison.

"Lieutenant Firena," a smooth voice called to him from down the hallway.

Hale stifled a grimace and turned to face Captain Ambrose. "Sir?"

The captain, sporting a uniform of white and sky blue, was a handsome, sandy-haired man with a neat brown beard. Hale hated him and everything he represented.

"Did you impress upon your old Guild fellows the importance of this afternoon's summons?" Ambrose asked, a gleam in his green eyes.

"I delivered the message, sir," Hale said, not willing to give the other man the satisfaction of knowing how much the trip had affected him.

"Excellent. Before you hurry off to your next task, I have need of you."

"Very well." Hale fell into step next to the other man, whose long stride ate up the polished marble floors of the Imbris palace. Well, it wasn't the Imbris palace anymore. The soldiers and officers who walked these halls didn't seem to fit, too bright and brash for the dark mahogany and gray stone of this place.

"Where are we going?" Hale asked as they rounded a corner into an unfamiliar building and headed down a narrow set of stairs.

"The dungeon," Ambrose replied. "We've got an old friend of yours."

Hale's stomach lurched at Ambrose's words; his mind raced to try to identify who the captive could be. "A guild member?" he asked.

"Indeed." They passed into a corridor of roughhewn stone, torches burning in iron sconces on the walls. A low moan echoed through the chill air, raising the hackles on the back of Hale's neck.

Ambrose slowed to a stop, turning to Hale. "I'd like you to speak with this fellow and take his measure. He claims to be loyal to Aprica, but I'm unconvinced. He served Imbris before the coup, and you know anyone loyal to that man is suspect."

"You just want me to…talk to him?" Hale asked.

Ambrose leaned closer, the torchlight limning the angles of his cheekbones, making them stand out in stark relief. His voice was low. "I want you to pretend you've snuck down here to speak with him. Tell him you might be able to get him out if he'll help you against us. See what he does. If he agrees to betray us, I have my answer."

"Who is it?" Hale asked, swallowing the bile rising in his throat.

"Grandmaster Beckett." Ambrose grinned slyly, holding a heavy iron key out to Hale.

Hale relaxed imperceptibly, taking the key from Ambrose's

outstretched hand. He didn't wish to see Beckett's head on a pike, but he wouldn't spare any tears if Beckett got what was coming to him. The man's betrayal of Callidus and the Guild had set in motion the chain of events that had led to Sable's death. "I'll do it."

"He's right down there," Ambrose said, pointing to a cell two doors down. "And Hale...I'll be listening."

Hale nodded stiffly, trying to resist the urge to look through the cells at the other prisoners. He didn't want to know. Not really.

Beckett's door opened with a screech of hinges. Hale slipped inside, closing the barred door behind him.

Beckett was sitting on a lumpy mattress on the floor, his watery blue eyes wild and wary. He didn't relax when he saw Hale, his fingers worrying a button on his stained suit. "What are you doing here?" he rasped.

Hale stood awkwardly in the cell, his head nearly touching the foul ceiling, wishing he had somewhere to sit. He approached slowly. "They don't know I'm here. I'm trying to find a way out. To do that, I need allies."

Beckett scoffed, his pale jowls quivering. If anything, the man had gotten fatter during his several-weeks confinement. "You look like you're doing fine...Lieutenant?" He pointed towards the gold bars on Hale's jacket, signifying his rank.

"Don't let the clothes fool you," Hale said. "I'm as much a prisoner as you are."

"And what do you think I can do for you?"

"You were well connected once. If I get you out, we could help each other. Get out of Maradis. Out of Alesia."

"Your inbred Guild family doesn't want you anymore?"

Hale rumbled in anger. He took a step towards the door. "I must have been mistaken."

"Wait!" Beckett cried, throwing out a hand towards Hale. He quieted. "What would I need to do?"

Hale wracked his brain for an answer. "Just be ready to go when the time comes. Be willing to do whatever it takes to get out of here. Even kill Aprican soldiers."

Beckett nodded, licking his lips nervously.

"Good," Hale said, striding back towards the door, anxious to be gone from this place. What was Ambrose going to do now that Hale had confirmed that the man was willing to betray the Apricans? He shoved down his guilt. He was sure it was the first of many distasteful tasks Hale would be required to perform. It was no more than he deserved.

Beckett called after him. "Hale. Can you do something for me? Do you...have that power?"

Hale stilled, his hand resting on the bars. Would the man ask him to take a message to his daughter, Marina?

But no. "No more bread," Beckett said. "I can't eat any more. Please. Just get me something else."

What? Hale's brow wrinkled. "I don't know what you mean."

"Every day they stuff me with it. Sourdough, rye, pumpernickel. Bear claws and croissants and doughnuts. I'm drowning in it. I can't eat any more. I think I'd rather die."

"They're feeding you too much bread?" Hale asked, still confused.

Beckett nodded, his face weary. "Please, no more."

"I'll see what I can do," Hale said before hurrying out of the cell.

CHAPTER 3

The letter Hale had handed Wren summoned her, Thom, and Grandmaster Callidus to the royal palace at 2 P.M. that afternoon. And so Wren found herself sitting in the silence of a rocking carriage, looking out the window onto the bleak Maradis afternoon. The gray winters had never bothered her before, not really. She'd had Master Oldrick's kitchen to keep her warm, and the world outside had seemed little her concern. This year, the rain seeped into her soul, bearing her down with heaviness and damp. It threatened to wash her away, and she was half-inclined to let it.

"Son of a spicer," Thom swore, peering out his side of the carriage next to her. His curse roused her enough to lean over to look out his window—a move she regretted instantly.

Her stomach somersaulted into her throat as she saw them, the line of gruesome heads on pikes decorating the palace gate like a string of yuletide lights. "I think I'm going to be sick," she said as her mouth turned dry and her breakfast heaved itself skyward.

Callidus pounded the ceiling of the carriage. "Stop!" he cried, his blue eyes wide with revulsion. The carriage lurched to a stop, and Wren toppled forward and then back, which didn't help the precarious situation in her stomach. She tumbled out of the carriage door onto the ground just in time to empty the entire contents of her stomach onto the slick, gray cobblestones.

The heads filled the periphery of her vision—from here she could recognize the twisted and rotting faces of the Imbris line: King Hadrian and his wife, Queen Eloise. Crown Prince Zane. Lucas's other older brothers—Casius, Maxim, Rikard, and Virgil. Poor, selfless Virgil—an image of him surfaced in her mind—Virgil in the library in his brown robes, petting Ella's cat. Then the image of him standing before Hale, bravely trying to save his father's life. A father who had never given him a second thought, who hadn't deserved his protection. Certainly not his life.

Wren wiped her mouth and shakily hauled herself back into the carriage, shutting the door to let it trundle the rest of the short way up to the palace doors.

Callidus's nose was wrinkled, his thick brows furrowed. "You smell like sick."

"Thank you for your astute observation, Callidus," Wren said, weariness washing over her.

"Are you all right?" Thom laid a gentle hand on her shoulder.

She nodded.

"If you have to vomit again, at least try to do it on an Aprican." Callidus sniffed.

Wren and Thom exchanged a look. "Was that... Was that a joke?" Thom asked, bewildered, as the carriage came to a stop.

"Surely not," Wren said. "Callidus cracking jokes? Then I would know the Huntress has come for us all and dragged us down to hell."

"It may come to that before the end," Callidus said, disappearing out the carriage door in a flurry of black.

"No way to go but forward," Thom said, gesturing towards the open door.

The royal palace seemed little changed from the last time Wren had been here, when she had come looking for Lucas and had ended up sneaking out a second-story window. Well, little had changed if one ignored the heads lining the wall and the Aprican blue and gold decorating the palaces' flagpoles and uniformed officers. And Wren very much felt like ignoring those items. After the trio announced themselves, the guards led them through the ornate hallways, past rows of bleached spaces where paintings of Alesian monarchs had once hung.

Their armed escorts showed them to separate rooms to be questioned. The thought of being split up made Wren's stomach churn yet again. She tried to rally her courage and found it thin indeed. But she had faced the Grand Inquisitor and the Block. She could do this.

The guards left her in a meeting room that was comfortably furnished with a plush sofa and chairs, a scene of a hunting party hanging on the wall over the wide fireplace. Thick drapes framed a wall of tall windows, and Wren gravitated towards them, letting the darting trails of raindrops soothe her anxious thoughts.

She wasn't sure how long she stood there before the door opened.

"Miss Confectioner?" A tall Aprican officer with a neat beard and close-cropped haircut stepped through the door, a pleasant expression on his face. "I'm Captain Ambrose of the Aprican Legion. And I believe you know Mister Willings?"

Wren hissed in a breath as the copper-haired man entered, closing the door behind him with a predatory smile. This man, formerly the king's steward...he had framed her for murder and tried to see her executed. He had escaped censure and continued to be a thorn in the side of her Guild. Gone was his Alesian green uniform, replaced with a simple charcoal suit. The pallid, pockmarked face and the air of malice remained. "Mister Willings," she managed. Her mind was racing, playing over the last time she had seen him. They'd been a room much like this one, and she'd begged, pleaded with Willings to warn the Imbris family that the Aprican forces were already within the city walls. To save them from the certain death that would meet them if they attended the public execution the king had planned. She'd wondered through the fog of her sorrow why Willings hadn't convinced Lucas and the others to stay in the palace, out of danger. Why when she'd warned Ellarose and Lucas herself, they'd seemed shocked to hear of the danger. But now, seeing Willings here in bed with the enemy, the awful truth was bared for her to see. The man was both a traitor and a coward.

"I suppose I shouldn't be surprised to see you here. The rats always know when to leave a sinking ship," she hissed at him. Virgil might still have been alive if this man hadn't betrayed them. Queen Eloise. Willings had been their most loyal subject, and when he'd seen that the tides of fate had been turning against them, he'd run. Dooming them all.

Willings's face turned purple with fury, and he moved towards her, his hand raised to strike her.

Captain Ambrose was faster. "Mister Willings," Captain Ambrose barked, his strong hand catching Willings's wrist mid-strike. "Miss Confectioner is here as Emperor Evander's guest. She is not to be mistreated."

"My mistake." Willings bared his twisted teeth at her, yanking his hand from Ambrose's grip.

Captain Ambrose grunted, squaring his body so it blocked Wren from Willings. "You're allowed to sit in on these discussions because of your background with Maradian citizens. If I for a moment believe your presence will not be helpful, you will be excused. Understood?"

"Understood." Willings crossed to one of the tufted armchairs and settled himself into it.

"Are you all right, my lady?"

Wren's skin crawled in Willings's presence; she felt his eyes on her. Felt the weight of his schemes and plots, the times he had tried to ruin her. He was no doubt plotting against her still. This time, he might succeed. She didn't know if she had the energy to fight any longer. She felt weary and raw and alone. And the thought that he could see it chilled her.

Ambrose's eyes crinkled at the corners as he smiled gently. "Now, if you would refrain from antagonizing my colleague here for the remainder of our meeting—"

"I will make no such promise," Wren said, not looking at Willings. "I will talk to you. I will talk to your general. I will talk to the whole damn Aprican army. But I will not talk to that man."

Ambrose sighed. "Master Willings, perhaps you would be better served by joining Captain Thomsian two rooms down, questioning the young lad."

Willings stood, a sneer on his lips. "Already, she wraps you around her finger. It would almost be impressive, Wren, if you weren't so predictable." He slammed the door behind him.

Wren blew out a deep breath.

"I think that went well," Ambrose said with a jaunty grin, hand on his sword hilt.

A weak laugh escaped Wren's mouth.

Ambrose gestured for her to sit, and she sank onto the sofa gratefully. "A bit of history between you two, eh?" He pulled a plate of cheese and bread off a credenza and set it on the coffee table before returning with a decanter of rose wine and two tiny crystal glasses.

"He killed a good man and framed me for the murder. I was almost executed. And that's not even the half of it."

Ambrose raised an eyebrow as he sat down across from her. He had a nice face, Wren thought. Open and honest, with straight brows that angled up towards each other, and a mouth with corners permanently curved in a smile. "Would you like something to eat?" he asked, gesturing to the tray.

Wren thought of her breakfast, abandoned by the palace gates. No, she didn't think eating was a good idea.

Ambrose poured two glasses of wine and offered one to her.

"No, thank you." She held up her hands to decline. "A bit early for me."

"Please." He waggled the glass at her. "I know that this meeting didn't begin how either of us intended, but I'd like to be able to work together. Just a quick toast, to start things right. I hear that in Alesia, friendships start over wine. Or food. Or both."

Wren relented, taking the glass from him. She didn't have it in her to argue. "That's true."

"To a long and prosperous partnership." He leaned in, clinking his glass against hers.

She took a small sip, meeting Ambrose's wide white smile with a weak offering of her own.

And then her mouth began to burn.

CHAPTER 4

Stupid, stupid, stupid! Wren glowered at Ambrose as the wine burned her throat. She buried her shaking hands in the folds of her dress, struggling to maintain control. She didn't want him to see he had unsettled her, though from the smug smile curving his handsome mouth, he knew. It didn't matter that she felt as fragile as a porcelain teacup, her thoughts foggy and dark. Taking food or drink from the enemy was stupid. She deserved whatever came next for her foolishness.

"I take it you're familiar with ice wine?" Captain Ambrose asked as he set down his own untouched glass on the table between them. Yes, she was familiar with ice wine. The Vintner's Guild's infused concoction acted as a truth serum, turning any lie to the taste of raw sewage on your tongue. She had experienced it only once before, when she had literally fallen into Guildmaster Chandler's secret meeting, and the man had demanded the truth behind her presence. It would wear off in a day, but that would do her little good right now.

Ambrose grabbed a slice of bread and a hunk of bronze cheese, popping both into this mouth. "We knew taking Maradis would be worth it for the food alone," he said around his mouthful. "But I'm still pleasantly surprised."

"I'm so glad," Wren retorted before realizing her mistake. Her lie soured in her mouth, the taste causing her stomach to lurch for the ceiling. "My name is Wren," she said quickly, relaxing as the flavor of the wine transformed into something like white chocolate raspberry.

"You'll have to watch that clever wit," Ambrose said. "The wine doesn't do sarcasm."

"Why is this necessary?" Wren asked. "I would have…" She trailed off. She was about to say, *I would have told you everything I know.* But that wasn't entirely true, was it?

"Thank you for illustrating exactly why it's necessary. Are you sure I can't interest you in something to eat?" He sliced off another wedge of cheese.

"My stomach is a bit off today. Please just ask me your questions," Wren said wearily.

"Very well. We know that you are a Gifted guild member. What is your gift?"

Wen cocked her head, examining him. How did the Apricans know so much? In the end, she supposed it didn't matter how they had found out about her or about the Gifted. It only mattered that they knew. "Good luck."

"Please name the other Gifted members of your Guild."

It felt wrong to lay bare their secrets after trying so long to keep them hidden. But she had little choice. "Thom, Callidus, Hale, me."

"Do you know the identities of any Gifted in other Guilds?"

Wren hesitated, her mind searching for a way out. Clearly, they'd already known about the Gifted in her Guild; they'd all been summoned here. Except Hale, that is, and he was working for them. But she didn't know what they knew about the other guild members. She didn't want to betray anyone—to doom them to this same fate.

"If it helps, your Guild is the last to be questioned. I doubt you will out anyone we don't know about."

Wren sighed. "The heads of the Brewer's, Cheesemonger's, Spicer's, and Distiller's Guilds. Patrick Imbris."

"Patrick Imbris. Yes. You are dating his older brother, Lucas Imbris, correct?"

"*Were* dating."

"It ended?"

"Well, I don't know. Are you still considered to be dating if your boyfriend fled for his life to avoid being brutally murdered by hostile invaders, and you may never see him again?"

Ambrose scratched his beard. "If you didn't break up before he fled, I think so."

"Then I guess we're still dating," Wren retorted.

Ambrose let out a little laugh. "Where is Lucas Imbris?"

"I don't know."

Ambrose frowned and leaned back in his chair.

She glared at him, some of her fire rekindling. He clearly thought she'd be the key to finding Lucas. *Not today, Captain.* For once, they'd thought ahead. Lucas was safe. For now.

Abruptly, Ambrose stood. "Thank you for your candor, Miss Confectioner. There's only one more item to attend to, and then you're free to go."

"And that is..."

"An oath of loyalty to Emperor Evander."

Wren's mouth went dry. She licked her lips. She didn't want to swear loyalty to that man. "Is it optional?" she asked with little hope.

Ambrose pulled a piece of paper from his pocket, turning it over in his manicured fingers. "Despite our reputation, the Apricans do not maim or harm needlessly. Emperor Evander is not a cruel man. We desire to partner with the Guilds—to work together towards a glorious future for Maradis and a unified Aprican empire. But before we feel comfortable allowing you to return to your Guildhall, we must be sure of your loyalty. The oath is a small thing, but it is considered mandatory."

"A simple 'no' would have sufficed." The unified Aprican empire. His words made her skin crawl. She sighed, holding out her hand for the piece of paper. Wren scanned the words, taking them in, letting them marinate deep into her soul. She couldn't lie to Ambrose. But could she say these words and mean them?

I [name] do hereby swear and affirm that I am loyal to the Empire of Aprica and Emperor Evander and all his successors. I solemnly swear I will take no action and speak no seditious word that harms or knowingly compromises the interests of the Empire.

"Any day now, Miss Confectioner," Ambrose said, crossing the room to pace the stretch of carpet behind her couch. His nearness unsettled her, but no more than the thought of taking the oath. But it wasn't the oath that troubled her. It was the realization that she could say the words...*and mean them.* She could speak these words as truth. Wren was tired of fighting. Of struggling and failing, of battling powerful men and watching her friends die for the trouble. She wasn't a warrior or a revolutionary or even a politician. She was a confectioner. And she was weary and ragged with sorrow over Sable. And Virgil. And Lucas's disappearance and Hale's betrayal and everything else. The Apricans could have Maradis. They could have her. She didn't have the strength left to fight.

And so Wren recited the words, the taste of white chocolate raspberry mingling with the salt of her tears.

Wren sat patiently on a bench in the palace antechamber, her hands folded in her lap. It was another twenty minutes before Thom came out and an hour before Callidus emerged.

They walked in silence through the front palace doors towards the waiting carriage, none apparently willing to be the first to share what had happened. What they had done.

Wren was stepping into the carriage when a familiar voice called her name. "Wren!"

She turned to find Guildmaster Chandler, grandfatherly head of the Distiller's Guild, hurrying their way, a short rotund woman at his side. Her hair was streaked with white and gray. Wren recognized her as the head of the Baker's Guild.

"Guildmaster." Chandler nodded at Callidus, extending his hand to shake. "Wren, Thom, you know Guildmaster Beatrix?"

Wren nodded, pulling her cloak tighter about her, burying her cold fingers in the woolen fabric.

"Hello," Thom said politely.

"Did you just come from your loyalty meetings?" Chandler asked.

A black cloud crossed Callidus's pale visage. "Indeed."

"I thought we went last," Thom said. "What are you doing here?"

"One of my guild members, Liam, never returned from his meeting," Guildmaster Beatrix said. "We're here to demand his release."

"Would he not swear loyalty?" Callidus's thick brow furrowed into one.

"He's meek as a kitten. He would have done anything they said. The emperor kept him. And I want to know why."

"Anything the Apricans want, we don't want them to have," Chandler said blackly.

Callidus's pale hand flew to his chest in mock surprise. "Why, Guildmaster, that sounds like a seditious word to me."

Chandler grunted in dark laughter. "The Confectioner Guild's stood with us before. We need you to stand with us again. Beatrix and I have talked to the other guildmasters and we're all in agreement. Well, except Pike. I can't find him, but I'm assuming he's up for a fight. If the ten Aperative Guilds stand together, we just might have enough sway to push back against the emperor's demands."

Beatrix nodded. "We should have been with you when you wanted to free the Gifted kidnapped by King Imbris. We won't make that mistake again. By standing aside, we ended up in a worse mess. They've got tails on us. They pretend like they'd trust us if we took their stupid oath, but it's a lie."

Wren's eyes widened. Apricans were tailing the guild members?

The Baker's Guildmaster continued. "No more. Together, we'll show Emperor Evander that he can't just take what he wants from us."

Callidus was nodding, a gleam of excitement heating the ice-blue of his eyes. "They may have our city, but they can't have our lives. The Confectioner's Guild is with you. To the end."

Thom cast a look of tense excitement at Wren, but she found she couldn't return it. Warning bells rang loudly in her mind. She had heard talk like this before, had been the one whispering it herself. It was the kind of talk that changed the tide of lives—of nations. And it was the type of talk that would get them all killed.

CHAPTER 5

Olivia stomped through the halls of the Guildhall, her turquoise skirt swishing about her. She'd finally convinced the comptroller to give her a look at the Guild's books, and what she'd seen was atrocious. Callidus hadn't collected rents on use of the Guild's artesian wells for the past two weeks. The Guild depended on that income—how did Callidus expect her to keep them all fed if he couldn't be bothered to collect their debts? "Fool man," she muttered, thundering down the stairs from the top floor. His office had been empty. Where was he? "Probably hiding in some kitchen," Olivia said under her breath, striding into the hallway that housed the teaching kitchens. "After I'm done with him, he'll wish he had a place to hide."

Olivia poked her head into two dark kitchens before she found one that was occupied. Lennon and Marina were within.

Olivia stifled a grimace at the sight of Marina. She didn't mind Lennon, but she and Marina had never gotten along. Seated on a stool, the girl was bent over a bowl, whisking furiously. Lennon was standing in the corner, his shirtsleeves rolled up, a canvas apron tied tightly around his narrow waist. His dark hair was mussed, his kind features sallow. But his fatigue seemed to melt away when he saw her paused in the doorway. "Olivia!" he said. "What're you doing here?"

"Looking for Callidus," she said. "Have you seen him?"

Marina turned. Her dark brown tresses were pulled into a high bun with a few wisps escaping, her dark-rimmed glasses sliding down her nose. "I saw Callidus, Wren, and Thom skulk off a few hours ago. I guess they were summoned to the palace," Marina said coolly. "No doubt they're on some new secret mission, leaving the rest of us to mind the shop without them."

Summoned to the palace? Why? Olivia walked over, examining what was on Lennon's tray.

"Coconut patties," he explained.

Marina rolled her eyes. "I told him no one likes coconut, but he couldn't be dissuaded."

"I think they smell heavenly." Olivia laid a kind hand on his arm, trying to soothe the sting of Marina's comment. "And I like coconut."

"What're you making, Marina?" Olivia then asked, trying to be nice. It was like pulling teeth, but her grandaunt had taught her to be polite. Olivia's thoughts stuttered like they always did when she hit a memory of her Grandaunt Iris Greer. The woman who'd betrayed them all and murdered her own twin brother. Olivia clearly needed to find a new role model.

"Rosewater meringues," Marine replied to Olivia's question. "And I better be done soon because I think my arm is about to fall off."

"Do you know anything else about this summons? What do the Apricans want with Callidus?" Olivia asked.

Marina narrowed her eyes. "Don't you mean what do they want with Wren and Thom? I'm so sick of those three galivanting about like the rules don't apply to them."

Olivia was starting to agree, though Marina's evaluation did seem a tad harsh. "Thom had been kidnapped. They were trying to rescue him."

"My father's been missing for two weeks. No one's lifted a flaming finger to find him," Marina snapped. "I asked Callidus to find out if the Apricans were holding him, but all I got was a non-committal 'I'll try.'" Marina said the last words with vicious mockery. "It's like if you're not in their special circle, they can't be bothered to care."

Olivia pursed her lips, wishing Marina's words didn't strike so close to home. Wren and Thom were supposed to be her friends, but lately they'd felt like strangers to her. She didn't even understand what had happened with Hale, not to mention poor Sable. It was like she'd woken one day and her home had been turned upside down, filled instead with murderers and mysteries and tragedy.

"They'll find your father," Lennon soothed Marina. "I'm sure Callidus is doing everything he can. It's probably just a misunderstanding."

"Absolutely," Olivia murmured in agreement. Lennon met Olivia's eyes, and she saw doubt there that mirrored her own. Before the city fell, Marina's father Beckett had thrown his lot in with King Imbris. And supporters of the late King Imbris...weren't faring well under the new regime.

Suddenly, Olivia needed to be gone from this place. She had troubles of her own without taking on Marina's. "If you see Callidus, will you tell him I'm looking for him?"

"Will do." Lennon nodded at her.

Olivia hurried into the hallway, turning on a whim into the conservatory. Its humid warmth washed over her, thawing the sudden chill that had just come upon her. Olivia took a steadying breath. This Guildhall had always been her home, but lately, it felt like foreign territory. The whole city felt strange and new. Dangerous. She'd thought she had friends, allies, but those seemed to have disappeared too. Wren was like a ghost, a phantom version of herself lost in her own private sorrows. Olivia sighed. Alone or not, Olivia needed to find her footing in this new world—and fast. Or she had a sinking feeling she'd end up like poor Guildmaster Beckett. Vanished without a trace.

Silence hung between Wren, Thom, and Callidus as the carriage shuddered to motion and pulled them back towards the thick of the city.

"What happened in your meetings?" Thom finally said, breaking the silence like an egg into custard. "Did you...drink anything?" Thom asked.

"Ice wine," Callidus said. "Nasty stuff. I refused and was gently told that refusing was not an option."

Wren pursed her lips. No need to share that she had fallen for it.

"They wanted to know about the other Gifted," Wren said. "And about Lucas and Trick."

"Same," Thom said. "And they want us to cooperate with the Aprican confectioners and share knowledge. Teach them our Gifts."

"Gifting can't be taught. They'll learn soon enough," Wren said. "Maybe they think they have more of us...with raw talent. It couldn't be all bad to have more Gifted around, could it?"

"Yes, what could be better than an army of magicians loyal to Aprica?" Callidus said.

Wren glowered.

"Do you think it's true, what Beatrix said? They're following us?" Thom asked. "Keeping tabs? It means...we can't leave, doesn't it?"

Wren tipped her head back against the interior of the carriage. "It's not like we have anywhere to go."

"Somewhere out there is safe from the Apricans," said Thom. "Lucas and Trick..."

"There's nowhere safe from the Apricans," Callidus murmured. "Not now."

"You two are just rays of blooming sunshine, aren't you?" Thom banged his fist on his knee. "If you don't think we should run, what do you think we should do?"

Wren lifted her head in surprise. She didn't think she'd ever seen Thom angry.

Callidus looked at them both, his dark eyes penetrating. "Isn't it obvious? There's only one thing to do."

Wren tended to agree. Keep their heads down. Stay alive. Hope the Apricans grew sick of the rain and headed home to bluer skies.

"What?" Thom asked.

Callidus's voice was as hard as steel. "We overthrow this king too."

Wren tipped forward, burying her head in her hands with a strangled laugh. Not this—not again. She had toyed with politics once, had treated it like a game. And look what had happened. Sable had ended up dead. Hale was an enemy. She had betrayed Lucas in her desperation—the Apricans had used the very key Lucas had given her to take Maradis, and all of Alesia. In winning, they had lost. "No," she said, the word muffled in her hands.

"No?" Callidus scoffed. "You were always the one leading the charge! I need you in this, Wren."

She looked up. "No. No. Just...no. I can't believe I'm the one having to be the voice of reason. I'm out."

"You're going to let them have everything? The city? The wells? The Gifted? Your infused chocolates? Your life? Because what, you're...tired?" Callidus said.

"Not because I'm tired. Because I'm weary to the marrow of my bones," Wren said. *How to explain?* "And I'm heartbroken. My boyfriend is in exile. My friends are dead. And...I don't want to end up like them."

Callidus shook his head. "We started something, Wren. We and the other Guilds. We can't leave things worse than they were when we started. We have to finish it."

"You can worry about your legacy as guildmaster. I'll worry about— "

"Yourself," Callidus retorted.

Wren wanted to grab him by the lapels of his black jacket and shake him. "We're just people, Callidus. I thought wanting to make something better was enough. But...it's too big. This is the might of the Aprican army. We're just...people."

Callidus shook his head, his gaze fixed out the window. "Anything that ever changed was done by just a person. I suppose—"

But Callidus's words were ripped from the air as a deafening boom rocked the carriage.

Wren's hand shot out against the carriage wall to steady herself, but it was futile. Another wracking boom sounded, the noise rumbling through her like an earthquake.

Then tipping...tumbling...and the world turned sideways.

CHAPTER 6

It was hard to make sense of this tumbled, smoky world. Wren blinked and tried to focus through the ringing in her ears and the pounding in her head. She'd landed in a tumble of gangly arms and legs between Thom and Callidus. She wasn't sure where one of them left off and the other began.

"What was that?" Wren gasped.

"The carriage tipped." Thom groaned, pushing off the side of the carriage, which currently served as the floor.

"Watch the glass from the window," Callidus said, uncoiling himself to come to a halfway-seated position. He reached out and picked a large shard of glass from Wren's auburn curls, tossing it into the corner.

Another boom sounded outside and a rush of heat swept past them, palpable enough to touch. Curls of gray smoke were beginning to creep through the seams of the carriage door in grasping greedy tendrils.

"Something's burning," Thom said, getting to his feet. Thom was tall enough to reach the handle of the carriage door above them. He wiggled it. "It's stuck."

With those words, the carriage seemed to shrink several sizes around them. "What?" Wren barely recognized her own high-pitched voice. The window above them was leaded glass, and though the glass had shaken free in the explosion, it was still crossed with diamonds of metal. They wouldn't be able to climb out if the door wouldn't open. She coughed. Smoke was filling the narrow space of the carriage with sickly pallor. Another pop outside made Wren jump, shying against Callidus.

Callidus stood and then reached down and helped Wren to her feet. His ridiculous coiffed hair was hanging low over his forehead, no longer defying gravity in its normal fashion. His pale face was grave.

"Can you jostle it free?" Callidus asked.

Thom banged on the door with his fist—once, twice, three times. It didn't budge.

Wren felt herself tilt, her vision blur. Despite the heat of whatever was going on outside, baking the side of the carriage, a cold chill washed over her, beading pinpricks of sweat on her brow.

"Don't leave us, Wren," Callidus said, grasping her elbows as she started to teeter over. "We're going to get out of here." He coughed, putting his arm over his mouth. "Sit down, stay low." He helped her to the ground, gently lowering her onto the shards of littered glass.

Thom continued to bang on the door above them, jumping, trying to hit it with his shoulder, anything. "It's not opening." He coughed into his elbow, looking around. "Can we get through the roof?"

"Carriages have a wooden frame." Callidus shook his head. "Maybe with an axe."

"Anyone have an axe?" Thom asked weakly.

"Any other ideas?" Callidus looked from Thom to Wren. Down below the smoke, her vision had cleared. She had an idea, sort of. She took a deep breath and screamed, "Help!"

Thom and Callidus joined her in a chorus of shouting and banging. Their flurry of activity fell silent as the first licks of flame undulated through a seam on the carriage's floor. Thom and Callidus shied away, backing up against the far wall with her.

"Anyone have any chocolate?" Thom asked weakly.

"We'll need more than lucky chocolate to get us out of here," Wren croaked. Her eyes burned, tears leaking from the corners.

"I just thought it would be nice to be eating chocolate when I died."

"That would be nice." Wren closed her eyes, trying to bring to mind the flavors of cacao and milk, rather than the bitter taste of ash and smoke.

The carriage rocked around them, and they all cried out. "What's happening?" Wren asked.

The door above them wrenched open, literally ripped off its hinges, exposing a hellscape of flame and smoke. And haloed by it all was a golden-haired man in an Aprican uniform. He reached down a hand. "Come on!"

"You first, Wren," Callidus cried, pushing her to her feet. She locked wrists with their rescuer and he lifted her out through the carriage door as easily as if she were a sack of flour. He deposited her on the side of the overturned carriage before bending back down for Thom and Callidus.

Wren's mouth fell open as she surveyed the scene. The entire city block behind them was awash in flames—buildings crumbling and debris littering the street. Oily black clouds chugged skyward—the drizzle of the gray Maradis day doing little to quench the inferno. Callidus was clambering out of the carriage now with the help of the Aprican, and Wren unsteadily made her way down from the carriage, cringing at the body of the horse that had been pulling them, a large chunk of wood protruding from its side, blood watering the cobblestone streets. She looked around for their driver and found him tossed across the street, groaning and stirring. She breathed out. At least the man was alive.

Thom was out of the carriage now and the three men were climbing down.

"Get back." The Aprican man pointed across the street, ushering them farther from the growing flames. They turned and watched the billowing flames from the other side of the street as their Aprican savior went to check on the driver. Two other carriages had been caught in the explosion; one was completely enveloped in flame and the other appeared empty, its horse cut from its harness. Cedar Guards and Aprican soldiers were running from down the street to put out the blaze.

"What in the Beekeeper's name was this?" Callidus breathed, his fingers laced through his hair.

"This is man's doing," the Aprican returned, surveying the scene. "Rebel scum don't care if innocents are killed." He spit on the ground.

Wren studied him. He was tall and broad like most Apricans, but with darker, dirty-blond hair cut strangely, longer on the top, with the sides cropped short, a tidy beard covering his round jaw. A faint scar shadowed one fine cheekbone. He met her gaze boldly, and she didn't look away. His eyes were the deep brown of raw cacao, rather than the crystalline blue of most Apricans.

"Rebels did this?" Callidus asked. "Why?"

"Half the flour stores in Maradis were in that warehouse," the man said.

"How do you know? This is the Guild Quarter. Why would there be grain stores here?"

"Because we just moved them here two days ago. To keep them safe from rebel attack."

Guess that didn't work, Wren thought.

"Who are these rebels? Why would they want the city to go hungry?" Thom asked. His face was streaked with soot, and ash was raining down softly, landing in the curls of his hair.

"They call themselves the Falconers. We've just started hearing whispers of the name, seeing pairs of wings scrawled on walls. Hungry leads to angry. And angry makes it easier to recruit to their cause."

"Swarms," Callidus said, seeming to deflate.

The Falconers. The Falcon was the royal crest of Clan Imbris, the clan of the late king. It seemed these rebels weren't taking the death of their monarch sitting down.

"You three inhaled a lot of smoke. Do you need a doctor? I can call another carriage to take you to the hospital."

"No more carriages," Wren burst out.

The man inclined his head, his hand resting on the sunburst on the pommel of his sword.

"The Guildhall is only a five-minute walk from here," Thom said. "We can make it."

"I'm happy to walk with you," the soldier said as they slowly turned from the mesmerizing scene of flame and smoke.

"A kind offer, but we can make it from here. I'm sure you must have more pressing business." Callidus's smile was tightlipped.

"Actually, I don't," the man said, sauntering between Thom and Callidus. It seemed this man wasn't taking *no* for an answer. Strange.

"Very well. I'm Guildmaster Callidus."

"I know who you are, Guildmaster. I'm Lieutenant Dashiell Cardas. You can call me 'Dash.'" The two men shook hands.

"Thom Percival." Thom waved.

Wren said nothing, her smoke-addled mind slowly working on something. How did a random Aprican lieutenant know who Callidus was? And where the grain was? And how was he in the right place to save them...? And why was he so eager to walk them home...?

"That's Wren," Callidus said. "Not sure what's gotten her tongue."

"You three went through quite a scare," Dash said. "It's not surprising the lady needs a moment to gather herself."

"I don't need to gather myself," Wren snapped, though in truth, she likely did. She had figured it out. "You're our tail, aren't you? You were right there, ready to save us—because you were assigned to us."

Dash grinned, flashing a row of small, white teeth. "I don't see any reason to hide it. We're going to be spending a lot of time together over the next few months. Might as well get to know each other. I know I'd rather be having a drink with you lot than skulking in the shadows all winter long."

"We're free Alesian citizens. We don't need a watchdog. Or a babysitter," Callidus said.

"Seems like it came in handy today, didn't it?" Dash pointed out, pulling a toothpick from his pocket and sticking it in his mouth.

Callidus didn't have a response to that.

"Change is always hard, but it won't be so bad, you wait. Everyone thought the sky was falling when the Apricans marched on Tarrasia, but it ended up being the best thing that could have happened to us."

"You're Tamrosi?" Thom asked.

"Born and bred," Dash said proudly. That explained the brown eyes and darker coloring.

"But you work for the Apricans," Wren said. "You're a traitor to your people."

"Ain't traitorous to secure a good job to provide for your family. I'm not the one blowing up buildings," he pointed out.

Wren opened her mouth to retort, but Callidus silenced her with a withering side-glare that said, *This is not the time for intellectual debates.*

Dash whistled as they turned from the cobblestones of Guilder's Row to summit the marble steps of the Confectioner's Guildhouse. "You Alesians sure like your sweets."

"You have no idea," Thom muttered.

Callidus paused, pulling himself up to his full height. He looked ridiculous, soot staining his narrow features, smeared by the mist like running mascara. "We owe you a debt of gratitude for saving us today. And if you've been assigned to us, the least we can do is make you comfortable. I will see that our Guildmistress finds you adequate chambers."

"Callidus!" Wren hissed.

He held up a hand and she glowered at it. Giving this soldier rooms in the Guildhall? Why not invite the emperor to a dinner party?

"That will be more than adequate," Dash said gallantly. "Thank you for your hospitality."

They walked up the stairs and into the antechamber of the Guildhall. Wren relaxed as the warmth from the building washed over her. A bath. She wanted a bath very badly.

"Who is this Guildmistress I should be seeking?" Dash asked.

"Ah, here she is now," Callidus said.

Olivia had just emerged from the far hallway and was striding their way with purpose. She pulled up short when she saw them, taking in their soot-stained clothes and faces. "What happened to you?" And then she took in Lieutenant Cardas, and her blue eyes widened, her pink lips forming a little O. Wren supposed Dash was quite handsome, if you set aside the fact that he was a professional stalker hired by the emperor.

"We had a bit of an afternoon," Callidus said with dripping sarcasm.

"Who...?" Olivia trailed off, still riveted by the Aprican soldier.

"Lieutenant Dashiell Cardas," he said, taking her hand and bowing low over it, gracing her knuckles with a kiss.

Wren rolled her eyes.

"He'll be staying here. Find him a chamber please, etcetera," Callidus said, heading up the stairs.

Wren gave Thom and Olivia a weary smile before following, the sound of Dash's low murmur and Olivia's tinkling laughter chasing her all the way. She heaved a sigh. It seemed that they'd just let a fox into the henhouse. And there wasn't a flaming thing she could do about it.

CHAPTER 7

There was a ship on the horizon.

Lucas squinted through the telescope, blinking to clear his vision. It came back into focus—a dark speck against a palette of gray and blue. It was too distant to make out what flag it flew. Lucas wasn't sure if it mattered. They were stranded here, but for a little sailing skiff that could hardly be trusted to get to the next island. If the Apricans had found them, they'd have nowhere to run.

Lucas drained the dregs of his coffee, grimacing as it slid down. The drink had gone cold. Had he been sitting up here so long? He couldn't remember. Time had a way of sifting through his fingers in this monochromatic house, with nothing but sea and fog around them. Or maybe it was the fact that for the first time in his life, he had absolutely nothing to do but sit with his grief. And it was driving him mad.

Lucas pushed to his feet and stretched, trying to calm his nervous energy. They were due for a shipment of supplies and news from Maradis. No reason to suspect the ship wasn't friendly. And no reason to excite or upset Trick and Ella until he knew.

He stood in a room lined in glass, atop a house nestled on a bluff, on an island shrouded in misty fog. He shoved his hands in his pockets and looked out the wall of windows before him. The house had been built by their great-grandfather. He hadn't been here in years, had all but forgotten about it until they desperately needed some place to lay low. It was the type of place the Imbris kings favored; they had remote outposts and safehouses all over Alesia and beyond—tucked-away corners of the world where they could plan and plot away from prying eyes.

This house was the only building on this island—if you didn't count the half-roofed boathouse. The island was one of a hundred in the Odette Isles, an archipelago off the coast of Nova Navis. The largest island was populated with a village of fishermen and craftswomen, but the farther you sailed from civilization, the smaller and more barren the islands became. The tail of the archipelago was perpetually foggy, as if a dark spell had been cast over it. The locals swore these islands were haunted—an ill omen at the least. They didn't venture near. It was how Lucas knew that the ship was here for them. Either it was their shipment of foodstuffs to replenish their larder, or it was the Apricans come to haul them back to Maradis in chains, if not execute them outright.

Lucas bent, looking back through the brass telescope, grimacing at the pull of the wound on his back. He was healing well, but still it pained him, throbbing and itching in turns. He straightened. The ship was closer, but he couldn't see a flag. Perhaps that was a good sign.

This room, like a little glass bird's nest on top of the house, was furnished by only a worn leather armchair and the telescope. Lucas had spent most of the last two weeks here, staring at the islands of craggy rock and proud cedar trees that stretched as far as the eye could see, all of it frosted in wisps of white fog. His brother Patrick had found his home in the kitchen, spending his days pulling together meals that were far better than they had any right to be with the few supplies they had, and spending his nights drinking through their grandfather's dusty wine cellar. Ella split her time between crying in front of the fire, snapping at her brothers, and sitting on a worn piece of driftwood on the bluff, staring vacantly into the sea. Ella had taken the murder of their parents and brothers the hardest—her grief was angry and red and raw. She felt too much, while Trick seemed intent on feeling nothing at all, his feelings buried under the busyness of keeping them fed or numbed by the sweet embrace of drink. Lucas didn't know what he felt, how he grieved. That was how it worked. It was hardest to know yourself.

Well, that wasn't entirely true. If he was being honest with himself, he thought he did know a few things. In the last two weeks, he had become a world-class worrier. He'd always had a fundamental optimism about the world—even when things seemed difficult, he was confident he'd figure them out. It would be all right. Now, he was certain of nothing. The shock of witnessing the coup, his parents' and brothers' deaths—it had given way to worry. Even with Trick's connections through the Vintner's Guild, it had seemed impossible that they would make it out of the city—surely, the Apricans would find them huddled in the hold of the cargo ship.

But they hadn't, and their ship had made it out onto open water. Lucas and his siblings had been transferred to the Heronette, a fast little vessel manned by a Captain Guinyson, a friend of Trick's friend Oban, who had arranged their passage out of the city. And even as the Heronette had successfully made the trip to Fletch Island, where they now resided, and deposited them with a few weeks' provisions and a promise to bring more, Lucas worried. Their fortune seemed uncanny, too good to last. Lucas worried about what would happen if the Heronette didn't come back. Would this be their life for the rest of their days, exiled to this sad little island? Lucas worried about what would happen if the ship returned and brought unfriendly faces with it. Because no matter how loyal Guinyson was to Oban…he was still a man. And men could be bought. Or tortured. Or killed.

And then Lucas worried about Maradis. He worried about what the Apricans were doing to the city and the people he loved. He worried about Wren. He closed his eyes, letting the image of her wash over him, the pale expanse of her skin, so soft and delicate beneath his fingers, the rich chestnut of her eyes burning with determination. Her smell of caramel and coffee and *home*. The fierce set of her thin shoulders as she squared off against men three times her size—not fearless, but all the braver for it. Wren had saved them—given them a chance to get off that platform and out of the square where the rest of his family had been murdered. And he'd abandoned her, leaving her with nothing but an old ring. She was smart as a whip, but the ring he'd give her was such an obscure clue, he wasn't sure even she'd be able to piece it together. He feared that she wouldn't, and he'd never see her again. He worried that she would, and she'd be punished for it. He worried about it all.

"Lucas!" Trick called from the kitchen below, startling Lucas out of his thoughts. "Do you see that? There's a ship!"

Lucas looked through the telescope again. The ship was close enough now; he recognized the blue stripe of the Heronette. He sighed in relief. Assuming there weren't Aprican soldiers hiding on that vessel, it would bring news and food other than stale bread and canned vegetables. "It's the Heronette," he called before turning and taking the steep steps down to the house's main level.

"Where's Ella?" Lucas asked, surveying the lunch Trick was putting together for them. His younger brother had managed to transform their sad store of vittles into appetizing-looking sandwiches with cured salami, pickled carrots, and creamy brown mustard. Lucas's stomach growled, reminding him it was well past noon.

"She's down by the beach on her log," Trick said. His brother's gray eyes were bloodshot, his face puffy. Lucas wasn't sure if it was from the crying or the wine, but he thought the latter. He supposed he didn't look much better. His own hair was getting long, and he hadn't shaved in weeks. He stifled a sigh. He'd thought he was doing the right thing by letting Trick and Ella grieve in their own ways, but maybe he'd been fooling himself. Maybe he was just being a coward.

Trick pulled off his apron, throwing it on the counter. "We should go down and warn her before they circle into the cove and scare her to death."

Lucas and Trick headed out the back door, grabbing coats and hats as they went. October had not been gentle this year, especially way out here. They picked their way carefully down the rickety staircase to the beach below. The beach in the island's little cove was rocky and strewn with kelp and bleached driftwood, not the type of place one would like to spend the summer. But it was the best place for rowboats to come ashore, and the curve of the island provided shelter from the wind for any boat that wanted to anchor there.

Wrapped in a coarse woolen blanket in the emerald green plaid of the Imbris clan, Ella was sitting in her usual spot. Her blonde curls were greasy and snarled from the wind. Her face was sallow and blank. The sight of her like this pained him deeply—it was as if her fire had gone out completely. And Lucas had no idea how to rekindle it again.

"Ella!" Trick called.

She turned slowly.

"The Heronette is back," Trick said.

Lucas offered her a smile, but she merely nodded.

Trick and Lucas sat down on either side of her, and Lucas wrapped his arm around her, pulling her into his side, rubbing his hand up and down her arm. "Are you warm enough, Ella?"

"Mm-hmm," she murmured, but she leaned her head against his shoulder, burrowing into him.

Trick scooted against her other side, wrapping his arm around Ella's waist, tucking his fingers inside the fringe of the blanket. They stayed like that, looking out across the glassy dark water, until the Heronette glided into view.

Captain Guinyson was a Maradis native and the son of an Alesian naval officer. The sight of him—with his bushy brown beard, navy cap pulled low, and gray woolen sweater—brought a smile to Lucas's lips. "He looks like home, doesn't he?" Lucas murmured.

"Isn't this home now?" Ella said flatly.

Trick and Lucas exchanged worried glances over her head.

"Ahoy!" Guinyson called as the rowboat ground up against the rocks. One of the sailors jumped out, pulling the boat in farther.

Lucas and his siblings stood to greet their guests. "We're glad to see you returned," Lucas said.

"Ready to eat something other than salami?" Guinyson asked with a warm laugh.

"You have no idea," Trick replied.

It turned out Guinyson had been busy filling his little vessel with goods from Port Gris, the capital city of Nova Navis. "Oban told me to treat you all well, so I brought what I could," he said, waving at the barrels of pickled meat, flour and butter, and canned vegetables and fruits. Trick almost looked happy pawing through all the new offerings. "What's this?" he asked, holding up a wire cage.

"Crab pot," Guinyson said. "We got you a net for fishing and a special shovel for clam digging, too. I figured you'd enjoy some fresh seafood."

"Thank you," Lucas said, grateful that he'd have something to fill his time. "What news from Maradis?"

The smile dropped from the captain's face. "It's what you'd expect.

I suppose it's not as bad as it could be. The Apricans are requiring people to swear loyalty oaths."

"Any news of the Guilds?" Trick asked eagerly. "The Vintner's—or the Confectioner's?"

Lucas looked sidelong at Trick. Why was Trick interested in the Confectioner's Guild? Perhaps because he knew Wren was in the Guild?

"More of the same," Guinyson said. "As long as our friends keep their heads down, they should be all right. Not everyone is, though."

"What do you mean?" Lucas asked.

"There's a rebellion brewing." The captain's brown eyes sparkled. "Some Maradians got ahold of the Aprican black powder. They've been causing a lot of trouble for our new rulers. They go by the name the Falconers," he said, casting a meaningful glance at Lucas.

Lucas's stomach twisted. The Falconers. On the one hand, it buoyed him to know that there were still people in Maradis loyal to his family, who were committed to resisting the Aprican occupation. But on the other hand, he didn't want anyone killing in his name. And if these people wanted an Imbris back on the throne...he wasn't sure he was willing to do that. To sit in his father's chair, to seize the mantle of power, violently no less...

"What do these Falconers want?" Lucas asked.

Captain Guinyson reached into his pocket and pulled out a letter. "You can find out yourself. I've got a letter for you from the Falconer himself."

CHAPTER 8

Hale wanted nothing more than to set this piece of paper on fire and watch it burn. But a summons from Sim Daemastra wasn't something you could ignore.

"Don't worry, Firena," Lieutenant Ambrose called from the end of the dining table, taking a swig of ale. "I hear he's real tender the first time."

"You'd know," Hale said, standing and grabbing the heel of pumpernickel bread from his plate. "Lead the way," he said to the servant who had delivered Daemastra's summons, ignoring Ambrose's scowl. The man was a buzzing fly—annoying but harmless. Hale knew that he headed where the real danger lay. Daemastra's workshop.

Sim Daemastra was holed up in the west wing of the palace, nestled against the sea wall. Hale hadn't set foot in this wing in the few weeks since he had been serving the Apricans and was struck by how empty the area seemed. Hushed. Why did the man need so much space? Perhaps because Daemastra and his patricians did most of the ruling? The emperor was rarely seen, confining himself to his chambers. Hale wasn't sure why Evander had even wanted this country if he wouldn't even set foot outside to enjoy it.

The page led Hale into a large, open kitchen filled with white-veined marble and ivory tile. Massive silver ice chests were set against the far wall, and a broad expanse of counters were covered with papers and measuring implements.

The page fled the room as Daemastra turned. The man looked much as he had when Hale had seen him at the Aprican camp a few weeks ago. Preternaturally smooth skin and white teeth, blond hair as thick as a pelt. He wore the same strange attire he had then, a bastard combination of a cuisinier's jacket and a priest's robe. He wore the same hollow smile.

"Ah! Mr. Firena." Daemastra strode over and shook his hand. The man's thin fingers were cold and dry. "So glad you could join me."

"Sure," Hale managed, trying to figure out what exactly struck him so wrong about this kitchen. It looked innocuous, but...then it hit him. The smell. The kitchen didn't smell of spices and chocolate and fresh herbs. It smelled like...a hospital ward. Chemicals and bleach. What was the man making in here?

"I suppose you're wondering why I've summoned you. I've requested a transfer of your post, and the emperor has granted it. You are to be my assistant."

Hale's blood slowed in his veins. "What?" His voice was flat. Yes, he knew he deserved to suffer pain and torment in this life for betraying his friends and failing Sable, but this?

Daemastra ignored Hale's poorly veiled shock. "I do important work here, Hale. I need someone with your talents and your discretion in my corner."

"I don't understand."

Daemastra pulled two stools out from under the butcher block island and motioned to one. "Please."

Hale found himself sitting, trying, he suspected unsuccessfully, to hide his distaste for this man.

Daemastra clasped his spindly fingers before him on the countertop. "I'm going to tell you something that very few people in this empire know. So few that if I catch a whiff of this around the palace, I'll make sure you meet with a very unpleasant end."

Hale nodded. He could hardly imagine an end that was more unpleasant than spending his life as this man's assistant. Gods, even Daemastra smelled bad. Like meat starting to turn.

"The emperor is not well. Not well at all."

That piqued Hale's attention, drawing him back from his self-pity. "What do you mean?"

"He has a degenerative condition. In fact, the only thing keeping him alive is a potion I concocted after years of effort."

"A potion?" Hale asked warily.

"Let us be frank with each other, shall we? We are to work closely together. I know all about the Gifting—the infusion of magic into food. Perhaps you think it is unique to Alesia, but it is not. Certainly more prevalent here, but no. Your mother was Gifted, as were a select few Apricans. I have been studying this magic for the last thirty years. Only in the last two has my work taken on such an urgent character."

"Studying it? How?" Hale wasn't surprised to hear Daemastra confirm what he himself had long suspected. Hale's mother's wines had been prized throughout Aprica. She had been Gifted.

"Cataloguing it. Identifying factors that influence its efficacy, its potency. Determining if it can be recreated, and under what conditions. Figuring out where the magic comes from."

"And have you? Figured out where it comes from?"

"Oh yes. I will explain it, all in good time. I know where it comes from, I know how to recreate it, I know how to combine different types into something new. The only thing I do not know is how to make it permanent."

"Why would you want to?"

"I have found a cure for the emperor's condition. But I must continue to make the potion every few days. The ingredients...are rare and hard to come by. I desire a permanent fix. That is what brought us here to Maradis. Where magic was born."

Hale blew out a breath, shaking his head. "You invaded...for our knowledge? Why didn't you just ask?"

"The secret of the Gifting was the most carefully guarded secret of the Imbris crown and the Guilds alike. Perhaps the only thing they could agree on. There would be no free exchange of information."

"Okay," Hale said. There was some truth to that. "But what's this all got to do with me?"

"You are extremely Gifted yourself. You know the Gifted in the city, you know the personalities. You can help...*persuade* them to lend me their aid in my quest."

"I'm no one's favorite right now. They'd as soon gut me in the dark as help me."

"I have a feeling that the winds of political favor will be blowing our way quite soon." Daemastra's wide smile made the hair on the back of Hale's neck stand on end. "Don't you worry about that."

"Fine," Hale said slowly. He didn't trust this man as far as he could throw him. As far as he knew, every word exchanged in this kitchen was a lie. But until he knew Daemastra's real angle, it was best to be cooperative.

"It's a lot to take in, I know. Take this afternoon to process and come back tomorrow at 9 A.M. We'll get started."

"Great," Hale managed, standing. "See you tomorrow." *You creepy old bastard.*

Hale hurried from the kitchen into the hallway, feeling like spiders were crawling up his back. He kept himself from breaking into a run through sheer force of will. He wanted away from the strange man.

He crossed another hallway and a distant voice called out down the corridor to his right. "Hello? Anyone there?"

Hale stopped, his heart in his throat. He wanted to keep walking, but something made him turn. He took a few quiet steps towards the voice, which called out again. "Hello?"

The voice was emanating from behind a heavy wooden door. In the center was a small window covered by crossed bars of iron. Hale peered in.

A face appeared directly across from Hale's and he jumped back with a startled cry. "By the Sower, man, you scared the sugar out of me!"

A thin, wiry man stood on tiptoes to peer through the little window. "Are you with them?" he asked, his voice thin and high. His graying hair was unkempt and he had a smudge of flour on one cheek.

Hale furrowed his brow. "Them...the Apricans?"

The man gave a manic nod.

"I...sort of," Hale said. "It's complicated."

"Can you get me out of here?" the man asked, turning the wild intensity of his gaze onto Hale.

"Who are you? Why are you being held?" Hale stalled.

"Name's Liam. And they're making me bake. Day in and day out. I only get a few hours to sleep. Bread, pastries, croissants, sticky buns, doughnuts—" Liam continued to name every kind of bread and pastry product under the sun.

What in the Beekeeper? Another strange comment swam to mind. Beckett pleading with him: *No more bread.* "Why do they need that many pastries? That much bread?"

Liam swallowed, looking away nervously. "They're special."

"Flaming hells." Hale stepped forward, his voice low. "You're Gifted."

The man's brown eyes locked onto his. "You know."

"Confectioner's Guild," Hale said, pointing a thumb towards himself. "What's your Gift?"

"Baker's Guild magic is the magic of love," he said. "My gift makes love grow and bloom. It's very wonderful magic."

Love? Hale's mind spun. That didn't seem too nefarious. Why would the Apricans want his man? Why were they keeping him here? "Could it make you fall in love with someone awful? Or someone you hated?"

Liam shook his head. "It only affects love that's already within you. I can't create love. Well..." He hesitated.

"What?" Hale hissed. "Tell me. I can't help you if I don't know."

"It might be nothing. But...there's something funny about the yeast they bring me. It's already working. I think they might be making something new."

"New?" Yeast? Hale thought of what Daemastra had just told him. That he understood the way the Gifting worked. He could recreate it. Combine it. This strange cocktail had Daemastra's tainted fingerprints all over it. But what was he making?

"Please get me out of here," Liam said.

Footsteps sounded down the hall.

"I'll see what I can do," Hale said. "But I've got to go now. Hang in there."

"Wait!" Liam hissed, but Hale hurried back down to the main

corridor.

Two Aprican legionnaires passed, one holding a tray of food. For their prisoner, no doubt.

Hale's mind raced as he walked through the hallways. This baker wanted Hale to help him. He wasn't sure he could do that. He wasn't sure if he could help anybody. Least of all himself.

CHAPTER 9

The next day, Wren found herself at another godsforsaken meeting. Callidus, together with all the guild heads, had received a summons he hadn't dared refuse—from Emperor Evander himself.

They arrived at the Tradehall a few minutes early and were ushered into one of the long meeting rooms. A table at the end of the room was piled with an array of breakfast pastries—sugar-crusted scones, flaky croissants, glistening puff-pastries with frosting drizzled across them.

Callidus glowered at the display. "Trying to bribe us with our own food. Blond bastards," he thundered.

"How about I get us some coffee?" Wren managed weakly, gravitating towards the carafes like a moth to a flame.

"Black," Callidus barked.

Wren fetched their coffees and they found two seats at the table. The room was filling in now with Guildmasters she recognized. Chandler and his pale artisan Bastian, one-armed Guildmaster McArt, Bruxius of the Butcher's Guild, Alban of the Vintner's Guild, Beatrix of the Baker's, and a few she didn't recognize. One swaggering figure was suspiciously absent.

"Where's Pike?" Wren whispered. The head of the Spicer's Guild, and their ally, had been grievously wounded in the attack that had killed Sable. But according to Callidus's sources, he'd been recovering.

Callidus frowned. "He should be well enough to attend, at least from what Rizio told me." Rizio, Pike's second-in-command, was absent as well. She didn't recognize any of Pike's Spicer's Guild members, with their silver piercings and dark scowls.

The guild members settled around the table, and the doors at the far side of the room opened. One man entered, the skeletal cuisinier Sim Daemastra.

"Where's the emperor?" Wren whispered.

"Do I look like the man's secretary?" Callidus retorted.

Wren sighed, taking a sip of her coffee.

Daemastra held up his long, spindly fingers for quiet. "Ladies and gentlemen. The emperor sends his regrets. He is an extremely busy man and was called away this morning."

That announcement was met by grumbles and mutters around the table.

"The emperor has asked me to appear on his behalf. As a fellow cuisinier, I can assure you that I understand the concerns that come with your position and responsibilities. The emperor values the Guilds highly and looks forward to working together. I must thank you all for coming to the palace individually to answer our questions; it has helped us immensely."

"So why're we here?" McArt called out.

"To the point. Good man." Daemastra smiled. His teeth were so white and perfect—large for his thin lips. Wren fought to keep the grimace off her face. Something was off about the man. "We wanted to quell any rumors going around. While the Falconer rebels have been a bit of a thorn in our side, we have made significant progress in rooting them out. There should be no more attacks like yesterday's explosion in the Guild Quarter."

"And what of the grain?" Guildmaster Beatrix asked. "I heard half the city's stores were lost in the attack."

"There will be no shortage of flour," Daemastra said smoothly, motioning to the mound of pastries behind him. "Indeed, I hope you have all helped yourself to this morning's delights. The emperor has the remaining grain under guard. We will work with each of your Guilds to provide access to your allotted quota."

Mutters rounded the table.

"I assure you, so long as your Guilds cooperate with our modest requests, life under Emperor Evander will be quite unchanged from what you are used to. But a word of caution on that front. The Spicer's Guild has somewhat...*rudely* rebuffed our request that they visit the palace to submit to questioning and pledge their loyalty. The emperor will not tolerate such insubordination. As of today, the Spicer's Guild is hereby disbanded. If you are aware of the location of a Spicer's Guild member, you are required to report that individual to the Aprican legion so they may be brought in for questioning. Anyone found harboring a member of the Spicer's Guild will be deemed complicit."

Sim Daemastra's words fell over them like a suffocating blanket of fondant. No one said a word.

Callidus's face was purpling, a vein growing in his neck.

Wren laid her hand on his arm—a warning. Nothing good would come from exploding at this man.

It seemed her warning wasn't enough. "Disbanded?" Callidus spluttered. "For missing a meeting?"

Sim Daemastra had the wherewithal to look apologetic. "The emperor requires absolute obedience during these delicate times. Perhaps later, when relationships are...*strengthened*...such a slight would not be as great a concern. But the Spicer's Guild has made their contempt for the emperor clear. There will be no quarter for such behavior."

Wren looked across the table at Chandler and McArt. They had been two of the most vocal critics of King Imbris's overreaching, but neither of them spoke up now. Chandler was picking crumbs of croissant off his plate while McArt stirred his coffee. Neither would meet her eye. She pursed her lips. Had they lost their nerve?

"The emperor bid me to share how much he appreciates your time and cooperation. Are there any other questions?"

Silence. Callidus was just shaking his head, his fists clenched by his sides.

Daemastra smiled, tucking his hands in his strange white robes. "Well then. I know you are all busy people. Please feel free to stay and enjoy the refreshments as long as you like." He turned and disappeared out the door, followed by his two Aprican guards.

It was a long moment before anyone moved. Bruxius got to his feet first, ambling over to the table at the front of the room to refill his coffee and grab another scone.

Callidus let out a little laugh of disbelief. "No one...not one of you had anything to say to our new overlords? No concerns about the change in policy?" His voice dripped with sarcasm like honey from baklava.

"I'm sure the emperor will secure the best interests of the Guilds, and Maradis," Beatrix said.

Wren's mouth fell open. What? What happened to standing together? A united front?

"Oh, you're sure, are you?" Callidus said, pushing back from the table and pacing behind his chair. "How long before he disbands one of our Guilds for looking at him the wrong way?"

"Don't give him reason to," Chandler said. "The emperor is a fair and righteous ruler. If we trust in him, he will bring glory to all the lands of the Aprican Empire."

Callidus stopped moving. "What?" he asked, exchanging a look of disbelief with Wren. "Is this a joke?"

"He's right," McArt said in his gruff tone. "We need to trust in the emperor." Murmurs of assent sounded around the table.

Callidus was shaking his head, his dark eyes wide. "And do the rest of you feel this way as well?"

Nods. Grunts of affirmation.

Wren looked around the room, craning her head to look at the corners, the ceiling. What in the Beekeeper's name was going on? Were they being watched, and they were the only ones not in on it?

"Wren, get up," Callidus said, straightening his gray waistcoat. "We're leaving."

Wren scrambled after Callidus, throwing one last look over her shoulder at the seated guild heads. Fear was coiling up from her center with grasping tendrils. Something was wrong. Very wrong.

Callidus radiated silent fury as he strode through the polished halls of the Tradehall.

Wren had to jog to keep up.

In the antechamber, Lieutenant Dashiell sat reading a copy of *The Maradis Morning*. He jumped up when he saw them, tucking the newspaper under his uniformed arm.

Callidus swore under his breath, holding up a hand to him. "We need a moment. Private business."

And then they were out the door into the dark windswept Maradis morning. Wren pulled her cloak tightly around her before the wind caught it. Dash was wise enough to stay behind in the warmth of the building, though she felt his eyes on them through the panes of the door.

Callidus turned on her. "I thought Chandler was with us."

She backed up a step. "He was! He is...I don't know what that was." Her mind was spinning, trying to make sense of what had just happened. "Just yesterday...you were there. He wanted us to stand united in opposing the emperor's policies."

"What changed between then and now? Because he sure as hell didn't seem to be standing united! They all seemed united against us!"

"I don't know," Wren said lamely. "Maybe...they're being blackmailed again? Like with King Imbris?"

"Or maybe the other Guilds have decided that the Confectioner's Guild has been on top too long and should be the next to go," Callidus suggested blackly.

"Chandler wouldn't... They wouldn't..." Wren stammered. They had been allies once. Friends. But who knew...in this new world. Perhaps it was Guild eat Guild in order to survive. "If that were true, why did he and Beatrix go to the palace yesterday? Why did they talk to us?"

"To throw us off the scent! To make us let down our guard and think we had allies."

"Maybe," Wren stammered. It didn't fit. Chandler wouldn't do that. Not after everything their Guilds had been through together. She had saved his life.

Callidus wagged his finger at her nose. "Until further notice, no talking with members of any other Guild without my permission or knowledge. Agreed?"

"Agreed," Wren said. Though she wasn't sure who she had to talk to anymore. All of her friends and allies were gone. Fled—or dead.

CHAPTER 10

Olivia paused in the antechamber, the tasks on her to-do list forgotten. There were a half-dozen Aprican legionnaires carrying boxes up the stairway into the Guildhall. What in the Beekeeper?

She caught sight of the man directing it all, acting like he owned the place. Who was he? Olivia clasped her hands behind her back, striding over towards him. "Good day, sir," she said, trying to keep her annoyance hidden. "What's all this?"

The man turned to her, his blue eyes shrewd and calculating. He was handsome, like all these Apricans seemed to be. Perhaps a bit generic-looking, she thought with savage evaluation. Though from the way he held himself, he thought himself the Sower's own gift to the female sex. "Captain Ambrose." The officer nodded to her, his smile a touch too wide. "And whom do I have the pleasure of speaking with?"

"Olivia Treekin, Guildmistress of this Guild. Usually all shipments go through me. I wasn't apprised of this one..." She let the sentence linger, her intent clear.

"My apologies, Guildmistress." Ambrose had the wherewithal to look apologetic. "It's a gift. Pastries from Sim Daemastra, the emperor's own cuisinier. An apology for the tardy return of one of your grandmasters."

"Which grandmaster?" That perked up her interest.

"Grandmaster Beckett," Ambrose replied.

"Beckett has returned?" Olivia's hand flew to her mouth. Despite Beckett's treachery towards Callidus, she was relieved to hear he was back. His ways were misguided, and he was a pompous ass, but he had the best interest of the Guild at heart. And most days, he was a lot easier to find than Callidus, who had a way of disappearing on her without a moment's warning. It would be nice to have a grandmaster around again to consult with when things came up. "Does Marina know?"

"If you're referring to the comely brunette girl with glasses, then yes, they had a somewhat awkward reunion when we first arrived." A smile twitched at the corner of Ambrose's mouth.

"I'll have to see that he has what he needs," Olivia said, wanting to be away from this man's oily charm. "I presume you and your soldiers can see yourselves out..."

"Indeed," Ambrose said. The uniformed soldiers were already filing down the stairs, their arms empty of burdens. "I suggest you enjoy some of the delicacies we've brought. I'd say they're tasty enough to impress even the Confectioner's Guild." Ambrose gave her a half-bow before pushing out the door, his soldiers in tow.

Olivia stood for a moment, shaking her head. What an odd interaction. Never mind, though. She was coming to realize that the Apricans were a strange lot. She shook off the feeling and headed up the stairs.

She found Grandmaster Beckett in the library surrounded by Marina, Lennon, and enough pastries to feed a small army.

"Grandmaster!" Olivia crossed the room. "Welcome back."

Beckett turned and to her surprise, pulled her into an embrace. Olivia suppressed her shock and gave him a hesitant pat on the shoulder.

"I couldn't be happier to be back home," Beckett said, smiling broadly. He looked a few pounds heavier, but other than that, none the worse for the wear. Olivia was surprised and relieved. She hadn't wanted to think what two weeks in an Aprican dungeon would do to a man. It seemed...nothing.

Beckett put his arms around Marina and Lennon's shoulders, pulling them to him. Both of them looked discomforted, but they pasted on smiles. The relationship between Marina and her father had always been rocky, but Olivia hoped that Marina and Beckett could use the events of the past weeks to start fresh. At least Marina still had a father, even if he was overbearing. Olivia was entirely alone in this world.

"We're happy to have you," Olivia said, shoving aside her moment of self-pity. The Guild was her family, and one of those members was home. It was a moment of celebration for all. "I'm glad to see you looking well. And bearing gifts, no less."

Beckett turned to the boxes of pastries that had been set out on the counter. "Have something! I can attest everything is delicious."

Olivia shrugged. Beckett released Marina and Lennon from his stranglehold, and the three of them peered into the boxes, surveying their options.

"Strangest reunion ever," Lennon whispered to Olivia, and even Marina smiled.

"Who knew the Apricans were so into carbs," Marina said. "You'd think they ban them from the Empire in order to maintain their perfect physiques."

"The Apricans are what we like to call 'lucky bastards,'" Lennon said, selecting a frosted donut. "They can probably eat enough for three men without gaining an ounce."

"Isn't that the truth," Olivia said, grabbing a cinnamon strudel. She'd seen Hale eat that much in a sitting and never exercise. Lucky bastard indeed.

She took a bite, holding her other hand out to catch the little avalanche of cinnamon crumbles and almonds pieces that fell from her pastry. It was delicious—perfectly flaky, with the nutty and sharp undertones of cinnamon and nutmeg. She could almost feel her taste buds radiating happiness, sending tingles of pleasure straight to her brain.

"Wow," Olivia said through her bite. She had never tasted so strong a flavor—like the sugar and butter permeated her being. She stumbled against the counter, suddenly feeling woozy. But the feeling was gone in a flash, so quickly Olivia was sure she had imagined it.

"This is some pastry," Lennon said, inspecting his donut with wide dark eyes.

It was. It was the best she'd ever had. And it was so considerate of the emperor to provide these gifts to them. It was exactly the type of thing their Emperor would do. He was always thinking of others—working tirelessly for the betterment of all who lived in the lands of the Aprican Empire.

Marina was looking at her father, her smooth face rapt with delight. "You must tell the emperor *thank you*. Tell him—he's a fair and righteous ruler."

Olivia found herself nodding. Truer words had never been spoken. "Yes." She nodded, overcome by her gratitude towards their sovereign. "A fair and righteous ruler."

Callidus knocked on the glass of the door and motioned to Dash sharply. The man slipped outside to follow them the short walk across the street to the Guildhall. It was ridiculous that he had even escorted them. The wind tugged at her and Wren corralled her whipping auburn tresses with one hand, her cloak in the other. A spitting rain was starting, the tiny drops stinging like needles against her skin.

A crowd was gathering down the street in front of the Sower's Temple, where Virgil used to work. Wren pressed her lips together in a tight line at the thought of Virgil. Hopefully, he was drinking mead at the Sower's right hand, smiling down at all of them. He deserved a blessed afterlife. As they always did, her thoughts of Virgil turned to thoughts of Lucas. Her chest tightened as she looked at the spot before the Temple's doors where she had once in her anger barreled into Lucas, sending them both tumbling onto the cobblestones. *Oh, Lucas,* she thought. *Where are you?*

She pulled her attention from the memory. "What's going on?" she asked, nodding her head towards the commotion.

"Not sure," Dash said, his steps slowing.

"I'm going to check it out," Wren said. Anything to distract herself from the grief and worry that tugged at her, from the thunderstorm of Callidus's mood.

Dash looked between her and Callidus, hesitating for a moment before falling into step beside her. "You seem the more pleasant company," he whispered with a wink.

"Don't count on it," she said blackly, heading down Guilder's Row.

The man reminded her too much of Hale for her to bear his presence easily. His friendly swagger, his unflappable good mood. Well, he reminded her of the old Hale. And that was an even worse reminder.

Before the ochre stones of the temple, a group of four Aprican legionnaires had set up a small tent and table. A heavy-ladened wagon sat next to them, the horse's head drooping in the rain.

"What's going on?" Wren asked a woman who stood with a little girl tucked in close to her skirts.

"The emperor is giving out free bread! You can take a loaf a person. Word is they're going to do it all winter! To make sure we all have full bellies."

Wren stood on her tiptoes, peering over the waiting crowd. The legionnaires were handing out what looked like loaves of bread wrapped in brown paper. She turned back towards the Guild, frowning.

"Why'd you look like you just swallowed a slug?" Dash asked as they walked back up the slick sidewalk. "Aren't you glad the emperor is feeding your fellow citizens?"

Wren nodded. "I guess." The gesture was surprisingly kind. So why did it leave an uneasy feeling in her gut?

"I told you life under the Aprican Empire isn't all bad. You wait. Things'll look up."

Wren ignored him as they walked into the Guildhall, lost in thought.

"You should get out of those wet clothes, my lady," Dash said with a pleasant smile. "And get something warm to drink. No need to catch a chill."

Wren glared at his retreating form. Why did he have to be so damn nice? It would be much easier to hate him if he were an ass like Ambrose or creepy like Daemastra. She pushed her wet hair off her forehead. In truth, something warm would be nice. She walked up the steps, headed towards the library. A cup of coffee. Then a long, hot bath. Things would make more sense after a hot bath.

Wren rounded the corner into the library and pulled up short at the heavenly smell of fresh baked bread and frosting. On the long marble countertop lay a cornucopia of baked goods. Olivia and Lennon stood at the counter surveying the plenty, Olivia giggling over a cinnamon strudel.

"What's all this?" Wren asked.

"Wren!" They cried in unison, turning. Olivia's cheeks were flushed and lovely. Lennon opened his arms wide with welcome, half a frosted donut in one hand, the other bite being rapidly chewed. "Come try something! A gift from the emperor to apologize for the belated return of Grandmaster Beckett."

"Beckett is back?" Wren asked, shocked. She hadn't thought they'd ever see him again. "Where is he?"

"He and Marina went back to his room to get him settled and talk," Olivia said.

"And he's...all right?" *Whole?* She wanted to ask.

"The emperor treated him like an honored guest," Lennon said. "He'll tell you himself! Now, seriously, you've got to try something."

Wren approached and surveyed the smorgasbord. They did look good. There were maple bars frosted with fresh maple syrup and what looked like tiny crumbles of bacon. Her stomach rumbled. She picked up the sticky maple bar, examining the craftsmanship. "What I don't get is, why would the emperor send all this to us? What is this? A baked good bribe?" She thought of the table with piles of bread being handed out. Perhaps that was exactly what this was.

"A bribe?" Olivia said around another bite of her strudel. "How could you think such a thing? The emperor is a fair and righteous ruler."

Wren froze, maple bar halfway to her mouth. "What did you say?"

"She's right," Lennon said. "If we trust in him, he will bring glory to all the lands of the Aprican empire."

Those words. She had heard those words before. Coming out of Chandler. And the other guild members. A heaviness settled over her—gluing her to the floor where she stood. What had Guildmaster Beatrix said? A baker's guild member was missing. A Gifted guild member.

The maple bar fell from her hand as the pieces clicked into place. This food was infused. The pastries at the Guild meeting. The bread on the street. It was all infused.

"Wren? Are you all right? You look like you've seen a ghost," Olivia said.

Lennon snapped his fingers before her face. "You're as white as a sheet."

"Who...else...?" Wren swallowed. "Who else has eaten these pastries?"

"Marina and Beckett. They were just delivered fifteen minutes ago." Olivia frowned. "What's wrong?"

"Callidus grabbed one with his coffee a few minutes ago," Lennon added.

"Callidus?" Wren's eyes widened. "Where did he go?"

"His office, I think."

Wren dashed from the library, spinning around the bannister to take the stairs up to the third floor two by two. The guards on the stairs leaped out of her way in surprise.

"Callidus!" she screamed as she tore down the hallway and burst through his closed office door.

Callidus sat at his desk, the cruller in his hand moving towards his lips.

CHAPTER 11

W ren dove bodily across the desk, batting the pastry out of Callidus's narrow fingers.

Callidus held his hands up, frozen in shock at Wren's sudden appearance before him. "What in the Beekeeper's name are you doing?"

Wren let her head fall down, relief washing over her like a sugar glaze. "Infused...pastry."

Callidus shot to his feet, retrieving the offending cruller. He held it between two fingers and examined it as Wren crawled off the desk, pushing her hair out of her face. "How do you know?"

"They're infused. All of them. The ones at the meeting this morning. The ones in the library. Olivia and Lennon were spouting the exact same nonsense as Chandler. What was it?" Wren paused. "Oh, right. 'The emperor is a fair and righteous ruler,'" she said, her voice as even as an automaton.

Callidus fell into his chair with a heavy thunk, staring at the cruller. Wren sat in the leather-wrapped armchair before him, weariness washing over her.

Callidus spoke. "They're brainwashing the Guilds. With pastries."

If she weren't so overcome with despair, Wren might have laughed. It sounded ridiculous when you put it like that. "That's not the worst of it. That crowd outside on Guilder's Row? They're handing out bread to the people. I bet they're doing it all over the city."

"They'll have the whole city under their control in a matter of days. But this... How...?" Callidus trailed off, rubbing his sharp chin with his fingers, his eyes distant.

"They have a member of the Baker's Guild. They must have discovered his Gift."

"Blooming hell," Callidus said. "This feels more like Vintner's Guild magic."

The thought chilled her. The Vintner's Guild—the magic of secrets and lies. "Maybe the Apricans have some new way of combining magics. We don't know. We've never really understood what gives one person the ability to create a certain type of infusion."

"What if they can put it in other food? Beyond bread or pastries? Who's to say that any of our food is safe?" Callidus asked, tossing the cruller onto the table, brushing the frosting off his hands with a grimace.

Wren blew out a slow breath. "He's already gotten to so many. All the guildmasters. Lennon. Olivia. Marina and Beckett."

Callidus looked up at that.

"Oh yes, Beckett is back," Wren said. "He's the one who brought the presents."

Callidus wiped his mouth with the back of a shaky hand. "Once it spreads, the rebellion will die naturally. There will be no chance of removing Evander from the throne."

"And we'll all be mindless drones, marching to whatever beat the emperor plays for us," Wren finished. She leaned forward, her head falling into her hands. This was worse. Worse than anything they had faced before. She hadn't thought it was possible, but here it was.

Callidus looked up with alarm. "Thom. Where's Thom?"

Wren and Callidus were out of their chairs and scrambling towards the door in the blink of an eye. They raced down the hallway, rounding the stairs, taking them at a breakneck pace. Lieutenant Dashiell was at the bottom, chatting with one of the guild guards. "Have you seen Thom?" Callidus cried.

"Dining hall." Dash crooked a thumb behind him. "What's wrong?"

Dining hall, Wren mouthed to Callidus in horror.

Without answering, they were off again, racing through the hallways, bursting through the doors into the dining hall. Thom was sitting at a table by himself in the empty hall, a forkful of pancake poised before his mouth. Wren ran forward, batting the fork out of his mouth. "Don't eat that!" she cried.

The fork spiraled out of his hand, skidding across the wooden floor. "Sweet caramel, Wren, what's gotten into you?"

Wren dropped onto the bench across from him. Please, by the gods, let that pancake be safe. "What do you think about the emperor?" she asked, her forehead scrunching in preparation for his stock answer.

"I hope the bastard chokes on a truffle and does us all a favor," he said. "Why?"

Callidus let out a triumphant laugh of relief, grabbing Thom by the shoulders and shaking him with excitement.

Thom looked between the two of them, confusion etched across his freckled face.

Dash trotted into the hall, his hand on his sword. "Everything all right?"

"False alarm." Callidus waved him away. He slid onto the bench next to Thom, adjusting his hair to return it to position.

Dash scowled at them, but he turned and left.

"Now will someone tell me what my pancake did to you?" Thom asked.

Wren answered in a whisper. "The emperor is spreading infused baked goods through the city. When you eat them...it changes you. You become his number one fan."

Thom looked between them in disbelief. "Is that even possible?"

"I assure you, it is. And it has happened," Callidus said grimly.

"How long does it last?" he asked.

Wren shrugged. "We'll see. But if people keep eating the infused bread, they'll keep getting re-infected."

"All the other Guild heads are under his spell," Callidus said. "And we can't trust anything in the city. Swarms, I hate to admit it, but the emperor's plan was genius."

"Evil genius," Thom said. "So...can I finish this pancake? It came from the guild kitchen, not from the palace." He motioned to the half sitting on his plate.

Callidus nodded sharply.

Thom retrieved his fork, wiped it on his napkin, and dug in.

"Callidus..." Wren's mind was working. "Not all the Guildmasters are infected. Well, at least we don't know that for sure. What about Pike?" The notorious head of the disbanded Spicer's Guild. He hadn't been at the meeting. Presumably, he hadn't eaten an infused pastry yet. "He might be our only ally."

"By the Beekeeper, I hate that Pike keeps turning up as our only ally."

"You should go see him," Thom said around a bite of pancake.

"You?" Wren asked, turning to Thom. "What are you going to be doing?"

Thom was chewing his last enormous bite and pushed up from the bench. "I'm going to warn my family. Maybe they haven't eaten the bread yet."

Right. Sometimes Wren forgot that Thom had another family.

"Go see to them. But come right back here. And eat nothing."

"Aye aye, Captain." Thom saluted, fixing his hat over his curls.

When Thom was gone, Callidus turned back to Wren.

"We have to at least see if Pike's infected," she protested.

"You're forgetting one thing," Callidus said. "The emperor has deemed Pike an enemy of the crown. If anyone is caught cavorting with him, they'll be arrested too. He's likely in hiding."

"We know where some of his hideouts are. It's worth a try. We should at least warn him."

Callidus grunted. "Fine. You're an expert at skulking about. How do you propose getting around our guard friend?"

Wren looked over her shoulder at where Dash had disappeared. That was right. If Dash knew they were going to meet with Pike, he'd be forced to arrest them. They'd have to ditch him.

"The direct way is the best way. We walk out the back door. Let's go." She stood.

"Now?"

"No time like the present."

The Unicorn Mercantile, a dance club on Nysia Avenue, was one of Guildmaster Pike's lesser-known business ventures. They had found him there once before, when he was hiding from King Imbris's watchful eye. Perhaps they'd find him there again.

The brick building sat empty and dark in the low light of mid-morning.

Callidus banged on the metal front door with his fist. "The place looks deserted."

"Pike's office was downstairs. He could be in there and you'd never know."

Callidus banged again, more insistent this time. No answer.

"Should we go around back?" Wren offered. "See if we can look in the window?"

"It's a club. There are no windows by design," Callidus said, pounding a third time, keeping up an even tempo, his fist echoing on the metal door.

The door cracked open as Callidus's hand was poised for another round. "What?" a deadpan voice said.

Wren squinted. She recognized the man. It was Pike's second-in-command, a dark-goateed man named Rizio.

Wren peeked her head under Callidus's arm. "Can we come in? Is the Guildmaster here?"

"Nope. And I'm not taking visitors." Rizio started to close the door.

"Please! We bring important news to share about the emperor."

Rizio sighed and closed the door. A chain on the inside rattled, and he opened the door, standing back to let them in. "Quickly. Prying eyes everywhere these days."

They descended the dark staircase into the still dance hall and beyond, into the bowels of the building, where Pike's office lay. The office was empty, desk drawers pulled out, files piled on the sofa and in boxes.

"Going somewhere?" Callidus asked, surveying the scene.

"It's not safe in Maradis for us anymore. The Guild has been disbanded. Time for us to return to sea. It's where we belong anyway."

Callidus spoke. "It's even less safe than you might imagine. For all of us. The emperor has a member of the Baker's Guild producing infused pastries and breads. He's distributing them all over the city. They remove your ability to think freely. By eating the bread, you become brainwashed to believe the emperor is the best thing for Maradis since...well, since sliced bread."

"Coward," Rizio said, his mouth twisting in distaste. "Politics. The Guilds have become like rats, scheming and maneuvering in the dark."

"Where's Pike?" Callidus asked. "Can we speak with him?"

"He's already left the city. He's safe."

"When do you leave?" Wren asked. She wanted to ask where Pike was but feared that was too blunt a question.

"I and the last of the spicers leave tomorrow. I appreciate you sharing your intelligence. We will be able to avoid any of the infused foods before we leave."

"It's been mostly bread, but you have to assume nothing is safe, save what you've prepared yourself," Wren said.

"Take us with you," Callidus said.

Shock coursed through her. He was thinking of fleeing? Abandoning the city? The Guild? A day ago, she might have welcomed a chance to run, to make a new start. A day ago she'd been weary. But that was before the emperor had shown his true colors. Now—she was angry. What he'd done was unconscionable. A horror on a level Wren couldn't have even conceived of. The emperor didn't intend to let Maradis rule itself. Their resources and their sovereignty weren't enough. He would have their very minds—their free will. They couldn't just stand by and do nothing.

"Callidus," Wren began, but he held up a hand. She fell silent, unease roiling within her.

"You don't even know where we're going," Rizio said slowly.

"It doesn't matter. It's too dangerous for us here right now. We need to regroup in safety. To make plans. We can pay you."

Regroup. That was promising. It meant Callidus didn't mean to flee forever.

The dark-haired man crossed his arms before them, considering. The silver rings in his ears glimmered in the low light of the office. "One hundred gold crowns for each of you."

Wren's eyes bugged out. One hundred! That was a king's ransom!

Callidus paled. "We're a wealthy Guild, but not that wealthy. Twenty."

"Eighty."

"One hundred for the lot of us," Callidus said.

Rizio rolled his eyes. "Fine. But you share a cabin. And no complaining."

"Done." Callidus thrust his hand out, and Rizio shook it.

"Where are we going?" Wren asked.

Rizio shook his head. "Better you don't know. In case you get caught. I'll just say...bring a cloak. A waterproof one."

Great, that narrowed it down to about everywhere between here and Aprica.

"Where shall we meet you?" Callidus asked.

"Our boat is the Black Jasmine, docked at the end of Pier 91 in the Port Quarter. Be there at midnight tomorrow or we leave without you."

CHAPTER 12

"Terrible idea," Hale muttered to himself as he hurried through the slick streets, heading for the Confectioner's Guildhall. Yet his feet were bearing him ever closer.

Hale couldn't shake his conversation with Liam and Beckett. And Daemastra most of all. Something was going on and it involved infused food. He would stake his life on it. He knew that he had made his choice—he was an Aprican stooge now. He knew that the Guilds—the city—blamed him for his current predicament. But old habits died hard. And so he found himself turning onto the wide avenue of Guilder's Row, the white marble Guildhall before him. Just a quick word to tell them they should be on their guard. That was all.

Hale started up the stairs to the Guildhall and spun quickly, hurrying back down when he spotted who was pacing before the doorway. Hale crossed the street and ducked into the shadow of the Tradehall before turning, blowing out a breath. He squinted to make him out. A legionnaire in sky blue, his brown hair cut short on the sides, a trim beard covering his jaw. The man looked furious, pacing back and forth like a rabid dog before the door. There was no way Hale could enter the Guildhall without that man noticing him. And Hale did not want an Aprican legionnaire to notice him.

Twin surges of relief and disappointment welled in him. "Well, that's that," he murmured under his breath. He had come, he had tried to warn them. But it wasn't meant to be. Wren and Callidus were smart. They had been through worse scrapes. Whatever Daemastra was up to—the Guild would be able to stay one step ahead of it. Hale hoped.

With a resigned nod, Hale shoved off the wall, heading back towards the sidewalk—where he was barreled into by a man hurrying by, his jacket pulled tightly around his throat, his hat pulled low.

"Watch where you're going," Hale shouted as he recoiled off the man, stumbling to catch his footing. The stranger hurried on without a word, not even looking back.

"Son of a spicer," Hale swore, shaking his head. At that moment, he noticed the man had dropped something. A letter. Hale picked it up and looked up for the man so he could call out for him. But he'd vanished.

Hale frowned and brushed off the creamy vellum on his pant leg. The letter was sealed with green wax formed in the shape of a falcon. The Imbris crest. He turned the letter over and froze. *Hale Firena,* it read.

Hale's senses surged to full alert, his awareness buzzing. He looked around, but no one was paying him any attention. His pulse raced in his veins as he broke open the seal.

Mr. Firena-

We are pleased to learn that despite your past misdeeds, you continue to have the best interests of Maradis at heart. As an Aprican soldier, you have unique access to intelligence that could be of use to the resistance. If you should ever come across information that you would like to share in order to assist in our efforts, we would be most obliged to receive it. If you do, place the information in an envelope underneath the seat of the Hippogriff carriage on the carousel at Gemma Park. Do not attempt to contact us. We will contact you.

Sincerely,

The Falconer

P.S. And, Mr. Firena, whatever you do, don't eat the bread.

Wren was stunned. They were leaving Maradis. "Is there no other way?" she asked Callidus as they emerged from the Unicorn Mercantile into the blustery slate day.

"I don't fancy becoming a mindless emperor-worshipper, do you?"

"Of course not." Wren sighed. "It just feels...like giving up." Which, if she were being honest with herself, she had been wanting to do for weeks now.

"Isn't that what you wanted?" Callidus asked. His tone was harsh. "Isn't that what you've been doing these past weeks? Withdrawing from the world, feeling sorry for yourself? It may be news to you, Wren, but you're not the only one who cared about Aiyani Sable. Or this Guild. Or this city."

Wren winced. The truth of Callidus's words cut as sharp as knives. She had been wrapped up in her own grief, callous to the fact that those around her were grieving too. "I'm sorry, Callidus," she said softly. "I'm just..." She trailed off. How to make him understand? She and Thom hadn't told Callidus that they had accompanied Hale to see the Aprican general the night before the city had fallen. She was afraid to.

"Just what, Wren?" Callidus asked, looking at her sideways over the high collar of his coat. A memory flickered, tugging at her. It was so much like the first time she'd ever seen him, in Master Oldrick's shop. She'd been afraid then, and she was afraid now. She was afraid to stay and afraid to go. Her fears were like glistening thorns surrounding her, a maze of brambles that she couldn't escape. As she shied away from one, another would pierce her. They crowded around her, their limbs growing tighter by the day. Soon she wouldn't be able to move at all. She wouldn't be able to breathe. She had to break free.

"I'm afraid that if I try to help, I'm only going to make it worse," she stammered out.

Callidus wrinkled his thick black brows. "It can't get much worse than this, Wren."

"Last time..." She faltered, but she shook herself, gathering her courage around her. "Last time I tried to make it better and it made it worse. All of this is my fault, Callidus. The city wouldn't have fallen if it weren't for me."

Callidus stopped in his tracks. "What are you talking about?"

So Wren told him, her words tripping over each other. How she and Thom and Hale had gone to make a deal with the Apricans to secure his freedom. How Hale had betrayed them and taken the key Lucas had given her to the secret passageway. She needed to confess her sins. She needed him to know. "So you see," she finished, "it wasn't just Hale who betrayed Maradis. It was me."

Callidus heaved a massive sigh and rubbed his temples with two long fingers.

Wren's stomach flipped nervously. "Please, Callidus, say something."

"What you did was stupid and reckless," Callidus said. He softened, looking up with those ice-blue eyes. "But you did it to save me. So I suppose I cannot fault you too terribly."

Relief flowed through Wren like a tidal wave. She sprung at Callidus, wrapping her arms around him, pressing her face into the scratchy wool of his coat. "Thank you. Thank you for forgiving me."

Callidus wrapped his arms around her, rocking her gently. "There's nothing to forgive. The Apricans were going to break through the wall in another few days. If you hadn't done what you'd done, I'd be dead. Along with Chandler, McArt, and Bruxius."

She felt about a thousand times lighter. How had she once thought Callidus was hard and cruel?

Callidus patted her gently. "Now let's get out of this rain."

They hurried the rest of the way to the Guildhall, only to be met by a golden thundercloud at the door. From the damp shoulders of his sky-blue uniform, it was clear that Dash had been waiting there for some time.

"You two!" he shouted at them, bounding down the steps to face them. "What do you have to say for yourselves?"

"We went for a cup of coffee," Callidus said, looking down his nose at Dash. "I wasn't aware it was illegal under the emperor's rule."

"For a cup of coffee?" Dash crossed his arms. "Sneaking out the back way? You must think I was born yesterday."

"To the contrary, I give no thought to when you were born. Now if you would excuse us, we'd like to get inside out of the rain."

Dash grabbed Callidus's arm as he tried to shove past the lieutenant. "Don't ever. Try to duck my watch again. There will be consequences."

"For him maybe," Wren muttered as she followed Callidus up the steps.

"I heard that," Dash said.

Wren looked over her shoulder in surprise.

He was right on her heel. "Oh yes. From now on we're as inseparable as salt and pepper. Enjoy."

Wren parted ways with Dash at her room, slamming the door in his face.

"Wren."

She jumped against the door, her hand flying to her heart. "Thom!" She let out a shaky laugh. "You scared the sugar out of me." She looked back over her shoulder and held up her finger to her lips. "Dash is out there," she whispered.

Thom was sitting at the table by her window, one long leg crossed over the other.

Wren rang the bell for a servant before taking the seat across from him. Some coffee would warm her up.

Thom grabbed a chocolate from the little bowl on the table. "Think these are safe?"

Wren shrugged. "I can't imagine the emperor's been everywhere."

A knock sounded on the door. Wren met the servant, poking her head into the hallway. "Just some coffee for me and Master Thom," she whispered, ignoring Dash, who was leaning against the wall, one booted foot crossed over the other, examining his fingernails.

The maid curtseyed and took off down the hall.

"Didn't you and Callidus just go out for 'coffee' an hour ago?" Dash crooked his fingers around the word "coffee."

"We Alesians drink a great amount of coffee. Perhaps you should do some research before you invade a country next time." Wren slammed the door again.

"How'd it go with your family?" Wren asked, dropping back into the chair.

Thom shook his head. "I was too late."

Wren deflated. "I'm so sorry."

Thom shrugged. "It might be safer for them. They'll toe the line, stay out of trouble. At least until we can find a solution. Did you talk to

Pike?"

Wren took one of the chocolates, unwrapping it. They were tasty, with a gooey center of just the right consistency and sweet milk chocolate on the outside. There was nothing worse than a caramel that dripped out of the center of its chocolate home. She could never understand confectioners who preferred that type of confection. But she was stalling. "We found Rizio. Pike's left the city. The whole Spicer's Guild has."

"Blooming hell," Thom said. "It's that bad, huh?"

Wren nodded before meeting his eyes. "We're going too."

"What?" Thom exploded.

Wren cringed. "Shh!"

Sorry, he mouthed. "You're leaving?"

"We're leaving. Or at least, I hope you're coming too. It's not forever. Just long enough for us to regroup and figure out what to do about this bread."

Thom was nodding. "I'll come. But only if we bring the others."

"What others?" Wren asked.

Thom rolled his eyes. "Lennon. Marina. Olivia. We can't just leave them here under the emperor's mind control."

"They're too dangerous to bring along. They could give us up to the emperor's men. They're not our allies right now."

"If they didn't know what we were doing until it was too late, then they wouldn't have a reason to fight us. We need to give the infused bread a chance to wear off."

"It would provide good information," Wren admitted. "To know how long it takes to wear off. But it's going to be complicated enough to get us out of the Guildhall with Lieutenant Babysitter watching our every move. To try to get three more..."

"When I was kidnapped by King Imbris, you didn't leave me to rot. You planned to get me out," Thom pointed out. "They're our allies."

"Olivia and Lennon are," Wren muttered. She sighed. "I'm not sure Callidus will go for it. But we can try."

"Good." Thom brightened.

"We can't go to Callidus without a plan, though." She clapped her hands. "So. What's your master plan to get us all out of here?"

Thom unwrapped another chocolate, grinning. "I was hoping you'd come up with one."

Wren groaned. "Take them out for a dinner in the Port Quarter? On one of Pike's ships? Then it starts going and before they're any the wiser, we're gone?" She let out a halfhearted laugh. It was a terrible plan. Hardly even worthy of the name.

"No one eats dinner in the Port Quarter. Plus, how would we lose Dash? And don't you think they'd wonder about our luggage?"

"Luggage." Wren scrunched her lip. "I forgot about that."

Another knock sounded on the door and Thom went to fetch their coffee. "We didn't ask for any food," he said, which warranted a murmured response from the maid. "Fine," he said, closing the door with one foot, a silver tray in his hands.

"They sent up pastries." He smiled sweetly. "Courtesy of the emperor," he said in a high-pitched voice. "Should I throw them in the fire?"

But an idea was blossoming in Wren's mind. "Keep them," she said as Thom sat down.

"Cream? Sugar?" he asked, and she shook her head.

"Black. Thom. I think...I think I have an idea."

"Thank the Beekeeper." Thom handed her an earthen mug, its contents warm and black. "Lay it on me."

Wren dumped out the chocolates onto the table and positioned the two croissants across from each other. "This croissant is the ship. This one's the Guild. The chocolates are us. And..." She snagged a sugar cube from the bowl and placed it with the chocolates. "This is Dash."

"Your plan looks delicious thus far."

She shot him a look. She added the little silver pitcher of cream to the pile of chocolates and sugar cube. "This is a wagon full of Guild goods. We tell Dash that we have been ordered by the emperor to transport these special products to a ship that will take them back to Aprica."

"What will be in the wagon?"

"We'll need to make some chocolate. But underneath, we can put our luggage."

"Nice," Thom said. "Won't we need some sort of paperwork? Official order or some such?"

Wren waved her hand. "We can forge it."

"Oh, of course. Silly me. Continue."

"We get Lennon and Marina and Olivia to assist us with the transport."

"Why would they come too?"

"I don't know, Thom. I haven't worked out every detail. We'll tell them…the emperor asked for them to supervise. They're so in love with him, they'll swoon all over themselves for the chance to serve."

"Things are getting shaky, but go on."

"We all take the wagon down to the docks, where it will be loaded onto the ship bound for 'Aprica.'" She moved her little convoy of chocolate and coffee accoutrements to the other croissant. "While Lennon, Marina, and Olivia are carrying the stuff into the ship, one of us distracts Dash and knocks him out. We tie him up inside the wagon." Wren dropped the sugar cube into the cream.

"Not it," Thom said.

"Now Dash is out of the way, our guild members are on the ship, together with our luggage. All we have to do is keep them on the ship and let Pike's men cast off."

Thom rubbed his jaw, pondering. "It's not terrible."

Wren blew out a breath. "Will Callidus go for it?"

Thom grinned. "What's the worst that could happen?"

CHAPTER 13

A pillow smacked Hale in the face.

"You're rolling about like a virgin getting his first lay." The soldier in the bunk above him peered down, his stringy, black hair hanging like a curtain. "Quit it."

"Sorry," Hale mumbled. He didn't remember the man's name.

The face disappeared and the bunk above him creaked as the soldier settled back down.

Hale sat up. He set his feet on the stone floor and cradled his head in his hands. There was no way he was going to sleep tonight. The Falconer's message was haunting him, playing over and over in his mind. Why was Daemastra keeping a Gifted Baker's Guild member hostage? What was he doing to the bread?

Hale hopped into his trousers, grabbing his boots and a flannel shirt. He padded through the dark barracks in his bare feet, pausing in the dimly-lit hallway outside to finish dressing.

It was well past midnight, what his mother had always called "the witching hour." A sad smile twisted on his face. His mother had been magic and she hadn't even known it. She would have been delighted. His father would have hated it.

Hale walked through the slumbering palace, not sure where he was headed. He just knew that his feet needed to mirror his thoughts—moving, moving.

He found himself in the empty hallways of Daemastra's west wing. Moving towards the cuisinier's kitchen, workshop, lair—whatever the man considered it. Daemastra seemed like the type of man who might work at all hours of the night, but Hale saw as he approached carefully that the room was dark.

He lit an oil lamp, carrying it with him, running his fingers over books, the utensils, and implements. He wasn't certain what he was searching for, only that there was something to find.

Hale opened the icebox, revealing a meticulously organized set of glass vials and jars of various sizes. Each was labeled with a name. He frowned, taking one out, looking at its contents in the light of the lamp. Some sort of white powder. He held up one of the big ones, the size of a large jar that you might keep peaches in. "Martin," the neat lettering read. He put it back, closing the door with a frown.

He continued his surreptitious inspection, pulling a book off the shelf. He flipped through the pages before pulling the next. Anatomy. Infectious diseases. Alchemy. Metalworking. Chemistry. There seemed to be no natural science that Daemastra hadn't studied. Perhaps the man truly was trying to discover a cure for the emperor's condition.

Hale put the last book back on the shelf. He tried to open a set of cabinets, but they were locked. Hale smiled. Locked cabinets had worthy contents. He looked around for something to pick the lock with and came up with a small knife and a paper clip. "Thank you, Wren," he said as he maneuvered the lock open. His smile faded at the thought of her, his elation dimming. What was going on back at the Guild? He sighed. That wasn't his home anymore. He had lost the right to care about them. This sterile workshop was his home now.

"Jackpot," Hale whispered as he pulled open the cabinet doors. The bottom shelf was filled with a dozen black notebooks. He pulled the last one off the shelf, flipping through it. Daemastra's script was small and neat, his documentation meticulous. Experiment 427? Hale's brow furrowed. Better start at the beginning. He retrieved the first notebook off the shelf, pulled up a stool, and began reading.

As the pages turned and the oil in the lamp burned off, Hale's horror grew. The notebooks went back a decade. It started with Daemastra's notes on the Aprican Gifted. Cataloging them, studying them. Experimenting on them—oftentimes against their wills. Which infusions had which result. Secrets, leverage. This man lived and breathed the Gifted. Infusions.

The notebooks documented Daemastra's own increased vitality as he began using infused products himself. Youth. Intelligence. The healing of the limp that had plagued him since a riding injury years back.

Hale moved through the notebooks, flipping through the pages, his eyes growing wider and wider. Daemastra's rise to power. Working as Grand Patrician Evander's cuisinier. Notes on recipes. Formulas. The coup that had ended King Vespian and Hale's own father—Daemastra had been integral in aiding Evander's rise to power. Hale's mother's name. Gifted potions to counter the emperor's condition. The emperor's condition...

Hale slammed the book closed. "By the Beekeeper's balls," he swore. He ran his hand through his golden hair. Daemastra *was* keeping the emperor alive. But he was also *poisoning him.*

"That crafty bastard," Hale whispered into the darkness. In a way, it was impressive. Daemastra had made himself indispensable to the emperor. Him, and his twisted obsession with cataloging and understanding the secret of the Gifted and their infusions. By infecting the emperor with a disease that only Daemastra and his "infused formulas" could keep at bay.

Hale slid the notebook back into its spot. He closed the cabinet, fumbling for far too long while trying to relock it. His heart was hammering in his chest. He was overcome with the desperate need to be away from this place—this room and the secrets it held. He hadn't had a chance to read through all the notebooks, to find out if they revealed what Daemastra was doing to the bread, but that seemed like a small concern in light of what he'd uncovered. If Daemastra found him here...there was no telling what the madman would do.

Finally, blessedly, the cabinet lock clicked shut. Hale blew out the lamp, replacing it where he'd found it.

Hale weighed his options as he hurried back towards the barracks. He shook his head, fighting with himself. There was really only one option, and it was lunacy.

But there it was. He needed to tell Evander. The man ruled an empire, and he was completely at Daemastra's mercy. The invasion, the imprisonment of Gifted members, perhaps Hale could end it all by telling the emperor the truth. Or perhaps he would lose his head.

Hale paused, chewing on his lip. He pulled a silver crown from his pocket. "Heads, I go talk to the emperor, tails, I go back to bed," he said to himself. His luck had never led him astray. He shoved aside the little voice that told him that luck may not stay with traitors to their friends and countries. He flipped.

Heads. Well, that settled it. Blooming hell.

He turned left towards Emperor Evander's wing. He had only glimpsed the man once since he'd taken over Alesia, since Daemastra had made Hale stand on that balcony behind the new ruler, forced him to look down upon the sea of people whose lives he'd helped ruin. Evander had changed much, no doubt thanks to Daemastra's poisons. Hale remembered Evander from his youth as a virile man with a hard set to his jaw, a man who hadn't smiled much. Actually, Evander had reminded Hale a lot of his father, though they'd been mortal enemies in Aprican politics. Now, the man was a shadow of his former self. A puppet.

A set of guards in white and gold uniforms stood outside the emperor's wing. "State your business."

"I need to speak to the emperor," Hale said.

"And I need a good lay," the man said. "Doesn't mean we're going to get it. It's past 2 A.M."

"I know, but I have intelligence for the emperor's ears alone. Extremely time-sensitive. If I don't get it to him, his interests could be irreparably harmed. Do you want to be the men responsible for one of the largest travesties in the history of the Empire?" Hale was laying it on a little thick, but the man's attitude rubbed him the wrong way.

The guards exchanged a look. "Could send him to the emperor's steward, let him decide," the one on the right said.

The other seemed relieved by this suggestion. "Steward Exita's chambers are at the end of the second hallway on the right. He will decide if you can interrupt the emperor at this hour."

"Thanks, mates," Hale said, offering a little bow. "You're a credit to your unit." He rolled his eyes as soon as he passed by the two men.

Hale didn't turn right at the second hallway. He kept going straight towards the next set of guards. "Here to see the emperor," he said.

"Not here," the guard said.

Not here? Shouldn't the other guards have just told him that?

"When will he be back?" Hale said through gritted teeth, trying not to let his annoyance show.

"Not sure."

"About now," a wizened voice said behind him.

Hale turned to find the emperor wrapped in a dressing gown, two more white uniformed guards behind him.

"Sir," Hale said. "I need to speak to you. It's a matter of utmost importance."

"Middle of the night." The emperor shuffled past him. He hardly came up to Hale's shoulder. It seemed Daemastra's poisons had been effective.

"Please," Hale said. He didn't want to tip his hand before the guards—he wasn't sure who might be in Daemastra's pocket.

"Go," the emperor barked, opening his door. The two guards were approaching Hale.

"You don't even have a moment for the son of Willum Firena?" Hale called as the emperor went to shut the door.

The emperor froze, turning to look at him. His eyes were milky, but Hale saw the recognition there. "Calladan, was it?" The emperor straightened.

"Hale," he said, his voice thick. He hadn't heard anyone speak of Calladan, his older brother, in years. "The younger son."

The emperor sighed. "Come in. Five minutes. I just drank a sleeping draught."

Hale shouldered past the guards, shaking one of the men's hands from where it rested in a less-than-friendly manner on his shoulder.

The emperor's chambers were huge, opulent, trimmed in gold gilt, with a dozen lanterns blazing merrily. The emperor waved Hale towards the fireplace before lowering himself into one of two large wingback chairs.

"I'll get right to it," Hale said. "Sim Daemastra has been poisoning you. You're not sick. Well, you weren't originally. He made you sick. I found it all in his notebooks."

The emperor looked at him through watery blue eyes, the lines on his face shadowed in the flickering firelight. Then he started to laugh—a wet, wheezing sound.

Hale leaned back, frowning as a hacking fit overcame the man.

When his deep, phlegmy coughs died down, the emperor looked back at him, seeming to weigh him. "I thank you kindly for your loyalty. I always respected your father, you know. Even though I had him killed. He was an honorable man."

Hale furrowed his brow at the non sequitur. "Your Majesty, what about Daemastra?"

"I'll tell you this, because in your old age, you get nostalgic. And I'm pleased to see you, this reminder of the old days. But this news, this revelation you bring me—is nothing I don't already know."

"What?" Hale leaned back, shocked. "You—You already know?"

"When you make a deal with the devil, don't be surprised when the devil comes to collect." The king pushed up one of the sleeves of his dressing gown, revealing wrinkled skin covered in sun spots. But beneath... Hale leaned forward, his eyes widening in horror. Lines of black twisted beneath the skin, as if snaking through the emperor's veins.

"You don't have to be a doctor to realize this isn't natural," the emperor said, pushing his sleeve back down.

"What...?" Hale stammered, trying to shake off his shock.

The emperor sighed. "I was young and power-hungry, and I let Daemastra off the leash, sanctioned his twisted...experiments. His obsession with the occult, with the Gifted, with infusions. He got me results, so I looked the other way and ignored his tactics. Before I knew it, we had run out of Aprican enemies to defeat. I was king, and I was satisfied. It turned out he wasn't."

"Why don't you have him arrested? Executed?"

"Besides the fact that I would die? That mattered to me for a while; it doesn't so much anymore. But my daughter, my grandchildren...I wouldn't want them harmed. Daemastra knows my leverage points. He's made it quite clear what would happen to my family if any harm befell him."

Hale shook his head. "So you do nothing? Let him have his way with Alesia?"

The emperor stood on shaky legs. "I suggest you do what I do. Stay out of his way. Beneath his notice."

"It's too late for that," Hale said softly.

"Then run," the emperor said. "You did it once. You made a new life for yourself here. You could do it again."

"I don't know that I could," Hale said. "Everything I love...it is...it was...here."

"Then this is your bed, and I suggest you get comfortable," the emperor said, shooing him towards the door. "That's all a man can do."

CHAPTER 14

"That is, without a doubt, the most idiotic, harebrained scheme I've ever heard. It will get us all killed. Or jailed. Or jailed and then killed." Callidus sat behind his desk, as dark as a storm cloud.

Wren and Thom sat before him, having just laid out their idiotic, harebrained scheme to ferry Olivia, Lennon, and Marina out of Maradis.

"Does that mean you'll let us bring them?" Thom asked, flashing his widest grin.

Callidus rubbed his temples. "They're not stray puppies." But Wren saw him softening, considering.

Wren and Thom exchanged a hopeful look but remained silent.

"Beckett is Marina's father. I'm not going to take her away from her family," Callidus said. "But Olivia...I do feel responsible for her in a way. After what happened with Kasper and Greer."

Thom gave a little victorious shake of his fists.

Wren smiled despite herself. "And Lennon?" she asked.

Callidus let out a long-suffering sigh. "Yes, and Lennon. In for a pinch, in for a pound."

"Yes! You won't regret this," Thom said.

"I doubt that very much," Callidus said drolly. "To pull this off..." He pulled out a little black notebook from the inside pocket of his jacket. "We'll need a forged bill of lading from the emperor for the goods, a whole hell of a lot of chocolates to use as cover, boxes to hide our actual luggage, and something to incapacitate Dash, Lennon, and Olivia."

"I figured we'd just knock them over the head," Wren suggested.

"Oh, did you? Do you want to be the one who has the honor of incapacitating Lieutenant Cardas without getting yourself killed?"

Wren and Thom looked at each other and shrugged. "We figured you'd do it," Thom said.

"No thank you, Thom, no thank you. We'd be just as likely to kill the lot of them than knock them unconscious."

"What do you suggest?" Wren asked.

"I know an apothecary who should be able to get us something that will put them under for a time." He scribbled in his notebook, scrunching his already thick eyebrows into one long line. "Yes, I think we can pull it off. If you two make all the confections, I can handle the other arrangements."

"Yes, Guildmaster," Thom said.

Wren and Thom stood in unison. It wasn't the worst of the jobs, to have to make the chocolate.

"And don't eat anything before tomorrow that you haven't made with your own hands. The last thing I need is to lose you two as well."

"Yes, Guildmaster," Wren said as they headed towards the door, winking at Thom.

"Why does it sound like an insult when they say that?" She heard Callidus muttering under his breath as she closed the door.

Wren and Thom spent the next twenty-four hours in the kitchen, mixing and boiling and stirring and pouring. They made amaretti truffles, buckwheat beehives, chai tigers, and spiked earl grey ganache. On and on they poured—orange blossoms and dulce de leche balls and toffee drops and gingerbread squares and peppermint swirls. They cooked until Wren's feet ached and her stomach yowled from hunger. They took turns stealing a few hours' sleep on the hard, little bench in the heat of the conservatory, the humid air melting away the aches in their backs and cricks in their necks.

Wren was swaying on her feet, placing the last of the mezcal macadamia chews into neat rows in tidy brown cardboard boxes, when Callidus appeared in the doorway to check on their progress. He looked over the stacks of boxes tied with twine and merely grunted. "I had the servants bring a packing crate up to each of your rooms. Pack only what you need and then we'll put the chocolates on top. Be ready in two hours." He disappeared into the hallway as quickly as he had materialized.

"If I didn't know better, I would think that grunt was a compliment," Thom said.

"If I didn't know better, I'd think you were right."

Wren and Thom trudged wearily up the stairs towards their rooms. Wren tripped over the first stair—only Thom's arm kept her from falling flat on her face.

"Did you infuse the chocolates?" Thom asked. "I know you're clumsy, but even you can usually conquer a set of stairs."

Wren looked crossly at Thom. "Some of them. It's hard not to when you're making that many." Wren's gift infused chocolate with good luck, but in the act of infusing, she gave up her own luck for a time. She certainly didn't feel very lucky right now.

"Wren, Thom!" Olivia stood at the second-floor landing above them.

"Hello," Wren said carefully as she and Thom summited the final steps to the landing. It was strange to interact with Olivia, knowing she was under the emperor's thrall.

"You two look positively dead on your feet," Olivia said, her pretty face twisted with concern.

"We had a large order of confections to make. An order from the emperor," Thom said.

"About that," Olivia said, walking beside them towards their room. "Why exactly did Callidus want me to come along? I normally handle deliveries to the Guild, not from it."

Wren's mind raced. "Um...I suggested you come along."

"Why?"

Thom and Wren exchanged a panicked look. Wren came up with the excuse. "Because...Lieutenant Cardas. He... I think he likes you."

"The Aprican Legionnaire? With the beard?" Olivia said. Her blue eyes widened.

Thom raised an eyebrow and Wren gave a hopeless little shrug. "Yep. He asked me about you. Since we all have to live with the Apricans now, I figure it can't hurt to get to know them."

"All right," Olivia said slowly, deep in thought. A smile crept onto her cherubic face. "You're right. It can't hurt to be friendly. We leave at what, eleven? A little late for a delivery, isn't it?"

"To keep out of sight of the Falconer rebels," Thom said sagely.

"Makes sense."

They had reached Wren's door now.

"I'll see you both in a few hours," Olivia said brightly, waving and heading back down the hallway.

"That was some first-class bullshitting. Dash has a crush on her?" He snorted a laugh.

"Hopefully, they'll be too busy flirting with each other to realize our cover story makes absolutely no sense."

"See you in two?"

Wren nodded.

As Callidus promised, one of the wooden packing crates had been delivered to Wren's chambers. Wren looked about, at a loss as to what to pack. She'd never had much in the way of worldly possessions, and since arriving at the Guild, she hadn't had a lot of leisure time for shopping. In her closet, she stripped off the chocolate-stained dress she wore and pulled on a navy-blue skirt and sky-blue blouse, cinching them both with a brown leather belt. She pulled on thick woolen stockings and laced up her good brown boots. Traveling attire, check. She looked through her meager closet, pulling out a few of the more sensible warm dresses, a few pairs of leggings and a thick sweater to sleep in. She ran her hands past the velvet dress she had worn to Callidus's Appointment Gala, and then the beaded gown she had worn to Crown Prince Zane's royal wedding. The black dress was heavy in her hands, its weight pulling at her. It had been a gift from Lucas. The first gift from Lucas. She wanted to bring it with her but knew it was completely impractical. There would be no need for fancy dresses where she was going. She didn't even know where she was going.

Wren leaned against the wall, pulling out of her blouse the chain that held Lucas's ring. She stroked the ring's carved edges, imagining him touching this very surface before he gave it to her.

"Where are you?" she whispered. "What if I never figure out what it means? What if I never find you?" She closed her eyes, trying to conjure up the image of him, to trace the contours of his features with her mind's eye. Dark hair laced with flecks of premature gray, soft gray eyes over a serious nose. A smile...a smile that melted her like chocolate in the sun. Checked suits, long fingers laced through hers, the rosemary-fresh scent of him. He was fading. She could see the pieces individually if she focused on them, brought them to the forefront of her mind. But the picture—the whole picture—was fuzzy. Wherever he was, was Lucas forgetting her too?

Wren shoved the ring back under her blouse, wishing her emotions could disappear as easily. She needed to finish packing.

She finished shoving clothes into the box—underclothes, a scarf woven in the forest-green plaid of the Imbris clan—a second gift from Lucas. A toothbrush and hairbrush and various bathroom implements, including some hairpins for any lockpicking she may need to do in the future. She took the coins she had saved up from their little hiding place on the bookshelf, adding them to the pouch on her belt. A deck of cards she had borrowed from Hale. Well, those were hers now. She packed the cards inside the crate and covered her measly worldly possessions with some crinkled paper before securely fastening on the lid. Perfect. Time to go.

Dash, apparently in good spirits again despite their unchaperoned outing yesterday, had commissioned a wagon for them. He seemed eager to prove his usefulness, which Wren supposed was better than him lurking about doing nothing. Thom and Lennon dutifully carried the crates of chocolate along with some of the guild servants.

"What does the emperor need all of this for?" Lennon asked, raindrops shimmering on his dark hair.

"He's having an All Hallows' Eve party for the ages," Wren said. "He wanted the best confections."

Thom winked at her, mouthing, "First class."

Wren made a shushing motion at him. She was almost starting to enjoy coming up with a load of hogwash to feed the others.

"That's the last of it," Dash said, dusting off his hands. "Shall we get going?"

"By all means," Callidus said, with an incline of his head. "After you."

The city streets were largely deserted this time of night, and they made good time to the Port Quarter. Their group was quiet, huddling under the wagon's canvas cover to keep out of the rain. Wren watched the silent buildings pass by—stones grayed with moisture, the light of lamps and candles turning the leaded glass windows into blinking eyes. When she had first come to Maradis, it had seemed a terrifying maze of strange faces and dark alleys. Now, despite its flaws, it had come to feel like home. When would she see it again?

Thom stared out the other side of the wagon, deep in thought. Was he wondering the same thing?

Wren shoved her hands in her pockets, half to ward against the cold, half to check, for the tenth time, that the little bottle Callidus had given her was still there. They each had one; the clear liquid was supposed to be strong enough to knock out a horse when inhaled through the nostrils. Wren had to admit that relying on a chemical was preferable to clubbing their friends over the back of the head and hoping nothing went wrong.

As it was, so very much could go wrong.

CHAPTER 15

T he Black Jasmine was a handsome three-masted schooner with a hull
of lacquered jet black. Its crew swarmed over it like ants, making final
preparations for departure. Olivia shivered in her cloak. She would have
refused this strange little job if it weren't for two things. The emperor
had requested it of them, and they needed to do whatever they could to
prove their competence to their new sovereign. And Dash. Olivia
looked sideways at the man from beneath the dark of her hood. The
Aprican lieutenant who was staying with them just happened to be one
of the handsomest men she'd ever seen. Yet another reason to rejoice
the emperor had come to save Alesia.

"Why isn't the emperor using one of the Aprican merchant vessels?"
Dash asked with a frown, pulling the horses to a stop.

"This one's supposed to be the fastest in Maradis," Callidus said
quickly. "He needs speed to get the confections there in good shape
before All Hallows' Eve."

The frown stayed fixed to Dash's face, but he hopped down from
the carriage bench. Callidus hurried after him. "I'll tell the captain we've

arrived," Callidus said. "Why don't you each grab a box and bring them on board?" Callidus strode down the dock, his black cloak flapping behind him.

Dash rounded the carriage to Olivia's side, offering his hand to help her from her seat. She didn't need the help, but it was considerate of him to offer, wasn't it? She placed her hand in his and he put the other on her waist, steadying her as she hopped down from the wagon. His hand was warm and broad, his thick callouses hard beneath the skin of her fingers. "Thank you," she murmured, breathing in his faint fresh smell of pine and sage.

"Of course," he replied, letting his hands linger for a moment. Or was she imagining it?

"Shall we?" Wren said, breaking the spell.

They circled to the back of the wagon and began unloading crates.

"Oof, these are heavy," Olivia said, pulling a crate off the wagon.

"Here, allow me," Dash said, taking it from her as easily as a pillow.

Olivia nodded, retrieving a smaller crate for herself. She headed down the dock behind Dash and the others, trying to ignore how finely his uniform cut over his muscled form.

Callidus was arguing with the ship's captain on deck, a dangerous-looking man who was gesturing towards the rest of them, with Callidus hissing in his face.

Olivia frowned and wondered what they could possibly be arguing about. Perhaps gold. She'd lost her cool with a vendor or two in her day when haggling over prices. Maybe the captain was trying to demand a higher price. It was important to get the best price for the emperor.

With a furious grunt, the captain, a dark-haired man with a silver earring, gestured to the end of the ship as they stepped off the gangplank onto the deck. "You can stack the cargo in the hold back there. The men can show you."

They followed a sailor down several teetering staircases into the dark hold of the vessel, where goods and barrels were piled against the walls. The man pointed to the far end and vanished into the low lantern light of the hallway. "Dash," Wren said. "Why don't you go with Callidus to grab more crates? We can arrange these ones down here."

"You sure you've got these?" Dash asked, setting his crate down.

"Definitely," Wren said sweetly. "Thanks for your help."

Dash grinned at Olivia as he passed by, and she found herself smiling back, her heart trilling within her. He was definitely flirting with her.

Olivia shuffled to the corner of the hold, dropping the crate with a crash, narrowly missing her foot. "I wish you hadn't sent Dash away," Olivia said. "What's in these confections, rocks?"

"Sure seems like it," Lennon said, moving behind Olivia to drop his own crate on top of hers.

Wren let out a stilted laugh. And then grabbed her.

Olivia froze in her shock as Wren clamped an iron hand over her face, another arm around her waist. Despite her frail appearance, the girl was startlingly strong.

"Wren!" Olivia tried to protest through the cloth her friend was holding over her nose and mouth. It had a sickly-sweet smell. She couldn't breathe with it over her face. Olivia struggled, trying to shimmy out of Wren's grip. What in the Beekeeper's name was Wren doing?

Olivia's head swam and her flailing became more desperate. Across the dark space of the hold she saw Thom grappling with Lennon. Olivia realized too late what was happening. Wren and Thom were betraying them. But why, she didn't know.

Olivia redoubled her efforts to break free, bucking like a wildcat, smashing her elbow into Wren's stomach.

Wren grunted in pain and her iron grip loosened.

Black was closing in on her vision now, but Olivia struggled against it, trying to push it back with clawing fingers. She wrenched out of Wren's arms only to find that her legs were lost to her—they weren't functioning at all.

Wren caught her before she hit the floor, lowering her to the sticky wooden slats of the hold. "It'll be all right, Olivia. I promise," Wren said. Her voice sounded distant—underwater.

Lies! A furious tear escaped the corner of Olivia's eye as she blinked rapidly, trying to fight the growing blackness. But it was a fight she couldn't win. The darkness swallowed her whole.

Olivia was down. Thank the Beekeeper. Wren let out a shaky sigh, pushing her hair from her face just in time to see Lennon rear back and punch Thom in the face.

Thom dropped like a felled tree, his hands to his face while Lennon hissed, sprinting towards the far end of the hold.

"Wait!" Wren said, tripping over Olivia's unconscious body to follow. Lennon stumbled up the stairs, running towards the freedom of the night air.

"It's for your own good!" Wren said as she raced after him. "Stop him!" Wren shouted as she leaped through the open door onto the deck, past a shocked sailor holding a coil of line.

Lennon was already across the deck and onto the gangplank. No, no, no. If she didn't stop him, he could call the Cedar Guard—or worse, the Aprican Legion—and lead them straight here.

Wren ran down the gangplank after them, almost bowling into Callidus, who was hurrying up the other way.

"What—?" he shouted, but she couldn't stop. If she stopped she'd lose him. Lennon was scrambling up onto the driver's bench of the wagon.

Lennon snapped the reins and the horses leaped forward as Wren caught up, grasping desperately onto the other side of the wagon, hauling herself up with raw strength she hadn't known she possessed. She half-flopped on Dash's unconscious body, slumped on the other half of the driver's bench. At least Callidus had managed to take out his target.

"Len—" she began, but he was ready for her. As she pushed up off of Dash, he released a savage kick that connected directly with her breastbone. The world slowed as the breath whooshed from her lungs, and she began to fall backwards, reeling through the open air towards the hard cobblestones below.

Her arms windmilled, grasping for anything she could find to keep her from falling. She connected with Dash's belt and clung to it desperately. But it only served to pull Dash's unconscious body off the bench, sending them both tumbling in a pile of arms and legs onto the hard ground below.

Light exploded in Wren's vision as she hit the ground. Her head cracked against the stones and her lungs felt like they had been rolled over by the carriage itself. Next to her, Dash stirred, letting out a groan. She tried to push to a seated position, but the world spun around her as fireworks exploded inside her head.

"Come on." Callidus appeared at her side, kneeling, pulling her up by her armpits.

She moaned in pain, but with his help, she got her feet under her. "Lennon," she managed.

"He's gone. We need to go now. He'll be reporting us to the legionnaires as soon as he finds someone. We need to be far from here when he does."

Getting back to the ship and up the gangplank took all of Wren's energy. Callidus lowered her gently against the rest of their crates that had been abandoned on the deck. Thom stood with horror on his face, no doubt watching Lennon gallop away into the night.

"Wren, I'm so sorry—" he began, but Rizio cut him off with a shout. "You flaming fools! This half-cocked scheme of yours will get us all killed. We'll have the Apricans upon us in minutes!"

"I suggest we be gone by then," Callidus said, his voice as cold as ice. "I'll double what we agreed for payment."

"Double it?" Rizio barked. "You should quadruple it!" But he stormed away, shouting at his sailors. The men had seemed to anticipate the command, as they had already thrown off the lines securing the Black Jasmine to the dock and were hoisting the sails.

"Are you all right?" Callidus asked, cradling Wren's head in his hands, opening her eyes wide to look in them.

"I'll live," she croaked. She could hardly see through the pain that drummed in her head.

"What a disaster." Callidus hung his head. "We never should have tried to bring the others with us."

"We got Olivia," Thom offered, standing over them with his shoulders hunched, his hands in his pockets.

Wren softened. "It was a mad plan. At least we're on the boat without Dash killing us. Nice job, Callidus."

"We're away from the dock," Thom said, seemingly desperate for some bit of positive news that they could attach to. "I bet—" But his words were cut off by a bloodcurdling cry, followed by a flurry of blue that crashed into him like a ton of bricks.

Dash staggered to his feet, his hair askew, his eyes wild and unfocused. The man had leaped from the dock to the boat!

Dash pulled his sword from its sheath with an ominous ring. "By order of the emperor..." He stumbled. Clearly, the combination of the drug Callidus had given him and the tumble from the carriage was still affecting him. He tried again as Thom scooted away from his swinging blade. "By order of Emperor Evander, I hereby arrest you." He pointed his sword at Callidus, who shied back a step. "I am commandeering this vessel."

In two swift steps, Rizio appeared behind the legionnaire and cracked him over the back of his head with the pommel of his dagger. "Commandeer this."

Dash's eyes rolled back in his head and he began to sway on his feet. He careened forward into the nearby rail, which did little to forestall his forward progress. He promptly pitched over the side of the ship, falling with a splash into the inky water below.

A moment of shocked silence hung over them.

Thom was the first to break it, racing to the rail to lean over and peer at where the legionnaire's sky-blue coat was visible in the water below. Thom looked back at them all. "Isn't someone going to help him?"

Rizio shrugged.

"He's going to drown," Thom said, looking from Callidus to Wren, who was still having trouble with the world not blurring into two or three versions of itself.

"He doesn't deserve to die!" Thom said, his hands up in disbelief. "No one. Seriously?"

"It's unfortunate—" Callidus began. But Thom was already vaulting over the railing, taking the long leap into the water below.

CHAPTER 16

Trick outdid himself with dinner that night. Lucas and Trick had retrieved a few dozen clams from the little beach on the island, which Trick promptly sautéed in a sauce of garlic and butter with chopped potatoes. Trick had opened one of the bottles of crisp white wine that had been sitting, forgotten, in the house's cellar. He steamed fresh dandelion greens Ella had collected and cut up the last of the fresh sourdough bread. They used it to sop up the delicious sauce from their plates until every morsel was gone.

When they were finished, they all leaned back, bellies big from the meal, the candles burning low. Lucas was loath to disturb the peace of the moment, even though questions were burning in his mind. Needing to be answered. Finally he broke down. "We should talk about the Falconer's letter."

Ella crossed her arms before her chest, her eyes flashing. "What have you decided?"

Lucas recoiled. She was so sharp now, all edges and points. There seemed to be little he could say that didn't raise her ire. "I haven't decided anything. It's all of our decision."

"It may affect Ella and me, but it'll be your life, Lucas," Trick said. "You're the one who has to choose in the end."

Lucas shook his head. "I'm making it all of our decision. We all agree or we don't do it. We're all the family we have left. I'm not doing anything to jeopardize that."

"Okay. But...do you want to be king?" Trick asked softly.

His brother had his own special type of sharpness too—an ability to cut right to the heart of things—to the truth you weren't yet ready to face. And that was it. The Falconer was raising a rebellion. To put Lucas on the throne. The man wanted him to return to Maradis to claim his rightful place as King of Alesia.

"No," Lucas admitted. "I don't."

"Then say *no*," Trick suggested.

"But it's not that simple, is it?" said Lucas. "Because I don't want to just abandon Alesia to the Apricans. I don't want to give up. We got out of the city to be safe for a time. We never intended to stay away forever. Did we?" In truth, their flight from the city had been such a hurried thing, they hadn't had time to think of the future. There had been no plans in place. There still weren't.

"You always were too noble for your own good," Ella said, downing the rest of her wine. "How do we even know we can trust this Falconer? It could be an Aprican plot to lure us out of hiding so they can kill us."

Trick shook his head. "If they knew where to send us a letter, they'd waste no time coming for us. I trust Oban and his associates. They wouldn't betray us to the emperor."

"We still don't know who the Falconer is, though. He could be a madman," Ella protested. "Or completely full of shit. He could have no support and no resources."

"It's a risk, certainly," Lucas agreed. "We'd be gambling our lives based on a promise in a letter from a man we don't even know."

Trick frowned, twisting his napkin. "When you put it that way, it doesn't sound like a good bet, does it?"

"If we said *no,* what would we do?" Lucas asked. "I've been thinking about it. We can't stay here. This island can't sustain us indefinitely. Most of the Western Reaches are under Aprican control. Nova Navis feels too close for comfort. I'm sure the Apricans will be coming for the peninsula next. Centu or east into the Ferwald badlands would be our best bets."

Ella wrinkled her nose. "I don't fancy myself a fisherman's wife, or living in a tent like a nomad."

"Neither have good climates for grapes," Trick said. "It'd be hard for me to make a living."

"It'd probably be too risky for you to hang your shingle as a winemaker anyway," Lucas said. "Too recognizable. Same for me as an inspector."

"We left the treasury behind in Maradis," Ella said. "So how would we live?"

Silence fell over them.

Lucas ran a hand through his hair, cursing his father, cursing the Apricans, cursing the whole damn situation.

"I don't know. Ella, what do you want to do?" Lucas blew out a sigh. Ella seemed the most fragile among them right now. He didn't want to make a decision that could break her.

Tears were shimmering in his sister's eyes, her chin quivering. "I want things back how they were. I want Mother, I want Virgy, I want my books and my cat and my friends and this all to be a bad dream." She shoved back from the table. "But I can't have any of that. So I guess I don't care." She turned and stormed up the stairs.

"I think that went well," Trick murmured.

Lucas loosed a shaky laugh, cradling his head in his hands. Poor Ella. In a way she'd lost the most. Because she'd lost her innocence, too. She'd had the bright incorrigible optimism of youth. And now she saw the world for what it really was.

"The truth is," Trick said, "I want to go back to Maradis. It's probably suicide, but it's our home. There are people we care about there. There are people...I care about."

Trick's tone was wary and thin, and Lucas looked up at his brother, his inspector's senses tingling.

"Who is she?" Lucas asked. He'd been a bad brother, if Trick had fallen for someone and Lucas hadn't even known. The weeks before Maradis had fallen had been madness, but still. He should have made time.

Trick hesitated, spinning the base of his wine glass on the table. "You mean...who is he."

Lucas's eyes widened as the import of his brother's words sank in.

Trick licked his lips and looked at Lucas, sitting as tense as a coiled wire.

Lucas softened, realizing the courage it must have taken his brother to share this piece of himself. Wishing Trick had felt safe to share it with Lucas a lot sooner. "Of course. Who is he?"

"Thom." Trick rubbed the back of his head, looking away.

"From the Confectioner's Guild?"

Trick nodded.

Lucas pondered, bringing Thom to mind. Trick and Thom had been held captive together at the orphanage; it made sense that they'd grown close. Become friends. And perhaps more. "Okay, I can see it. Tall. Cute freckles. Strong hands." Lucas waggled his eyebrows.

Trick smacked his forehead in mortification. "Tell me you are not going to check out guys for me now."

"Isn't that my job as older brother? I need to screen these fellows and make sure they're worthy of you."

"Do not go all Inspector Imbris on him." Trick pointed at Lucas threateningly, but he was fighting a smile.

"No promises," Lucas said. "Does he...feel the same?"

The smile slipped from Trick's face. "I'm not sure. Maybe? I didn't have a chance to talk to him before everything happened."

"He'd be a fool if he didn't. You're a catch."

Trick rolled his eyes. "You have to say that because you're my brother."

"True. But I also happen to mean it." Lucas softened. "I'm really happy for you, Trick."

"Thanks, Lucas," Trick said, and Lucas understood what he meant. For everything.

"Confectioner's Guild, who knew?" Lucas joked. "They've got all the good ones."

Trick nodded. "Apparently. Does this mean you've decided? We're going back to Maradis?"

Had he decided? Lucas still didn't want to be king. But perhaps he would, if it meant freeing the city he loved. Perhaps he could find a way to make it tolerable. At the least, he knew he had to go back. He couldn't face a world—a future—where he never saw Wren again. Where he couldn't see her mischievous smile, laugh at her wry sense of humor. He wanted strolls to the Farmer's Market hand-in-hand and lazy Saturday mornings with coffee and pastries from Bitterbird Cafe. He wanted the heat of her mouth on his and the chill of her ridiculously icy fingertips curling against him for warmth. He wanted Wren. And he wanted Maradis.

"You'd be a good king," Trick said. "More so because you don't want it. Alesia would be lucky to have you."

Lucas nodded, feeling the weight of the decision settle upon him. "So we're going back to Maradis. To overthrow an Emperor."

"And to find our confectioners," Trick said with a grin.

CHAPTER 17

"Firena, get up." Someone kicked Hale's foot, which was hanging over the side of his bunk.

"Hmm?" Hale lifted his head, peering at the interloper through slitted eyes. "What?"

"Sim Daemastra's asking for you. Now."

A surge of adrenaline coursed through Hale's system, jolting him awake. "All right," he said, running a hand through the tangles in his long hair.

"Now," the legionnaire said before moving on.

Though morning light streamed through the narrow windows, Hale was groggy with fatigue. He blew out a breath. His conversation last night with the emperor felt like a strange dream.

He quickly dressed, running to the washroom to splash water on his face and relieve himself.

He strode towards Daemastra's wing, pulling his hair back into a bun. Gods, he hated this uniform. It made his skin crawl. Maybe the emperor was right. Maybe he should run. Get as far away from here as he could. He could suffer punishment for his betrayal in some other way, rather than helping the monsters who'd killed his father and invaded his city. Hale sighed. No. He was one of those monsters now. This was what he had sown when he'd sold out his city and his Guild. He didn't deserve escape.

Hale rounded the corner into Daemastra's workshop and came to a startled stop. Talking to Daemastra were two men he hadn't expected. One he knew—Steward Willings—and one he didn't—a brute of an Aprican legionnaire even taller and more muscular than he. A scar across the man's upper lip seemed to twist his expression into a permanent sneer.

"Ah, young Firena. So kind of you to join us," Daemastra said, clapping his bony hands together. "You look positively exhausted. Trouble sleeping?"

Alarm bells rang in Hale's mind. Did the man know something? But no, how could he? The emperor would have no reason to sell him out to Daemastra. But he had no reason to protect him either… "You try sleeping in a barracks with twenty snoring men," Hale replied.

"Very good. I understand you know Mister Willings. And this is Lieutenant Oosten. They're both assisting me with a special project."

"What kind of special project?" The hairs on the back of Hale's neck prickled in alarm.

Willings replied. "Sim Daemastra is creating an elite force within the Legion. The Golden Guard. Only the strongest and most capable warriors have been chosen." That snake, it made sense that he had cozied up with a leech like Daemastra.

"I get why he's here"—Hale nodded towards the hulking soldier—"but why you?"

"Hale." Daemastra tsked. "Mister Willings will be leading this force for me. Overseeing their training and their…conditioning."

It was all Hale did to suppress a snort. Willings was a weasel, yes, but soldier, no. These men wouldn't respect him. Why had Daemastra made such a poor choice? He was normally more…shrewd.

Daemastra continued. "I've been working on a special formula. Something that will give my Golden Guard an edge over the rest."

Sly smiles stretched across both men's faces, chilling Hale to his core. Flaming hell. Daemastra planned to give these warriors some sort of infused concoction. What would it do to them?

Oosten seemed entirely clueless as to what he was signing up for, standing like a statue, his meaty arms crossed before him.

"Oosten, if you please, would you mind sitting down in this chair?" Daemastra said, going to the icebox to retrieve a syringe. The chair Daemastra spoke of reclined like the chairs of the Dentist's Guild, but, Hale saw for the first time, it came equipped with leather restraints. Hale's stomach flipped.

Hale was overcome with the mad urge to warn the soldier, but he didn't even know what he was warning him against. So he stood mute as Daemastra injected a strange milky liquid into the soldier's arm.

Willings leaned forward, his dark eyes shining with anticipation.

Oosten began to shake, his huge body wracked with convulsions.

Willings and Hale stepped back, but Daemastra stood still, pulling one of his little black notebooks off the counter and writing in it.

Soon enough, the convulsions stopped. But something else was happening. The man's face was transforming—his features pulling and twisting. The wrinkles by his eyes, the scar twisting his lip—they smoothed out, leaving him youthful and...handsome. The soldier's body was growing too, his muscles bulging even more than they had been, his legs lengthening until the chair creaked from the weight.

Oosten groaned, gritting his teeth against the changes, panting through perfectly-straight blindingly-white teeth.

Finally, the metamorphosis was over.

The room was still and silent but for Oosten's ragged panting.

Hale shut his mouth, realizing it had been hanging open. This—This was Gifted magic? He had never seen anything this profound. The magic of the Confectioner's Guild was a subtle thing, sneaky and sly. There was nothing subtle about this.

"Marvelous," Willings said. His pockmarked face was rapt with possibility as Oosten swung his huge feet onto the ground. He towered over Hale, over all of them, his face devastatingly handsome, vibrating youth and health. He was like...a god. Like the Sower come down from his golden fields to the ground to sup with mere mortals. This...whatever this man was...people would worship it.

"Try out your new body," Daemastra said, motioning towards the man.

Oosten jumped, nearly crashing into the ceiling. He darted into the corner of the room, impossibly fast. "Everything's so clear," he said. Even his voice was attractive—a deep and resonant baritone. "I...I understand so much."

"What's 435 multiplied by 9087?" Daemastra asked.

"3,952,845," the man responded, as if Daemastra had asked him to add one plus one.

Willings looked towards Daemastra, who did a quick calculation in his notebook. Daemastra nodded in appreciation. "Correct."

"Remarkable," Willings said, reaching out and petting the man's chiseled arm.

"The best of the Guilds. Strength and prowess from the Butcher's Guild. Beauty and virility from the Distiller's. Intelligence from the Cheesemonger's and health from the Cuisinier's. Wit and magnetism from the Brewer's Guild. It should last several hours, per my prior experiments. Go test it out. Take good notes, Willings. I'll expect a full report."

"Absolutely," Willings said eagerly.

Oosten was holding a silver tray, examining his face in the dull reflection. "I'm prettier than him." He pointed to Hale.

"Indeed." Daemastra chuckled. "Enjoy. Now, there will be some adverse effects when it wears off. Nausea, vomiting, achiness. Take it easy and rest the remainder of the day."

Oosten nodded eagerly and ducked out the door.

Willings hurried after.

Hale stood in stunned silence as the men left. He had to admit, he was impressed. Truly, none but a madman would risk such a strange concoction...but it was remarkable.

"Impressive, is it not?" Daemastra said.

Hale managed a nod.

"Once the formula is complete, we'll be able to create a whole legion of super soldiers. Young, virile, intelligent. The best humanity has to offer."

"Will they even be human at that point?"

"Of course." Daemastra's voice was smooth as silk. "Just...improved."

"And I'm sure you've never thought of using this on yourself," Hale countered.

"What man doesn't want to be young and handsome forever? I wouldn't deprive myself of the benefit of the culmination of my life's work." Daemastra turned, putting his notebook back in the cabinet with the others.

"And the emperor?" Hale asked. He was dangerously close to a forbidden topic, but he couldn't help himself.

"Of course, the primary aim of this work is to find a cure for the emperor's ailment. He will be the first recipient once I am sure it is safe."

"Of course," Hale parroted. Daemastra's plan was beginning to come into focus. Once he became god-like, he could dispatch the emperor, claiming the monarch had finally died of his wasting sickness. And who would the people of the Empire look to for new leadership but the man who had stood beside the emperor through thick and thin? Emperor Evander only had one daughter, and she'd been married off to a minor Aprican Patrician years ago. Her children were still young. They'd be no match for Daemastra.

Daemastra interrupted his circling thoughts. "Hale, you're a tall fellow. Would you grab that pitcher on that shelf?" Daemastra pointed to a glass pitcher on the top shelf.

Hale suppressed his irritation but crossed the room, reaching up to retrieve it for the strange man.

He felt a prick in his arm. He looked down to find Daemastra pulling a syringe out of his bicep.

"What—?" Hale began, but the ground tilted beneath him. The pitcher fell from his hand, shattering on the ground. The sound was far away. "What did you do?" he managed.

"Now, Hale, it's best to sit down." Daemastra steered him towards the ominous reclining chair.

Hale collapsed into it. His heart was thundering in his chest, his blood boiling in his veins. He tried to shake off his daze. "What did you do?"

Daemastra narrowed his gaze. "Do you think anything goes on in this Empire that I am not aware of? Did you think you could visit the emperor without my knowledge?" Daemastra paused, but it seemed more of a rhetorical question, because when Hale didn't answer, the man continued. "I had hoped we would be able to work together as allies. But I see that your old allegiances still hold sway over you. It's my fault, really, for overlooking it. It's my job to see you're properly motivated."

"What did you do?" Hale tried again. His voice sounded strange. Like he was underwater. He looked down at his body, to make sure it was still there. His hands... He held up a hand. Black veins were creeping down his hands, like oil-slicked spiderwebs. Black like he'd seen beneath the emperor's paper-thin skin. "What did you do?" He raged again, trying to push out of the chair, but the room was spinning.

"Since you and the emperor are so friendly, I thought you'd appreciate the same treatment. I've infected you with the same poison. If you don't get the antidote from me on the dot every morning, you'll die a quite gruesome death."

"Why...?" Hale managed. "Why me?"

"I need your luck to perfect my formula."

"Fine," Hale said, fighting through nausea and panic. The man was well and truly mad. "I'll cook for you. As much as you want. Like the baker. Just give me the antidote." The part of his mind that was still lucid cursed at him for sharing that he knew about the baker. The rest of him didn't care. It would reveal anything to stop feeling this way. Self-preservation was a powerful force.

Daemastra chuckled. "Hale, there's so much you've yet to learn. The formula doesn't used infused food. It needs something much more potent." Daemastra pulled up a little wooden tray on the side of the chair, using the leather restraint to strap Hale's hand down. He quickly secured the others straps around Hale's chest and feet.

Hale tried to fight—to fend him off—but he was so weak. Delirious. "What...you mean?" His tongue was thick in his mouth.

"Do you know where magic comes from?" Daemastra stood by Hale's side like a patient tutor. Something glinted in his hand.

Hale tried to focus on it. A knife. A butcher knife. He jerked away, but the straps held him. He was as weak as a mewling lamb.

"I didn't either," Daemastra continued. "It took me years of experimentation to determine where it comes from. The pure, unadulterated essence of a Gifted. It's in their bones, Hale. Their bone marrow, to be precise."

"What?" Hale managed. Fear coursed through him as the swirling room focused and narrowed to a pinpoint. On the knife in Daemastra's hand.

"Don't worry, Hale. I always start small. I may need more in time. All of it, if you're what I'm looking for. But for now, I'll start small."

The knife flashed in the air, dropping like the blade of a guillotine.

CHAPTER 18

Wren had never been at sea before. Now that she was here, she wasn't firmly convinced that she ever wanted to be at sea again. She stood at the bow of the ship, her feet braced against the endless undulating waves. She kept expecting a vessel flying a flag of sky blue with a sunburst of yellow to appear behind them on the horizon, but so far, none had. The Black Jasmine was blessedly fast. There was only the sullen gray sky above, the endless slate-blue water below, frosted with whitecaps like peaked meringue. It was disconcerting, being so exposed. Here, it felt like the Piscator could reach his hand up at any moment to pull her down into his watery kingdom.

"Breakfast," Thom said, coming up to stand beside her against the rail. He held out a meager offering—a hard biscuit and a cup of oily-looking coffee.

"Thanks." Wren took both, licking the tang of salt off her dry lips.

"Hardly Guild fare."

"At least it's not infused with magic to make you fall in love with the emperor."

Thom clinked his dappled ceramic mug against hers at that.

"Are they still at it?" Wren nodded back towards the stairs to the lower cabins.

"I almost think they're enjoying it at this point," Thom said.

Callidus and Rizio had been shouting at each other the better part of the night. Between their row and Olivia and Dash bellowing from the little locked cabin they'd been thrown in, it hadn't been a restful night below deck.

Wren had emerged onto the deck before dawn, desperate for some peace.

The sailors on deck eyed her with a mixture of disdain and downright hostility, no doubt thinking these new charges were far more trouble than they were worth.

The wind gusted and Thom shivered, wrapping a thick navy blanket around his shoulders more tightly. It was the type that looked more scratchy than warm, but she supposed beggars couldn't be choosers, now that they were as good as refugees.

"You still chilled? Should we go below?" Wren asked.

Thom's face was pale, his hair gnarled and unkempt from his heroic plunge into the harbor's frigid waters. "It's more peaceful out here, but I should probably go inside. I just can't seem to get warm."

"I need you healthy," Wren said, following him across the deck, washing down a bite of dry biscuit. Sweet caramel, the coffee was strong. Almost undrinkable. Did they just boil the grounds in the pot? "I still can't believe you jumped in after him. I didn't know you had it in you."

"Neither did I," Thom said. "We used to swim in Lake Viri a lot as kids, so I figured I wouldn't drown. I just didn't realize how blooming cold it would be." After Thom had plunged after Dash, he had managed to right the unconscious man, holding him aloft in the dark water. A frenzied shouting match between Callidus and Rizio had resulted in a life ring being thrown down, secured under Dash's armpits, and they had both been hauled up on board. They'd stripped off the men's wet clothing and bundled them in blankets next to a stove in the captain's cabin, where Wren and Callidus, after securely tying Dash, had rubbed the life back into the two men's icy limbs.

"How's Dash doing?" she asked.

"All right, I think. He's mostly sitting in sullen silence, though he did thank me for saving him. Olivia..." Thom shook his head. "She's another story."

When they had added a warmed-up Dash to Olivia's little cell in the lowest hold of the ship, Olivia had glared at them through angry red-rimmed eyes, calling Wren and Callidus traitors and thieves and worse. Wren hadn't stuck around to hear more; it was too disconcerting to hear such vitriol coming from Olivia, normally such a sweet person.

"She seemed to have calmed down a little," Thom said. "But she's furious at us."

"Do you think she'll ever forgive us for stealing her away from the Guild?" Wren wondered out loud.

"I think so." Thom coughed. "Once the infused bread wears off."

Wren hoped he was right. "Shall we see if we can find Callidus?" Wren asked, searching for a change of subject as they plunged into the dark gloom of the hallways.

"If we must." Thom let out a rueful laugh.

Their Guildmaster wasn't hard to find. Raised voices sounded at the end of the narrow hallway, emanating from the Captain's cabin.

Wren went first, knocking on the door with more confidence than she felt.

"What?" two stern voices barked from inside.

Wren and Thom exchanged a silent look of mirth. "They're perfect for each other," Thom whispered.

"It's Wren and Thom," she called.

Callidus appeared in the open doorway, his hair disheveled, dark smudges under his eyes.

"We were hoping to talk with you," Wren said.

"About?"

"I don't know, where we're going, what we're going to do with our prisoners...you know, our entire future?" Wren said, exasperated.

Callidus rolled his eyes but stepped aside, allowing them entry.

Rizio's state room was the only place in the ship that had a little breathing space. The thick wooden paneling was painted white, and a soft rug with a Centu design of rolling waves cushioned their footsteps. A large bed was built into the back wall, which was lined with small leaden windowpanes.

Rizio stood at the small table in the corner, holding a mug identical to the one in Wren's hand. "How are you feeling, Thomas?" Rizio asked, his dark eyes keen.

"Okay," Thom said, slowly sidling towards the little stove in the other corner of the cabin.

"Ask my cook Nicolas to give you some hot broth. Take some to the other man, too. It's important to keep your core temperature up. Exposure to the Piscator's hallowed hall is no small thing."

"So, where are we headed?" Wren asked.

"Centu," Callidus said. "According to Rizio, there's a small bay on one of the eastern islands that is well known for being an...off-the-record meeting area. It's called Forgotten Bay."

"I believe I called it a den of cutthroats and pirates," Rizio said, settling into one of the little chairs and crossing his booted feet.

"Yes, well…" Callidus looked at him crossly. "Pike is there meeting with some of the Centese representatives. To see about them supporting an effort to retake Maradis."

"Why don't they just meet in Centa Kana? Isn't that the capital?" Thom asked.

"The Apricans have spies everywhere," Rizio said. "In every government. Going through unofficial channels is the only way we can talk without risking exposure."

"How long till we get there?" Wren asked.

"Another day if the winds are fair," Rizio replied.

"And Pike will be willing to meet with us?" Wren asked. After everything that had happened with Sable, she didn't think anyone from the Confectioner's Guild was a favorite of Pike's right now.

"I believe so. You have assets to offer."

Assets? Wren wrinkled her brow, doing a mental inventory. Their infused foods, gold, their wells...perhaps some contacts at other Guilds...it seemed a meager offering to secure Pike or the Centese government's assistance. Callidus and Rizio were both staring, their dark eyes boring into her. "What?" she asked, stepping back inadvertently.

"Will you show Rizio the ring?" Callidus asked.

Oh. Rizio didn't want the Guild or even her. He wanted Lucas Imbris, the missing heir to the Alesian throne. A legitimate face to lead their resistance. Her hands felt heavy as she lifted the chain from around her neck, slipping it over her head. The ring hung between them, swinging softly like a pendulum.

Rizio examined the ring, turning it over in his hands.

She knew what he was looking at; she'd memorized every inch of the ring by heart. A stylized falcon's head grasping a milky white stone in its curved beak. On the band of the ring, the falcon's wings were etched, wrapping around each side. The falcon was the Imbris family crest. Lucas's note had said that the ring would lead her to him. But Lucas must have been overestimating her prowess as a detective. To her, the ring seemed to be the most generic clue she could imagine.

"Interesting design," Rizio said, handing it back to her. "Have you talked to the jeweler?"

"No. I have no idea who made it. It didn't come with an instruction manual."

"His mark is right on the inside," Rizio said.

"What?" Wren asked.

She, Callidus, and Thom crowded closer, drawn like moths to a flame.

"I'll show you." He took the ring back and turned it over, pointing with his pinky to the inside of the ring, where the metalwork held the stone. "See this little leaf? It's not just a decoration, it's the craftsman's mark. I don't recognize it, but someone in the Forgotten Bay might. Actually, there's a jeweler I know named Hiryo who might be able to help."

Wren looked up, delighted. "That's the first real clue we've gotten. Thank you!" Hope swelled in her. Lucas. Could it really be that simple? Find the craftsman, find Lucas. And if they could find Lucas, they would have a chance. To take back their city. And their lives.

CHAPTER 19

Hale's pinky finger throbbed. Except it didn't. Because it was gone. He couldn't stop running his fingers over the bandage, over the emptiness where a finger once had been. It wasn't the missing finger that bothered him, so much as the fear that Daemastra would decide he needed more precious parts.

Hale's footsteps dragged as he headed towards the workshop. The place had taken on new meaning to him—its horrible secrets laid bare. He hadn't been able to sleep at all last night, part for the throbbing in his hand, part for the realization of what those jars in the ice box were.

Do you know where magic comes from? Daemastra had said. *It's in your bones.* How much bone would it take to produce a canning jar full of powder? A lot. More than a person could spare—and live. Hale's mind rebelled at the thought, at the realization of who this man was. Who he now served. He should run. He should run and never look back. But he already had strange black lines creeping across his bicep, from the tiny red dot where Daemastra had stuck him. He needed the antidote if he wanted to live. And gods help him, for whatever reason, he wasn't ready to let go of this flaming mess of a wreck he'd made of his life. He was too cowardly to die. So he dragged his feet, but he walked. Back into the lion's den.

Voices sounded inside Daemastra's workshop—raised voices. Angry voices. Hale slowed, pausing by the door. Daemastra's calm, even tones contrasted with Willings, his words laced with panic and anger.

"Oosten is dead!" Willings said. Hale froze. Oosten, the huge guinea pig they'd tested their formula on?

"Did you perform the tests as I instructed?"

"Yes, of course. But you're missing—"

"How did he perform?" Daemastra seemed as if he were speaking to a small child.

Willings let out a frustrated hiss. "He performed remarkably."

"Good. Then the experiment was a success. We know the formula works."

"The formula kills people," Willings protested. "Are you going to drink that stuff? Because I sure as hell won't."

"The formula is missing a key ingredient," Willings said. "Two, if I have my way, but only one that really matters. We need to make it permanent."

"I thought it *was* permanent."

"No." Hale could almost hear Daemastra's eye roll. "I told you. In its current form, the formula is only temporary. It puts a tremendous strain on the body and mind as it transforms it. When it returns to its weakened state...I thought it might be too much for some. We need the magic of time to make it permanent."

Magic of time? Hale wondered. *Which Guild was that?*

"And do you have a plan for getting this last ingredient?"

"The Spicer's Guild. One member in particular if my research is accurate, which it very usually is. The guild head."

"You disbanded the Spicer's Guild. They all fled the city," Willings pointed out.

Daemastra clicked his tongue in frustration. "Well, that wasn't my intent. I thought by disbanding them, they'd lose their legitimacy and we'd be able to scoop them up without questions. Unfortunately, they were craftier than I gave them credit for. A mistake I will not make again."

"So where are they? Do you have a plan for getting this Gifted?"

"I am working on it. In the meantime, keep training our Golden Guard and preparing them for the transformation process. As soon as the formula is concocted, I want to be ready to administer it."

"Very well," Willings said, storming out of the room.

Willings started, almost running into Hale. Hale's cheeks heated, as he had obviously been caught eavesdropping. "I didn't want to interrupt," he said lamely.

Willings only sneered at him. "Down in the mud with the rest of us, aren't you, Firena? What would your precious Guild say if they saw you now?" He pushed past Hale, and Hale moved stiffly into the room, trying and failing to ignore how much Willings's comment stung.

"Hale." Daemastra smiled at him, flashing his too-white, too-straight teeth. A fleeting thought flashed through Hale's mind as he wondered if Daemastra had stolen those teeth from poor Gifted, too. Was there any original part of this horrid man? Or was he a strange amalgamation? "How are you feeling?" Daemastra asked.

"I've got black running down my arm and I'm missing a finger, so I've been better," Hale snapped. He was here. That needed to be enough for the man. He didn't need to be polite too.

Daemastra's smile didn't falter, but his eyes glittered dangerously. "Well, I can help one of those things." He turned and retrieved a small vial from a cupboard. "Drink this," he said, handing it to Hale.

Hale did as instructed. If the man wanted to kill him, he would have done it already. The liquid tasted bitter, like chewing raw dandelion leaves.

"Good. Now. About the sample I took from you," Daemastra said.

Hale tensed.

"It wasn't what I'm looking for. Your luck is...limited," Daemastra twisted his too-smooth face.

Hale let out a bark of laughter. "You could have just asked. My magic only works on cards or dice."

Daemastra nodded, frowning. "Helpful if you need a little extra coin, but that's not what I'm looking for. The formula needs good luck that influences all situations. Who in the Confectioner's Guild has such magic?"

Hale stilled.

Daemastra continued. "Need I remind you that if you don't tell me, I can choose to withhold tomorrow's antidote. And then I'll just find out anyway."

Hale licked his lips. They suddenly felt dry. "Wren," he said softly.

"Of course. One of the three who have fled the city."

"They've fled the city?" Hale's eyebrows shot up. He tried to keep his features neutral, showing only surprise, not the relief that was welling deep within him.

"You didn't know?" Daemastra seemed amused. "On the outs, are we? Well, yes. For now, they're gone. But I have a feeling they'll be back."

Hale sent up a prayer to the Sower. It seemed like he had been doing that a lot the past few days. Pike and Wren were the two Gifted Daemastra needed to complete his formula.

Chickadee, he thought, wishing Wren could hear him, wherever she was. *Stay far, far away.*

Olivia had been trapped in this postage stamp cabin for an entire day. If she had to go another day, she thought she might lose her mind.

"You're making me dizzy," Dash said, lounging back on the hard bunk, his fingers intertwined behind his neck. "Come sit down." He patted the bunk next to him.

Olivia sighed and plunked down by his feet, slumping over to rest her head in her hands. At least the company wasn't entirely unpleasant. She supposed if you had to be trapped in a tiny cell on a rolling ship, doing it with a handsome Tamrosi man was the way to go.

"How are you feeling?" She leaned over, placing her hand against Dash's temple. His skin had been flush when they'd first been brought to the cell, but the color seemed to have receded. "It seems like your fever's gone down."

Dash looked at her, his brown eyes like pools of molten chocolate. "I'm not sure. Perhaps you should keep checking."

Her body flushed and she pulled her hand back.

Dash let out a husky laugh before scooting to a seat, leaning back against the wall of the cell. "I'll live. Thanks to Thom, anyway. I'm healthy as a horse."

"Good." Silence fell over them, but it was warm, like a comfortable blanket. They'd spent the last day talking, sharing about their pasts and families, likes and dislikes. Their conversations had circled deeper—fears, dreams, hopes for the future. Everything Olivia learned about Dash made her soften to him more. He had been born the son of a blueberry farmer outside Terrasia, the Tamrosi capital. His father had died in the Red Plague two years earlier, and they'd had to sell the orchard in the following years to make ends meet. Dash had joined the Aprican army the next spring and sent the majority of his pay home to his mother and two younger sisters. He counted himself lucky that he'd never had to kill a man in battle, and he hoped he never would. He'd gotten the faint scar on his cheek from falling out of a hayloft at the age of seven. He hated pickles, he hummed lullabies in his sleep, and he had the edge of a tattoo peeking out from the cuff of his shirtsleeve that Olivia longed to see the rest of.

"Shall we play a game?" Dash asked.

"A game?" Olivia raised an eyebrow. "What kind?"

Dash stroked his beard, considering.

He had good hands—strong and broad, with neatly-trimmed nails and deft fingers. Olivia found herself watching his hands far too often. She scolded herself. If he caught her staring, she'd be mortified.

"Have you ever played I Spy?"

Olivia wrinkled her nose. "In here? It'll be a short game, won't it? I spy with my little eye something brown."

Dash pretended to ponder. "Is it wood?"

"How did you know?" Olivia slapped her knee in mock surprise. "You're a master at this."

Dash laughed—the sound warm and deep. "I spy with my little eye..." He caught her eye and held it. "Something beautiful."

Olivia pulled in a sharp little breath.

A key jangled at the lock and Olivia tore her gaze from Dash's, grateful for the distraction.

The door opened and a bare-footed sailor entered the room, bearing a tray with two dinner bowls. A thin figure was silhouetted in the hallway behind him. Wren.

Olivia's lip curled. Her former friend who had betrayed her, stolen her away from her home and city and Guild. Who still hadn't told her why.

Wren stepped into the room. Her face was wan, her auburn hair tangled as if from salty air.

"How are you feeling?" Wren asked quietly.

The sailor deposited the tray on the little corner shelf and went to stand by Wren, crossing his arms before him. Her bodyguard, it seemed. As if Wren needed protection from Olivia or Dash. She was the one who had attacked them!

"A little cabin fever, but well enough," Dash replied.

Olivia ground her teeth. She'd already said her piece to Wren. No need to repeat it now.

"Olivia," Wren said carefully. "I know you're very angry, but I was wondering if you might tell me what you think of Emperor Evander?"

Olivia exchanged a look of disbelief with Dash. This again? "Why do you keep asking me that?"

"It just... It matters to me," Wren said. Typical Wren non-answer. Olivia was trying to recall if there was ever a time when Wren had been completely honest with her. She wasn't sure she could think of one.

She let out a frustrated hiss. "Emperor Evander is..." She paused. Her mind felt foggy and confused when it came to the subject of their new ruler. She'd felt so strongly before, but now... She put her hand to her temple. "I'm—I'm not sure."

A look of relief broke across Wren's face, lighting her up like a sunbeam. "Good. That's good."

Dash was frowning, watching her closely. "What's going on?"

Olivia shook her head, trying to clear it.

"I'll explain everything in another day. Tomorrow we'll be arriving at Forgotten Bay, in Centu. Olivia, I think you'll be able to come out of this awful cabin by the time we arrive."

Olivia wanted to get out of this cabin more than anything, but... She looked at Dash. "What about Dash?"

Wren pursed her lips. "I'm sorry, Dash, but you're still an Aprican legionnaire. We can't risk releasing you."

He didn't seem surprised.

"That's not fair," Olivia protested. "I don't want to be released until

Dash is."

"Olivia, don't be mad. You're part of the Guild. He's the enemy."

"He's been a better friend to me than you as of late." Olivia crossed her arms over her chest. She knew that was a tad bit melodramatic, but Wren still hadn't apologized to her for what she'd done.

"We'll discuss this tomorrow. You might find you've had a change of heart," Wren said. She nodded to the sailor. "Let's go."

Dash stood, retrieving the two bowls and handing one to her before sitting down beside her.

"You would really do that for me?" Dash asked softly. "Give up your freedom? Stay in this cell?"

Olivia took a bite. The stew was watery, but it had a pleasant flavor of curry and cardamom. "They can't hold you indefinitely. Maybe I can help them see that."

"That would be the kindest thing anyone has ever done for me," he admitted. "But I won't let you do it."

"Good thing you don't have the power to *let* me do anything," Olivia countered. "I make my own choices. I'm my own woman."

Dash nodded, his gaze intent upon her. "What if there was a way we could both be free?"

Olivia's spoon froze halfway to her mouth. She let it fall. "What do you mean?" she whispered.

"If I could get us out of here when we get to Centu, would you come with me? We could find our own way back to Maradis. Get you home."

Her heart skittered in her chest. Dash was asking her to run. It was madness. She'd only known him for a few days. But she trusted him more than she trusted Wren and Callidus and even Thom right now. "Yes." She found herself saying, a smile stretching its way across her face.

CHAPTER 20

Rizio called down to Wren, Thom, and Callidus when they caught sight of land. They emerged from their narrow berths, donning boots and cloaks before making their way into the frigid misty air above deck.

Thom was moving slow—his face pallid and clammy. He had developed a ragged cough over the last day.

Wren shoved down her worry. So long as they kept filling him with soup and tea, he'd get over whatever it was. He was young and strong.

Wren's first glimpse of the Centese archipelago was distinctly underwhelming. Desolate islands of slate stone thrust up from the glassy sea—their barren forms shrouded in mist. The hush of the morning was broken only by a call of a stray gull as the Black Jasmine glided silently towards land.

The ship drew closer to the nearest island, heading directly towards the sheer rock face.

Wren and Thom exchanged a look of concern. Why was Rizio heading directly for the island? Though the sea was calm, there were still bound to be rocks in the shallow water at the island's edge. Wren's pulse quickened the closer they got to the island until it was almost too much to bear. She looked back at Rizio standing calmly at the wheel, the collar of his wool jacket turned up against the cold. She needed to say something. He was going to kill them all!

But then he spun the wheel and the ship turned, gliding into a narrow opening between the rock as the sailors scrambled to bring in the sails. The passageway was nearly invisible from afar. No wonder this place was called Forgotten Bay.

The only thing more surprising than the hidden entrance to Forgotten Bay was what she saw once inside. The island cradled a sprawling metropolis of ships and humanity. A spiderweb of docks stretched across the water, creating a veritable floating city. Ships with their tall masts were nestled next to wooden outbuildings with colorful tile roofs and open squares where vendors in narrow boats hocked their wares.

"What in the name of the Beekeeper is all this?" Thom marveled, leaning forward over the rail. He pulled a little pad of paper out of his pocket and began sketching with the nub of a charcoal pencil.

Wren leaned her elbows down on the rail and took it all in as their ship glided past rows and streets of docks crowned with strings of colorful lanterns. Dark-haired Centese in bright red and green silks chatted on the edges of docks or haggled over goods, handing their wares from boat to boat. Wren found herself grinning. She'd never been anywhere but her hometown and Maradis before, had never thought of much beyond finding someplace safe to hunker down. But this—this was marvelous. This was why people traveled.

The Black Jasmine sidled alongside an open stretch of dock and the crew sprang from the boat, clambering down onto the dock to secure the ship to her new berth. A moment of trepidation struck Wren. She hadn't thought much beyond escaping Maradis. But now they had. And they were here. What were they to do if Pike didn't help them? Would they...settle here? She shoved the thought aside. Pike would help them.

Callidus strode towards Rizio, Wren and Thom hurrying in his wake. "We go see Pike, correct?" Callidus asked. "You know where he's staying?"

"I do," Rizio said. "We'll go now. The sooner I can get you off my ship, the better."

Thom and Wren moved to follow the two men, but Callidus turned on them. "No. Not you two. I'll talk to Pike myself. The last thing I need is you two bumbling through things."

"We're coming with you." Wren protested. "This involves our lives too."

"No." Callidus's voice was hard. "It may shock you, but I am the Guildmaster of the Confectioner's Guild and I do not need your assistance with everything I do." He pointed his finger at both of them in turn. "Stay."

"We're not a pair of terriers," Thom said, crossing his arms before him.

Wren's frown followed Callidus and Rizio down the gangplank and out of sight.

"What should we do while we wait?" Thom asked.

"We're not waiting."

"Wren—" Thom groaned, pulling his cloak tighter about him, rubbing his nose with his sleeve.

Wren held up her hands. "I won't follow Callidus and Rizio. But Rizio mentioned a jeweler who might be able to help us identify Lucas's ring. Callidus can't object to us being efficient with our time."

"I suspect Callidus could find an objection to just about anything we do. We don't know where in the city this guy is, either."

"There can't be too many jewelers named Hiryo in this city. How hard can it be?"

Thom seemed to consider, but when his shoulders slumped, Wren knew she'd won.

"Do I have to come with you?" he asked. His shoulders were drooping even more than normal; his face was sallow.

Wren bit her lip. He did look like he should be back in bed, but she didn't want to venture out alone in this totally new territory. She summoned her courage around her. She could do this alone. "No, you can stay. Rest up."

It seemed luck was with her, for when she asked one of the sailors for directions to Hiryo's shop, he pointed to a building just one dock down.

The door tinkled when she opened it. "Hello?" Wren called, taking in the glass cases filled with an assortment of glittering gems.

A little man hurried out from the back wearing enormous glasses, his head as bald as a baby's. He spoke rapidly in a strange language Wren could only imagine was Centese. Curses. She hadn't thought about the language barrier. "Alesian?" she asked with an apologetic smile, stepping up to the front counter.

"Some." The man switched to Alesian, and Wren let out a sigh of relief.

Wren pulled the chain over her head and pointed at the little leaf that Rizio had shown her on the inside of Lucas's ring. "Do you know who made this ring?" She spoke slowly and apparently, a touch loudly.

"Can hear fine," the man said before clicking another layer of glass over his glasses, giving him a bug-eyed look. He examined it under what must be some sort of magnifying lens. He straightened, handing the ring back. "Master Ishiya."

Excitement bloomed within her. A lead. "Where can I find this Ishiya?"

"Dead," the jeweler said.

Wren's excitement fizzled within her. "You're sure?"

The man nodded, like she was an idiot. "Dead."

"Is there anything else you can tell me about the ring? Like the stone. What's inside it?"

The man frowned, examining it. "Nothing." He proceeded to say something that sounded like he had a mouthful of rocks.

"I'm sorry?" she asked.

"Ru-til-at-ed quartz," he said again, sounding out the syllables as if she were an imbecile. "Nothing in it. Grows like that."

Rutilated quartz. She'd never heard of it. Well, it was something. "Anything else?"

"Only..."—he squinted, looking at the ceiling—"ten mines with this stone. Rare."

"Oh!" Maybe the location of the mines were a clue?

"Can you make me a list of where these mines are located?"

He held out a hand to her. She looked at it, confused. She put the ring back in it. "You want to see it again?"

He scoffed, tossing the ring down on the glass counter. "Money."

"Ah." Wren's cheeks heated. Of course he wanted payment for his information. She reached inside her belt pouch and passed over a few copper crowns. "Good?" she asked.

He nodded, sliding the coins off the counter and pulling out a notepad. He began scrawling out a list for her.

Wren looked out the shop's window as motion drew her eye. A man and woman racing down the dock, the woman's blonde locks streaming behind her. Son of a spicer! It was Olivia and Dash.

Wren launched into action, grabbing the ring and the list. "Thank you!" she cried to the jeweler as she plunged out the door into the gray morning. She wasn't sure what she was going to do when she caught them…Dash was a blooming Aprican legionnaire. But she couldn't just let Olivia disappear into Centu.

Wren skidded around the wooden building. A few paces away, Dash and Marina were huddled together, examining the various routes. "Wait!" Wren called, cradling her aching lungs with an arm.

The two whirled and, catching sight of Wren, launched into a run. *Flame it!*

Dash glanced over his shoulder, and seeing her still on the trail, knocked over a cart full of strange black fruit as he passed, sending a herd of the balls rolling into her path.

The little shopkeeper swore at her as she waded through, trying to avoid slipping or squishing any of the fruits.

Olivia and Dash had rounded another corner, and now their merry little chase was headed straight towards a floating market—a U-shape of docks filled with hundreds of narrow vessels loaded with produce, fish, flowers, and spices. Dash and Olivia showed no signs of slowing and plunged straight into the market, leaping onto the first of the boats.

Wren soldiered forward, following them onto the boat, where a startled oyster fisherman had just recovered from Olivia and Dash's passage.

Screams and cries lit the path she had to follow, and so without thinking of the madness of what she was doing, Wren scrambled from boat to boat, pushing off people and piles of goods, scraping her shins and tangling her skirt. Dash and Olivia were through the other end, and Wren redoubled her efforts, pulling her foot out of a crate that it had just gotten stuck in. She grabbed a cleat on the far dock and pulled herself up, scrambling to her feet, looking for her quarry. But all she saw was a banner of red sailing down towards her, enveloping her in yards of canvas.

Wren flailed with her hands, finally ridding herself of the covering. It looked like the banner for the market. They'd cut it down! Dash and Olivia rounded a far corner down an alley and Wren took off after them.

At the end of the market, people were gesturing angrily, shouting at four men who now stalked down the docks. They wore black trousers and white shirts and had red armbands tied around bulging muscles. Thick necks. Angry faces. Swords at their sides. A vendor pointed for the men. Directly at her. "Sweet caramel," Wren swore. Some sort of police force.

They entered the alley Olivia and Dash had disappeared down. It was a dead end. Dash and Olivia were scaling the side of one of the buildings—Dash was already up on top, reaching down his hand to help Olivia up.

Wren sprinted forward and clambered up the boxes, grabbing Olivia's ankle and pulling with all her might.

Olivia looked down in shock as Wren pulled at her with a silent apology. Olivia's hand slipped out of Dash's grip and she tumbled backwards into Wren.

They hit the hard boards of the dock like a ton of bricks. The force stunned Wren, driving the breath from her lungs, and exploding stars before her eyes. A groan escaped her lips.

Through blurry vision, Wren saw Dash nimbly scale back down the building before leaping to Olivia's side, checking her over gently. Wren felt a sudden pang of longing for Lucas as she rolled onto her side, pushing herself up to a seat gingerly.

"Don't run anymore," Wren said. "Please. Olivia, I want to help you."

"You kidnapped me!" Olivia hissed.

"Well...how do you feel about Emperor Evander?"

"He could go hungry in hell for all I care." Olivia was practically spitting. "And right now, I feel the same about you, Wren."

Relief welled through Wren even as Olivia's words stung her. The infusion had worn off.

But then a thought struck her. If the infusion had worn off, why had Olivia tried to run?

"Olivia, you were brainwashed," Wren said. "I'll explain everything back at the boat." She pushed to unsteady feet.

"You're not going anywhere," a menacing voice said from the mouth of the alley. Four huge men darkened the entrance, blotting out the light.

And so they found themselves, hands bound before them, being walked through the docks of the Forgotten Bay at sword point.

"It's just a misunderstanding," Wren said. "Callidus and Rizio will hear about it and come get us." *She hoped.* "Olivia," Wren said softly. "I'll explain everything when we get back to the boat, I promise."

"I can't imagine what you could say that would make this right," Olivia sniffed, tilting her face away.

Wren could understand that. But then again, the existence of magic wasn't something one normally imagined.

The men with swords funneled them into a little holding cell that was barely big enough for the three of them.

A severe woman wearing the same uniform, with the exception of a brilliant red coat, sidled up to the bars. "Destruction of property," she said in broken Alesian. "Disturbing peace. Wait here for judgment."

Judgment? Wren mouthed as the woman turned. "Wait!" she called, but the woman was already gone.

She turned back to find Dash leaning against the wall, and Olivia leaning against Dash.

"What are we going to do?" Olivia asked, her voice thick.

Wren leaned against the bars and closed her eyes. Why did it seem like everyone always looked to her? She didn't know what to do. "I guess when this judge person comes, we explain that the whole situation was a big misunderstanding and beg their forgiveness."

"Brilliant," Olivia said, setting her jaw.

Stony silence charged the air between them as the minutes ticked by.

"Prisoners!" The woman in the red coat reappeared in the doorway. "Judgment. Stand against wall."

"That was fast," Dash muttered.

A tall, dark man stalked into the room. Shining black boots came to his knees over black trousers, a sword belt slung low on a hip. Above those, he wore a purple velvet coat with silver embroidery and epaulets.

Dark eyes narrowed over a knowing smirk framed by a goatee.

"Come," the woman barked, motioning at the man.

Wren let out a laugh of delight.

The man was Pike.

CHAPTER 21

"You!" Wren said.

"You," Pike replied. His voice was low.

Pike was the judge? "How...? What...? Never mind. Just get us out of here."

Pike hooked his fingers through his belt loops and strolled closer. "When I heard a pack of wild Alesians were running about destroying half the city, I should have known you'd be responsible."

Wren wanted to protest but held her tongue. "Will you please release us?"

Pike squinted through the bars, examining them. "Perhaps I should just leave you in here and sail away to a land of fine food and beautiful women."

"I'm hoping there's a 'but' in that sentence," Dash muttered.

"But...I might want to go back to Maradis at some point. And old Cally says you're the only one who can find Imbris. So I guess I'll let you out."

Wren slumped in relief.

"Although..." Pike stroked his goatee. "I could just leave you here, gather things together, and then come back for you when I'm ready for Imbris. You won't be able to cause trouble in the meantime and I'll know just where to find you."

"Pike." Wren leaned her forehead against the bars, swallowing her pride. "Please. I promise I won't cause any trouble."

Pike examined them. His face looked weathered and he had a smattering of gray hairs at his temples. Either Wren hadn't noticed before, or they were new. But that wasn't the change that struck her. Beneath his veneer of danger, Pike had been playful, even kind. But that levity was gone. A different Pike stood before her. It seemed the ripples of Sable's death stretched even to Centu.

He shook his head. "All right, I'll let you out, but you three don't even bat an eyelash unless Callidus or I say so. Agreed?"

The three in the cell muttered their agreement.

Pike turned to the fierce little woman and spoke to her in Centese. After an exchange of rapid, heated words, the woman relented and stormed to their door, unlocking it.

"She didn't seem very inclined to release us," Wren said as she came out of the cell.

"I told her you were mental invalids who couldn't be legally held accountable for your actions."

Wren pressed her lips together, hiding a smile. "It's blooming good to see you, Pike."

Outside the guard station, the sun had slipped over the horizon, leaving the velvety blue of twilight. Lanterns were being lit across the stretch of docks, yellow oil lanterns on tall poles, and colorful paper lanterns stretched across walkways, a thousand glowing lights like colorful jelly beans. It reminded Wren of the lantern parade for All Hallows' Eve in Maradis, and she felt a twinge of longing. Would she ever see Maradis again?

"Rizio's crew has transferred your cargo and possessions to my ship, the Phoenix. Callidus and Thom should be there," Pike said. Two of his sailors were leaning against the wall and pushed off when they sighted

Pike. Wren didn't think Dash would try anything stupid, but she was glad that they had more manpower just in case.

Wren nodded. "Now are you going to tell me how the heck you came to be judge in the middle of a foreign country?"

Pike shrugged. "I'm not. Money buys justice in Centu. I'll be adding it to Callidus's tab."

Wren blanched. Great. Callidus would just love that.

The Phoenix was a sleek three-masted ship painted in orange and black. The masthead was a lifelike bird in flight, its beak cawing in triumph. Wren was struck by a sort of kinship for the mythical bird. She prayed their Guild could find a way to rise from its ashes. Their city too.

"Callidus will be waiting in my quarters," Pike said as they ducked below deck. "Aprican, what's your name? Dash?" Pike paused before another door. "You'll be in here."

"Locked up I assume?" Dash asked, grimacing.

"Until we decide what to do with you," Pike said.

Olivia's face blackened, and she opened her mouth to speak.

"Take it up with Cally," Pike said. "Not my call."

She closed her mouth and crossed her arms over her chest in a way that signaled that she would very much be taking it up with Callidus.

Callidus was in Pike's captain's quarters, a black cloud hanging above his head.

"Drinks? I'll get drinks," Pike said, quickly spinning and heading towards a sideboard built into the ship's wooden walls as Callidus approached them.

"You!" His voice was hushed with rage. "Can you imagine my mortification as Pike and I were meeting with the Centese delegation, then they get called away to deal with a group of runaway foreigners in the city? And it's you!"

"I didn't want them to escape," Wren said lamely, her cheeks heating. What a disaster of an afternoon.

"Well, at least you got that right. Why did you bring her?"

"The pastry wore off," Wren said. "Olivia's back to normal."

"And yet you ran?" Callidus turned his wrath on Olivia. "What were you thinking?"

Olivia tilted her chin up in a haughty angle, looking him straight in the eye. "I am the Guildmistress of the Confectioner' Guild. I am a free woman. You have no right to detain me. If I wanted to leave, I was free to leave."

Wren had to admit she was impressed. Though she did notice Olivia's hands shaking in the folds of her skirt.

"All grown up, are we? Olivia, you need to trust us. We took you from the Guildhall for your own good. It wasn't safe there."

"That makes no sense. Dash said he was just there to watch and keep us safe. If you want my cooperation, it's time you told me the truth. About what the hell is going on. Your little secret enclave," Olivia said, motioning towards them.

Callidus cast a glance sideways at Wren.

"I agree," Wren said. "We need to be united."

"Whiskey for you, for you, for you," Pike said, handing each of them a glass filled with amber liquid. "For when you're done tearing each other to shreds."

Callidus let out a long-suffering sigh, taking a healthy swallow of the whiskey. He hissed. "Fine. We talk to Pike. Figure out our next move. Then we'll tell you everything."

"Promise?" Olivia asked.

Callidus rolled his eyes. "Yes, I promise. Do you want to pinky-swear on it? Or is the word of your guildmaster sufficient for you?"

"Your promise will suffice." Olivia said, taking a sip from her own glass, her blue eyes still glittering dangerously.

"Now, should we move to the more important matters at hand?" Callidus asked.

Pike nodded. "Of course, dear Cally."

"Don't call me that." Callidus pinched the bridge of his nose with long fingers.

"Very well. Would you like to share the bad news, or shall I?"

"Be my guest."

"The Centese aren't willing to help us."

Wren's stomach dropped into her feet as Pike continued. "The Centese are cautious. They haven't maintained their sovereignty all these centuries by getting involved. The late King Imbris strong-armed them into that marriage by convincing them that joining Alesian and Centese strength might keep the Apricans at bay. Clearly, that has not panned out. While the princess managed to escape the Aprican attack, the Crown Prince was killed. They are not going to assist us unless things are going so well that we basically wouldn't need them anymore."

"I'm sorry." Olivia held up a hand. "What exactly are we doing here?"

"Did you think this was a book club?" Pike asked. "This is a covert meeting of revolutionaries. We're retaking Maradis."

Olivia's mouth formed a little O. "The three of you?"

"The four of us," Wren said. "You wanted to know. You wanted to be included."

"I wanted to understand. And I still don't," Olivia said.

Pike, Wren, and Callidus exchanged a look. No time like the present. It was Pike who went first. "Magic is real, child. Real enough to kill for, to conquer countries for. And Maradis is the most magical city in the whole damn world."

Olivia let out a little bubble of a laugh, looking first from Callidus to Wren and back to Pike. No one said anything.

Her smile faltered. "What kind of magic?"

So they explained everything. The Gifting. Infused food. The binding wine. The Accords, King Imbris, the truth behind Kasper's death and the Guild's power. Emperor Evander and his twisted cuisinier, whose plans no one understood yet. And the infused bread that had taken hostage the minds of an entire city.

"But...magic bread? It's so farfetched," Olivia protested, her sweet face pale. She'd taken in the truth in stoic silence. Wren wished she could comfort her, knowing that the truth behind her granduncle's death must have shaken loose difficult emotions. But there seemed to be a chasm between her and Olivia now. One she wasn't sure they'd ever be able to bridge.

"I've never seen anything like it," Pike agreed. "It seems like some sort of bastardized combination of Baker's Guild and Vintner's Guild power. Baker's Guild, best we know it, has the power of love and fertility. Combined with the Vintner's Guild power of lies...it's like the love and the lie combined, sown in the minds of everyone who ate the bread.

"But thanks to you, Olivia, we know the infusion will wear off in approximately twenty-four hours," Callidus said.

That was good. But Wren was thinking of how much Pike knew about the Guilds. About what each of their Gifts did. "What do the Spicer's Guild infusions do?" Wren asked. "It can't truly be the magic of death."

"Can't it? I have to keep some secrets," Pike said.

"No, no, no." Callidus held up a hand. "We need to stop acting alone. In silos. If we're to take back Alesia, there can be no more secrets. It's time for the truth."

Pike heaved a sigh. "It is not the magic of death. Yes, we sell poison. But ours is the magic of time."

"Time?" Callidus asked.

"Slowing it down, speeding it up, in powerful doses, even stopping time itself."

Wren's mind whirled. "So does the person stop? Or does the world around the person stop? Or do you go back in time? I'm so confused."

"It depends on what spice you're using. Just as I imagine your luck varies depending on the confection."

A memory flared to mind—of Sable lying on Pike's couch, her lifeblood seeping out, Hale curled over her pale form. "Could you...?" She trailed off, her voice whispering.

Pain flashed behind Pike's eyes. "I know what you're thinking. If I had been awake...maybe I could have..." He turned abruptly, striding across the cabin. He hung his head for a moment, his back to them. When he turned, his face was carefully blank. "We've bared all our secrets to Olivia. Now I think it's time we talk resources. Even if we get help from the Falconers on the inside, and the people join us in a glorious revolution, we need men who know how to fight to go up against the Aprican legion."

They looked around. "We can't trust anyone in the city," Wren said. "We have to assume they'll be working against us."

"Does Imbris have any followers?" Pike asked.

"I don't know," Wren said. "I still don't know where to find him. I got a lead, but it only narrowed it down some. He could be in a number of places."

"We have coin," Callidus said. "Could we pay men from Centu to help?"

Pike rubbed his jaw. "Centese are great on sea, not great on land. We need someone who can go toe to toe with the Apricans in the streets. I might...know of someone."

"Who?" Callidus asked.

"A mercenary. Last I heard, he was in Nova Navis. He'd have men, or be able to get them. If there's gold in it, I think we could get him."

Callidus's thick brows drew together. "A mercenary? Can we trust him?"

"Don't think we much have a choice," Pike said.

"So should that be our first stop? See if we can get this fellow to join our cause?" Callidus asked.

"Unless you want to sit around here eating bonbons." Pike retorted.

Callidus pursed his lips. "What's this fellow's name?"

Pike grinned. "They call him the Red Badger."

CHAPTER 22

The journey to Nova Navis was supposed to take three days. And Olivia sure as hell wasn't going leave Dash locked up alone in a tiny cabin for the whole time.

While she knew she wasn't going to convince Pike and Callidus to let Dash out, there was no reason they shouldn't let her in.

She gathered her nerve and knocked on the door of Pike's chambers. She entered when she heard the muffled invitation.

"I'd like to be allowed in Dash's cabin," she said, her shoulders thrown back.

One of Pike's eyebrows arched towards his hairline. "You want to be thrown in that little closet? There's not much room in there."

Olivia crossed her arms before her. "At least I'll be with someone who hasn't been lying to me my whole life. At this point, I trust him more than the lot of you."

Pike snorted. "You realize we had no choice, don't you? Revealing the Gifting was a treason punishable by death."

Olivia faltered. She hadn't realized that. "Well...they should have found a way. At least my granduncle. I lived in the Guild my whole life, with magic all around me, and he couldn't even tell me?" *He should have found a way.*

"The road to the Piscator's hallowed halls is cobbled with 'should haves.' If you want to keep a grudge, that's your business. Ask for Saad, my first mate. He'll show you into the cabin."

Olivia nodded her thanks and headed to the door. A gust of briny air swirled past her as she made her way back onto the broad deck of the Phoenix. In the brisk bright light of the day, her resolve faltered. Was this idea madness? Maybe they'd lied to her, but they were still the Confectioner's Guild. They were the closest thing she had to family. And who was Dash? An Aprican soldier she'd known all of a few days. It had been madness to run off with him, but she had just been so angry. All her life she'd toed the line, done exactly what was expected of her, and where had she ended up? Kidnapped. Lied to. Alone in this world. Dash had seemed a way out. Something un-Olivia. And right now she was very tired of being Olivia.

Sailors scrambled around her as Olivia stood on the deck, her legs braced against the roll of the ship. She ducked under a boom, curling her fingers around the smooth varnished wood of the ship's rail. She took a breath to center herself. She didn't know if she could trust her judgment anymore. Her grandaunt had been like a mother to her—and she'd been a murderer. The girl she'd thought was her best friend was a liar. A magical liar. So what if she was wrong about Dash?

But...there was something about him. A sincerity that people didn't always have. A kindness that was rare in powerful men who could take what they wanted without thought of what it cost others. Dash had been sweet and funny and genuine. And when he looked at her, a heat coiled within her that she had never experienced before. And so she needed to make a choice. The unknown of Dash or the known unknown of the Guild. She believed that Wren and Callidus and Thom would have told her if they could have. And she believed that she would forgive them in time. But she also believed that Dash was a good man. An ally. She believed that he just might care for her.

Olivia hissed in frustration, smoothing back her hair, trying to corral the strands whipping around her. Why couldn't she have both? For all her life, it'd been loss after loss after heartache, yet she'd managed to cling to her optimism and positivity. She wasn't inclined to let it go now.

She wanted it all. She wanted her home back. She wanted love. She wanted to be the heroine and not just the servant.

A sailor hurried by and Olivia grabbed his arm. "Point me to the first mate?"

"You got 'im." He was tall and lean and weathered, in the way that a length of rope might be after years of fading in the sun.

"Take me to the prisoner's cabin."

She trailed behind the first mate back down into the hold.

When the door opened, her heart trilled in her chest at the sight of Dash playing a game of solitaire. His quarters on the Phoenix were only slightly more luxurious than those on the Black Jasmine, but it seemed that Pike or his sailors had been kind enough to give him a stack of books and a deck of cards.

The door clicked behind Olivia with a jangle of keys.

"What's going on?" Dash asked. "I thought—I don't know what I thought."

Olivia crossed the tiny cabin and sat next to him, closer than was strictly necessary. The heat of his thigh cut through the layers of her dress and set her heart racing. "I believe there's something you need to know."

Dash's face grew blacker and blacker as Olivia explained the truth that she hardly believed herself. The Guilds' magic. Real magic. And more importantly—the emperor. What he had done to Olivia. To Maradis.

Dash shook his head. "I don't believe it."

She paused. "You actually don't believe it? Or…is that a rhetorical statement?"

He let out a shaky laugh. "I don't know. There's talk around the legion about Daemastra. Sometimes people would disappear." He shook his head. "There were rumors, but…how do you believe something like that?"

Olivia nodded grimly. "I know exactly what you mean."

Dash rubbed his beard in an unconscious motion. "What now?" he asked.

She shrugged. "We're going to find a mercenary. They plan to try to take back the city."

Dash's eyes widened and he blew out a breath. "That's a tall order."

She nodded. "If you could take back Terrasia, wouldn't you do it?"

"I don't know." Dash was still. "The leadership in Terrasia was corrupt too. It always seemed like exchanging one faceless tyrant for another."

"I know what you mean," Olivia said. "But it changes things to know that he's taking people's free will. Their very thoughts. Somehow it changes things."

"I don't know why you're telling me all this. I'm the enemy."

"That's the thing," Olivia said carefully. "I don't feel that you are. I feel more kinship with you than with my own Guild right now."

"They lied to you. It's understandable that you feel betrayed."

"Do you think, now that you know... Would you ever think about joining us?" she asked hopefully, trying to keep her voice nonchalant. *You know, just betray your country, your oaths, your very life for a girl you've known for a few days and a country you've just arrived in. No big deal.*

"What would you have me do?"

Olivia paused, her excitement growing. *I would have you kiss me,* she wanted to say. I would have you swear your loyalty to the Guild, and me, and profess your love with such vehemence that I cannot help but believe you. But instead she said, "Talk to Callidus and Pike. They could use a legionnaire on their side. Someone who knows the ways the Aprican think and the way they deploy their soldiers. Someone who knows their battle strategies and tactics. You could be instrumental in helping us take back the city and stopping Daemastra and the emperor."

"And you ask me this for the city?" Dash asked carefully. "For Alesia?"

"Of course." But his question. It sounded...loaded. She hesitated, feeling perched on the edge of a knife. *She wanted it all.* So she plunged ahead—caution be damned. "I would also have you aid us because I've enjoyed our time together. And I would wish to see you standing beside me on the bow of the ship rather than stuck in this cramped cabin. And perhaps, someday, back at the Guildhall. Or on Nysia Avenue, taking me to dinner."

A smile quirked the corner of his mouth. "I should like to take you to dinner. And dessert and breakfast and lunch after that. And every day following."

She hissed in a breath, her senses suddenly alive with his nearness. The melted chocolate of his eyes, the presence of him—sturdy and sure.

Dash's hand came up slowly. He cupped her face, and in that moment, she felt more alive than she ever had before. She wanted to laugh with the stupidity of it. They'd just met.

His calloused thumb stroked along her cheek, leaving a trail of tingles in its wake. "I'd like very much to join you and your Guild. But mostly you. I think I might fight the Huntress herself for you."

And then he kissed her.

The world seemed to rock beneath her and Olivia wasn't sure if it was the movement of the boat or the fire in her heart. Kindled—come to life—at this man's touch.

Wren felt unmoored, as if at any minute, a gust of wind might blow her away. Perhaps being back on land would ground her, bring her back to herself...but she doubted it. She tried to identify what it was that made her feel this way. Being away from Maradis? From the Guild? From Lucas? Maybe it was all of that, and none of it. Somewhere in all of it, she had lost her sense of herself, had flown too high, had thought she could change the fates of men and kingdoms. Who had she been kidding? She had only just barely ever been able to take care of herself, and she had done that by being small and unseen. Yet somehow, in all of it, she had become a person people looked to. For answers. It had been a heady feeling at first, the power, the excitement, but now it weighed on her. What if she made the wrong decision? What if more people died?

Wren dragged herself down the hallway she shared with Callidus and Thom. She knew she was due for the mother of all lectures from Callidus, but she wanted to check on Thom.

Callidus sat on a little stool by Thom's bedside.

Thom was asleep, his eyes closed, a sheen of sweat on his pale face.

"How's he doing?" Wren asked, lingering in the doorway to their cabin.

Callidus's head swiveled her way. "Pike's sailor said that Thom's likely suffering from pneumonia. He's given him a tonic, but if it doesn't work, we'll need to get medicine in Nova Navis."

"Pneumonia?" Wren closed her eyes against her worry. Master Oldrick had caught pneumonia several years back, and it had taken him a month of fevered nights, warm broth, and bedrest to recover. It wasn't a gentle illness.

Thom let out a wracking cough and Callidus reached out, dabbing at his brow with a damp rag.

"Callidus," she said softly.

Callidus wiped Thom's brow again. "What?" he asked.

"I'm sorry," she told him. "I'm sorry for running after Olivia and Dash. If I ruined our chances with the Centese…"—the words stuck in her throat like thick taffy—"I'll never forgive myself."

Callidus reached behind him and pulled out another little stool from beneath her berth. He patted it and she sank onto it gratefully.

"Wren," he said. "There's something I've learned. It took me many years, and some days I think I still haven't learned it fully." He turned to her, the blue of his eyes filled with something unexpected. Compassion. "You can't control everything. You can plan, you can hope, you can pray, you can try. But sometimes in the end, it's not enough. That doesn't mean there's anything wrong with you. Because I don't know about you, but I'm just a mortal. And a confectioner at that. And all I can do is all I can do."

Wren let his words wash over her like a soothing balm. They brushed against a dam within her that she hadn't known existed. A sob broke free from her lips. She clapped her hand over her mouth to hold it in, afraid to let that dam burst.

"What happened with Sable, with Hale, with Thom…none of it is your fault," Callidus continued.

Wren nodded, fighting back tears. When she spoke her voice was thick. "It's never enough. I'm tired of feeling like I'm not enough. I keep thinking if Sable were here, she would know what to do. Or Lucas. Or even Hale. The old Hale. They could have convinced the Centese to ally with us. Or have stopped the emperor from taking over Maradis."

Callidus shook his head. "It's easy to think that way. I do all the time. But I think you and I are more alike than we realize. We may not have Lucas's pedigree, or Hale's charm, or Sable's savvy, but we keep trying, damn it. We don't give up. If that's my legacy, then it's one I'm proud to leave behind."

Wren nodded. "I think…me too."

Callidus rubbed his hands on his legs. "Hand me my mandolin, will you?"

Wren reached behind her and pulled out the black case from where it was tucked against the wall.

Callidus flipped the buckles and pulled the polished tear-drop instrument out of its blue velvet lining. His fingers plucked the strings lovingly as he tuned each one.

"Do you think Olivia will ever forgive us?" Wren asked. Olivia had stormed out of Pike's cabin after their meeting, refusing to speak to Wren. They hadn't given her the binding wine, but Wren hadn't wanted to remind anyone of that fact. Let her tell Dash. Let her tell the world. She was sick of keeping secrets. She was sick of getting tangled in her lies.

As Callidus started to pluck an easy melody, he replied, "She's angry right now. But Olivia is a lot like Kasper. And he saw the best in everyone and everything. Give her time. She'll come around."

Tension unwound from Wren as she sat, listening to the rise and fall of Callidus's tune. She had entered this room full of trepidation and doubt. And now, though she still felt scared and uneasy, there was something else there too. Determination. They would find Lucas. They would find this mercenary. They would find the Falconer. And together, they would take back their city.

Or at the very least, they'd die trying.

CHAPTER 23

Hale walked stiffly from the King's Hill Quarter towards the Lyceum. His sword was on his hip. Around him marched a phalanx of Aprican legionnaires. Blond and brawny and faceless. Yet they had ten fingers and he had only nine. He thought that was the only distinguishing characteristic between them. An explosion had rocked the Lyceum Quarter just a half hour before. The Falconer up to his old tricks. It seemed the man had been right about the bread. Though Hale had known something was off, between Beckett's strange comment and the captive baker, he hadn't been able to put two and two together. Not fast enough.

It was a subtle thing. Hale hadn't noticed at first, locked in the palace as he was. But here, out in the streets, he saw the infused bread's horrible effects for what they were. Banners, posters, buttons, all declaring the wonder of the emperor and the Aprican Empire. People cheered as they passed, faces rapt with delight. It was almost too much to bear.

Maradis wasn't perfect, and certainly King Imbris hadn't been, but it had been a city filled with differences. A city that celebrated those differences—from the clothes on a man's back to how he took his coffee. And now they were a faceless mass. An amalgamation of people robbed of their individuality. Hale felt sick. Bile rose in his throat as a little boy dashed forward, waving. The Falconer's cause was hopeless. How could he defend this city when people didn't even realize who the real enemy was?

This was what Hale had done. This was what his deal with the devil had reaped. Part of him thought of letting the poison overtake him. Let it be done. He didn't know how he could go on like this.

They crossed a wide intersection of Third Avenue, and Hale was suddenly overcome with the need to be away. To be away from these soldiers. Away from the sound of boots and the clanking of swords. Without thinking, he turned, angling off onto the other street. One of the legionnaires called after him, but no one followed. They had their orders. Report to the site of the bomb, not follow their wayward brethren.

Hale's feet drew him forward. He didn't know where they were taking him until he reached the wrought-iron gates of the Holyhive Cemetery. His heart—whatever shattered remnants of it there were—twisted in his chest. Of course his feet had brought him here.

He walked to the Guild plot, the little patch of grass and stone that held confectioners, guildmasters, and grandmasters from centuries before.

Sable's headstone was the freshest. Bright and shining. The flowers they had laid at her funeral were shriveled and dead.

Hale gathered them up and carried them back up the lane to deposit them in a trash bin. He snapped the stem of a hydrangea bush, pulling off a single sprig. The flowers were brilliant blue—cobalt, like the color Sable used to love to wear.

He sat before the stone, placing the bloom gently upon it.

"Well, it's as you predicted. Without you here, I've fumbled everything. It's all gone so wrong. More wrong than I ever imagined. I'm not supposed to live this life without you," he said.

He almost expected to hear the velvet of her voice, the whisper of a ghost. But there was nothing.

"I don't know what to do, Sable. What would you do?" He let out a little laugh. "I know what you'd do. You wouldn't let it stand. When you saw wrong, you couldn't help but want to fix it. But I'm not like you. I never was. I'm not as brave. I don't fight for the plight of the weak who can't fight for themselves. I'm a gambler. I care about money. And luck. And comfort. And I cared about you. But now you're gone."

He sighed. "Don't you see? I can't do this without you. I need a sign, Sable. I need a sign from you."

At that moment, a cry pierced the quiet of the cemetery. The cry of a hawk. Hale craned his neck, searching the gray sky for a glimpse of the bird. It sounded again. There it was. Not a hawk. A falcon.

The bird circled. And dove.

Hale's eyes widened in shock as he watched the raptor dive towards the earth, pulling up at the last moment with a prize in its talons. A fat golden mouse.

A bubble of disbelieving laughter escaped him. He looked up at the sky and closed his eyes, soaking in the feel of her imagined presence. "You never were subtle, were you? But I wouldn't have had it any other way."

Wren sat against the mast of the ship, her cloak pulled tightly around her. She'd been in their little room below deck for hours and needed some air, to be away from Thom's incessant cough and her worry for Lucas. She didn't know now how that story would end. If she'd ever see Lucas again. If he'd ever forgive her for the part she'd played in his family's downfall.

"Can I sit here?"

Wren looked up to find Olivia standing above her, uncertainty playing across her lovely features.

"Of course," Wren said.

Olivia sank onto the deck behind her, leaning against the mast.

A glimmer of hope lit inside Wren. She and Olivia hadn't said two words to each other since Pike, Callidus, and Wren had shared the truth of the Gifting with her. Was she finally ready to talk?

But Olivia said nothing, seeming content to pull her knees against her chest, staring out across the sea.

"How's Dash doing?" Wren asked, twisting around to face her.

"He's as well as could be expected," Olivia replied. "He'd be better if you'd let him out of that cabin."

Wren bit her tongue, holding back her protestations that it wasn't her call. If Olivia blamed Wren, so be it. Whether it was fair or not. "I don't know if we can do that," Wren said. What to do with Dash was one of many problems that weighed heavily on her conscience. She didn't think they had it in them to abandon him somewhere, or sell him into slavery, or kill him. Maybe Pike was ruthless enough to do that. But she and Callidus? No. But where did that leave them? Abandon him in a cell to rot? How long might this rebellion last? Or even more dangerous—trust him?

"This is his life," Olivia said. "You can't just keep him in a cage like an animal."

"He was never supposed to come. If he hadn't been so damn zealous in his duties..."

"It's who he is."

"You know him now?" Wren turned her head to examine Olivia.

"I think I do."

"And you trust him?"

"Yes. I told him everything," Olivia said coolly.

Wren winced. Another person who knew the secret of the Gifted. She sighed. What did it matter anymore? Perhaps Callidus was right. Perhaps it was time to let the truth be free.

Olivia went on. "He wants to help us. Think of the knowledge he has as a member of the Aprican legion. He could help us take down the emperor."

"Or he could double-cross us," Wren protested. "How do you know we can trust him? That he's not lying? Playing you?"

Olivia's voice grew soft. "I...I just do."

Wren closed her eyes. Gods, this was bad. It seemed that Olivia was falling in love with the man.

"I know what you're thinking," continued Olivia. "That I'm a foolish girl who fell for a man whom she just met. Whom she hardly knows—"

Wren cut in. "I don't think you're a foolish girl. I just don't want you to get hurt if he turns out to be a different person than you thought. He has a reason to lie. To play upon your sympathies."

"So did you, Wren," Olivia said. "When you first came to the Guild. But I chose to trust you."

"But—" Wren protested.

"Lucas chose to trust you—to risk his life for you—even though he'd only just met you."

Wren took a steadying breath, trying to banish the pain that squeezed her heart at the mention of Lucas. Her hand drifted to the ring beneath her dress.

Olivia continued. "Sometimes you can sense something about a person. Even if your head tells you it's crazy, your heart knows otherwise. That they're worth taking a chance for. I felt that about you. I feel that about Dash. He's a good person. He wants to help us." Olivia's blue eyes were bright with fervent belief.

Dash *had* been kind to them when he'd been free. He was Tamrosi, not Aprican. Word of the emperor's dark magic might be enough to put anyone off his cause. Wren found herself nodding. "All right. If you trust him...I'll talk to Callidus about releasing him. But no promises..." But Olivia was already squealing in delight, her hands clutched to her bosom, her eyes bright. "Thank you."

Wren nodded. "I'm sorry it took us so long to tell you the truth."

"I'm still mad, but I get it," Olivia said. There were tears sparkling at the corners of her eyes. "Wren?"

"Yeah?" Wren said, fighting the lump rising in her own throat.

"Thanks for kidnapping me."

A startled laugh escaped Wren. "That's what friends are for."

CHAPTER 24

Nova Navis was a barren, windswept moor of high cliffs and gray glass. Wren stood at the rail, watching it grow larger on the horizon. Her body swayed with the rolling and tossing of the sea, her hair tangled in hopeless knots in the whipping wind. They were nearing the rocky shore now, and the sailors crawled over the deck behind her, pulling on ropes and lines while Pike shouted orders.

Callidus appeared next to her at the bow, followed by Thom, who held Callidus's arm for support. His coloring was still off, but he looked better, his eyes brighter, his back straighter.

Olivia and Dash lingered on the bow of the ship, Dash having changed into a brown sweater and olive trousers, along with sturdy boots. Wren hoped it wasn't a mistake, letting him out of his tiny cell of a cabin. But Olivia was right. It was time they started trusting her. And how much trouble could he really get up to out here in the middle of nowhere?

"How are you feeling, Thom?" Wren asked.

"Sick of lying in bed," he replied, letting out a muffled cough.

"Maybe a little fresh air is exactly what you need."

"Fresh air and a fire sounds great," Thom said.

Some of the sailors were headed to the shore to make a bonfire and forage for supplies. Saad, Pike's first mate and unofficial ship doctor, had thought it would be good for Thom to head to shore and dry out some of the damp.

Wren stifled a sigh. Thom needed to get better. His illness was one more weight on her already-heavy conscience.

"So that's Nova Navis," Callidus said. "Doesn't look like much."

"Good wool," Thom said.

Wren let out a laugh. "What?"

"It's what my ma always said. She was a laundress. Held up better than the rest. Colors kept bright. Good wool. Maybe I'll get me a sweater."

"I think we should all get sweaters, don't you, Wren?" Callidus crooked one substantial eyebrow at her.

She smiled, wrapping her arm around Thom's arm and leaning into him. "You can have all the sweaters you want when this is all over."

"Do you think it will ever be over?" he whispered so softly, the wind almost carried the words away.

Wren and Callidus exchanged a look. Even though Thom was her age, she felt the need to protect him somehow. Shield him from the truth. Callidus apparently felt the same.

"When this is over, you're going to buy Salted Cream from your former master. And I'm going to open up a confectionary next door. We'll have lunch on the grass by Lake Viri every afternoon. And Callidus will come visit us after his guild council meetings and eat ice cream with us."

A splash from the bow of the boat startled them.

Pike and his crew had dropped anchor in a horseshoe bay that was somewhat protected from shore. The anchor chain clinked as it slid off the deck into the gray water. The Black Jasmine was just sliding into view on the horizon.

"You ready to go badger hunting?" Pike strolled up, a rolled cigarette smoking in his hand.

"Ready as we'll ever be," Callidus replied.

The little skiff ground against the rocky beach of Nova Navis. The two men who had been manning the oars jumped out, frigid water splashing around their ankles as they heaved the rowboat the rest of the way up onto shore. One of the men helped Wren out, followed by Callidus, Pike, and Thom.

The rocky shore crunched beneath her boots as she stepped over slimy strands of kelp abandoned by the sea. A sparsely forested cove stood before them, stretching up towards the higher moors of Nova Navis.

They had packed enough for two days walking, though Wren vehemently prayed it wouldn't take that long to find the mercenary. Every day that ticked by wore at her, filled her imagination with potential horrors being perpetrated on Maradis and the other Guilds. What were Chandler and McArt and Bruxius doing? Marina and Lennon? Was Willings having his way with the Confectioner's Guild, pillaging its coffers and its staff? And then there were her thoughts of Lucas. He was out there somewhere. Her hand strayed to the lump beneath her shirt. Would she ever solve his riddle? Would she ever find him?

Her heart thudded in her chest as she followed Pike up a faint trail through underbrush of rushes and sedges. Everything looked cold, harsher than even the slate gray of Maradis's winter. What type of man lived out here?

"I know you said that he's rumored to live along the coast to the south of Port Gris," Callidus called to Pike. "But do you have any more specific notions about where to find him? We won't be just wandering about, will we?"

"Best I hear it," Pike said, "you don't find the Red Badger. The Red Badger finds you."

"Funny you should say that," a gravelly voice called out from the trees next to Wren. "Cuz ya found him."

Wren stumbled into Pike, who had pulled up short before her. Out of the woods, men materialized around them, arrows and spear tips pointed their way. "Easy now, fellas," Pike said. "We come in peace."

"We'll be the judge of that," the same voice said. Wren now saw that it belonged to a huge bearded man clothed in brown leather and furs, weapons strapped to every conceivable place on his sizable frame. If this was the type of mercenary they had come to hire, Wren wasn't sure if she should be terrified or grateful. This was a man who seemed like he could stand up to the Aprican legion without blinking. She just wished he wasn't pointing his sword at her.

"I should clarify," Pike said. "We come with an offer for the Red Badger. And gold."

"Very well. We'll take you to him."

The mercenaries, whom Wren thought numbered at least a dozen, bound their hands with leather straps and prodded them forward. "Is this really necessary?" Pike asked, to which the mercenary leader narrowed his gaze.

"Protocol. Red Badger has made a few enemies over the years. Can never be too careful."

Wren and Callidus had pleaded with the men to leave Thom behind, but they seemed disinclined to grant any special requests.

They emerged from the stand of trees to find a flat plane of scrubby grass with a dozen horses grazing. The leader pointed to a few of his men, who split off from the group to approach each of them. Out of the trees, Wren could see their captors more clearly. They were strong and fit, with grizzled faces and lean muscles under their leathers. The men were a mix of ages and nationalities—the man who approached Wren was an older, dark-haired man who had the complexion of a Magnish clansman, while the man who approached Thom seemed no older than they were, with the blond hair of an Aprican. There was even a female warrior, as lean and muscled as the men, with her brown hair threaded in several tight braids over her shoulder. Somehow her presence, though still hostile, made Wren feel a tiny bit safer.

Wren's eyes opened wide as the man approached her with a cloth in his hand. "Commander likes his privacy. You'll be blindfolded until we get there."

A person has a lot of time to think when tied up and blindfolded on the front of a horse. Wren's breathing came in shallow hitches as she tried to rein in her circling worries. What if this badger person wouldn't help them? What if he robbed and murdered them? What would happen to Maradis then? To Lucas? Her hand jerked up in an unconscious motion to grasp the ring hanging above her heart, but the rope restrained her.

Lucas. She half-feared, half-hoped that the incessant ache inside her at the thought of him would dim with time, but it was becoming more pronounced. Like a splinter burrowing deeper. He was so calm, so reasoned. If he were here, he would take her in his arms and banish her worries with his kisses. To her shame, she found herself crying beneath her blindfold. She tried to keep her shoulders from shaking, but the feelings were pouring out of her now, and she began to sob for the first time in weeks as the sorrow and helplessness seeped into her.

The man behind her grunted, then shushed her. She felt an awkward pat on her shoulder. "No need to be afraid. If you're here to do business with the Commander, we won't hurt ya."

Wren's tears turned to a disbelieving laugh. The man was comforting her! He thought she was crying out of fear for the situation. More laughter bubbled up, bursting from her, mingled with more tears.

"What's that?" the gravelly voice barked from ahead.

"Think mine's lost it," the man from behind her called out.

Thom's hacking cough joined the chorus of her manic giggles.

"Think mine's dying," another said, from the direction of Thom's cough.

"Better be a lot of gold in it," the leader said while Wren continued to laugh.

Wren's body ached when the horse finally stopped beneath her. She felt the saddle's weight shift as her captor swung down from his saddle and then he was grasping her around the waist, hauling her down too. Her knees almost buckled as he set her on the ground, but he steadied her until she got her feet under her. She took unsteady steps forwards, longing to see the world around her. The smells of a cookpot and the sound of a crackling fire oriented her slightly. They were in some kind of camp. And that was the sound of chopping wood. The mercenaries were calling out greetings to other men, and other male voices, even a few female, called back.

"Sal!" a deep voice called out, with a hint of a Novan twang. "Did ya go fishing? What catch have ya brought me?"

"Folks lookin' for the Red Badger," the man replied. "Seems they have a need of your services."

"A job! We're getting a bit too fat around here anyway," the other man called, his voice cheerful. That voice...it struck a chord in Wren's memories. It was familiar somehow. "Take off those blindfolds. Let's greet our guests properly."

Wren's captor took off her blindfold and she blinked as her eyes adjusted to the sudden brightness. He slit the cords at her wrists and she rubbed them as she looked around and saw her friends all accounted for. They were in the yard of a tidy village.

The man who must be the Red Badger strode forward, grasping hands with Pike. His hair was brilliant red and hung in curls around his ears. He was tall and broad, heavily muscled with a sword-belt buckled around his trim waist. He was handsome, Wren realized with a blush, extremely handsome, with angled cheekbones and fine brows crowning bright blue eyes. The feeling of familiarity wouldn't leave Wren. She felt herself drawn to Pike's side, longing to examine the Red Badger more closely.

"Welcome to the Warren, as we Badgers affectionally call it. You are?"

"Maximus Pike, Guildmaster of the Spicer's Guild of Alesia."

The redhaired man grinned at Pike's title. His smile lit up his face, filled with straight white teeth. Except one. A chipped front tooth.

Wren's knees went weak.

"I'm the Red Badger. But you can call me—"

"Ansel?" she breathed his name—half a prayer, half a curse.

CHAPTER 25

Suddenly, Wren was a little girl again, all knees and elbows, painfully thin, painfully naive. Even back then, Ansel had been a gatherer of souls—poor, unfortunate wretches like herself who flocked to the apparent safety in the shelter of his wings. She'd met him the same night she'd run from the orphanage, from the horror of a future she had been thankfully too naive to fully comprehend.

She hadn't known back then, but Maradis was divided up into territories—gangs of thugs and ruffians ruled the streets, but below, in the shadows, feral children ran in packs like wolves. The Cyclones ruled the Lyceum Quarter, the Hounds of the Huntress everything from west of Nysia Avenue and north of Council Street. The Jackabees took the Central Quarter, the Harlequins the Guild Quarter. And the Red Wraiths, Ansel's little gang, took the Port Quarter.

Ansel found her curled under the corner of a bridge, eyes red-rimmed with tears, nose streaming. The rain was pouring down in sheets that night, the street before her running like a river. Ansel wore a black rain slicker, its collar turned up against the wet.

He and two of his other followers came dashing out of the rain, laughing and cursing, pausing under the bridge for the rain to let up. When he caught sight of her, an electric charge went through her. His eyes were as blue as ice, yet she grew warm when they fell upon her. The only thing more striking than his blue eyes was his red hair. Wren thought it strange that the gods had chosen to paint this boy in such vibrant color when they left the rest of them mute brown.

"Hey," Ansel called to her, ducking low as he approached, his hands out like he was calming a spooked beast. Which in a way, he was. "You have anywhere to stay tonight?"

Wren didn't answer, only pulling her knees in closer to her body, tightening the grip of her shaking arms wrapped around them. She had been fooled once by such an offer. She wasn't going to be fooled again. She finally managed an imperceptible shake of her head.

"We have a place not far from here," Ansel continued. "Lots of kids like us stay there. Some girls too. It isn't much, but it's dry. You're welcome to come with."

One of the others, a dark shadow of a boy who looked half-Centese, groaned at him. "C'mon, Ansel. Ye can't take in every stray. She can't do nothin' but sit there. Don't need more mouths ta feed."

The redhaired boy, this Ansel, didn't answer, crouching low. He waited.

"'M fine," Wren managed, her body shaking from cold. She didn't like the look of that dark-haired boy.

"You don't seem fine," Ansel replied. "C'mon. Just one night."

Wren shook her head again. People didn't do nice things for free. She had learned that the hard way. If this boy was offering her something, he wanted something. She wasn't a fool.

"Look," he said. "Just an offer. We're in a warehouse a few blocks down on Edmund and Seventh Streets. Says 'Excelsior Soaps' on the side in white. Can ya read?"

Wren nodded. She could read some.

"If you change your mind, you're welcome," he said, standing.

"You're telling her where the Wraithhouse is now?" The dark boy groaned.

"Can it Nik," Ansel barked. "She's obviously not Cedar. Do I run this gang or what?"

The dark boy cast a sharp look back at her before the three disappeared into the rain like the wraiths they were.

Wren sat and shivered for a long while before unwinding herself and following them into the rain, towed by some invisible force that she only later recognized as Ansel's gravitas.

The warehouse was just as he'd described it, sitting brooding and quiet on the corner, the white lettering on the side stained gray by the night's rain. She crept into an alley around the side and clambered up a dumpster onto the rickety fire escape, creeping silently to the upper floors. From there, she peered in a window, squinting to see through the condensation fogging the inside of the glass. There were lanterns dotting the wide floor inside, and kids laid out on pallets and blankets. A deck of cards was spread across the cement floor between two kids, and a fire chugged in an iron stove in one corner. From Wren's perch on the cold, sharp steel, it looked like heaven. She leaned closer, holding her breath, looking for the redhaired boy from before. Where was he?

A face appeared behind the glass, causing Wren to jump backwards with a cry, slamming into the railings of the fire escape. The redhaired boy pushed the window up with a creak. "It's a lot warmer in here," he said with a wry grin. He held out a hand into the rain. She looked from it to him. He had a chip in one of his front teeth. The chip had done it, in the end. It had given him an earnestness that couldn't be faked. So she found herself putting her hand in his and letting him pull her through the window onto the balcony inside.

So began two fairly happy years, relatively speaking. Wren found her place in the Red Wraiths. The dark-haired boy, Nik, never took a shine to her, but the other orphans and street kids were nice, even friendly. They taught her the ways of the world on the street—the best places to beg, which cuisiniers and bakers saved their day's leftovers for the gang, the Cedar Guard's routes, and more. Wren was a hopeless fighter, uncoordinated and small, but she turned out to have a fair hand at lockpicking and quickly excelled, becoming Ansel's preferred partner in crime. She was lousy at pickpocketing, as she didn't have the boldness the skill took, but she played the part of the poor waif or distraction very well with her big eyes and protruding collarbones.

As the months ticked by, she found herself drawn to Ansel more and more, like a flower's face follows the sun. And it seemed he was drawn to her too. Ansel began picking her for solo jobs, and sometimes the two of them wouldn't go right back to the Wraithhouse but would dart around town—running through the piers, swiping a cinnamon stick from a vendor, or sitting on the grassy hillsides overlooking Spirit Bay. And from the sidelong glances of some of the other wraiths, they began to notice too.

It all fell apart one bright October day. The air was crisp and clear, the chill breeze rustling dry leaves in a kaleidoscope of orange and red. The leader of the Jackabees, a cruel blond-haired boy named Harlson, had been testing the boundaries between their territories for weeks. It seemed he was ready to test his mettle against Ansel, because that morning, Nik ran in, reporting that he'd spotted Harlson and another Jackabee all the way on Longshore Drive, in the heart of wraith territory. Ansel, Nik, and two of their other toughest brawlers ran to meet the threat.

There was a dangerous glint in Nik's eye that left an uneasy feeling in Wren's stomach. So she followed them, keeping to the alleys and shadows. So she saw when Ansel met Harlson, confronting him about his encroachment. She saw when Nik turned on Ansel and the other wraiths—watched with horror as a horde of Jackabees appeared from the side streets to join the fray. She saw Ansel, battered and bloody, on his knees before Harlson, the other boy's fist twisted cruelly in his beautiful red hair. Wren watched with white-knuckled fear, desperate to do something but knowing it would be useless against the might of the other gang.

Ansel finally held up his hands, admitting defeat. He smiled his chip-toothed smile, his teeth red with blood. "Whatcha want, Jackabee?"

"Half your territory. To the Raven Club." Harlson announced gleefully.

Wren silently cursed. If Ansel agreed, the Jackabees would be only blocks from Wraithhouse!

"That it?" Ansel asked.

Harlson looked at Nik, who nodded at him, glowering at Ansel. "And your woman. That auburn-haired girl."

Nik grinned toothily at Ansel.

Wren's heart stuttered in her chest. Her. They were talking about her. Did Nik think she meant so much to Ansel? Was he doing this to hurt him? Emotions roared within her, fear and guilt and...hope. Did Ansel feel for her how she felt for him?

"Wren? She's nothin.' Ya can have her," Ansel said. "Free of charge.

What're we really talking here? The Raven Club is too far."

The rest of Ansel's negotiations blurred in her mind, drowned out by the ringing in her ears. Ansel...had given her away. Thrown her out like trash, handed her over to that brute Harlson like a pair of old shoes. She flattened herself to the wall, her breath coming in gasps. She'd been a fool. Yet again. Trusted another man...cared for him...and for what?

She dashed down the alley and cut through the streets, away from the Jackabees, away from the Wraiths and Ansel and the Port Quarter. She kept running and running until her legs burned beneath her, until she crossed into the Guild Quarter. She never looked back.

"Wren." Callidus snapped his fingers before her and she started, her eyes focusing on his pinched face. "What's gotten into you?"

The color had drained from Ansel's face, his brash bravado swallowed by the shock of her presence.

"Wren?" he asked, taking a shaky step towards her. For a moment, he was that boy again. The boy offering a hand in the rain, a chance. But it had been a mistake then. It would be a mistake now.

"No." She shook her head, backing away. "No, no." She bumped into the chest of the man behind her, the man whom she had ridden with from the bay. She turned to Callidus, to Pike, feeling wild and panicked, penned in by these walls of men around her, leather and muscles and swords. "We're leaving. We are not working with him."

"What's gotten into you?" Callidus asked, laying a hand on her shoulder. "Are you ill?"

Thom was the one who looked ill, standing slightly to the side of them, his pale face covered with a sheen of sweat.

"He can't help us," she said, her voice shrill, sounding hysterical in her ears.

"A moment." Pike grinned widely at Ansel, who was standing in stony silence, his muscled arms crossed before his chest.

Pike drew her aside, turning their backs to the other men. "Get ahold of yourself," he hissed. "There is no other option. Don't ruin this."

"He can't be trusted," she whispered back, her breath ragged. "He will betray us."

"How do you know? Do you know him?"

"He betrayed me once. I'm not going to let him do it again," Wren said. "The answer is no. I'm out. We're out. We find another way."

Callidus was inching closer to them. "What in the Beekeeper's name is going on?"

"Wren has history with this man," Pike said.

"We can't work with him," Wren said, tugging on Callidus's sleeve.

Callidus's gaze darkened. "Wren, we were just hauled over half of Nova Navis blindfolded on horseback, and you're telling me you want to turn around, pack up, and go find another horde of dangerous men to help us retake our country?"

"Please," she said. "If you've ever trusted me, trust me now."

Callidus seemed to consider and Wren held her breath, clenching her hands into fists at her side to keep them from shaking. *Please, Callidus,* she thought. *Trust me.*

Callidus's shoulders slumped and he pushed his drooping hair back from his forehead. "Fine. We'll find another way."

Wren heaved a tremendous sigh, the tension draining from her.

Pike rolled his eyes and threw up his hands, letting out a string of curses in a language that sounded like Centese. "Just because you cupcakes refuse to work with him, doesn't mean I do. You don't think I've grappled with worse than this pretty boy? I'm staying."

Wren's mouth dropped open and Callidus glared at him. Pike was their manpower, their ride to find Lucas. But there had to be another way. Her mind spun, grasping for something, any way to get out of this. To keep their alliance with Pike and take back Maradis. Without allying themselves with someone who had thrown her away like a scrap of paper in the wind. She looked over her shoulder.

Ansel twisted his bottom lip between his fingers while he watched her, and the familiarity of it took Wren's breath away. "We don't wanna do business with anyone who doesn't wanna do business with us. But, Wren, I'd like to talk to ya."

"No, thank you," she said firmly, taking a step back. It didn't matter. She'd find a way later. They needed to leave. She patted Thom's shoulder, motioning for him to move. "We'll be on our way."

And then Thom toppled forward, crashing to the ground.

CHAPTER 26

It was Ansel who caught him. In a blink, the mercenary darted forward, catching Thom and lowering his lanky limbs to the ground.

Wren's mind moved sluggishly through the haze of surprise.

"What's wrong with 'im?" Ansel asked. "He's burning up."

Callidus was at Thom's side next, helping Ansel roll Thom onto his back.

"He's got pneumonia, best we can figure," Pike said.

"We told you not to bring him," Wren scolded Sal, the bearded man, who was now craning his head to take in Thom's prone form.

"We have a healer here who can look at him. Unless you're still planning on leaving this moment," Ansel said, looking pointedly at Wren.

She bit her lip. Staying meant getting sucked into Ansel's orbit. But they couldn't drag Thom back to the ship now. Not until he was stabilized. Against her better judgment, Wren nodded quickly. "Help him. No favors. We can pay."

Ansel motioned to a few of the other men, who picked up Thom's limp body and carried him towards one of the strange huts. Wren followed, getting her first glimpse of the little town.

About a dozen wooden houses in a semi-circle were built right into the hillside, their roofs covered in grassy earth. They faced the leeward side, sheltered from the western winds. Forming the other side of the semi-circle were outbuildings that looked like a barn, a smithy, and a smokehouse. In the tidy open area between them were cooking areas, firepits, and in the distance, fenced fields that housed both livestock and sparring men.

Wren and the others followed the men who carried Thom into one of the huts. Inside, they found a cozy room adorned with oil lamps and dried herbs. A wizened old woman prodded at Thom, who had been transferred to a table. "Can't have all ya in here," she barked, shooing them back out the door. "I'll summon ya if anything changes."

Anxious not to leave Thom but recognizing sense, Wren backed out the door.

Ansel was standing outside, his eyes roving over her form. "Why don't ya come with me? Warm ya up, get ya a bite to eat and some ale."

"We don't need anything from you." Wren crossed her arms over her chest.

"Speak for yourself," Pike said. "I'm starved."

Callidus looked over his shoulder at her before following in Ansel's wake. Wren stood frozen for a moment, her mind vacillating between the little cabin with Thom and the larger cabin the others had disappeared into. She finally huffed and followed after the others. She was thirsty. She supposed some water wouldn't hurt.

The large cabin on the end seemed to be used as a dining hall. Inside were low-slung tables and benches. It was surprisingly tidy, and a ginger-haired woman in an apron and kerchief hurried over to the table they had gathered around. Wren glowered at Pike and Callidus as she slid onto the bench next to Callidus, daring them to say anything. Thankfully, they didn't.

"Got a venison stew with pearl onions and carrots," the woman said. "Shall I bring four bowls?"

"Ya, please, Greta." Ansel flashed his smile at her, and the chipped tooth made Wren's heart stutter. How had he come to be here? From the Red Wraiths to the Red Badger, worlds away? She wanted to ask, but she didn't want to talk to him. To be sucked in. She knew how charismatic Ansel could be. She didn't want him softening her with platitudes and explanations. She knew what he had done. She had heard the words with her own ears. She knew what he was.

The serving woman returned with four bowls of hearty stew, along with a board full of cheese and crusty potato bread. "The boys hunt all the meat local. And Greta is one of the finest cuisiniers in Nova Navis," Ansel said. "Enjoy."

Wren looked down at her stew. It did look delicious: hearty chunks of meat and little onions glistening like pearls. She took a bite and was surprised at the complex mix of spices—pepper, tarragon, and...was that a hint of nutmeg?

"So," Ansel said. "Why ya lookin' for mercs?"

"None of your business," Wren said.

"Ya made yourself clear earlier," Ansel said, "but it can't hurt to have some idle conversation. Or shall we all sit here in silence?"

Wren glowered.

Pike and Callidus each cast her glances that she knew meant 'stop being so rude,' but she didn't care. They didn't know Ansel. She did. This is what he did.

"We're considering a...countereffort against the new Aprican emperor," Pike said. "We need men."

Ansel whistled. "I hear the people are fallin' to his side like dominos. You'd be up against tremendous odds. Highly disciplined fighting forces, nearly unlimited financial resources. City fightin' is difficult terrain if it came to an actual skirmish." He smiled around a bite of bread.

She took another bite of stew. Between the stew and the heat of the fire, a warmth suffused her that she hadn't felt in days. Her muscles began to uncoil, loosening the tension that had filled her at Ansel's nearness. Could she really get back on that boat and sail to gods-knew-where? Without Pike as their ally? Would they even be welcome back on the vessel if Pike insisted on working with Ansel and Callidus refused? And could Thom make the voyage to the Beekeeper-knows-where they would head to next? How long would he have to convalesce here? They'd already been gone from Maradis a week.

"How many men do you have?" Pike asked.

"'Bout two hundred," said Ansel. "But they fight like a thousand. Each man—and I've got a few ladies—is handpicked and trained by me. Loyal. Fierce."

"Two hundred," Callidus said. "The Apricans have thousands."

"About ten thousand, I hear," Ansel said. "Though some of those'll be headed home now that the city is won. Alesia has at least five. If those men could be rallied, the right plan put in place, the right man to command 'em, the Aprican occupying force could be crippled."

"Especially if the emperor began to think the city was subdued," Callidus said, exchanging a glance with Pike. "He might let his guard down."

"We'd have to find a way to...neutralize certain defenses," Pike said. The bread. He was talking about the bread.

"When you are hired, how do you and your men get from place to place? I didn't see any sailors around here?" Pike asked.

"I know a captain over in Port Gris," Ansel said, referring to the capital of Nova Navis. "She's got a fleet that's carried us in the past. I trust her."

"She?" Pike raised an eyebrow.

"Oh ya." Ansel grinned. "Quite a firecracker. Hell of a sailor."

"And how much have you charged, in the past, for you and your merry band?" Pike asked.

"He can't be trusted," Wren muttered into her soup.

Callidus turned to her. "Should we really discuss this now?"

"I don't care if he knows I think he's a two-faced snake," Wren said.

"I admit," Ansel said, "I ain't always been one hundred percent upstandin' in my business dealings. But I don't know what ya think I've done. Ya disappeared into thin air. Far as I knew, ya were dead."

"Is that before or after you sold me to the Jackabees?" Wren was on her feet now, her hands planted on the table.

"What?" Ansel's face drained of color. For the first time since they had arrived, she thought she saw some of that young boy he had been years before.

"Maybe we should leave these two to talk," Callidus said, standing.

"I'm not done with my stew," Pike protested, but he let Callidus haul him up.

"Greta will get ya more if ya ask nicely." Ansel motioned back towards the kitchen.

Pike took his bowl with him and the two men pushed through the double doors.

Suddenly, the room felt very small. Even with the table between them, blocking Ansel from Wren, the air felt charged. Ansel's ice-blue eyes were fixed on hers, pinning her to where she stood. She had been through so much, yet still this man made her feel like a little girl, foolishly following her first crush anywhere.

"I was there that day," Wren said. Her voice was steady, much to her relief. "When you went to confront the Jackabees with Nik. I had a bad feeling, so I followed you. I saw when they ambushed you. I saw when they beat you. And I heard when Harlson asked for half your territory. And me. And you gave both to him without a second thought."

Ansel pushed up from the table, pacing away from her, and then turning. "I was lyin,' Wren. If I'd said *no,* they'da known…" He looked down, tracing the pommel of his sword. It was fashioned in the shape of a snarling badger head. "They'da known how much ya meant to me. I'd have said anythin' to protect ya. I gave up half our territory, just so they'd let me go—so I could get back to the Wraithhouse and warn ya. But when I got back, ya were gone. Nowhere to be found. We thought they'd taken ya. We…*I* went crazy. I rounded up the rest of the Wraiths and we went for them. That night. The Jackabees. To find ya. It was bloody. There was so much fighting; a lot of the Wraiths died. But ya weren't there." Ansel rubbed his jaw, his eyes distant. Like he was still seeing the blood of those children. Like he still had it on his hands.

He continued. "Nik, he said ya were already dead. That they'd found ya and beaten and dumped your body in the bay, over by the piers. I took a few of the lads who were left, and bloody and hurtin,' we searched everywhere. We never found ya. We thought ya'd died. Been picked clean."

Ansel's words struck Wren like arrows from a quiver. Could that be true? That he had thought she'd been dead? That he had searched for her? That it had all been a desperate ruse…?

Her world was tilting on its axis, shifting beneath her. She had hated Ansel for so long, his betrayal had festered inside of her, poisoning her like a cancer. Don't trust anyone…they betray you. No man will ever think you're worth fighting for. Could it be possible that she had been wrong?

No! Her mind rebelled at the notion. Ansel was playing her like he always had. She was a fool to fall for it. "You're just saying that," Wren said. Her voice was shaking now.

"Am I?" Ansel stepped around the table, looming over her. She wanted to shrink back from him but held her ground. "Maradis was ruined to me. The wraiths had gone to hell, and I couldn't be in a city that killed ya. Me and a few of the lads stowed away on a boat. Made our way to Port Gris. Turned out I had some family here. A grandmother I hadn't known. Started rebuildin' my life."

Wren found herself shaking her head. Lies, they were lies. They had to be. For how could she even think about trusting him again?

"Bran is here, one of my seconds. Ya remember him from the Wraiths? Ya don't believe me, ask him what happened that day with the Jackabees. Ask him...whether he thinks I woulda handed ya over to Harlson."

Wren's heart thumped in her chest. Branley. She did remember him.

"And if ya don't believe him..." Ansel started unbuckling his leather breastplate under one arm, pulling it over his head.

Wren jumped as it thunked onto the table. "What are you doing?" she asked.

Ansel pulled his white shirt off, tossing it into a ball on top of the armor. His face was flushed. "If ya don't believe me, or believe him, believe this. I got this to keep ya close. Always."

Wren's breath left her as she stared at Ansel's taut torso, lean and strong from years of sparring and fighting. Across the center of his chest, right over where his heart must have been, was an intricate tattoo rendered in black ink. A tattoo of a wren in flight.

CHAPTER 27

Wren was drowning. Drowning in Ansel's words, his presence, in the stark black ink of the tattoo, proclaiming that the anger she had felt for the past four years had been for nothing. Had been...a misunderstanding. Wren backed up. "I need some air." Her feet propelled her past Ansel, through the door out into the damp chill Novan afternoon.

Pike and Callidus were outside, huddled close to a fire, Pike finishing his second helping of stew.

"Did you figure out whether you hate him or not?" Pike asked, his dark eyes furrowed.

Wren ran her fingers through her hair, its ends knotted from the blustery ride. "Maybe? I don't know," she said, shaking her head. "There's someone else I need to talk to." Wren squinted towards the paddocks beyond the little village, where men and women were sparring with whirling staves. "And I think I see him. Wait here."

"Can't wait," Pike called in a simpering voice after her.

Even back in their Wraith days, Bran had been big. Now, he was huge, with thick cords of muscle raining down blows upon his opponent in a merciless tempo. His round face was ruddy with effort, and his dimpled cheeks were covered with a thick beard braided at the ends and tied with little silver beads.

"Bran," she cried, stepping up on the lowest rung of the fence circling the field.

Bran looked her way, shock registering in his hazel eyes.

His opponent took advantage of the moment and whacked Bran hard in the ribs.

Bran doubled over with a grunt of pain, resting one hand on his knee, the other held up in a sign of surrender. "Low blow." He coughed before standing and taking in a deep breath.

"Never take your eyes off the fight," his opponent said with a wide grin.

"Right you are. Now you're learning," Bran said. "Switch partners. I need a minute. I think I see a ghost from my past."

"A wraith," Wren called.

Bran let himself through the gate and swept her up in a bone-crushing hug. "Gods, it's good to see you."

"Ribs..." Wren croaked.

"Figure it's payback for that little swipe." Bran set her down, a wide grin breaking across his face. "I knew we had company...but I never in a million years would have thought..."

"The feeling is mutual," Wren said.

"Can I get you something hot to drink? You're freezing." He ran his hands over her shoulders in a vigorous motion. "Some things never change. You never had any insulation on you, did you?"

"None left for the rest of us after you took it all." Wren punched him in his sizable arm.

Bran guffawed, and the sound warmed her. It *was* good to see him. She had locked Ansel and the other Wraiths into a little dark corner of her mind after she had fled, but those memories were all resurfacing now. They had been her family. And with the exception of Nik, she had loved them like family. Well, with the exception of Ansel. That had been more complicated.

Bran led her into one of the small cabins. The interior held a main living room with two worn chairs pulled close to the fireplace. Bran went to work setting the fire and Wren wandered about, examining the sparse furnishings. Everything was faded and worn, but somehow inviting. On the windowsill, Wren found a crude carving of an elk, one of its horns broken off. "You still have this?" She turned to Bran, running her hands over the rough cuts of the wood. She could almost feel the boy's chubby fingers, frustrated that he couldn't get the chisel to work just right. She remembered him making it, sitting by the little cast-iron fireplace in the Wraithhouse while a particularly nasty storm drummed its fingers on the metal roof.

"Had to gauge my progress. This here's some of my latest work." He pointed to an exquisite carving of a braying elk over the mantle, its proud antlers rendered in lifelike detail.

It drew her and she ran her fingers over the grooves of the elk's fur, the velvet of the antlers. "It's extraordinary," she breathed.

"Can't go on killing people forever," Bran said, setting a kettle over the growing flames. "One day I'm gonna give this all up and open my own shop."

"I know exactly what you mean," Wren said, sinking into one of the chairs, its sagging cushions enveloping her. "Except the killing part."

"So." Bran sat too. "Our little Wren, flown home. How, after all these years? Why?"

Wren closed her eyes. "I didn't know you were here, that Ansel was here. We came looking for mercenaries for hire. I'm a member of the Confectioner's Guild, and some of the Guilds are looking for aid to try to take back the city."

"Confectioner? Like candies?" Bran wrinkled his nose. "You're too real for all that fancy stuff."

"Says the man carving intricate elk statues," Wren joked. "In truth, I didn't find it. Confectionary...it found me. It saved me. After..."

"Yes, that. After what. Why did you leave? Ansel...it almost destroyed him. "

Wren's mouth dropped open. "Are you... It's true? You went looking for me? Fought the Jackabees?"

"Hell yes. Ansel was like a man possessed. The red wraith come to life. He bashed Harlson's head in with a rock. That snake Nik said they had beaten you and left you for dead. We pawed through garbage along the piers for days, but after we couldn't find you, we had to face facts.

You were dead. Few of the other lads drifted away to join other gangs, few of us stayed with Ansel. We realized we couldn't go back to the city, not with what Ansel had done. It had upset the balance of the gangs. And we'd had it with Maradis anyway."

Wren pressed her lips together. So Ansel's story was true. The rumbling of boiling water from the kettle was the only sound between them, and Bran got up, removing it with a towel before moving into the corner to pour. When he returned, he placed a blissfully warm mug into her chilled hands before sitting down.

"Where'd you go, Wren?" Bran asked softly. "Why'd you leave us?"

She looked at him. There was old pain in his eyes, and fresh pain too. They had thought her dead, and now it seemed she had left them. "I overheard Ansel saying he would trade me to the Jackabees. Hand me over like nothing. So I ran."

Bran softened. "You really thought Ansel would do that to you? You and Ansel... He felt like a king with you at his side. Didn't you know how he looked at you? He never woulda traded you for anything."

Wren looked into the fire, tears prickling in her eyes. "Sometimes it's hard to see...what's right before you."

"Well, isn't that the way of the world?"

"And the tattoo..." She looked at Bran. "On Ansel's chest? Is it really...?" She trailed off. Seeing Ansel and Bran again...it brought it all raging back, the raw want and need of the Wraithhouse, the way her heart seemed only to beat for Ansel, her eyes always searching for him. The memories of her time with him were so vivid—the color brighter, the smells more pungent. Perhaps it was the potency of young love, or the heightened pain of his supposed betrayal, but when she thought of Ansel, her feelings buffeted her. Even after all this time.

"For you? Of course the tattoo's for you. Failing you was his biggest regret. I reckon once you two get over the shock of seeing each other, the fact that you're alive and well and happy will bring him great joy."

"I'm sorry," Wren said, guilt washing over her. How had she gotten it all so wrong? "For leaving. For putting you through...what you went through."

"Sounds like you went through quite a bit yourself. It was a long time ago. We were stupid kids playing at being gangsters. We ended up right where we were supposed to be."

"Good," Wren said, taking a sip of her tea. She coughed. "Does this have whiskey in it?"

"'Course! What kinda operation you think we're running here?"

She laughed.

"Seems like you landed yourself in a good spot too, current circumstances aside," he continued. "Do you have someone taking care of you? You married?"

"Married? No," Wren said. "There was...is...someone..." She sighed. "I don't know where he is right now."

"That sounds like a story," Bran remarked, taking a sip of his own tea.

Wren let out a little laugh. "It's been a strange few months. We're trying to find him, but all I have to go on is this." She pulled the chain out from the neck of her dress, showing him the ring.

"What's this?"

"Your guess is as good as mine. A clue. As to his whereabouts. But it's about the most generic clue ever. The stone is rare but still it could be found in a dozen places. The falcon...it's his clan crest. Could mean anything."

"That's not a falcon," Bran said, turning the ring in his hand to study it. "The beak is wrong."

"What?" Excitement lanced through Wren's body like lightning. "What is it?"

"I think it's a cormorant. Sea bird."

"How do you know?"

"The beak is longer. Hooked on the end. But I'm no expert. Let's ask old Mac. He fancies himself a real ornithologist."

"A what?" Wren asked as she hurried after Bran, setting her tea down on the counter.

They crossed to the smithy, where a gnarled old man was hammering the dents out of a breastplate.

"Mac, Wren, Wren, Mac." Bran did the introductions. "Wren has a question that might stump even the most avid bird-lover."

"Oh?" The man raised a furry white eyebrow, straightening.

Wren took the chain off, holding out the ring. "Do you know what kind of bird this is?"

Mac wiped his dirty hands on a cloth before picking up a pair of spectacles from a far table. He peered at the ring. "Cormorant," he said.

"Ha!" Bran said with a broad grin. "I knew it!"

Pike and Callidus had drifted over and were standing behind them now.

"What's going on?" Callidus asked.

"Not just any cormorant." Mac was still turning the ring over, examining it. "See the etching around the eyes? It's supposed to denote a patch of white, I reckon. This is no ordinary cormorant. It's a hooded cormorant. They're natives of the Odette Isles. Rare birds. Big birds."

"The Odette Isles. You're sure?" Wren's blood was racing in her veins. The Odette Isles were one of the places the rutilated quartz could be found. But more than that. They were close by.

"'Course I'm sure! I grew up there."

"Do you know if the Imbris clan has any property on the islands? Say, a summerhouse or cabin?" Wren asked.

Mac rubbed his scraggly white whiskers. "That does sound familiar. One of the little islands...Fletch Island, yes, that's what it's called. They own the whole thing, I think. We didn't go there."

Wren sprang at the man, pulling him into a tight embrace. "Thank you, Mac," she said. He smelled like smoke and oil.

Mac patted her on the back. "Nice to find someone as enthused as I am about birds."

She released him and took the ring from his offered hand. She turned to Pike and Callidus, practically jumping up and down.

"Did that old man just tell us what I think he did?" Pike asked.

Wren nodded, clutching the ring to her chest. "We just found Lucas."

CHAPTER 28

W ren needed Lucas. And Alesia needed him too. And to get him back on the throne, they needed the Red Badger. Her checkered past with Ansel melted away at the prospect of seeing Lucas again, at the chance of righting the wrong she'd done to him and to Maradis. She'd make a deal with the Huntress herself if it meant getting to him. Plus, Bran had confirmed Ansel's story. It seemed she had misunderstood him all those years ago. Wren shoved down the flood of emotions that threatened to surface. How different her life might have been if she hadn't run that day. She wouldn't be a confectioner. She would never have known of her Gift. Never would have met Sable or Hale or gotten mixed up in King Imbris's plans. She never would have met Lucas. Would she have stayed with Ansel and the Wraiths? Would she be in this camp with him right now at his side? Or maybe they never would have left Maradis, would have fought the Jackabees and the other gangs for their turf. Maybe they'd all be dead.

Wren shook off the endless possibilities. It wouldn't do her any good to think of what might have been. She'd made her choice. That first one, and all the rest that had brought her here. This mess was her life. She would make the best of it.

"Let's go talk to Ansel," Wren said, looping the chain over her head, tucking Lucas's ring back into her blouse.

"You've finally come to your senses?" Callidus asked.

"I've finally come to my senses." Wren nodded. "Thanks for your help." She waved to Mac, who made a dismissive motion with his hand. His gap-tooth smile followed them back across the camp and into the dining hall.

Ansel was leaning against the hearth, staring into the fire. The flames were glinting off his red curls, and now that she wasn't so shocked or angry, she could see what a handsome man he had become. Strong, capable—a real leader among men. No, his business was still not entirely respectable, but Ansel's ability to make a person feel secure amongst the thrill of danger was always one of his most magical qualities.

She was grateful he had put his shirt and leather armor back on. She didn't think her ragged heart could handle the sight of the tattoo again. She closed her eyes, fighting through the image of Ansel's chest filling her mind's eye.

Lucas, we're coming, she thought desperately. She needed him now more than ever. His sure, calm presence, his soothing smell of rosemary. At the thought of seeing Lucas again, her memories of him took flight like a flock of birds freed from their cage. He would know what needed to be done. He would help her find her true north once again.

"Commander." Bran pulled up short, his spine lance-straight. "It seems our guests have reconsidered the use of our services."

Ansel turned, his piercing gaze sweeping over each of them before resting on her. "All of ya agree?"

"We do," Wren said, swallowing.

"Finally." Pike shook his head. "We need you and all your men. And ships to carry you. We have a destination. The Odette Isles. You know them?"

"'Course," Ansel said. "A day's sail from Horseshoe Bay, where ya anchored. But few travel those islands. It's said they're cursed, haunted by spirits who call ya to your doom on the rocks."

Pike waved a hand. "Superstitious nonsense. You'll still sail there, right?"

"If the money's right, we'll sail into the teeth of hell itself." Ansel grinned wide.

"My kind of man," Pike said. "Now, there is the matter of price—"

The old woman who had been treating Thom appeared in the doorway, interrupting Pike. "Ansel dear, I thought your friends might like to know that the young lad is doing much better. He's awake and lucid, if they'd like to see him."

Callidus put a hand to his chest, relief etched on his face mirroring Wren's. "Pike, do you mind handling this while I visit Thom?" Wren asked.

"I'd like to go as well," Callidus said.

"Off with you," Pike said. "This is the fun part, anyway."

Wren and Callidus hurried after the old woman.

Inside the small cabin, they found Thom sitting up in bed, drinking broth from a wooden bowl. Wren rushed to him, throwing herself around him as Thom held out the bowl, trying not to spill. "Easy there." He laughed.

She pulled back, amazed. His color had returned and he no longer had the sheen of sickly fever about him. Even his voice sounded better, not so raspy and dry.

"How dare you scare us like that?" Wren said, giving him a playful punch on the arm.

"Easy on the invalid!" Thom cried, but he smiled.

"Glad you're back with us," Callidus said.

"You're not going to be back to your old self for another few days," the old woman said. "Plenty of hot food and clean water, lots of sleep. And sprinkle some of this in his food before every meal until it's gone." She handed a leather pouch to Callidus.

"Thank you for helping him," Wren said. Seeing Thom back to himself was a huge weight off her shoulders.

"Anything for a friend of Ansel's," the woman said before pushing back through the door and leaving the three of them alone.

"So," Thom said, picking up his bowl of broth. "What'd I miss?"

After an hour of heated negotiations between Pike and Ansel, they had a settled on a price for the service of the Red Badgers. From the somewhat nauseous look on Callidus's face when Pike had given him the number, Wren suspected it was the better part of the Confectioner's Guild's coffers. But if it helped them win Alesia back, no price was too steep.

Ansel had sent a rider to Port Gris to locate Captain Griff, who would bring ships to carry them from Horseshoe Bay.

They had dinner in the dining hall with Ansel and his mercenaries. Even Thom made it to the table, Callidus hovering over him like a mother hen as he walked creakily to the bench.

Wren found she rather liked the men and women that made up Ansel's little band of mercenaries. They were nothing like she had expected. Respectful, good-natured, funny as hell. They laughed and joked throughout the meal, ribbing on each other good-naturedly, even poking fun at Ansel. Their life here was tidy and comfortable. Warm. It reminded her of the Wraithhouse.

Wren, Thom, Callidus, and Pike were given their own little cabin just outside the main ring of houses, and before heading off to bed with the others, Wren took a deep breath and walked over to Ansel. She needed to do this. "Can I talk to you for a moment?"

"'Course," Ansel said, getting up from the bench and walking with her to a quiet corner of the dining hall. His nearness threatened to overwhelm her. His aura of power and confidence had always drawn her in like a moth to the flame, and she felt its pull even now. *Steady,* she told herself. *You're not that little girl anymore.* "It seems I owe you an apology. I talked to Bran, and he confirmed what you told me. I'm sorry I put you through that. All of you. Thinking I was dead, having to leave Maradis... It wasn't easy for me either, just know that. Hearing those words from your mouth...they broke me. For...a long time—"

"I'm sorry too," Ansel said. His words were soft. "I shouldn'ta said those things. Even if I didn't mean the words, even if they were a lie... ya shouldn'ta heard that. I'd only ever wanted ya with me, Wren."

"I know that now," she managed, a lump growing in her throat.

"I was a stupid kid tryin' to survive. To take care of everyone else when I couldn't even take care of myself. But ya didn't need me, Wren. Ya made it. Seein' the woman you've become"—Ansel reached out and stroked her cheek with his thumb, sending a shiver through her—"it brings joy to my soul. You're a survivor. Ya didn't realize your strength back then. But I see it now. To know that you've found a place….it makes me glad." His hand dropped.

"Thank you." Her words were a whisper. She cleared her throat. "You too. This place, these fighters...it suits you. I never thought a den of killers could be so...inviting."

Ansel chuckled. "I've always been good at hospitality. I'm glad we'll be goin' with ya. Fightin' at your side. It's a good cause. We'll fight for anyone who pays us, but we prefer a worthy cause."

"It is. The emperor...it's not right what he plans to take from Maradis. From its people."

"And you think this...Lucas Imbris will be able to help the cause? To rally the people?"

"He's nothing like his father. He's kind, and honorable—you'd like him."

"Sounds like ya know him well." Ansel cocked one red eyebrow.

Wren's hand drifted to the necklace around her throat. "I do. I... He's..." She cleared her throat and looked him in his bright blue eyes. "I love him," she declared, the words a shield against Ansel, against the havoc his presence had wreaked in her heart.

A sad smile drifted across Ansel's face. "Then we better go get him."

Lucas stood with the icebox open, a frown on his face. The kitchen was shadowed around him but for the single oil lamp, the floor chilled beneath his bare feet. What time was it—4, 5 A.M.? You'd never know it from the heavy dark sky. He'd woken hungry, but nothing in the house looked good. They'd quickly eaten through the best of Greyson's provisions and were now back to canned food and sardines. He settled for a glass of water, poured from the pitcher on the island. He sat down on the stool, staring morosely before him, the darkness twisting the furniture into strange shapes.

A few days before, he and Trick had celebrated their decision to return Maradis and fight alongside the Falconer, their hearts soaring. The excitement had very quickly fizzled as they realized how long they'd have to wait. It would be at least the two weeks before Greyson returned with his next shipment, and even after they got to Nova Navis, they'd have to figure a way to smuggle themselves back into Maradis without being caught. Once they were at the city walls, they could use Trick or

Ella's keys to access one of the secret passageways back into the city. But it was a long trek between Port Gris and Maradis, with no doubt at least a few Aprican checkpoints to cross.

Lucas sighed. He'd been thinking on it for days, his mind racing and spinning. But without more information from Greyson, they couldn't plan anything.

He ran his finger around the rim of the glass, his mind wandering to Wren, his memories of her sugar scent and the silk of her skin. Where was she now? Had she fled Maradis too? Or was she living in the city under Aprican rule? Did they know she'd had a hand in getting him and his siblings free? Worries crowded at him. They hadn't been able to say goodbye, not really. He'd been in and out of consciousness from the wound on his back as Trick's friends had transported them in a wagon to the port. He remembered the murmur of her voice, the flicker of her wide chestnut eyes. His groggy move of pulling the ring from his finger and pressing it into her hand. That was it. There was nothing else until he had come to on Greyson's ship. Now, the ring seemed a fool's errand. How could she ever figure out such an obscure clue? He wished he had a way to get her a message. Or to find out her fate.

He rotated his shoulder in its socket, feeling the pull of the skin of his back where the wound had been sewn shut. It was mostly healed now. Trick had removed the stitches a few days ago. Ella had offered, but he hadn't trusted the gentleness of her hand.

A light flickered in the dark windows outside the house and Lucas's head jerked up, his eyes searching for what he'd seen. He sat still, his breath stuck in his chest. He peered into the darkness, slowly scanning the wide set of windows on the main floor of the house. Nothing.

He let out a shaky breath. The flicker must have been his imagination.

But there it was again. Like a flash of a lantern. He leaned forward, squinting.

Glass shattered behind him as the back door exploded inward, kicked off its hinges.

Lucas flew to his feet and twisted just fast enough to catch glimpse of a man in a pale blue uniform. And then a sharp pain bloomed on the back of his head, and his world went dark.

CHAPTER 29

They had left that afternoon, sailing the majority of the way to the Odette Isles under the dark of night.

Captain Griff was a short, thin, tough-as-nails woman with steely eyes and wild, red hair. She'd brought six ships with her to ferry Ansel's men to the Odette Islands, and then on to Maradis. The ships were sturdy two-masted brigantines with crisp white sails and scrubby ginger crews. It seemed most of the sailors were Novan. The sailors and the mercenaries had clearly sailed together before, because the excruciatingly long process of boarding all the men and supplies had been interspersed by cries of recognition, claps on the back, and good-natured ribbing.

As they neared the Odette Isles, a layer of heavy fog fell over them like a quilt. The mood on the ship dampened with each passing minute.

Pike stood by the wheel of the Phoenix, talking to Griff, Ansel, and Callidus. It was a strange group they had collected, each skilled in their own way, each dangerous. Wren stood off to the side, not sure if she belonged. Would they include her at all in the planning once she had retrieved Lucas for them? That was her primary use here, wasn't it?

"Strange place, the Odette Isles." Dash appeared at the rail next to her. With his clothing changed to nondescript trousers and shirt and his long, brown hair pulled into a ponytail, she hardly recognized the Aprican legionnaire anymore. Somewhere he'd gotten hold of a toothpick, which was stuck in the corner of his mouth, just like the first day she'd seen him. He was handsome, with kind eyes and an easy manner. Wren could see what Olivia liked in him, and the feeling unsettled her. Callidus may had agreed to give him the free reign of the vessel, and to consider his assistance with their plans to retake Maradis, but he was still a legionnaire. Wren couldn't forget. He couldn't be trusted.

"Everyone keeps saying it's haunted," Wren said.

"I don't believe in such things."

"Me either," Wren said. "There's plenty of horror in mankind alone. Don't need to add supernatural horrors to the mix."

Dash looked at her out of the corner of his eye. She didn't meet his gaze, instead staring back into the endless fog.

"Life hasn't been kind to you, has it?" he remarked.

"Sometimes I think I'm especially unlucky," Wren said, trying to ignore the irony that her Gift presented. "But other times life surprises me. Not sure anymore that I've had it any worse than anyone else."

Dash said nothing, instead leaning down on the rail, looking out into the silent dark water beneath them. The occasional crack of a sail in the wind, the creak of the rigging, and whispered conversations of those on deck were the only sounds that accompanied them through the mist. It was eerie.

"I'm sorry you're here, Dash," she said. "It wasn't our intent."

"I'm not," he said. "I might not have gotten to know Olivia otherwise." A secret smile curved across his face.

Wren turned to him. "Don't hurt her, Dash." Her voice caught in her throat. After all Olivia had been through, after all she had lost, Wren thought another betrayal might break Olivia. Gods, it would break her. They were all stretched thin by grief and hardship and sorrow. They needed people they could count on. Trusting him was such a risk. Not just for the cause. If Dash betrayed them—

"I won't." Dash rested his hand on hers, and though Wren tensed, he looked at her with such earnestness in his eyes that it overwhelmed her. His hand was large and warm, a strange comfort atop her frigid fingers. "You have my word."

"The word of an Aprican legionnaire?"

"The word of a Tamrosi blueberry farmer who found a girl who takes his breath away."

Silence passed between them as Wren thought on that. Was it so impossible to believe that people could change? That Dash was a good man who had gotten swept up into the legion when he'd had no other option? Wren thought of Hale, her heart squeezing painfully.

"Okay." She nodded. "Okay."

"Good. Hey..." He trailed off as his eyes slid past her, peering into the mist. "Is that...?"

Wren turned to where he looked, squinting into the fog. It moved and undulated, revealing nothing of the secrets it held. Until...yes, she saw it. A solid object. A tree. "Land!" she cried and the sailors exploded into action, trimming the sails to slow the ship. The cry echoed down to the other ships in the line. It was dangerous to move at full speed in such thick fog with rocky shores about.

A gray, craggy coast appeared from the mist on their port side, which Wren had learned in sailor's lingo meant left. The island brimmed with towering cedars and firs, catching wisps of mist in their needles like cotton candy. A tall, thin black bird sat on a rocky outcropping jutting into the water. It had a white patch around its eye. A cormorant. It opened its hooked beak and let out a strange, clicking cry that sent a pair of icy fingers running up her spine. She shivered. What a sad solemn place for Lucas and his siblings to be hiding. She prayed they would find them here—safe and unharmed.

Wren shoved her damp hair back from her forehead and walked to the others. "We're looking for Fletch Island, according to Mac."

"Funny place for a summerhouse," Ansel remarked.

"But a good place to lie low," Pike said. "Your man is here, Wren. I have a feeling."

Ansel looked sharply at her at that, and Wren blushed.

Thom and Olivia emerged from below deck, a red plaid scarf rolled around Thom's neck. They came to stand by Wren and she twined her arm through his. "Glad you're feeling better," she whispered.

"Me too," Thom said. He leaned low and murmured into her ear. "Had to make myself presentable for Trick." He winked at her, and she smiled. Of course. Thom must be feeling just as excited to see Trick again as she was to see Lucas.

"We have an old map of the islands." Griff was smoothing the map's edges. "Best I can figure, we're here." She pointed to an inlet between two of the outermost islands. "This one is Fletch Island. There should be a place to anchor around the other side. We're making for that, and then we'll send some skiffs out to see what we can see."

"I'm going," Wren said. "I should, so Lucas knows we're friendly."

"I'll go too," Ansel said. "For backup."

"Fine," Wren said. "We should take one more."

"I'd like to go," Thom said, straightening.

Callidus opened his mouth to protest, but Thom hurried on. "I'm well. I've been useless this entire trip. Let me help. Let me do something."

Callidus gave a reluctant nod.

One of the sailors ran up to Pike. "We've spotted a structure."

Wren's heart leapt into her throat. This was it. Lucas. She could feel him out there in the distance, almost close enough to touch. She longed to press her head against his chest, to strangle him with a hug. Gods, she just wanted to see him. To know that he was alive and well and real.

The time it took to anchor the ships, drop a skiff in the water, and row to Fletch Island felt like an eternity. Wren's knee bounced up and down with excitement, and she had to clasp her hands together to keep them from shaking. Lucas. Everything in this world made more sense with him at her side. She had made it through these last few weeks by the skin of her teeth. She hadn't known if she could make it. But Lucas had never doubted her. He made her feel like she could do anything. Be anything. Even happy.

Wren leapt out of the rowboat before Ansel had even pulled it up on shore, her boots splashing in the freezing water. Ansel sprang out after her, catching her arm, ricocheting her back around towards him. "Wait," he hissed. "We don't know what's up there. We go together."

Wren wanted to scream with frustration, but some still-sane part of her recognized the wisdom of his words.

The path up to the house felt never-ending—a zigzagging line of stairs set into the sandy soil of the island. Up and up they went until they reached the broad expanse of windows at the front of the house. They were nearly at the top of the island now, and Wren knew the view must be breathtaking. She didn't turn and instead continued forward towards her single-minded goal. Lucas.

Finally, blessedly, she burst through the carved wooden front door. It was unlocked. "Lucas!" she cried, her breath ragged from the climb.

Thom called from right on her heel. "Trick! Are you here?"

The house showed signs of use—the furniture was uncovered and free from dust. A vase of scraggly yellow dandelion heads sat on the table in the dining room to her left. An open book, turned over to mark the page, sat on the sofa in the living room on the right.

"Lucas!" she cried. "It's Wren!"

"Wren." Ansel placed a hand on her arm, stilling her. He pointed down the hallway. Broken glass littered the tiles of the kitchen floor.

Wren's breath caught in her throat.

She and Thom exchanged a panicked look.

"We check the first floor," Ansel whispered, motioning down the hallway. "Then the second."

They moved silently through the house. The hammering of Wren's heart and the thunking of their boots on the polished oaken floors seemed deafening enough, sure to alert any intruders. They rounded into the kitchen and Wren's hands flew to her mouth. The back door behind the kitchen was hanging off its hinges, the glass of its leaded window shattered.

Apricans, was all Wren could think. She whirled, breaking past Ansel's protective grip, dashing back to head up the stairs. *No, no.* To come all this way, to find Lucas gone...or worse. Her thoughts were wild with fear as she took the stairs two by two. She tripped, falling, bashing her shin, but she scrambled forward, ignoring the pain that exploded through her leg. At the top of the stairs was a hallway with a series of bedrooms, but there was another spiral staircase at the end. "Lucas!" she screamed, heading for the staircase.

"Wren!"

She could hear the others pounding up the stairs behind her, their steps sounding like thunder.

She spun up the stairs into the upper room of the house, a room encased almost entirely in glass. From up here, she could see in every direction, all around the island. The fog was starting to burn off, and a ray of sunshine broke through, displaying the green treetops below. And something in the distance. A ship. A fancy gold telescope sat on a stand in the corner, no doubt to watch birds or whales or whatever the idle rich watched for fun. Wren spun it around, peering through it, searching desperately for the vessel in the distance.

There. It came into stark relief. A three-masted vessel with sails being hoisted for a quick departure. Flying a light blue flag with a golden sunburst in the center.

The Apricans. The Apricans had Lucas.

CHAPTER 30

"We have to catch them." Wren whirled on the others as they summited the stairs behind her. She felt like a wild woman. Unmoored.

"That's a fast ship," Ansel said, leaning forward to look through the telescope. "And they've gotta head start."

"We have to try!" Thom said, shoving Ansel aside to peer through the telescope. "They'll kill them."

"Agreed. We haveta at least give chase, right?" Ansel shrugged.

A moment passed before they all flew into action, flying down two sets of stairs and out the front door, careening dangerously fast down the steep staircase to the beach. They leaped into the rowboat and Ansel dug his heels into the sand, manhandling the skiff into the waves before leaping nimbly in behind.

Wren could hardly sit still. Ansel was rowing quickly, his thick corded muscles working tirelessly, but it wasn't fast enough. Images of that day rose in Wren's mind, of Virgil gutted by Hale's sword, of Queen Eloise's eyes bulging as an arrow pierced her through her swan-like neck. She closed her eyes to the memories, but they wouldn't go. The emperor had declared that the entire Imbris line was to be exterminated. And he had just found the last three.

She felt someone take her hand and opened her eyes to see Thom, his face pale and grave. He didn't look her way, instead merely holding on. She squeezed his hand, her frigid fingers grasping his so tightly they turned white. *Please,* she prayed to whoever might care to listen. *Don't let me get here moments too late.*

They were nearing the Phoenix now and Ansel called to the crew. "Ready the sail and be quick about it! There's a ship on the other side of this island we need to catch."

The men on the deck scrambled into action.

They bumped alongside the Phoenix's lacquered hull and hurried up the ladder to the deck.

"What's going on?" Callidus asked as he met them at the rail, together with Pike, Olivia, and Dash.

"There's an Aprican ship. They got them," Thom said, the words choked.

"Swarms," Pike swore, spinning on his heel to stalk across the deck, yelling at his men.

Olivia's hand hovered before her mouth, her blue eyes wide. "Do you think...?"

"That they're still alive?" Wren let out a hard laugh. "For now. There wasn't any blood in the house. They took them—they didn't kill them. But who knows how long that will last. If we show up on their tail..." She hadn't even thought of that. By giving chase, would the Apricans decide to cut their losses? Kill the Imbrises where they stood? What were their orders?

"Dash, do you think they would kill them? If they think we were going to be able to free them?" Wren asked.

He ran a hand through his hair. "The order is likely to retrieve them dead or alive. Preferably alive, to go through the pomp of a public execution. But if they thought they were going to lose them..." He trailed off.

Wren felt a sob rising in her throat. She fought it with all her might. She stalked to where Pike, Griff, and Ansel were crowded around the map.

"To get out of the islands, the quickest way is to go through this channel between Fletch and Robinette island," Pike said. "To come back out the other way, they'd have to come past us. It's narrow, and they'll have to be careful. Should slow them down. Maybe enough for us to catch up."

"The brigantines have a shallower keel than that Aprican vessel. We should be more maneuverable in there. If we can catch them before they get out the other side, there's a chance."

"There's a possibility that if the Apricans see that we're winning, they'll kill the Imbrises," Wren said.

The three looked at her, unblinking. "You want to back off?" Griff asked.

Wren's mind raced. They were all looking to her. For leadership. To make a decision. A decision that could mean Lucas's life, if it was wrong. A decision like the one that had killed Sable.

"They're goners if we don't get 'em back now, right?" Ansel said. "I'd take maybe dead over surely dead any day."

Wren nodded woodenly. Yes. It was true. She felt a surge of gratitude at Ansel for laying out the choices so clearly before her. "We have to at least try," she said.

The time it took to round the island felt like an eternity. And when they finally made the turn into the narrow inlet between the two islands, the Aprican vessel was almost through, out into free water. Wren's fingernails dug into the rail and she looked up at the sails, cursing them to move faster. *Hold on, Lucas,* she thought. *We're so close.*

But they weren't close, not at all. They weren't going to make it. In open water, the sleek Aprican ship would eat up the distance, pulling ahead. They'd never get Lucas back.

Wren had never felt so helpless. There had to be something she could do to help.

And then a thought struck her like a ton of bricks. There *was* something she could do. Something forbidden and secret and *magic.*

Wren turned and raced across the deck.

Ansel raised an eyebrow as she passed and turned to follow as she half-ran, half-slid down the stairs below deck.

"I've seen that look before," Ansel said. "What're ya up to?"

"We need a little luck," she said, throwing open the door to the cargo hold where their crates of chocolates were sitting quietly in the corner.

"Ya need a whole wagonload of luck," Ansel retorted.

"Exactly." She rounded on him, holding out her hand. "Give me your knife."

"Wren—"

"Your knife!"

Reluctantly, he handed it over.

She wedged it into the crack under a crate's wooden top and levered it down, popping the top off. Arrayed underneath were neat boxes of chocolates stamped with the Confectioner's Guild gold seal.

Wren handed back the knife to Ansel and opened the box. She recognized the dulce de leche chocolate balls she had made. She grabbed one and shoved it in her mouth. The milk caramel sweetness barely registered as she chewed and swallowed, grabbing another one.

Ansel looked at her like she had lost it. "Stress eating?" he asked.

She shoved the box at him. "Eat one."

"I'm more of a peppermint twist kinda guy myself—"

"Eat!" She shook the box at him, and he took one tentatively. "Come on," she said, making for the upper deck.

Back on deck, Wren raced first for Olivia and Dash, the closest victims. "Eat one." She thrust the box at them. "Is this...?" Olivia asked, but she broke off as Wren shook the box again. "Eat!"

They obliged.

Callidus and Thom next. "Wren, what are you doing?" Callidus hissed, looking around. "Someone might notice that something's off... about these chocolates. Not everyone on this ship knows. We're not supposed to use them."

"I don't care. And that was before anyway, under Imbris. Now he's dead and we need luck. A miracle. I am going to make this the luckiest ship in Nova Navis."

Callidus heaved out a breath, but he and Thom each took one.

Wren made her way around the ship until all her chocolates were gone. Then she turned to watch the vessel, shaking hands and clutching the empty box to her chest. Let it be enough.

Griff had a spyglass to her eye and lowered it before raising it again.

She handed it to Pike. "What do you make of that?"

Pike let out a laugh of delight. "They've run aground! They hung up on something! Guess these islands are bad luck after all." He lowered the spyglass and winked at Wren.

An earsplitting grin broke across her face as relief flooded her, leaving her weak and shaky. It had worked. Thank the gods.

Her elation was short-lived. As the Phoenix, the Black Jasmine, and the rest of Griff's fleet drew closer to the Aprican vessel, cannons extended from the side like iron fingers.

"Blooming hell. They have black powder." Griff swore. "Tell me this thing has more powerful guns."

The first cannonball slashed into the sea about a hundred yards before them, sending up a column of water.

"I've got something better. Centese dragon fire," Pike said, his dark eyes gleaming. "Catapults at the ready," he shouted, and Griff directed Pike's sailors to hoist flags that would signal the other vessels to array in defensive positions.

"Fire," he shouted, and trebuchets on the bow and stern sent pots of dragon fire sailing across the water towards the Aprican vessel.

One of the pots smashed into the side of the Aprican vessel in an explosion of green flames.

"You could hit the hostages!" Wren turned to Pike. "We don't know where they are."

"You want me to just sit here and wave at them while they fire at us? Ask them to come over nicely? Lucas is a tough lad. He'll figure out where not to be," Pike said. "Load another round!"

The Aprican ship was at a marked disadvantage, as it was trapped where it sat, run aground on a hidden obstacle in the water. And its guns didn't have the reach Pike's catapults did. At this rate, Pike would destroy the Aprican ship, sending everyone aboard to their deaths. The dark waters around them were frigid; those aboard wouldn't last long if they plunged into the icy depths. Thom had shown them that.

Wren bit her lip, turning to look at where the little skiff had been pulled up alongside the stern. Someone needed to get them. To be there, in case Lucas, Trick, and Ella went into the water. She was moving before she realized she'd decided. Luck was thrumming through her veins from the two pieces of chocolate she had eaten. She could row right through the middle of the battle without a scratch—she knew that down to her toes. Lucas might not be so lucky.

"What madness are ya up to now?" Ansel met her at the stern as she began lowering the skiff with the pulley system.

"If they go into the water, they only have minutes. Someone needs to be there."

"You're goin' to row into the middle of a war zone?" Another catapult snapped on the deck of the Phoenix, tossing Wren against the rail. "This guy really worth that?"

"Yes," Wren said, her hands moving on the rope.

"I better help ya get 'im then," Ansel said.

"You're coming?" Wren asked.

"My grandma could row faster than ya, with those skinny arms. I'm comin.'"

Wren felt a surge of gratitude at Ansel's presence as she hurried over the side and down the ladder. They had fallen into their old pattern so easily. It was so familiar. She had forgotten how good it had felt to have him to protect her, to watch her back. Ansel was like a fire. He warmed you just by being close.

She shoved the thought aside. Lucas. She needed to get to Lucas.

The Aprican vessel was listing in the water now, flames licking up the rigging with greedy fingers. Callidus caught sight of their little rowboat as they passed into the space between the two vessels. Wren could hear his shouts on the wind, but the words eluded her. No doubt he was telling her she was crazy, that she was going to get herself killed. He might be right.

Luckily, the sailors on the Aprican vessel were too busy to notice their approach. Ansel pulled their little rowboat up alongside the stern as the Aprican ship sent another cannon shot at Pike and Griff's fleet. The cannonball just missed one of the other brigantine vessels, which had gotten dangerously close.

Complete chaos greeted Wren and Ansel as they pulled themselves up onto the deck. Flames and black smoke were billowing from half a dozen spots on the deck, and men shouted orders while others ran with buckets of water, trying uselessly to put out the deadly flames. "Where do you think they're being kept?" She pulled her cloak up to her mouth, breathing through it, coughing.

"No idea," Ansel replied, pulling his sword from his scabbard.

So Wren went on instinct, trusting the luck of the chocolate to guide her way. They scrambled over the deck, past surprised sailors who were too busy to do anything but mark their passing with wide eyes and shouts. They plunged into the low hallway and ran straight for the captain's quarters at the stern of the vessel. The hallway was thick with smoke.

The door to the chamber was locked. "They're in here." Wren pointed, coughing. "It's locked."

Another blow hit the vessel, tossing Wren and Ansel hard against the wall.

"Get back," Ansel said, and with a powerful kick, he splintered the wood of the door jamb, flinging the door back on its hinges.

Wren rushed into the room after Ansel.

"Who in the Sower's name are you?" It was Ella. Sweet caramel, it was Ella. Wild-eyed, messy-haired, but haughty as ever.

"Your rescuer, m'lady." Ansel gave a little bow.

"Wren?" That voice...

Wren looked around wildly, and when her eyes focused on him, her knees went weak beneath her.

Solid. Real. Alive. Lucas.

She ran and threw herself into his arms with force that felt stronger than the cannonball shots.

Lucas.

"How—?"

"No time," she cried, plastering his cheeks with kisses. "Gotta go."

"I sure am glad to see you," Trick said, and Wren was grinning, and then they were running together into the hallway, and Wren couldn't keep the smile off her face because she had them. They were going to make it.

A deafening crack rang out, as if the world were ending around them. The hallway tilted sideways, throwing them against the wall, which was quickly becoming the floor.

She didn't know who shouted the words. Maybe it was her.

"We're going down!"

CHAPTER 31

"Ansel broke Wren's fall.

Wren tumbled into him as the ship threw itself sideways, landing an elbow in his stomach, a knee in another soft part.

He groaned beneath her, cursing as she pushed herself off him. Ella and Trick were in front, half-stumbling, half-crawling towards the open hatch through which they'd come in. Lucas offered a hand, and Wren took it, grasping it like a lifeline while offering her other back to Ansel. "Come on!"

Ansel heaved himself up and together they barreled out onto the tilting deck amongst roaring flames and screams of the crew.

"Nice rescue," Ella said, but Wren ignored her, so fixed was she on the rowboat, bucking in the roiling water behind the sinking ship. No one had taken it yet. "Quick," she said, and they ran across the slanting deck towards the little skiff. Men were leaping off the sinking vessel into the water, but Wren ignored the splashes and cries, trying to drown them out. The rowboat was all that mattered.

The Aprican ship was low in the water now, and there were only a few steps down the ladder needed to get to the boat. Ella went first, then Trick, then Wren, Lucas not wanting to release her hand to let her down the side. But she was over and he followed in a blink. When it was Ansel's turn, he didn't even need the ladder, he just stepped over the rail of the ship into the rowboat. The ship was sinking rapidly now, and it began to pull at the line of the rowboat, threatening to drag it down.

"Untie us!" Lucas cried.

"I'm tryin.'" Ansel grunted, working at the knot on the cleat. The tension was too much, and the knot wouldn't yield. "Get back," he said, and he stood, unsheathing his sword and hacking once, severing the rope as everyone ducked out of his way.

Wren let out a breath of relief as Lucas began rowing quickly away from the wreckage.

She cast her gaze on Lucas, drinking in the sight of him. His salt-and-pepper hair was shaggy, and he had a short, dark beard shadowing his face. He wore olive green canvas trousers, a flannel shirt, and a pair of work boots. He looked even leaner than he had been, making his face seem harder, more angular somehow. But despite the changes, her heart filled to bursting at the sight of him. His gray eyes swam with a warmth and earnestness and concern that was all Lucas. And even as he rowed, his gaze was glued to her, a grin wide across his face. "Lucky you showed up when you did," he finally said.

Wren let out a breathless laugh, and tears sprang to her eyes. She nodded.

"Damn, it's good to see you, Wren," Trick said, his smile a mirror image of Lucas's. "Thought we were goners back there."

Wren looked at Ella, but there were no similar professions of gratitude from her. Ella huffed and looked out across the islands. "Well, at least with you here now, Lucas might shave off that ridiculous thing on his face."

A smile caught at the corner of Wren's mouth. That was probably the nicest thing Ella had ever said to her.

"I don't mind it," Wren said. "I think it looks nice."

"Of course you do," Ella said. Even in her coral trousers and tied denim shirt, she managed to look like a princess, her blonde curls exploding like a halo around her. "I've tried to explain that only a certain kind of man can pull off a beard. Like...well, like your new friend here.

Wren, are you going to introduce us?"

Ansel had been watching the exchange with interest, most of his interest focused on Ella. "Name's Ansel," he said. "Folks call me 'the Red Badger.' Head of the fiercest band of fightin' men in all of Nova Navis."

Ella sniffed, though she was clearly examining him with interest. "A mercenary. Why am I not surprised Wren would be consorting with such riffraff?"

"Don't mind Ella," Trick said cheerfully. "She could find fault with the Sower himself. Wren, is anyone else from your Guild with you?" Trick regarded her with such a look of cautious hope that Wren knew in that moment that Thom had found his match.

"Callidus, Thom, and Olivia." Wren nodded.

"These are all ours, I presume?" Lucas nodded behind him to the little fleet of ships.

"Head towards the Phoenix," Wren said, pointing at Pike's flagship. "They're filled with pirates and mercenaries. Ella, you'll be right at home."

Those on board the Phoenix greeted the Imbris siblings with hugs, handshakes, and claps on the back. But best was seeing Thom and Trick catch sight of each other and careen together in a bone-rattling embrace.

Lucas looked at Wren and smiled, pulling her against him, murmuring into her hair. "I'm not the only one glad to be rescued by the Confectioner's Guild."

"Well, we are rather gallant," Wren managed, wrapping her arms around Lucas, running her hands up the straight arrow of his spine, the hard plane of his back. He was warm and real and *here*. When she thought how close she'd come to losing him...it felt a miracle. Finally, luck had been with her. It had been drilled into her head that the use of infused chocolates was forbidden, but now that King Imbris was dead, she'd have to remember she had a potent weapon at her disposal.

"Let's talk below," Callidus said, shaking hands with Lucas. "If Wren can manage to untwine herself from you."

"I think we can talk while twined, if it's all the same to you," Lucas said, pulling Wren closer to him. "We've got lost time to make up for."

Callidus rolled his eyes but turned, motioning them below decks. "Thom," he barked, ignoring the fact that Trick and Thom were standing against the rail, their foreheads pressed together, Trick's hand wrapped securely around Thom's shoulder.

Wren couldn't hear the words Trick spoke, but from the intimacy of their postures, it seemed clear that Trick and Thom would be making up for lost time as well. It was funny how nearly losing someone made all the excuses melt away.

They crowded into Pike's captain's quarters, filling the space with bodies. Lucas, Trick and Ella, Wren and Callidus, Pike, Ansel, and Griff. Thom and Olivia and Dash. Allies new and old alike.

Lucas refused to relinquish Wren's hand, which was perfectly fine with her. The feeling of having him with her again was surreal. She wanted to banish all these people for a time, to make them vanish one by one until it was just her and Lucas. She would press her mouth—her body—against his, letting his touch drain the stress of the last few weeks away… But that would have to wait.

"We are very, very glad to have you with us," Callidus said. "When we saw the Aprican vessel…well, we feared."

"That was some bit of heroics," Pike said, nodding to Wren and Ansel. "I'm worried you're going as crazy as a loon, Wren."

"It was a one-time thing," Wren said with a shaky laugh. "I'll behave myself from now on."

"Impossible," Lucas whispered in her ear, his breath tickling her, casting goosebumps across her skin.

"Things are different now," she whispered back.

"Ahem." Callidus interrupted, shooting her a dark glance.

She leaned away from Lucas with a sigh.

"How much do you all know about what is going on back in Maradis?" Callidus asked.

"Very little," Lucas said. "We had allies in the city who were feeding us information and supplies."

"We hadn't heard anything in a week," Trick said, cutting in. "We were intending to make our way back to Maradis, but we didn't get the chance. A force of Apricans busted through the back door."

"Trick promised his friend was trustworthy," Ella said, casting a black glance at Trick, "but he was the only one who knew our location. He must have betrayed us."

"Perhaps not by choice." Callidus explained what had gone on back in the city, with the infused bread brainwashing the citizens of Maradis into worshipping Emperor Evander and the Apricans.

Wren watched Griff and Ansel with veiled interest as Callidus told the tale, as those two were the only ones, Wren guessed, who didn't know of the existence of magical food. They both seemed to take it all in stride. Perhaps her illustration with the chocolates had helped make them believers.

"Flaming hell," Lucas swore when Callidus finished. "Our contact must have been turned and given up our location."

"So who can we trust?" Ella asked.

"You're lookin' at 'em," Pike said.

"What about the Falconer?" Trick asked Lucas. "Do you think the Apricans got to him, too?"

"You know who the Falconer is?" Wren asked. They still didn't know the identity of the leader of the rebel group back in Maradis who had been disrupting things before they'd left.

"We don't know who he is, but we had been in brief contact with him through our friend. He wanted to help us get back into the city. Retake the palace. He'd been building support for us."

"And blowing things up," Callidus said.

"It would help to have a man inside the city," Ansel said. "Can we getta message to 'im?"

"There's no way of knowing if he's been affected by this...bread stuff," Lucas said. "Is there?"

"Maybe..." Wren said. "The infused bread had a fairly consistent effect on people. If we could get a message to him, perhaps we could gauge from his reaction whether he's been affected."

Olivia piped up. "I could help. I know what it felt like...to be under the influence. I think I could craft a set of questions that would reveal whether he's compromised."

"Worth a try," Lucas said. "We'd need to get someone into the city, though."

"Happy to oblige," Ansel said. "My lads could nip in, easy as pie."

"Let's say this Falconer is on our side and willing to help us. We need to talk about a plan. How can we win Maradis back from Evander's forces?" Pike asked.

"We need to neutralize the infused bread," Wren pointed out. "It needs to be our highest priority. Without it in play, we'd have considerably more allies. Be able to reach back out to people who we once thought were on our side. The other Guilds. The contact that was supplying you all with food and information."

"Agreed," Pike said. "But do we know where this Gifted baker is being kept?"

"Probably close to Sim Daemastra, the emperor's infused goods expert. The palace, most likely," Wren said.

"Likely won't be close enough. We need to know before I risk my men," Ansel countered.

"Obviously." Wren glared at him.

Ansel grinned back at her.

Lucas looked between them, his brow furrowing.

"We need to go back to Maradis. Find this Falconer. Then find the baker's location and neutralize him," Callidus said.

The group exchanged glances.

"Agreed," Pike said.

"Agreed," said Ansel.

"Agreed." Wren sighed.

"It's not enough," Lucas said.

"It's just a first step," Wren said.

"That's not what I mean," Lucas said. "My father *lost* his throne. The Apricans didn't take it, not really. He was a tyrant, at the end. The people wanted something new."

"Lucas—" Ella said, but Lucas held up a hand to silence her.

Wren furrowed her brow. Lucas was right. She'd wanted King Imbris gone as much as anyone. Had helped the Aprican cause in her own way. She still didn't know what Lucas would think of her when he found out the role she had played. If he'd ever forgive her. Suddenly, the firmness of his hand in hers felt fleeting once again. Ephemeral.

Lucas continued. "I'm not saying he was evil, but he lost the trust of the people. Even if we free people from this compulsion, we can't just go in and slaughter the Apricans, taking the city back by force."

"Works pretty well, actually," Ansel said, crossing his thick arms before his chest.

"I'm not saying it couldn't be done," Lucas protested. "I'm saying we shouldn't do it that way. Maradis belongs to the people. We need to give them a say. Let them decide."

"What are you proposing?" Callidus asked.

"Tell people the truth. About the infused goods. About the emperor, and how he's been manipulating them. Tell them...if they help us take back the city, that we will turn it over to them. Set up a system of free elections. No more emperor. No more king."

Silence hung in the room. "You can't be serious," Ella whispered. "The common people don't know how to rule. They'll run Maradis into the ground."

"Then it's our job to educate them. Set up a system that will help them rule. It could work. Enough lies. Enough swords. I don't want to be king. But that's not why I'm saying this. Maradis needs a better way. Alesia does."

Wren thought of her family, her father, working until his mind and body broke, indebted to the royal town that gave them succor. Paying for scraps of wood to heat their hut when trees were plentiful in the forest all around them. She thought of the children living in the royal orphanage, desperate for any protection. The thousands who had died in the Red Plague while the king had barricaded himself in his palace with the cure. Yes. Things needed to change. "I think it's a beautiful idea," Wren said.

"Encouraging the people to revolt would make our job easier," Pike said. "Don't know how the rest will work out, but the truth seems as good a plan as any."

Lucas nodded, looking to the others.

"I go where ya pay me to go." Ansel shrugged.

"Same," Griff said.

Ella shook her head, looking at the wall. "Lucas, you were always such an optimist."

"I like it," Trick said. "Leave a legacy the Imbris clan can be proud of."

"I like it too," Callidus finally said. "Strong men have used their power to exploit the weak for too long. Evander's just one of a long line of tyrants who have ruled us. I'm with Lucas. It's time to give Alesia back to the people."

CHAPTER 32

Strangely enough, the decision to scrap the monarchy was less controversial than how to get into the city. Pike, Ansel, Griff, and Callidus debated for the better part of an hour, arguing about the best approach.

Wren perched on the side of Lucas's chair, his arm wrapped around her, his thumb stroking circles across her palm. That simple motion filled her senses, sending heat coiling deep within her body. It was all she could think about. How good it felt to have him back. How badly she wanted to get him alone.

"We're just going to sail right into the harbor," Ansel finally announced.

"That's your grand plan?" Ella scoffed.

"The port is open. We take one of Griff's ships, which won't be recognized. We walk right in under their noses."

"All of you think this is best?" Lucas asked.

They exchanged glances, nodding.

"Fine. We'll hide in the hold and sneak into the city after dark," Lucas said.

"Oh no." Pike held up his hands. "You Imbrises are not going anywhere near Maradis. "

"But—"

"They're right, Lucas," Trick said. "Until we know what the situation is, we're safest out here."

"But the Falconer—"

"You don't have to be the one to contact him, right? You weren't before?" Callidus asked.

"No." Lucas frowned, hesitating. "He said if we want to reach out to tape a letter to the bottom of the sleigh on the carousel at Gemma Park."

"It's so very cloak and dagger," Ella said, rolling her eyes.

"Then it's settled. Someone else will reach out with this message," Callidus said. "Remember, we don't know if he's compromised."

Lucas clenched his fists. "I hate not being able to do anything! We've been sitting on that island for the past few weeks..." He sighed, running a hand through his hair. "Fine."

"So, who'll be coming with me?" Griff asked.

"I'll go," Ansel said. "I ain't been in Maradis in years. No one will suspect me of anythin.'"

"Anything but your regular hijinks?" Wren said. For some reason, the idea of Ansel going alone didn't sit well with her, though she couldn't put her finger on why. "I'll go too," she said.

"You could be recognized too," Callidus said.

"It's too dangerous," Lucas protested.

"Ansel and I skulked around the city for years. We know how to work together and we know where to go to avoid watchful eyes. He shouldn't go alone. If anything happened, we wouldn't know." She looked at Callidus, trying to communicate with her eyes. *If he goes alone, what's to stop him from betraying us to the Apricans—so long as they can pay a higher price?* She'd trusted Ansel during her time as a wraith, but those days were a distant memory. Better to keep an eye on him while she got to know the man he'd become.

Lucas raised an eyebrow at Wren, and she shot him an apologetic look that she hoped said, *I'll explain everything later.* She hadn't yet had a chance to tell Lucas about her history with Ansel, and she felt a strange hesitation within her. She shoved past it. There was nothing to worry about. It was all in the past. Lucas would understand that.

"Fine," Callidus said.

"Okay." Wren stood, grabbing Lucas's arm. "I think this meeting is over."

Wren towed Lucas up on the deck, where the wind whipped her hair and cloak around her. They were underway again, leaving the fog-shrouded Odette Islands behind.

Lucas turned his body so he blocked the wind, pulling her cloak around her and holding it closed before her chest. He looked wild and untamed with that beard, with the dark shadows under his eyes and his legs braced against the tossing of the ship. "You found me," Lucas said. His slate gray eyes reflected the sky, filled with light as he regarded her. "You figured it out. You'd make an excellent inspector."

Wren smiled, pulling the chain and the ring out from beneath her dress. She held it up and he examined it, taking it in his fine fingers. "Rutilated quartz. Hooded cormorant. Creepy bird," she said.

"My great-grandfather, on my mother's side, grew up on the northernmost island. This was his ring. I knew you'd figure it out." He grinned at her, and that smile split her heart in two.

Wren wrapped her arms around him, leaning into the warm planes of him. "I'm so sorry. About everything. Virgil. Your mother. Gods, Lucas, it all went so wrong."

"Hush. It's not your fault." He stroked her hair, cradling her head to his chest. Guilt spasmed through her even as she breathed in the scent of him, the feel of Lucas here in the flesh. But she did bear part of the blame. Wren and Hale had gone to the Aprican camp that night to make a deal with the devil. True, she had turned back, but her idea had led Hale down that path. She should have known that he wasn't stable, that he wouldn't be able to make good decisions. She had dropped the key to Maradis in their enemy's lap.

Even as Wren had fantasized about holding Lucas again, this secret had shadowed her thoughts, her dreams. Because she needed to tell him. And by telling him, she very well might lose him.

She'd tell him tomorrow. She just wanted one day to enjoy his presence. To be happy. Was one day too much to ask?

"Wren." Lucas pulled back.

Her heart stuttered and for a moment, she wondered if he had somehow managed to hear her secret thoughts.

But he continued. "Who is that man? Ansel? How do you know him?"

She sighed. "We knew each other when I was young. When I lived on the streets. He formed a kind of family with some of us. He was like a brother to me for two years." But even as the words came out, Wren wished she could take them back. That wasn't entirely true, was it? But there was nothing between her and Ansel now, nothing for Lucas to worry about. She had just gotten Lucas back, and there was no need to complicate things so soon, was there?

"A brother," Lucas said slowly. "What happened? Why haven't you ever spoken of him?"

"A misunderstanding," she assured him. "We've worked it out."

"I don't like him," Lucas said.

Wren let out a bark of a laugh. "I'd be surprised if you did. He's a cocky bastard."

"You knew him a long time ago. Are you sure we can trust him?"

"I'm not sure we can trust anyone anymore," she said.

"Except us." Lucas kissed her forehead.

"Right," she whispered, closing her eyes. "Except us." Except the little voice inside her head was whispering too, *You can't trust anyone, Lucas. Not even me.*

The twilight breeze blew unseasonably warm, and everyone was in fine spirits. They had accomplished their mission of retrieving the heir to the throne, vanquishing an enemy vessel in the process. The Phoenix's cuisinier, an old sailor as gnarled and twisted as the walking stick he used, made a particularly tasty stew, using the last of the ship's halibut. The spices of cardamom and chili warmed her, as did Lucas's presence, as he sat tucked securely at her side. One of Pike's men struck up a tune on a fiddle, and a bottle of some powerful liquor was passed around.

The sailors started dancing, a hornpipe with pantomimed motions of hoisting the sails and climbing the rigging. Wren and Lucas and the others clapped along, drawn into the enchantment of the fiddle.

And then Callidus appeared with his mandolin, a shy smile on his face, his black locks falling over his eyes. A great cry went up and after a brief discussion between the musicians, a new tune was selected, a reel that wove the dancers around each other like a pretzel.

Callidus's fingers flew across the strings, and Lucas looked at Wren with amazement. "He's phenomenal!"

"I know." She laughed. "Little known secret."

"Care to dance, Miss Confectioner?" Lucas stood, offering a hand to her. "Let's see what a mess we can make of this."

"Challenge accepted."

Lucas and Wren wove in among the other dancers, Dash and Olivia, Ansel and reluctant Ella—even Pike and Griff took a turn. The steps were simple enough, and though Lucas and Wren managed to step on each other a few times in the beginning, they began to catch on, whirling and laughing amongst the other dancers. When the song ended, Lucas tilted her back and kissed her thoroughly.

Wren and Lucas collapsed back in their seats, and Wren caught sight of another couple across the circle, twined together as if the crowd were a distant thought, and the world was only the two of them. Wren's heart squeezed with joy as Trick brushed Thom's blond curls off his forehead, leaned in close, and kissed him.

"Look," Wren said, a breathless laugh bubbling forth.

"Good for them," Lucas said as he wrapped his arm around her, pulling her close, his nose nestled in her hair. "Trick and I spent many glasses of wine discussing the finer features of the members of the Confectioner's Guild."

Wren looked sideways at him, smiling. "You knew?"

"He told me," Lucas said. "He was nervous as hell about telling Thom."

Wren snorted. "Same for Thom."

The warm buzz of Lucas's whisper in her ear pulled her from her thoughts. "Do you think we can sneak away unnoticed? I'd like to show you how much I've really missed you."

Wren threaded her hand in his and pulled him across the deck, away from the revelers. Her, Thom, and Callidus's cabin would be empty. They had time.

With Lucas at her side, the world felt right again. As if her vision had cleared, the fog of doubt burned away by the sunshine of his presence. He brought out the best in her. He was all she needed to be happy. Lucas and a little chocolate shop somewhere. Not politics or the fates of nations. Not covert operations, or mysteries to solve, or crises to avert. Just life. Love. Could she have that?

They ducked below deck, and Lucas pressed her against the wood planks of the hallway, his hungry mouth on hers. She reveled in the taste of him, the spice of the stew, the bite of the liquor on his lips. His hands roved over her body, searching, desperate, tangling in her hair, grasping the back of her neck to pull her closer.

"My cabin's that way," she gasped, managing to pull back from him, from the blood thrumming in her veins and addling her mind.

"Too far," he said jokingly into her neck, trailing kisses over her ear, her neck, down onto her collarbone.

"Come on." She pushed him.

With a little growl of frustration, Lucas took her hand, leading her down the corridor. She shoved into their little cabin.

"Cozy," Lucas said, spinning her back against the door, slamming it shut.

Wren's breath hitched in her throat as Lucas pressed the hard length of himself against her. She felt lost in him—his arms, his kiss, the sweet rosemary scent of him. His beard scratched her face, but she didn't care. She twined her fingers in his hair and pulled him close. She didn't think she could draw him close enough.

He hoisted her into his arms and she wrapped her legs around his waist as he walked to the bed. He laid her down gently before lowering his weight on top of her.

He drew back, kissing her eyelids, her nose, her lips, punctuating each word with a kiss. "You are without a doubt, the craziest, bravest woman I've ever known. Once again, I owe you my life."

"Don't mention it," she said jokingly, swallowing at his sudden seriousness.

He shook his head reverently, tracing the line of her collarbone with a finger. "I won't let you diminish what you've done. You saved us. Ella, Trick. You saved our lives again."

"It was selfish really," she managed, her voice catching in her throat. "You see, I don't want to live life without you."

He kissed her gently, his gray eyes searching hers. "Whatever happens from here, I'll be by your side. Always. You have my promise."

Wren pulled his mouth to hers, burying his words with a kiss. Shoving down deep her fear that it was a promise Lucas couldn't keep.

CHAPTER 33

Spirit Bay and the Port of Maradis looked no different than they had left it. The low gray sky, the drizzling rain. The thick wall of rocks forming the breakwater, the red cranes unloading ships of goods for the city. The jutting skyline of office towers and churches.

Yet somehow, it felt different. Wren didn't know what was waiting for her within those walls. Apprehension filled her.

"She's a pretty city," Captain Griff said from Wren's side, putting a booted foot up on the lower rail of her ship, the Sea Witch. Ansel and Wren had transferred aboard to head into the city.

"Have you spent much time here?"

"Just a day or two here or there when I was delivering goods. I've a friend who lives here." Nostalgia flashed in her green eyes. "Well, haven't talked to him in years. An old friend."

"You never thought to berth here?" Wren asked.

"Alesia's Merchant Guild charges the hell out of everyone, but their own members worst of all. I make more money calling Port Gris my home base. Plus, never liked it in cities. Too dangerous."

"Too dangerous?" Wren asked. "How could life at sea be less dangerous than living in a city?"

"Cities are filled with people," Griff said.

True enough.

"You should probably get below deck," Griff said. "We're approaching the breakwater. You can sit in my cabin. They usually just inspect the hold."

"And if they inspect more?" Wren asked, suddenly feeling that this was a very bad idea.

"Then I'd hope that luck of yours holds."

But Wren thought it would. She'd gone below deck and snagged two more truffles before they'd left the Phoenix.

Ansel waggled his fingers at her as she ducked below deck. They had decided it would be best if Wren kept out of sight, given the slight chance that someone would recognize her. For all she knew, the emperor hadn't noticed their absence, but on the rare chance that he had…she didn't want to compromise the mission. They needed to get in touch with the Falconer. And pray he hadn't been turned.

Griff's captain's cabin was austere and neat, unlike Pike's with its array of colorful trinkets, Ferwish lanterns, and Centese rugs. There wasn't a speck of dust on the practical furnishings—everything was dark colors, sturdy fabrics, items hooked or corralled onto surfaces so they wouldn't slide off when the ship tossed with the waves. There were a few pieces of evidence that Griff liked nice things—a crystal decanter of wine, a silver hairbrush. And her bed. An oversized thing loaded with pillows. Wren looked at it longingly. Lucas hadn't let her get much sleep last night. A smile curved onto her face. Well, that was probably the only activity that she was willing to give up sleep for.

Shouts outside and a shuddering movement told her that they'd docked. She looked out the porthole to see Aprican legionnaires strolling up the dock. Her hands tightened in her skirt inadvertently and she backed away from the window. She ran to the door and closed it, trying to steady her nerves. It was fine. Griff had said they would only search the hold. Just to be safe, Wren retrieved the bit of wax paper from her pocket and popped one of Thom's truffles into her mouth. She closed her eyes in delight as the chocolate melted onto her tongue. It was flavored with crushed violet flower and mint.

Wren pressed her ear to the door as she chewed the second truffle, a burnt caramel bergamot with a topping of candied orange zest, trying to make out what was being said. It was impossible; all she could hear was the pounding of boots and the stern timbre of male voices. Wren went to the little bar and retrieved one of the crystal glasses, pressing it against the door to hear.

"I assure you—" Griff's voice sprang into sharp relief. "There is no need to search my cabin. It's entirely against precedent."

"Under King Imbris," the man was countering. "But King Imbris doesn't rule Maradis any longer." Footsteps were coming this way.

The glass almost fell from Wren's hand, but she managed to catch it. She ran and returned it to the table before looking around frantically. Apparently, two truffles weren't going to be enough. Where could she hide on this cursed vessel? Wren frantically searched through drawers and cabinets, but everything was packed tightly with goods and gear.

The voices were at the door now. Wren's panicked sight caught on the giant pile of pillows. She dove for it, worming her way under them, curling against the headboard in a little ball.

The door opened, and a handsome blond man with short hair strode in, Griff behind him, her eyes wild. "I assure you," Griff said. "I don't smuggle and I don't have stowaways. There's nothing to find."

"I'm sure you understand why I have to do more than take your word for it." The man began opening cupboards and cabinets, stomping on boards to test for hidden troves. He approached the bed and leaned over the pillows, pushing against the headboard, testing for squeaks.

Wren held her breath until she thought her lungs would burst, peering through a tiny crack between pillows.

The man leaned back, apparently satisfied, and turned to another part of the room. Captain Griff caught Wren's eye, her own widening in recognition. She quickly stepped up and moved a pillow slightly, cutting off Wren's vision, standing next to the bed.

Finally, after the minutes stretched on, the man appeared satisfied.

"Very well, Captain," he said. "Thank you for your cooperation."

"You finished?" Griff asked stiffly.

"Indeed."

The two of them left the room, and when the door clicked shut, Wren let out a shaky breath.

Wren stayed under the pillows until Griff and Ansel returned to the captain's quarters.

"Made yourself a little nest, did ya?" Ansel asked, pulling a pillow off of her, revealing her face. "Looks comfy. Room for two?"

"With you? Never," Wren said, pushing out of the pillows and standing, straightening her dress.

Griff threw back a finger of amber liquid in one of the crystal glasses. "Too close for comfort," she said.

"What were they looking for?" Wren asked.

"Didn't say," Griff said. "But they're watching these docks like hawks. Not sure if you'll be able to sneak off undetected."

"Wren and I are excellent sneakers," Ansel said, slinging an arm around Wren's shoulder.

The gesture reminded her of Hale. She angled her body, sliding out from under his arm. "We've gotten through the hard part. We need to try. This might be our only chance to make contact with the Falconer."

Griff poured herself another drink and threw that back too. "Fine. It's your neck on the line. If you're sure.

Wren wasn't particularly sure. It *was* her neck on the line. It always felt like her neck on the line lately. She longed for the interminable days in Master Oldrick's shop making row after row of confections. "Think I can get a nip of that?"

"Now we're talkin'!" Ansel said.

Wren just rolled her eyes.

They waited until midnight, when the guard shift changed. The docks seemed surprisingly well lit, leaving few shadows for skulking. Wren and Ansel, dressed in dark cloaks, tiptoed off the vessel onto the dock, hurrying across the wharf and ducking behind a stack of boxes.

Wren's skin was charged with heightened awareness.

Ansel motioned when the coast was clear and they darted across the open space between the docks and the nearest warehouse building, sheltering in its shadow.

"Just like old times, right?" Ansel said with a crooked grin.

"Except then it was only street kids and Cedar Guards we were on the lookout for."

"True. You've moved up in the world. Come on."

They skirted between buildings, keeping to the dark alleyways and side streets. As they left the Port Quarter, Wren let out a breath, beginning to relax. Here, they could pass as citizens out for a late-night stroll.

Until they passed a streetlight with a sign posted on it. Wren froze.

"Ansel," she said, grabbing his cloak and wrangling him backwards. "Look." It was a wanted poster. With her face at the top. Hers, and Callidus's, and Thom's.

He let out a low whistle. "Thousand gold crowns? Wren, you're an expensive lady."

She huffed. "I can't believe they're actively searching for us. What have we done wrong?"

"Defyin' the might of the emperor," Ansel said in a deep voice, puffing his chest out.

"Shut up," she said.

"Who're all these other fellows?"

"Spicer's Guild members. Pike, Rizio...I don't know the others. They're wanted for questioning too."

"The emperor seems to want to talk to ya real bad. This change anythin'?"

Wren bit her lip, considering. They were already in the city. This was still the best chance of contacting the Falconer. "No. We're here; we need to keep going. Let's just be careful."

"You're the boss."

Wren pulled her hood farther up around her features. Luckily, a cloaked woman was an unremarkable sight in this drizzle.

"Pretty deserted out here," Ansel said, a frown curving his handsome face. "Even at this hour, I'd expect a few lads out carousin.'"

"Agreed. I doubt there's been much carousing since the Apricans showed up."

"It hasn't changed," Ansel said, looking around. "Not really."

"You haven't been back since..." Wren trailed off.

"No. Went to make my fortune elsewhere."

"Seems you've done well," Wren said begrudgingly. She wasn't surprised. Ansel was the type of person who always landed on his feet.

"It's a big world out there, Wren. I'd be happy to show it to ya."

She looked at him with surprise. It was hard to see past the shadow of his hood. "What do you mean?"

"Ya and I both know this city's goin' to hell. Your boyfriend may think he's got a chance of changin' things, but when do things ever change?"

Wren pursed her lips, saying nothing.

"It's admirable that he thinks people will rise up, support their own rule, do the right thing. But it's a pipe dream. Ya and I both know that."

"It could work," Wren said. Her voice was small.

"You've seen what people're really like. We both have. Imbris has led a life of safety. He's got the privilege of believin' people are capable of creatin' a utopia where they rule themselves. It's a fantasy. The strong'll always take advantage of the weak. It'll just have a different face."

"So you'd have me what, just run away?" *With you?* She wanted to add.

"This ain't your fight. The people are gonna tear each other apart. But only after they tear Imbris apart first. Ya don't haveta be there when it happens. Ya don't haveta see it. This ship is sinkin,' Wren. Get out while ya still can."

"If that's true, then why are you helping us?"

"Your guildmaster is payin' us a small fortune to be here. We'll do our part, but we're not responsible if it ain't enough. When I see the writin' on the wall, me and my men're gone."

"How honorable of you," Wren said. They had made it to Gemma Park now and were walking one of the cobblestone paths through the trees. The park was quiet, as if the trees themselves were holding their breath. Waiting. Waiting for what?

"There's no honor in dyin' for a foolish cause. There's only one person you've gotta look out for in this world. You. Ya used to get that."

"And I used to be alone and friendless, too."

"Friends won't keep a warm in the grave. You've got me. And the boys ain't so bad. Come with me. I'll take ya wherever ya wantta go in this world. Wren—ya and me—we had somethin.' We can have it again." His words soaked into her, sticking like honey.

Wren bit her lip. Once, she would have given anything to hear words like this from Ansel. But those days were long gone. Weren't they? But some of what he said...rang true. Did she truly think that Lucas's plan would work? Could people rule themselves fairly? And if it became clear that she wouldn't be able to do anything, would she stay? To fall with them? And then there was the dark cloud hanging over her. Her role in the Aprican invasion. What if Lucas learned the truth and wanted nothing to do with her? Would finding safety at Ansel's side be such a bad choice then?

Wren caught sight of the carousel in the distance and was overcome by a profound gratitude for it. She didn't need to answer these questions. Not right now. "Look," she said. "We're here."

The carousel sat dark and still in the grassy clearing. Benches surrounded it, a closed-up stall standing behind with a garish sign offering popcorn and popsicles.

"Do the honors?" Ansel asked, pulling a letter from the pouch at his belt. They had all drafted it together. It was vague, but hopefully not too vague. Asking the Falconer to share his thoughts on the emperor and confirm his loyalties. Hopefully, the truth of the Falconer's condition would be evident from any response he gave.

Wren stepped up onto the carousel. The creatures depicted were those out of myth: unicorns, griffins, a rearing water horse, a winged sphinx. Wren found the sleigh pulled by a hippogriff. She knelt down beneath it, and there she found a little ledge. She tucked the letter atop it. Here, it would stay dry until the rebels hopefully came to claim it.

She stood and hopped off the carousel. "Done," she said. "What now?"

"Don't suppose we have time for a pint?" Ansel asked with a grin.

"I think that would be pushing our luck. Back to the ship." Wren pulled Ansel along, back down the trail into the trees.

"You're no fun."

"We're not here for fun."

Wren didn't hear the twig snap until it was too late. Until a black hood was thrown over her face and a blow to the head knocked her unconscious.

CHAPTER 34

Wren wasn't sure how long she'd been out. She came to in a dark room, her hands and feet bound. The stone floor was cold beneath her, leeching the warmth from her body. It smelled musty, and dust tickled her nose. Ansel was beside her, stirring. She nudged him with her elbow. "Ansel."

"Ah, you're awake," a male voice said from across the dark room.

Wren jerked to attention, peering into the gloom. She couldn't make him out. Her eyes had adjusted to see that they were in some sort of...cellar? Yes, a wine cellar.

"Why have you taken us?" Wren asked. "Who are you?"

"I'll be asking the questions here." That voice. It was familiar somehow. But from where? Her hazy mind struggled to place it.

"Tell me your thoughts on the emperor," the man said. "Do you support his cause?"

The question made Wren sit up. It was the exact question she would have asked in his position, if she had wanted to know whether her captive were compromised by the emperor's infused bread.

"I don't think he's a kind and magnanimous ruler, if that's what you're wondering," Wren said. "I think he's a greedy tyrant who saw what he wanted and took it. I think he doesn't belong in Maradis."

The man seemed to consider that.

Ansel groaned at her side, coming to.

"You're the Falconer, aren't you?" Wren hazarded a guess. "We came looking for you. Tell me what *you* think about the emperor."

The man's voice grew low—dangerous. "I think he's overstayed his welcome. And as soon as this city is out from under his spell, he'll realize just how unwelcome he is."

"Untie us," Wren said. "If you are the Falconer, or work for him, we want to help you. We're on the same side."

"You're sure?" the man asked. "Just what would you do to rid this city of the Apricans? How far would you go?"

Wren grew cold. What did he mean? "I won't say what price I'm willing to pay unless I know what's being asked. I'm not inclined to make blind deals in the dark."

"Very well. Just remember, as you said, we're on the same side."

Another man approached and untied Ansel's bonds, and then hers.

"What the hell is this?" Ansel asked.

"The Falconer," Wren whispered. "He found us."

She stood on shaky legs, helping Ansel up.

They followed the man up a curving staircase at the end of the cellar. At the top, Wren squinted against the light. They were in a kitchen. A nice kitchen—with immaculate white marble countertops, a six-burner stove, and hanging pots of polished copper.

A man stood across the kitchen from them, a wide wooden island between. He was bald and moved slowly, as if he were very old. This was the Falconer?

He turned slowly, and when she saw him, Wren's blood froze to ice in her veins. Now she knew why the voice sounded familiar. The Falconer...was Grand Inquisitor Killian.

"You're dead," she whispered, backing away inadvertently, bumping into Ansel's broad torso.

"Not for lack of trying," he said, a crooked grin crossing his face.

He was much changed. His features looked slightly wrong, as if he hadn't been put together right after Hale had beaten his face to a pulp outside the orphanage. His muscled physique had withered, and it was clear he was still recovering from the grievous wounds he'd received that night. He held a wobbling cane in one hand, and with the other leaned heavily on the countertop.

But the rest of him—the calculating eyes and the brash grin that seemed to say there was no line that wasn't worth crossing. Those things were all Killian.

Wren shook her head. This couldn't be happening. "Even if you're truly the Falconer, why the hell should I trust you?"

"You said it yourself. We're on the same side. You need me. My contacts in the city. And I need you. You can get to Imbris." A sly smile crossed his face. "If you haven't already."

Wren's shock was wearing off and fury was filling its place. "You killed my guildmaster. You tortured me. Framed me for murder. Tried to lock me in a cage."

"All done at the king's orders. I don't work for him anymore. I work for—"

"You murdered Sable!" she yelled, slapping her hands on the countertop, leaning towards him. Though the blade had been held by a Black Guard, the ambush that had cost Sable her life had been arranged by Killian. Everything she'd lost—Sable, Hale, Virgil, and the queen—this man had had a hand in all of it.

"I paid for that mistake," he hissed back. "I am paying for it every day. Look at me." He motioned to his twisted limbs. "Firena left me for dead in this broken body. There's not an hour that goes by that pain doesn't radiate through some part of me."

"Good," she spat. "It's no less than you deserve."

"This isn't about our past. It's about the future—"

"I'm not listening to you," she said, drifting towards Ansel. She was glad he was here, felt moored by his presence. "There's nothing you can say that would make me trust you."

But a new voice joined in. A female voice. "Perhaps there's something I could say."

Wren turned to find the last person in the world she expected. "Mistress Violena?" She didn't think she could take any more surprises.

"What...? How...?"

"Come." The elderly woman gestured. "Have some refreshments. I'll explain all."

Wren's fire snuffed out. "Fine," she said, closing her eyes for a moment, trying to still the panic Killian's sudden appearance had wrought in her.

Mistress Violena led them into a well-appointed sitting room with a broad stretch of windows overlooking Lake Crima's sparkling azure waters. Wren hadn't noticed in her upset where they were. It was a townhouse of some sort, richly appointed with beautiful artwork and furnishings. "Is this your house?" Wren asked, sinking onto a velvet sofa.

"It is. My city home." Mistress Violena motioned to a servant who had been standing silently in the corner, and the man disappeared.

"And you're...part of the Falconers? You're working with Killian?"

"I am." She wore a dress of slate gray that reminded Wren of the Maradis sky, and her short, white hair was slicked against her scalp. Wren wasn't sure if it was the color or the circumstance, but Mistress Violena seemed...dimmed. Perhaps it was the loss of Sable, whom she had helped raise and had loved like a daughter. Wren didn't think she had reached the end of the repercussions of that loss.

The servant returned with a pot of tea and three cups. Wren waited until he had poured and left before speaking again. "How? How can you work with him? You know that he...he as good as killed Sable. You know that, right?"

Mistress Violena sighed. "I do. And I mourn Sable every day. But this is about more than one person. This is about all of our lives. Our future. I had to ask myself. If it could save Maradis, would I make a deal with the devil? And I knew the answer was *yes*."

Wren shook her head. "But how do you know you can trust him?"

"Self-interest. His. He was one of King Imbris's most loyal supporters. He knows who the other loyalists are. He won't last under an Aprican emperor."

"And so you just...forgive him? For what he did? Let him stay in your house?"

"I don't have to like him. Or forgive him. I just have to work with him. And that I can do. You can, too."

Wren took a sip of tea, suddenly feeling very weary. It was good. Peppermint. She closed her eyes, sighing. "What does he propose?"

"Shall we ask him?" Violena asked, her shrewd eyes watching Wren.

"Fine," Wren replied.

Killian limped into the room, leaning heavily on his cane. He lowered himself into the other chair opposite Wren and Ansel. Ansel placed a hand on her back, lending his support.

"Violena has convinced me I should hear you out," Wren said.

"She's a very persuasive woman," Killian said. "You see, first we need to win back our allies."

"You're talking about neutralizing the infused bread."

"Exactly. Without it, the emperor's stranglehold on this city will weaken significantly."

"How do you propose to do this?" Ansel asked.

"We know where the baker's being held."

"You do?" Wren perked up. "How?"

"We have a man on the inside feeding us information. It seems that Daemastra is up to some...*very unusual* experiments."

"What kind of experiments?" Wren was almost afraid to ask.

"He's combining magic from different Gifted craftsmen. Different infusions. To create new magics."

"Like the bread. Combining the magic of lies and the magic of devotion."

"Exactly. Our contact says the man is creating some sort of supernatural soldier with the different infused foods."

Wren's stomach dropped. She exchanged a look with Ansel.

"Whatcha know about these soldiers?" Ansel leaned forward, his forearms on his knees.

"Not much. The formula isn't complete yet. Apparently, he's looking for members of the Confectioner's and Spicer's Guild to complete it."

"The wanted posters..." Wren said, her gut roiling. Gods. What did that man want with them?

"We need to take out the baker first. Then we can hopefully rally our allies and neutralize these other experiments," Killian said.

"Take out... You mean *rescue*," Wren said. "I thought this baker had been kidnapped. That he was being forced to work against his will."

"Of course, we'll try to rescue him. If we can. If not, though...he has to be eliminated."

Wren shook her head. She couldn't think about that right now. Murdering a guild member for having the misfortune of being used for his gifts? It seemed wrong. "Who is your contact inside? Can he be trusted?"

"I think he can be trusted, though you may disagree." Killian grimaced in pain, adjusting on the couch. "My contact is Hale Firena."

Wren's hand flew to her heart. Hale. She had tried not to think of him in the past weeks, of his stone-faced words to her on the steps of the Guildhall, his blue uniform trimmed in gold. "Hale is helping you?" she whispered.

"He doesn't know it's me. He's helping the Falconer," Killian said. "But yes. It seems he's not as enamored with his new employer as you might think."

If Hale was helping the Falconer from the inside...then maybe he'd come to his senses. Maybe he was back to his old self, just trapped in his current circumstances. Maybe they could get him back. Her thoughts shifted beneath her, becoming ever more complicated. So many moving parts. So many lives. In saving Maradis, could she somehow save Hale too?

"So how'd ya propose to get this baker?" Ansel asked, interrupting the whirlwind within her. "What's the plan?"

"We still have a few barrels of black powder. All we need to do is find the right target, and we have a distraction that will keep the Apricans busy while we retrieve this baker."

"My men could help," Ansel said. "They've done this sorta mission before."

"Who are you?" Killian asked

"Ansel. They call me 'the Red Badger.'"

Killian raised an eyebrow. It seemed he had heard of him. "Made some new friends, have we, Wren? Who else is on your team, if I may ask?"

Wren exchanged a glance with Ansel. Were they trusting him? She looked at Mistress Violena. She may not have trusted Killian, but she trusted the woman, and she supposed it was true. Sometimes you needed to make a deal with the devil.

"Callidus and Thom. Pike and his men. The Imbrises. An Aprican legionnaire. And two hundred of Ansel's mercenaries on six ships."

Killian whistled softly. "You collect dangerous men like candy, Miss Confectioner. The infused bread cost me three-quarters of my forces. If we free the city from its compulsion, I'll have four hundred fighting men, including a number of nobles who have significant resources."

"I think the other Guilds would come around, too," Wren said, ignoring Killian's strange comment.

"If we coordinate our attack from inside and outside the city, we just might be able to get to the emperor. If we can kill him, the Apricans' hold on Alesia will crumble," Killian said.

"It's possible." Ansel nodded.

Hope surged through Wren. With this unholy alliance, they just might manage to take back their city.

CHAPTER 35

Wren's soaring hope fell like a bad soufflé as they began discussing the logistics of getting everyone into the city safely.

"There are four tunnels under the city," Killian explained, "leading from various points on the wall inside. Each of the members of the royal family has a—"

"Key," Wren said, rubbing her temples. She'd known she would have to tell Lucas. She had meant to. But it didn't mean she relished the thought. "The tunnels are compromised. The Apricans have a key."

Killian raised an eyebrow. "How?"

"It's a long story," Wren said. "And Willings is working for them, so I think it's safe to say he informed them of the location of any tunnels they didn't know of."

Killian leaned back stiffly, stroking his chin thoughtfully.

Wren played it over in her head. *So, Lucas...funny story...you know how an invading force captured the city and murdered most of your family? Turns out I gave them the key to get in...* She let out a pained sigh. Would he ever forgive her? If she were him, she wouldn't forgive her.

"Is there another way in?" Ansel asked.

Killian and Violena exchanged a glance.

The elegant woman wrinkled her nose but nodded.

"There is," Killian said. "Leads from the port directly to the palace. The Imbris clan wanted to be able to make a quick exit at any time. There are multiple tunnels in and out of the city and the palace. It's how the Falconers were moving around before."

"Do you think the tunnels might be compromised?" Wren asked.

"I'm certain they are. But there are likely no more than a few guards you'd have to dispatch, versus trying to get past the guards at the port, and then navigate the entire city."

"It sounds preferable," Ansel admitted.

"There's just one thing you should know," Killian said. "They don't smell very good."

"When do we leave?" Wren sprang to her feet. Maybe she wouldn't need to tell Lucas right away after all.

"*We* ain't goin' anywhere," Ansel said, standing and taking her shoulders gently in his hands. "Remember that wanted poster? There's no need for ya to risk yourself. Killian can show me the way."

"But—" Wren protested.

"But nothin,' Wren. It's an unnecessary risk." This close, Ansel smelled of spice and leather, so different from Lucas's fresh scent. His hands felt hot on her flesh, strong and real.

She looked down, warring with herself. She didn't like the idea of letting Ansel leave here alone. True, he hadn't betrayed her, but Ansel had always had a way of looking out for himself. And hadn't he said in the park that if things went sideways, he'd find his way to the door? But their plan was coming together. There was gold to be had. She would need to trust him, one way or another, before this was all done.

"Wren?" He took her chin in his hand and tilted her head up so she was looking into his clear blue eyes. By the Beekeeper, the man had grown up well. Those copper curls, the rugged planes of his face. He was vital and devastating and so very *Ansel*. "Will ya see sense?"

"Fine," she said, and it took all her willpower to wrench her gaze from his. "Just bring them back safely."

Lucas was not pleased when Ansel came back alone. He didn't trust that man—too sure, too cocky. He reminded him of Hale in a way. And though he had come to tolerate Hale, respect him even, he'd never liked him.

But Ansel promised they'd found the Falconer and a safe place to lie low, where Wren was waiting for them. And they'd get nowhere if they didn't take some risks. This whole flaming plan was a risk.

"Are you sure we can trust him?" Trick whispered as they waited for a rowboat to be lowered into the dark water.

"Absolutely not," Lucas murmured back.

"He and Wren go way back," Thom said, his hand securely clasped in Trick's. Those two had been inseparable as peanut butter and jelly since the Imbrises had been rescued from the Aprican vessel. "He wouldn't do anything to put her at risk."

"It's not Wren I'm worried about," Trick said, mirroring Lucas's thoughts.

The man was a mercenary. Who was to say what he was willing to do? Lucas had seen the way Ansel looked at Wren—he watched her like a beggar eyes a feast though a window. Would the man be willing to eliminate a rival if it meant securing what he wanted?

"Well, I think he's handsome," Ella said, her bright eyes watching Ansel's bunching muscles as he finished lowering the rowboat.

"Ready?" Ansel called, a brash grin on his face. He held out a hand to Ella. "Ladies first."

Ella glided forward, placing her hand in his.

"If Ella likes him, we're in even more trouble than I thought," Trick whispered.

Lucas couldn't help but agree.

The night was dark and quiet, the oars cutting quiet slices through the black water. They all seemed to hold their breaths as they neared shore. Ansel had explained that there were tunnels beneath the city that were known to the Falconer. No—to Killian. In a way, Lucas wasn't surprised that the man was alive. He was like a cockroach—impossible to kill. And if Killian was anything, he was cunning and ruthless. Killian was a bastard, but he was their bastard. He was a welcome ally right about now.

Lucas coughed as Ansel drew near the tunnel that would take them under the city. He threw his arm over his nose, breathing into the crook of his elbow. "What is that smell?" he asked, his words muffled by the fabric of his shirt.

"Oh, did I not mention?" Ansel said. "These here are the sewer tunnels."

Thom groaned audibly next to him as they all regarded the sewer tunnel that yawned over them with fetid breath.

"You've got to be kidding me," Ella said. "We're supposed to go...in that?"

For once, Lucas shared Ella's opinion.

"Sorry, princess," Ansel said. "The outlet opens into a bunch of tunnels. Dry tunnels. It's the best way. Unless ya fancy getting' captured by the Apricans."

Ella let out a little moan. "I fancy waking up in my bed and realizing this was all a horrible dream."

Lucas had to give it to her. That did sound nice.

"Why can't we use our keys and go through one of the dry, non-smelly tunnels?" Ella pouted.

Ansel shrugged. "Wren said they're compromised."

"Compromised?" Lucas frowned. "That would have meant they got one of the keys." Perhaps they had taken them off the bodies of some of his other family members. But how had the Apricans discovered what the keys opened? A chilling thought struck Lucas. "Thom, does Wren still have her key?" He still wanted her to be able to flee the city if things went wrong.

Thom shifted uncomfortably, running a hand through his curly hair. "Um, you'll have to ask her."

"What's the hold up?" a voice hissed out of the dark behind them. Pike. There were two other rowboats of people lined up to enter this hellhole. Pike, Callidus, Olivia, and her new boyfriend, Dash—Lucas wasn't sure where that fellow had come from—and some of Pike's and Ansel's men. Griff and the rest of the men and sailors would shelter behind Dash Island, waiting for the word

Ansel rowed forward into the gloom. The smell was horrendous.

Trick pulled a torch out of their pack and struck a flint against the wall, lighting it. The tunnels were low, bowing over them in an archway formed of slick stone and cobwebs.

Ella had her eyes closed and the hood of her cloak up. She held the fabric before her nose, breathing through it.

The low path through the water opened into a tall junction between several tunnels. Lucas looked at the map Killian had drawn for Ansel. "There." He pointed towards the left junction. "It's that tunnel."

While the paths of sludgy water continued into the depths of the sewer, the tunnels were wide enough here for a person to walk on the small ledges that bordered the channels. Ansel rowed the boat into a little alcove with a ladder against the wall.

"Looks like these paths were made for the workers that would be maintaining these tunnels," Lucas said.

"Worst job ever," Trick said.

"Agreed," Thom said.

Trick went first, helping Ella and Thom out of the boat onto the ledge. Ansel tied off the rowboat on the ladder as Lucas stepped out himself, his long legs carrying him across easily. Ansel came last. They retreated farther into the sewers while the others tied off and stepped out of their boats. It was a difficult thing, trying on the one hand not to fall in the brackish water while on the other not to touch the slimy wall that hugged them.

"I don't know about you, but I'd just as soon get out of the Piscator's armpit and back up to solid ground," Pike said, appearing behind them.

"Agreed."

"Let's move." Lucas and Ansel spoke at the same time. They looked at each other, seeming to fight a silent battle for alpha status. Finally, Ansel inclined his head stiffly. "You're the prince. Lead the way."

Wren's relief was strong as hundred-proof whiskey when she saw Lucas walk through Violena's front door. She ran and threw herself against him, burying her face in his damp cloak as he rocked her back and forth.

"Happy to see you too," Lucas remarked wryly, giving her a kiss.

Wren wrapped her arm around his waist and led him into the sitting room, making room for the mass of cloaked figures that were parading through the door. Everyone filed into the sitting room after hanging up wet cloaks and jackets and removing muddy boots. The room was filled to the brim and toasty from the fire cracking in the hearth. Wren perched on the arm of a sofa next to Lucas as Violena's few servants took drink orders and returned with hot teas, whiskey, and wine. Another put down a board heavy-laden with creamy cheeses and arrayed charcuterie, together with toasty baguettes.

"By the Piscator, it's good to be back in Maradis," Pike said, diving for a loaf and ripping off the heel.

"It's safe?" Wren asked.

Violena gave a nod, and Wren took a piece of the bread and a slice of prosciutto, popping them both into her mouth.

They exchanged pleasantries and introductions while they ate and thawed themselves from the cold night, discussing the foulness of the tunnels, the hospitality of Griff's sailors. Wren wrinkled her nose at Ella's dramatic rendition of the sewers. She didn't relish having to go into those.

Wren had worried about what Pike would think about working with Killian, given his role in the ambush that had led to Sable's death, but it seemed that her concern was misplaced. Perhaps the head of the Spicer's Guild had cooperated with enough double-crossers, enemies, and cutthroats that one more was of little note. When the cheese board (and a second) had been wiped clean, Pike leaned back in his chair, letting his silver belt buckle out one notch. "Are we all sufficiently sated to talk about the elephant in the room?"

Callidus sighed, dabbing his mouth with a napkin. "Yes. What comes next? We need to decide."

"We find Liam, the captive baker. We rescue or neutralize him. And after that, we kill the emperor," Killian said.

Trick spluttered into his wine. "Just like that?" He coughed.

"Killian is right," Ella said, popping a blueberry into her mouth. "With the emperor dead, the Apricans will turn on each other, vying for power to fill the vacuum. If we show any signs of concentrated resistance, they should retreat."

"Well, obviously it would be great if we could turn all the Aprican troops into gumdrops. But—" Callidus began.

Ansel broke in. "Can ya do that?"

Callidus shook his head crossly. "No, we can't do that. It was just hyperbole—"

"Too bad," Bran said to Ansel. "That would really simplify things."

"Agreed," Ansel said.

"Let's stick to the realm of reality, shall we?" Killian said. "We know where Liam is, thanks to our contact on the inside." Killian winked at her. Hale. Wren hadn't had a chance to mention it to Lucas. Would he be willing to trust Hale's intelligence after Hale had killed his brother? Yet another unpleasant truth she'd need to share with him. The list was growing long indeed.

Killian went on. "Assuming we can find Liam, the Gifted bread should run out in...how long?"

"It took about twenty-four hours for the infusion to wear off in Olivia's case," Wren said, casting a glance at her friend. Dash and Olivia shared an emerald-green armchair, Olivia seeming perfectly content to sip her hot toddy in the comfort of Dash's strong arms. Wren shoved down her trepidation about the match. About Dash. They had chosen to trust him. Second-guessing that choice served no purpose.

"Assuming they don't have any bread stored anywhere," Thom pointed out.

Everyone frowned at that.

"I've got that taken care of," Killian said. "One of my men learned of the location of their stockpile of infused bread. We could use a diversion when we head in to get Liam. We'll blow it."

Wren considered. It could work.

"The annual All Hallows' Eve parade will take place in three days. Our source inside the palace has told us that the emperor will be participating. It's the perfect time to get to him," Killian explained.

"To assassinate him?" Callidus said flatly. "He'll be surrounded by guards."

"We have men of our own." Killian pointed to Ansel and Bran. "Plus, there's going to be a diversion."

"What kind of diversion?" Callidus asked.

"Well, that's what we need to come up with. Another explosion perhaps?"

Silence fell over the table as people contemplated. Wren took a sip of her coffee. She needed a refill; the dregs of her cup were lukewarm. But the thought fled from her mind as an idea flashed into existence. "We tell people the truth about the Gifting," she said. "About infused food. That's our diversion."

"Tell people that magic is real? No one would believe it," Callidus said.

"Then show them," Wren said. "We have all those chocolates we made back on the Phoenix. Many of them are infused. It's traditional to throw candy at the All Hallows' Eve parade. So we do. We throw infused candy with a written explanation. All over the city."

"It would be mayhem," Pike said.

"Exactly," Wren said. "Just what Killian needs. Lucas." She turned to him. "You say you want to turn the government over to the people. But they can't rule if they don't have all the information. The people need to know about this if they are going to have any chance of actually ruling fairly, not just becoming another dictatorship."

"It would be dangerous for the Gifted," Callidus said.

"It's already dangerous for us," Thom said. "I agree with Wren. It's time to come out of the shadows. It's time we tell the truth."

Wren looked around the room, at the people who had become her allies, her friends. She could hardly think of a stranger amalgamation of personalities. But here they were. Bound together in a singular goal.

Callidus sighed and nodded. "The Beekeeper help us."

Thom nodded, taking Trick's hand in his with a questioning look.

Olivia nodded too, taking a deep breath. "Kasper died because of this secret. Let's make sure it never happens again."

Pike shrugged his shoulders. "It'll mean big business for the Guilds. We'll finally be able to sell our infusions. I'm in."

Ansel crossed his arms over his chest. "I'll do whatever, long as ya pay me."

"Same," same Bran.

So it was up to Ella, Trick, and Lucas. The Imbris children looked at each other.

"I agree," Trick said. "If we're going to do things a different way, let's do it a different way." He patted Thom's hand.

Lucas nodded.

Ella rolled her eyes and sighed. "Fine."

"So we're agreed then," Killian said. "Come All Hallows' Eve, the secret of the Gifting will be a secret no more."

CHAPTER 36

The next hours were a whirlwind of planning and preparation. As it turned out, assassinating an emperor and outing the best-kept secret in Alesia took a bit of doing. Ansel and Bran, the only members of their little group who weren't wanted by the crown, would spend the next few days shuttling information and supplies between the safehouse and the ships, where Griff and her crew, as well as Ansel's and Pike's men, waited patiently. They would retrieve the crates of infused chocolates, and somehow, through chocolate-infused luck and prayer, get them through a port inspection.

Lucas had a contact who worked at the *Maradis Morning,* the city's newspaper. Lucas had been fairly certain that the man wouldn't be infected by the emperor's infused breads, as the man was allergic to gluten. Lucas thought he could arrange for the newspaper offices to be left ajar, giving them access to the paper's printing presses to make enough fliers to rain from the sky, trumpeting on high the truth—that in Alesia, magic was real.

It was nearly dawn when they retired, Violena finding them each rooms. Wren and Lucas trudged up the stairs to their chamber, eyelids drooping.

Once inside, Lucas tilted over onto the bed, collapsing into its voluptuous embrace. He groaned in delight. "Yes," he said. "A thousand times yes."

"Compared to my berth on the Phoenix," Wren said, settling onto the bed next to him and closing her eyes, "this is heaven."

"Mmm," Lucas agreed.

Wren burrowed into his side, nestling herself in the crook of his arm, resting her head on his shoulder. Sleep tugged at her.

"Wren," Lucas murmured.

"Yep?" she replied, her eyes still closed.

"Do you still have my key?"

Suddenly, Wren was wide awake. Her eyes flew open as her stomach sank like a stone. "No," she whispered.

"What happened to it?" The words were drowsy.

Wren squeezed her eyes shut. She was overcome with the urge to lie. To keep this perfect moment, to hold it tight. True, they were in a fight for their lives against a powerful enemy who wanted them dead. But here, in this house, in Lucas's arms...everything was right. And if she told him, she might never feel this again. She exhaled as tears pricked her eyes. She couldn't keep lying. Not forever. "The Apricans took it."

"How?" It seemed to wake him up. He cocked his head, looking at her.

She drank him in with her eyes—the relaxed stretch of his lean body next to hers, his tousled salt-and-pepper hair, his slate-gray eyes. Memorizing the moment. "There's something I need to tell you," Wren said, pushing herself up on her elbow.

"What?"

"Remember when Hale and I went to Dash Island, and you were so mad because we could have been captured?"

"How could I forget?" Lucas said. "I could have throttled that blond asshole for taking you."

"Well..." She swallowed, feeling Lucas slip from her fingers. "We were. Captured, that is." Her words tumbled one over the other as she explained what had happened—General Marius and Sim Daemastra, escaping the Aprican camp through the tunnel—Callidus's sentencing after Sable had died, her helplessness and desperation to stop it. Going into the tunnel with Hale. She left Thom out of it. She didn't want to ruin his and Trick's relationship too. It was Thom's choice to make, whether to be honest or not. Faster and faster, the words fell, Marius's ultimatum, Hale's betrayal. Her escape from captivity and the harrowing trip back into the city under the noses of their invaders.

When it was all done, she looked up at him, at the stony mask that had transformed his features. The hard set of his jaw, his muscles working furiously.

"Say something," Wren pleaded. "Anything."

"My mother," he said, so quietly she almost missed the words. "Virgil..."

"I know." Guilt twisted her heart, wringing it out until it felt empty. "It's my fault. If I hadn't gone, Evander wouldn't have gotten the key. Wouldn't have known about the passageways and been able to sneak in. Lucas, I'm so sorry." She grasped his hand, pressing it between hers. Tears were falling now, salty and bitter. "You have to know how sorry I am. I was just trying to help. I thought... I don't know what I thought."

"You thought you'd sell my family out to our enemies?" Lucas pulled his hand from her grip, recoiling away from her, off the bed, pressing himself against the far wall. As if he couldn't get enough space between them. "You just thought you'd, what...lie to me? Kiss me and lay with me like everything was all right—all the while knowing my family is *dead* because of you?" He spun around, his hands covering his mouth, his face, running through his hair.

"There just wasn't...the right moment." She sobbed, knowing it was a weak excuse. She had been selfishly putting off this conversation. "I was worried...I didn't want to hurt you. To ruin things between us."

"Well, you have a funny way of showing it." He whirled on her, his fists clenched at his side. "After *all* we've been through, you should know that the one thing I can't stand for is more lies from you! If you'd told me straight up...I don't know. Maybe...I don't know. I might have been able to move past it. But lie to me..." He shook his head. "The truth. That's all I ever asked for from you, Wren. And that's what you seem perpetually incapable of giving me." He stormed past her and yanked the door open before slamming it shut behind him.

A picture fell off the wall from the force of the blow—its glass shattering.

A sob escaped Wren's mouth and she slapped a hand over her lips, trying to hold it in. She shook her head in disbelief, broken. The truth—Lucas had said he wanted the truth. Well, now he had it. And it seemed it had cost her everything.

CHAPTER 37

Olivia didn't sleep well that night. Her stomach flipped with nervousness when Dash opened the door to their assigned quarters to reveal a large four-poster bed. Would Dash expect...? Her thoughts galloped away from her. Yes, Dash set her blood burning in her veins, and she wanted to be with him fully...at some point...but in a stranger's house, with people all around...?

Dash wrapped his arms around her from behind, kissing her cheek. "I'll take the floor," he said.

Relief flooded her that she wouldn't have to explain her troubled thoughts to him. "There's no need," she said, turning in his arms and rising on her tiptoes to meet his lips in a kiss. "You've been sleeping in a cell for the past week. It's plenty big for both of us to sleep."

"If you're sure," he murmured into her hair.

"*Just* sleep," shd said.

But lying beside him, she was hyperaware of his presence. The large shape of him stretched out beside her in the dark, the rhythmic rise and fall of his broad chest, the cut of his cheekbones. She wanted to run her hands over his face, through his hair, to marvel at his realness. But she dared not wake him.

Since she'd been a girl, she'd longed to find a man like Dash. Handsome, gallant, brave, and kind. Yet now that she had him, she couldn't deny an uneasiness in her stomach. She had sworn to Wren that Dash was trustworthy. The whole reason that he was here was because of her—because she had vouched for him.

But what if she was wrong? Olivia hadn't even seen her own grandaunt's treachery. What if Dash was fooling her too? He was an Aprican legionnaire. And tomorrow, they were sending him back into the palace—back amongst his fellow men. He was the one who had best knowledge of the layout of the palace and location of the Aprican troops. But what if he had been fooling her? What if it was all a lie? What if the only goodbye Olivia got was a force of Aprican legionnaires knocking down the townhouse door?

She squeezed her eyes closed against the horrors her imagination readily supplied. She tried to focus on the things that were real. The hours they'd talked in the dim cabin before Dash had ever known he might be released. The sweetness of his kiss, of the way she caught him gazing at her, like he wasn't quite sure she was his. The same way she found herself looking at him.

She blew out a shaky breath. Dash was an honest man. The son of a blueberry farmer. They could trust him. She could trust him. She repeated the mantra to herself—a whispered prayer in the dark. One that desperately needed to come true.

The night sky hung as black as Lucas's mood. Lucas had done his best to avoid Wren for most of the day, but the townhouse was flaming small. It seemed everywhere he turned she was there, her wide eyes brimming with tears and silent apologies. He couldn't face her. He just couldn't. He could hardly make out the layered depths of what he was feeling— but one emotion rang out loud and clear within him: Fury. He was furious with her for lying to him. *Again.* He couldn't be anywhere near her. They had dangerous work to do, and he needed his head on straight. He'd process everything after they took back Maradis. If they weren't dead.

The tension in the carriage was thick enough to choke on. The *Maradis Morning* offices were in the Industrial Quarter, all the way to the south of town. It was too far to walk, too far to go in the infernal sewer system. So they were risking a carriage, knowing that there was a chance that they could be stopped. And if that happened, it would all be over.

The monstrous machines of the presses required many hands to work, so those of them who weren't trying to rescue Liam, the baker, had come with him. Callidus, Olivia, and one of Ansel's mercenaries rode with him; Trick, Thom, Ella, and another mercenary in the carriage behind. Wren, Ansel, Pike, and Dash were headed into the palace, and Ansel's second-in-command, Bran, had headed back to the ship that morning to retrieve the last of the infused chocolates and fill the rest of their group in on what was going on.

Callidus was looking at him from across the carriage with a contemplative look.

"What?" Lucas snapped. He didn't want to be analyzed right now.

"Strange vibe in the townhouse today. If I'm not mistaken, you and Wren didn't say two words to each other. Everything all right?"

Lucas's hands tightened into fists at his side. "No, everything's not all right."

"Would it help to discuss it?" Callidus asked stiffly. The man didn't have much of a bedside manner, did he?

"Nope." Lucas shook his head, looking at the carriage curtains, wishing he could open them so he had something to look at.

The carriage was quiet for a moment. Then Olivia spoke. "Whatever it is, I'm sure you can work through it. Wren loves you."

"Love has never been our problem," Lucas said through gritted teeth. Why had he ended up in a carriage with two of Wren's fans?

"That girl—" Callidus began.

"Woman," Olivia said, interrupting. "She's a woman."

Callidus rolled his eyes. "That *woman* saved your life twice in the last month. She would go through fire and brimstone for you. She faced the might of a king *and* an empire. For you. Not often you find a girl— woman—like that."

Lucas pursed his lips. He knew Wren was brave and loyal. He'd never doubted that. But she was reckless, too. With people's lives. With the truth. It had gotten his family killed. It had gotten them all into this predicament.

Callidus spoke carefully. "If you're angry about what I think you're angry about...consider that it's like being angry at someone for leaving the back door open before a tsunami hits. Perhaps it was easier for the water to get in, but it was going to get in all the same."

Lucas shook his head. "But maybe the family would have had more time to get to safety if the door hadn't been open."

"Or maybe they all would have stayed snug in their beds without that warning, and they all would have been lost."

Lucas met Callidus's icy-blue gaze. There was compassion there, but he didn't want compassion right now. He wanted anger. He wanted to wrap it around him like a cloak, to cover himself with it until nothing else could get through. Sure, maybe he'd be dead too if Wren hadn't done what she had. But maybe they'd all be alive. Virgil. Mother.

"It's your life," said Callidus. "It's your decision. But I'll say one last thing."

"Please, enlighten me," Lucas said dryly.

"Don't wait too long to figure out how you feel. It's plain to see that there's someone else vying for the position of Wren's better half, and *he's* not hesitating," Callidus said.

Lucas's mood sank even lower at the mention of the redheaded mercenary.

"He's talking about Ansel—" Olivia said.

"I know he's taking about Ansel," Lucas snapped. "He can't keep his flaming hands off her." Lucas's eyes flicked to Ansel's mercenary, a tall bearded man with the coloring of a Magnish. The man had the wherewithal to stare at the curtains, leaving them to their conversation.

"You don't need to be rude," Olivia said, drawing herself up. "We're just trying to help."

Lucas closed his eyes, taking a long-suffering breath. He couldn't be held responsible for anyone else's feelings right now. "I'm sorry, Olivia," he said with as much gentleness as he could muster. "I know you mean well. I just can't think about this right now."

"Forgiven," she said primly. "Just...don't miss your chance, Lucas."

They lapsed back into uneasy silence as the carriage trundled beneath them, the clop of the horse's hooves sounding deafening in his ears.

Callidus and Olivia's points, though uninvited, held a ring of truth.

Yes, he was furious at Wren. He wanted to rage and scream at her for what she'd done—the risk she'd taken. She could have been killed. She could have gotten *all* of them killed. But then, part of him wanted to bury his head in her shoulder and cry, to breathe in her scent of sugar and vanilla. To mourn with her. To taste the salt of her tears on her lips as they navigated this madness together.

But now...Olivia's words rang in his mind. *Don't miss your chance.* Dread pooled in the pit of his stomach. Maybe he already had.

Wren's misery made poor company as they moved through the foul-smelling passageway towards the palace entrance. She shoved down all throughs of Lucas as she walked between Ansel and Pike, Dash bringing up the rear. Now was not the time. If she'd kept moving after Sable had died, she could keep moving after Lucas turned his back on her. At least he was alive. And that meant there was a chance of fixing it, however remote it seemed.

The day had been spent preparing and planning. Arguing. It seemed everyone was against Wren going with the group to retrieve the baker Liam, but she had insisted, standing her ground. She had convinced them that she might be easier for Liam to trust than Ansel or Pike. They didn't need to know the true reason for her stubbornness. Wren wanted to be there to ensure that nothing untoward happened to the poor Gifted baker. She could see Ansel or even Pike being more cavalier with the man's life. She would do everything in her power to make sure that no one else died on their crazy mission.

The tunnels were still and quiet but for the scuffle of their footsteps and the occasional drip of water echoing against the walls. Killian's Falconers had triggered an explosion in the warehouse holding the infused grain a half hour ago. That was their diversion; now the rest was up to them.

By a stroke of luck, the tunnel let out in the west wing of the palace, which was also, according to Hale, where the baker was being kept. Dash had confirmed that it was the area of the palace Daemastra had claimed for his own.

Wren's heart hammered harder in her chest the closer they got. They hadn't seen any guards, like Killian had warned them to watch out for. Every corner they turned around, she kept waiting for someone to jump out, despite the infused chocolates each one of them had eaten, and the four she carried in her pocket, wrapped securely in wax paper.

But there was no one. This place was empty but for the scuffling of rats.

Finally, they reached the dead end that Killian's map showed as their exit point. There was a ladder with iron rungs heading up the side of the wall.

"I'll go first," Ansel said.

Ansel summited the ladder and turned a crank that opened the trapdoor above them. The crank screeched with protest, and they all winced. Ansel waited for a moment as they all stood stock still, listening for signs that someone had heard the noise. Nothing. Ansel cracked the trapdoor, and a sliver of light shone into the darkness of the tunnel.

Sweat prickled Wren's skin, despite the chill of the tunnels. She wanted out of here.

"It's clear," Ansel said, throwing the door open and climbing through. The rest of them made quick time of it, and they found themselves in a storeroom. Dash was last through, closing the trapdoor. From this angle, it was indistinguishable from the rest of the floorboards.

Ansel peeked into the hallway next. He motioned to them that it was all clear. "Dash, take a gander and see if ya can tell where we are," Ansel hissed.

Dash followed instructions, poking his head into the hallway. He closed the door again. "We're near the bathing pools. If Killian's source is correct, we're a few hallways over from there the baker is being kept."

"You know the way?" Pike asked.

Dash nodded.

"Lead on." Ansel gestured.

The stone hallways were deserted.

As they went to turn a corner, Ansel pulled Dash back, shoving him against the wall.

The sound of boots on the stones sounded down the corridor. Wren peeked around the corner, sandwiching herself between Dash and Ansel. Her stomach dropped. It was Hale, his face hard, his uniform buttons gleaming in the flickering torchlight.

She pulled back against the far wall, trying to keep her breathing in check. Hale was here. In the same wing as Daemastra. The same wing as the baker. Was he helping the Apricans with their strange experiments, or trying to undermine them from the inside?

"Clear," Ansel said.

Wren followed in their wake, her mind sluggish after the sight of Hale.

"You all right?" Pike asked.

She nodded woodenly. She didn't know. She hadn't been prepared to see him in this place.

"I think I found 'im," Ansel said.

Wren let out a breath. Could it be that easy?

"Wren, do the honors?" Ansel asked, nodding towards the lock.

Wren knelt down, taking her lockpicks out with shaky fingers.

"You've got this," Pike said.

She worked at the lock, springing it free. She stood and pushed the door open.

The man inside was gaunt and haggard, heavy shadows under his eyes. He sat up from a hard bunk where he lay. "Already?" His voice was hoarse. "I've just had an hour. I'm supposed to get at least two hours of sleep. Please." He looked near tears.

"We're not here to take you to the Apricans. We're here to rescue you," Wren said. "Come with us."

"What? Who are you?"

"We're from the Confectioner's Guild," Wren said.

"And Spicer's," Pike said, cutting in. "We need to get you out."

Ansel strode into the room and hoisted the man to his feet. "Come on, man. We can do introductions after we get ya outta here."

"How's the city?" Liam asked, letting Ansel half-walk, half-carry him into the hallway. "I've feared...what they've been doing."

"It's not great," Pike said. "You've pretty much brainwashed the entire populous."

"Oh," the man said, his voice quiet, his jaw going slack.

"But that ends now," Wren said.

They hurried around the corner and pulled up short. Wren let out a squeak of fear and disbelief.

They were face to face with a pack of Aprican soldiers—their spears leveled.

Behind them stood a smug-faced Willings. "Oh, Miss Confectioner, if only that were true. But alas. You aren't going anywhere."

Dash stood up straight and saluted. "Lieutenant Dashiell Cardas, reporting in. Please inform Captain Ambrose I've brought him two fugitives and a person of interest."

CHAPTER 38

"Traitor!" Ansel shouted, leaping into action before Wren's mind had time to even register the threat. Dash had betrayed them. Flame it all to hell, she'd known...she'd told Olivia... Her thoughts spun from her as the flash of swords pulled her back into the moment.

Ansel's blade swung directly at Willings's ginger head.

Willings dove out of the way, his eyes going wide with fear. Wren didn't blame him. Ansel was a sight to behold.

Willings's men did a bit better than Willings. The front man, short but stocky, in the Aprican uniform of sky blue, had his sword out in a blink, parrying Ansel's wicked strike.

And then, chaos reigned.

Pike threw himself into the fight, hitting at Willings's men with the force of a whirlwind.

Willings scrambled to his feet, coming for Wren and Liam, who had backed against the far wall.

Dash seemed to be holding himself back out of the fray; perhaps some small decent part of him couldn't bring himself to come to blows with those he'd supped with just hours before.

Wren kept her arm under Liam's armpit, holding him erect. The man was weak with exhaustion and hunger—he was in no shape to fight. He was in hardly any shape to run. It would be up to Wren.

She pulled a dagger from her belt, letting its solid shape strengthen her resolve. She wasn't much of a fighter, but neither, it appeared, was Willings. "I should have known I'd find a bottom feeder like you here," Wren practically spat. "Always riding on better men's coattails. You're like a parasite."

"Better a parasite than a little bird. So easily crushed. Give him over to me," Willings said, a short sword in his hand. He circled her warily, not seeming to want to test his skills against her own.

"You can't have him," Wren said, baring her teeth. Best be bold, oversell her skills here. "You've exploited this man long enough."

"Another dozen men are on their way to our position right now," Willings said. "You'll never get out in time. There's nowhere to go but the gallows for you, confectioner."

"Funny," Wren said. "I could say the same about you." She lunged at him with her knife, and as she predicted, Willings scrambled back, rather than blocking with his own sword.

She grabbed Liam with her other hand and yanked him forward, past Willings, towards the storeroom they had come out of. Ansel and Pike had downed several Aprican men, but if Willings had been telling the truth that there were reinforcements coming, they had only moments to make their escape.

Out of the corner of her eye, Wren saw Ansel turn his wrath towards Dash, and the man held up his hands, backing up.

"Ansel!" Wren called. "Leave him."

Liam's breathing was ragged as she pulled him along behind her, scooting around a corner, only to be confronted by another band of soldiers hurdling down the hallway towards them.

"We'll never get out," Liam moaned.

"We're not far." Wren puffed, pulling him down the hallway and wrenching open the door to the storeroom they had come out of. Ansel and Pike ran down the hallway, naked blades in hand, and skidded to a halt behind.

"What are you doing?" Liam asked, his eyes wide. "We'll be trapped in here!"

"No, we're not," Wren said as Pike wedged a chair up against the door handle to stop the soldiers who were already crashing against the door.

Ansel pulled open the trapdoor and motioned to Liam. "Inside!" he hissed.

The man scrambled forward with wide eyes, dropping into the tunnel below. Wren quickly followed, then Ansel and Pike brought up the rear.

"What is this place?" Liam asked.

"The sewer," she said. "If we can get through to another exit, we're home free."

"I can't swim," Liam said, misery etched across his face.

"We won't have to swim," Wren said. "Come on."

"Quit your complainin', man," Ansel snapped, close on their heels. "We're tryin' to save your life. Sorry we couldn't drive up front with a comfy carriage for ya."

Wren couldn't help but agree as she grabbed the torch they had left burning at the base of the trapdoor and they ran forward through the dark tunnels. An explosion sounded behind them, and they all flinched inadvertently.

"They're in," Pike said. "But they don't know which way we've gone."

"They can tell from our light," Liam said. "It'll lead them right to us."

The pounding of boots behind them was growing louder.

"He's right," Ansel said. "Come here." He shoved both Liam and Wren into a little alcove and tossed the torch into the water, snuffing it, plunging them into darkness. "We'll be right around the corner," he whispered.

Wren and Liam scrunched down into the alcove, pressing themselves against the slimy wall.

The bootsteps had slowed. It seemed their pursuers were making a more leisurely investigation of the tunnels. "Come out, come out wherever you are..." Willings's nasal voice called in the dark. Wren shivered and Liam clutched her hand. His own was shaking like a leaf in a gale.

"I won't go back," he whispered.

"You won't have to," Wren said. She wanted to pull the chocolates from her pocket but feared that the crinkling of the paper would give them away. "Trust me."

A light was blooming at the end of the tunnel. They were getting closer. What had they been thinking, trying to hide here? If the Apricans happened to come this way, they would see them—they'd be totally exposed.

The light grew closer, and Wren's breath hitched in her throat. Even knowing Ansel and Pike were nearby, she worried it wasn't enough. It was two men against how many? If it was too many, they'd be slaughtered.

Wren felt like she was going to explode. Liam's hand was clutched in hers, his breathing coming in short little bursts of air.

The light was just feet from them, and Wren could see Willings's face now, his pockmarked skin cast in garish shadow.

Wren squeezed her eyes closed, wishing that it could make her invisible.

And then a roar sounded from down the tunnel, and two men hurdled through the blackness, crashing into the group of soldiers behind Willings. Ansel and Pike were like berserkers in the night, tossing men bodily into the channels of dirty water, slicing others clean through with bloodied swords.

"Come on!" Wren cried and grabbed Liam's hand, darting past Willings towards another tunnel that she prayed led towards Violena's. In the mad dash of their flight, she wasn't one hundred percent sure where they were in the maze of the sewer.

Wren could have wept in relief as she saw two men tearing after them and recognized the brawny forms of Ansel and Pike.

"Did you get him?" Wren asked breathlessly.

"Redhaired bastard? Scuttled off," Ansel said. "More men're coming; we've gotta go."

"More?" Wren said with dismay, skidding to a stop in front of a wide channel of sluggish water. She pulled the crumpled map from her pocket, looking at it, willing it to reveal its mysteries to her.

"Now's not a great time to be lost..." Pike said, looking back. Shouts were ricocheting off the tunnel behind them, growing nearer.

Liam had his eyes closed, moaning softly.

"There." Wren pointed across the wide stretch of water. "We're a few tunnels down, but if we cross this, we should be just one or two turns from the entrance to Violena's."

"Across?" Ansel said with dismay. "Ya know what's in this water, right?"

"It's this or the sword," Wren said, and with a cry of disgust, she leaped into the center of the river.

She gagged as she came up for air, stroking quickly towards the other side. It wasn't far, and as long as you didn't think about what might have been floating in the water with you...it wasn't so bad. Splashes and curses sounded behind her, and she knew that the others had joined. She reached the other side and with all of her strength, hauled her wet self up onto the slimy stones. She gasped and turned to see Ansel and Pike crossing the channel. Liam was standing on the other side, his eyes wide with terror.

Oh, gods. He had said he couldn't swim.

"Come on, Liam!" she cried. "Go back. Help him. He can't swim."

Pike swore and turned, swimming back across the channel with sure strokes. He pulled himself out of the water with a heave. "Come on, man," Pike said, shaking like a wet dog. "I'll help you across."

It was then that another half-dozen Aprican soldiers manifested from the blackness behind Liam.

"Pike! Liam!" she screamed. "Jump!"

But Liam appeared frozen to the spot. A soldier seized him, three others leveling swords at Pike. He lifted his hands slowly. "Easy, mates."

Liam struggled against the soldiers, his eyes meeting Wren's. She recognized what she saw there because she had felt it at times too—in some of the darkest moments of her life. Despair.

"Liam, no!" Wren cried, and the moment seemed to slow as he reached for one of the soldiers' belts and seized a knife. But instead of stabbing the soldier or fighting his way free, he turned the knife towards his own stomach and plunged it in to the hilt.

Hale was stunned. The baker was free. Or possibly dead. But wherever he was, he wasn't in that oppressive kitchen, baking his fingers to the bone anymore. Someone had freed him. But who?

It had to be the Falconer. It had been a risk—passing every piece of information to the man. Making his way to Gemma Park, to the carousel. It was risky even leaving the palace anymore, strange and unsettling to move among the people of Maradis, to hear the same whispered words, the same flat professions of admiration and love for the emperor. He had thought what Daemastra had done to him had been bad. What he had done to the baker. To the icebox full of Gifted he had ground up into dust. But what he had done to the people of Maradis, robbing an entire city of their free will, their very faculty to think and dissent and engage...it was something else entirely.

Yet somehow it seemed Daemastra had missed a few. While the Falconer's attacks had diminished significantly after the infused bread had swept through the city as soundly as the Red Plague, they hadn't stopped. And that meant that there was hope, however small and insignificant a thing it seemed.

The sounds of fighting had roused Hale from his bunk, where he'd dosed the afternoon away. They had been too quick for Hale to catch a glimpse of who it was. Except one. A man Hale had seen before... He wracked his brain to place him as the man strode past him liked he owned the place. The foreign haircut, long in the middle and shorn on the sides. The stern set of his handsome face... There it was! The memory bloomed to life in Hale's mind. He had seen the man once before on the steps of the Confectioner's Guild, pacing before the door. The day Hale had gone to warn Wren. Hale craned his neck at the man's retreating form. Who was he?

Hale found himself before Liam's little cell, the door hanging open. He'd tried to give the man what comfort he could—bringing him extra rations, a book to read. Not that Liam had much time to do anything but bake and collapse on his bunk in an exhausted haze.

Voices sounded down the hall and Hale pushed inside the room, closing the door partway so he couldn't be seen. Boots echoed on the floors as the men drew closer. It sounded like several. Half a dozen soldiers, maybe?

Hale recognized one of the voices and his eyes narrowed. The nasal words of Willings floated to reach his ears. "—all the guard and legionnaires should be looking out for her. And the redhaired man she was with."

"What should we do with this one?" a man asked.

"Take him to the morgue. He's dead," Willings said.

Hale risked inching forward, peeking out the bars of the cell door, keeping his form in the shadow. Who was dead?

His heart sank as he saw Liam's gaunt form hauled between two soldiers, blood trailing behind. *No.* Hale's heart seized in his chest. Poor man. He'd almost made it. So what had happened to the rescuers?

A gasp of shock escaped him as he saw who walked between the next two legionnaires, their swords leveled with deadly precision. "Pike?" Hale whispered, twining his fingers through the bars, craning his neck to see as they rounded the corner towards Daemastra's workshop.

He pressed himself back against the wall, his mind racing. Guildmaster Pike was here. Captive. What did that mean? Was Pike working with the Falconer? A thought struck him and his mouth went dry. There were only two more ingredients Daemastra needed to make his formula. Luck and time. With Pike here—if the man's magic was what Daemastra needed—the madman would be one step closer to transforming himself and his soldiers into gods. And perhaps he'd forgo luck, if he was this close.

Hale had to know what was happening. He needed to get near that room.

He passed several of the legionnaires as they hurried from Daemastra's workshop. He didn't blame them. There was something about that place that made a man's skin crawl. He'd felt it even before he'd known what it was. The ground-up bones of dozens of Gifted, kept in refrigerated jars.

Hale sidled up to the wall beside the door, listening to the voices inside. Pike. Willings. Daemastra.

"I'm so pleased you could join us Guildmaster Pike." Daemastra was purring. "I've been looking forward to meeting you."

"And I hadn't thought of you at all," Pike countered.

A smooth chuckle from Daemastra. "I doubt that, Guildmaster. I doubt that very much. There's so much I want to ask you. So much information you have to share that will aid the Empire. The identity of the Falconer, for instance. The location of the rest of your guild members and the missing members of the Confectioner's Guild. Perhaps even, if I'm lucky, the location of our missing heir to the throne."

Flame it! The man knew where Wren and Callidus and Thom were? It was worse than he thought.

"And then, an item of personal interest," Daemastra went on. "The nature of your Gift."

"If you think I'm going to tell you anything, you're more deluded than you look," Pike spat at him. "You can go straight to the Piscator's watery hell. You and your dog here and your whole blooming empire."

Pike's defiance warmed Hale and a grim smile crossed his face.

"Your spirit is admirable. In fact, it's no less than I was expecting from the notorious head of the Spicer's Guild. But I'm afraid I'm going to have to dispense with the pleasantries. You will tell us what you know because you'll have no choice. Willings, I believe I have a bottle of ice wine in my chambers. Would you send for a servant to fetch it?"

"Gladly," Willings said, and Hale launched into action, sprinting down the corridor and slipping into the nearby empty kitchen. Hale watched from the dark room as Willings passed, a smile baring his crooked teeth. Ice wine.

Hale slumped against the wall, horror welling within him. Wren, Thom, Callidus. Lucas and his two remaining siblings. The last resistance in the city. If Pike knew anything about any of it, they were all doomed. And there was nothing he could do to stop it.

CHAPTER 39

Ansel pulled Wren along through the wet Maradis night. Her body was numb, her mind more so.

The Apricans hadn't followed them across the disgusting stretch of sewer water; they had seemed fixed on getting Liam and Pike back to the palace. Liam hadn't been dead when Wren and Ansel had turned the corner, the slimy stones blocking her final glimpse of Liam's pale visage and Pike, his face a mask of fury.

Wren wasn't sure whether she was praying for Liam to die a clean death or to live. She didn't know anything anymore. Her mind was shrouded by fog, by shock, by exhaustion. She needed...she didn't know. She had thought that getting Lucas back would bolster her courage, her resolve to do what needed to be done. But now she'd lost him. And seeing that knife thrusting into Liam's gut...she didn't know if she had that in her. Would she kill herself, to avoid being used by these monsters? Or would she take the coward's approach and live—knowing that her magic was being twisted and used for evil?

They turned the corner onto the street that housed Violena's townhouse, and Wren recoiled.

Ansel pulled her back into the shadows between two buildings, pressing her against the hard brick. Aprican soldiers milled on the steps of the townhouse, and the door was open. A carriage stood in the street before the house, another blue-clad soldier sitting at the reins.

"What's going on?" she whispered.

"I think the safehouse ain't safe any longer," Ansel said.

A hand fell on her shoulder and a screech escaped from her lips as she whirled into the darkness of the alley—to face the other figure there. "Shh!" the man said, clapping one hand over her mouth, resting a finger against his own lips.

Her blood thrummed through her veins as she registered who it was, relaxing slightly. Bran. She nodded and he lifted his hand.

Ansel and Bran shook hands as Wren sagged against the wall, her hand pressed to her chest.

"What's this?" Ansel nodded back towards the scene on the townhouse steps. They were leading Killian out now, his gnarled form flanked by two huge Apricans.

"Think one of the shipments got flagged goin' through the port. The soldiers must have followed it here. I got my last wagonload here and found this. I parked around the corner. I think they're from customs, doing an inspection. Could be that they don't know what they've really got is the Falconer. Maybe that slick bastard will be able to talk his way out of this."

"One can hope."

"What happened in the palace? Where's Pike? Dash?"

A bubble of deranged laughter escaped Wren's lips. In her shock at Liam's bloody suicide, she'd forgotten about Dash. And poor Pike. He was probably back in the palace, being tortured for information right now. Gods, it was partly her fault. She'd told him to go back for Liam.

Ansel put his arms around her shoulders, and unconsciously, she relaxed into his warmth.

"We ran into trouble," Ansel said. "Dash chose his side. They took Pike."

Bran shook his head. "Damn. That's a loss. At least the Imbrises and the others are safe, right?"

Ansel shook his head. "Pike and Dash both know our plans. We haveta assume that if Dash doesn't spill all, they'll get the information from Pike with infused foods. No one's safe."

Wren felt her resolve crumble even more beneath her. Gods. "The newspaper office," she said, horror welling in her. Lucas, Callidus...images of Aprican guards kicking down the door to the *Maradis Morning* lanced through her mind. Lucas and Trick and Ella, blood seeping across the polished wood of the floor. Thom and Callidus, dragged to the palace to be used like laboratory animals. She pressed a hand to her chest, as if the gesture could keep her lungs from seizing.

"Wren," Ansel said. "It's all right. Just breathe."

She was shaking violently now. Ansel and Bran loomed over her with matching concerned expressions, and suddenly, she needed to be away. She pushed past them, farther into the dim of the alley. "A minute." She gasped, leaning over, fighting for breath.

She had no flaming clue what to do. How to fix this. Their desperate plan was falling apart, the thin slice of hope slipping from her fingertips. As Wren grappled with her racing thoughts, struggling for breath, a memory surfaced. Sable's words—one of the last things she'd said to Wren the night she died. *I can barely see the two steps in front of me, let alone the whole path. All I can do is walk those steps, and then the next two, and the next two. And hope I end up somewhere worthwhile.*

The pressure in her lungs eased. Wren could see the next step—the path they must take. After that, she had no flaming idea. She stood and turned, marching back towards Ansel and Bran. In a hushed whisper, she announced, "Bran, get us to the *Maradis Morning*. As fast as humanly possible."

The printing presses for the *Maradis Morning* were housed in a large warehouse in the Industrial Quarter, not far from the Block, the prison Wren and Lucas had had a brief stay in. She shivered as she, Bran, and Ansel passed its high walls, trying to forget the feel of Killian pressing a hot needle under her fingernail. She couldn't believe they were working with him now—that she was worried for his safety, wondering if the soldiers had found the chocolates they'd stashed in the basement. But everything was upside down, wasn't it?

When they reached the warehouse building, Wren let out a shaky sigh. They'd caught a glimpse of two Cedar Guards in the distance at one of the intersections they'd passed, but the roads had been blessedly clear. Perhaps their luck was holding—for now.

Wren hurried from the carriage and pushed through the back door of the newspaper building. It creaked audibly, and she winced.

The cavernous space was filled with black beasts of printing presses, her friends around them, shirtsleeves rolled up, smears of ink on their hands and faces. Wren exhaled a deep breath in relief. They weren't too late. The Apricans hadn't found them here yet.

"Wren!" Callidus's pale face popped out from behind one of the glistening machines, his hair flopping over his forehead. "What are you doing here?"

The others emerged too and gathered around them—Lucas keeping his distance, his face impassive.

A lump rose in her throat as she faced the prospect of admitting their defeat to her friends.

Ansel laid a hand on her shoulder. "They were waiting for us. We lost Liam in the fight. Pike was captured."

Dismayed murmurs and exclamations peppered the room—disbelief warring with anger.

Olivia's hands flew to her mouth. "Dash?" Her blue eyes were wide and pleading.

"He turned," Wren managed, the words as hard as granite.

Olivia shook her head as if to ward against the truth, her face crumpling.

"I'm sorry," Wren managed.

"We haveta assume Pike is compromised. He knows our plans. He knows where we all are," Ansel said. "It ain't safe for ya to stay here."

"But we're not done—" Trick protested.

"It doesn't matter," Ansel said. "We haveta abandon this plan. For now. For all we know, Dash or Pike spilled and there are Apricans headed here right now. We need to get ya somewhere safe."

"And where is that?" Lucas asked. "If Pike is compromised, so is Violena's."

Wren exchanged glances with Bran and Ansel. There was one place they had thought they might be able to lie low—*if* it was as they'd left it. But that was a big if.

Wren began. "We think—"

It was that moment when a door across the room flew open, kicked down by a powerful blow. A dozen Aprican legionnaires, led by Captain

Ambrose, poured into the warehouse, their naked blades glinting in the lamplight.

Ansel, Bran, Lucas, and the others leapt into action, but the resistance was short-lived. Ansel and Bran dashed for the front door, their swords out, trying to clear a path for them. But a dozen soldiers materialized in the front, too, followed by the sneering face of Willings.

Wren stood in shocked stillness, her gaze locked on Willings, her blood roaring in her ears. It was over. They'd be taken to the palace—to Daemastra and the emperor—to whatever twisted experiments the men wanted to perform.

Wren looked at Lucas. Oh, gods. Lucas. They'd execute him. Helplessness flooded through her, as cold as ice water.

"Quite the morsels we've caught in our web, eh, Ambrose?" Willings crowed.

"The emperor will be pleased. Pleased indeed," Ambrose agreed, swaggering forward. "Is this not one, but two...nay, three Imbrises? All that's left of the royal line, ripe for the picking." He lingered near Ella, grasping one of her golden curls, examining it before letting it drop.

Ella spit in his face.

Ambrose backhanded her across her cheek. Her head snapped to the side, but she didn't cry out, didn't even wince at the blood that appeared in the corner of her mouth.

"Don't you flaming touch my sister," Lucas growled.

Ambrose turned a dark smile towards Lucas. "You're not in a position to be making demands. Now, where are the Gifted? Oh yes." Ambrose strode up and seized Wren by the wrist, pulling her forward. Lucas and Ansel both tensed, Ansel's hand on his sword hilt. She gave a little shake of her head. If they drew blades, it would be a blood bath. They were outnumbered practically three to one.

"Those two." Willings pointed to Thom and Callidus, still standing behind a curtain of soldiers. Coward.

"Come, come." Ambrose motioned them forward with cocked fingers. Thom and Callidus reluctantly joined her, Thom's hand lingering in Trick's grip as long as possible.

"And that one. The middle Imbris." Willings said.

Trick reluctantly stepped forward, but Ambrose held up a hand. "Not you. Your family line takes precedence over your Gift, unfortunately for you. You stay."

Unfortunately for him?

Ambrose motioned to his men. "Tie them up."

Wren watched as the soldiers went to quick work, binding her friends' hands and feet. She needed to think. She needed a plan. She needed some infused cheese, like they'd slipped her in the Block. No, infused chocolate... Wren reached quickly into her pocket and seized the little wax paper satchel of chocolates, letting it tumble down her skirt onto the floor. Perhaps it was the only help she could give them.

Just in time, for a soldier seized her hands, wrenching them behind her back and tying them tightly behind her. She didn't even struggle. Resisting this was useless. They were out of help. Out of allies. Alone.

Wren caught Olivia's wild gaze for a moment, and she motioned with her head to the packet on the ground.

Her friend's blue eyes widened imperceptibly.

"It was a valiant little resistance you put up here. But the fun is over now," Ambrose said. He waved a hand. "Burn the place to the ground."

"No!" Wren cried, lunging forward.

Ambrose caught her with iron arms around her waist, hauling her up into the air, dragging her back. She kicked and screamed as they pulled her from the warehouse while the other soldiers went to work pouring out oil from black canisters.

Wren collapsed into the corner of the carriage they shoved her into, tears leaking down her cheeks. Thom and Callidus were shoved in next to her while Willings climbed in across from them with an Aprican guard next to him.

She wanted to scream at Willings, to rail and shout and scratch his face with her nails. But her body had gone weak, numb with the realization of what was happening. Lucas was going to die. Lucas, and Olivia, and Ansel and Trick and Ella. Four little chocolates weren't enough to stop the might of the Aprican empire. A sob escaped from her throat.

"Don't cry, little Wren," Willings said gleefully.

"The Huntress take you," Wren swore, turning away. She couldn't look at his smug face anymore.

"I don't envy you," Willings said. "Before long, you'll be wishing you had let King Imbris have his way with you. A lifetime in a cell making chocolate for Imbris will seem like a dream vacation compared to what Daemastra has in store for you."

CHAPTER 40

Lucas wanted to scream. He hadn't come this far just to be outmatched by flaming Willings.

The heat from the flames was beginning to reach them, now just the warmth of a crackling campfire. But they were spreading quickly and held the promise of more—a blistering inferno that would destroy all they held dear.

"Anyone got any bright ideas?" Ansel asked. He and Bran were tied the tightest, back to back.

"I got a knife in my boot," Bran said. "If someone can get to it."

Ella was closest. "I can." She rolled onto her knees and slowly scooted forward, her pale blue dress leaving a trail through the dust. She thunked onto her side next to Bran's feet, almost teetering over before righting herself.

"My lady," Bran said with a grin as Ella leaned back, trying to fumble her way into Bran's boot.

"In your dreams," she said, rolling her eyes before letting out a smile of victory. "Got it!" She awkwardly pulled a small dagger out of the boot, holding it askew in her bound hands. "Now what?"

"Now give it here," Ansel said, sticking his hands out to the side. "I'll cut through our ropes."

Ella maneuvered the knife into his hands.

The flames were growing taller around the perimeter of the room and had almost reached a giant stack of paper piled next to the printing press. "Hurry up," Lucas said. "If the fire reaches that paper, we're done for."

"Oh really?" Ansel snapped. "I was goin' at a leisurely pace, but I guess now I'll pick it up a bit. I mean, I'm supposed to go on break in a few. Hope I finish up before then."

"Shut up!" Ella and Olivia shouted at the same time.

"I agree, mate," Bran said. "Less talking, more cutting."

"I can do both." Ansel sulked under his breath but sawed harder. The bonds snapped free, and Ansel turned, working his way quickly through Bran's.

The flames were licking the piles of papers now, which lapped up the fuel greedily. "Come on," Lucas said under his breath. Not that he knew how they were going to get out of this. The Apricans had barred the doors—he had heard the leader give the order himself.

Bran's hands came free, and Ansel handed him the dagger, unsheathing his own sword. They quickly freed their legs and raced to free the others.

When Lucas's hands were free he threw an arm over his mouth, breathing through his shirt. Thick, black smoke filled the room, stinging his eyes and turning everything blurry.

"Where to?" Ella asked, breathless, clinging to Lucas. He put a protective arm around her.

"Up there!" Trick pointed to a stairway leading to the balcony. It wasn't yet covered in flames. "Maybe we can get out on the roof."

"Wait," Olivia cried as Lucas took her hand, pulling her up. "Wren dropped something!"

"Leave it," Lucas hollered, but Olivia broke free and scrambled across the floor, shying away from the flames licking towards her. She grabbed a little white pouch and ran back. "Go!"

The group pounded up the stairs, running through the burning building.

Sweat beaded on his brow. The heat was intense. Lucas's instincts cried for him to run, to flee, to get out of this place.

Ella stumbled on the stairs and he was there beside her, pulling her to her feet. Tears were streaming down her face, from the smoke or fear, he didn't know.

They summited the stairs and came onto a wide balcony. Offices lined the back wall of the warehouse, flames reflecting in their glass walls.

"Look." Trick pointed. "A ladder to the roof."

They ran for it, and Ansel scaled up the iron rungs, twisting the handle that opened the trapdoor up to the roof. It wouldn't budge.

"Sower's balls," Bran swore.

"It's stuck," Ansel said. He leaned into the handle, his corded muscles straining, his face red from the effort. It didn't budge.

Ella let out a little sob.

"No go," Ansel said. "We need another way."

They turned, fleeing back towards the stairwell, but it collapsed before them in a shower of sparks and crackling wood.

Lucas shied back, clinging to the balcony. He hissed, pulling his hand back. The metal was as hot as a stove.

Olivia was fumbling with the little pouch she had picked up.

"What are you doing?" Lucas cried as he spun around, his mind whirling, his eyes searching for an exit. Anything. Could they go out a window?

"Eat it." Olivia shoved the pouch under his nose.

"Ain't really time for a snack," Ansel shouted over the roar of the flames, but Lucas ignored him, his eyes latching on to the contents. Chocolate. Completely melted—but still chocolate.

Lucas's and Olivia's eyes met, and they both dove in, scooping the molten chocolate out with their fingers, shoving the pieces into their mouth. Lucas shoved past her with sticky fingers—back to the ladder on the wall. To the trapdoor to freedom. They just needed a little luck.

He wrenched the handle, pulling with all its strength. And it *moved*. Slowly at first, just an inch. But then more. It moved, twisting in his grip, freeing itself. Lucas threw open the trapdoor, gasping in the fresh cool air that poured in from above. He scrambled out of the opening onto the roof, reaching down to help the others come through.

Ansel was the last one, and as he moved to climb up the stairs, the ladder gave way, the entire balcony they had been standing on collapsing with a groan.

Lucas shot his hand out and made contact with Ansel's wrist, grasping the other man. The mercenary's weight pulled at him, Lucas's shoulder straining in its socket. Below Ansel—below both of them—was nothing but a sea of flames. "Hold...on..." Lucas grunted. "Bran!" he cried. Ansel's wrist was slipping in his sweaty, chocolate-covered grip. For a moment—a flicker of time—Lucas thought Ansel was going to fall. That he couldn't hold on. But the moment passed, and Bran was there on the other side of the opening, grabbing Ansel's other wrist. Together, with gritted teeth and straining muscles, they pulled the man up onto the roof, all collapsing in a pile together.

"Come on." Trick pulled Lucas to his feet. "This roof won't hold much longer. Ella found a fire escape."

Together, they fled down the rickety iron stairs, the sound and heat of the inferno radiating through the brick walls of the building.

Lucas could have kissed the ground when his feet touched it.

"We need to get out of here," Trick said. "The fire department will be here soon. We don't know whom they're loyal to."

"We can't go back to Violena's," Ansel said.

"So where?" Lucas asked.

"The Guildhall?" Olivia offered.

"It hasn't been long enough for the infusions to have worn off yet," Trick said. "It'd be risky."

Ansel exchanged a look with Bran. "I know a place. It's been a few years, but if it's still there...we'll be safe."

Lucas sighed. He hated trusting this man, but it seemed they had no choice. They were covered in ash, and all wanted fugitives. They needed to get off the streets. "Lead the way."

The Wraithhouse turned out to be an abandoned warehouse full of dust and ghosts. It was easy enough for Ansel to break the padlock on the rusty doors and let them inside with an ominous creak. The interior wore a thick coating of dust that swirled up with their steps.

Olivia sneezed.

Ansel and Bran had strange looks in their eyes as they surveyed the place, the remnants left behind of a life lived: a bundle of worm-eaten clothing, a moldy blanket, some cans of food petrified on a little shelf below the window.

It struck Lucas, then, that Wren had lived here too. For two years of her life she had scraped and scrounged in this dark underbelly of the sparkling city he had grown up in. True, his childhood hadn't been a dream. His constant terror of his father had seen to that. But this...it made him wonder if he would ever truly know Wren. All the way through. He watched the redhaired mercenary as he looked over the old building as if surveying his kingdom. Lucas wondered if he could ever know the part of her that Ansel did.

With little grace, Olivia collapsed onto the bottom stair of the staircase leading to the second level, a tear winding its way through the soot on her face. She buried her face in shaking hands. Trick went and sat by her, his hand on her back offering silent comfort.

Their escape had been a close thing. The adrenaline of the moment was leaving him now too. Now that they had achieved some semblance of safety, he felt empty and heavy all at the same time. He wanted nothing more than to curl up on the floor and go to sleep.

"Bran and I will see about getting' us some food and water," Ansel said, taking charge. At this moment, Lucas didn't really care, and so he let him.

"The plan has changed, but our objective's the same. Break into the palace, rescue Wren, Thom, and Callidus, and kill the emperor," Ansel said.

Ella let out a harsh laugh. "Oh, is that all?"

"Ella—" Lucas started.

"Don't *Ella* me, Lucas," she said. "The plan was shit before, and it's double shit now. We've lost the printing presses; we've lost Killian, so we've lost our diversion; and we've lost the chocolate. Except that little melted puddle we still have. I think the plan is pretty much in tatters." Her voice rang in the stillness of the warehouse.

"So what would you have us do?" Trick stood. "Turn ourselves over to be executed? We have to do something."

"I'm tired of doing something." Ella closed her eyes, sighing. "Can't we just go back into exile? Live out our lives...on the beach or something?"

"We saw what would become of us," Lucas said. "They found us. It's not an option."

"We just need to reform the plan," Ansel said. "What're our resources?"

Silence.

"Killian showed me the signal to start the attack by his people. The Falconer's Gambit, he called it. So we could still use it as a diversion," Lucas offered.

"The cart we took to the newspaper office had two crates of infused chocolates in it," Bran said. "I doubt they noticed it on their way to kill us. We can go back and get them."

"The infused foods should wear off in the next twelve hours," Olivia said. "Maybe we can call on some of our old allies."

"Olivia's right," Trick said. "There were people at my Guild who were with me once. With us. Maybe they can be again."

"We still have my men, and Griff's boats," Ansel offered.

"You're still with us?" Lucas asked, his eyes narrowing.

"We don't get paid if we don't get Callidus or Pike back," Bran said.

"And I ain't leaving Wren," Ansel said. His voice lowered. "Not again."

"So that's the plan?" Ella asked, incredulous. "Blow some stuff up, run into the palace with a bunch of mercenaries, and hope that the Guilds will have woken up enough to back us?"

"It's about as likely to succeed as the first plan," Trick said.

"So not at all," Ella retorted.

Olivia stood, staring down Ella. "At least we'd be doing something. I don't know about you, princess, but I'd rather die fighting for my home than cowering any longer."

Ella narrowed her eyes but didn't take the bait. "You may get your chance," was all she muttered.

Lucas let out a breath. Gods, his sister could be trying at times.

"When can you have your men to the palace?" Lucas asked.

"If Bran and I head back to the ship, we'll haveta rendezvous at Dent Island. But most of the men could attack by sea, which is easier than getting' all of 'em through the entire city unseen. So...by midnight tomorrow."

So soon. Gods. "How do we know that you won't just head back to the ships and leave us?" Lucas asked.

"Don't ya trust me?" Ansel grinned wolfishly.

"Not particularly," Lucas said.

His smile died on his lips. "Fine. If it settles your nerves, I'll stay with ya. I'll send Bran back. That work?" He turned to Bran, who nodded.

Lucas crossed his arms over his chest. "Have Bran send some of your men into the city. A dozen. To help us get into the palace if we have to fight our way in."

"Very well, Your Highness," Ansel said.

"Midnight tomorrow," Olivia said. "I'll see which of the Guilds I can talk to by then."

Lucas rubbed his stubble-covered jaw, frowning at the smear of black that came off on his fingers. "So we have a plan. Tonight, let's try to get some food in us and sleep. Maybe a change of clothes, if we can manage it. Tomorrow at midnight, we rescue the confectioners, and retake the palace." *Or die trying.*

CHAPTER 41

H ale couldn't refuse a summons from Daemastra, as much as he might have wished to. When the man called, he came.

He braced himself for what he knew he would see as he rounded the corner into Daemastra's workshop, but even then, it was like a punch to the gut to see Guildmaster Pike strapped to the strange chair. He blew out a breath as he tried to school his features into some semblance of neutrality. He didn't want Daemastra to know that he knew the man. That they'd once been considered allies, after a fashion.

Pike was unable to hide his surprise when Hale stepped into the room. "Hale?" he asked, looking shrewdly at Daemastra. No doubt performing the mental calculus, wondering if he could leverage Hale somehow to get himself out of this predicament. Hale wanted to tell him not to waste his time.

"How'd you get mixed up in all this?" Pike asked. Dark circles ringed his eyes; his voice was hoarse.

"It's a long story," Hale managed. Part of Hale didn't want to know what secrets the man had spilled under the influence of the ice wine.

The other part was desperate to grab the man by his shirt and shake him until he told. Had he given up Wren? The Imbris heirs? Had he given Daemastra the magic he needed to complete his formula? He stilled his hands at his side.

Daemastra smiled his tight-lipped smile. "You two know each other?"

"We're acquainted," Hale said.

Captain Ambrose appeared in the doorway, his uniform starched and perfect. "Sim Daemastra. A moment."

Daemastra inclined his head and strode into the corridor to speak with Ambrose.

Hale wasted no time, hurrying across the room to Pike's side. "Does he have Wren? Thom and Callidus?" he hissed at Pike.

Pike nodded wearily. "Probably. They sent men to round them up."

Hale cursed under his breath.

"Your magic. Did you tell him of your magic?" Hale whispered.

"Not yet. He wanted to know the location of the others first, and then some soldier interrupted him. What does he want with me? With my magic?"

"Tell me what your Gifting is, and I'll tell you," Hale said.

Pike narrowed his eyes. "Why?"

Hale looked towards the door, his heart hammering. He still heard Daemastra's and Ambrose's voices in the hallway. "This is the room where you will die. And your bones will be ground into dust to power Daemastra's twisted magic. He thinks your power will make infusions last forever. He thinks he can turn himself into a god. Tell me that's not the case."

Pike had gone pale. "Help me! Get me out of here!"

"I can't even help myself," Hale said. "We're both doomed. But maybe...if you tell me, maybe I can stop him. Somehow."

Pike hesitated, but then his head drooped. "I'm a cursed man anyway, without her. I suspect you know a thing or two about that." Sable. Pike had loved her too.

Hale nodded. "This world...it's a shadow without her."

"Sometimes I want to stand at the edge of a cliff, just to feel something again. Something other than sorrow. Even if it's fear. Or pain."

"If you're on the cliff, make it mean something. Tell me. Your Gift. Could it freeze time? Stop things?"

Pike shook his head. "No. My Gift speeds up time. It would make an infusion pass more quickly if there was truly some way to combine them."

Hale blew out a breath. "Is there someone in your Guild who has the power to stop time?"

Pike glanced towards the hallway. "Yes," he said, his voice low. "In the breast pocket of my jacket, there's a vial. Get it."

Hale reached inside the man's velvet jacket, his fingers brushing several small vials.

"Which one?"

"The one with the black cork," Pike said.

Hale peered into the darkness and pulled it out. A tiny vial with a black cork.

"That." Pike nodded towards it. "That would do what the man wants. It is a member of my guild's make. I've kept some with me, since I was stabbed. To...slow things down if I was ever wounded again."

Hale pocketed the vial. "Lie," Hale said. "Tell him what he wants to hear. That your Gift would extend the power of an infusion and make it permanent."

"I can't," Pike said. "Even if I'm willing to sacrifice myself, I drank the ice wine. I can't lie. But..." His eyes lit up. "Grab the other vial. With the white cork."

Hale reached in his pocket again and pulled it out.

"It's my infusion. It should speed things up. Make it wear off. Then I can lie and he won't know."

Hale pulled the stopper off and tilted it into Pike's mouth.

Daemastra rounded the corner back into the room.

Hale straightened hastily, his hands flying behind his back, corking the empty vial. He slid it into his pocket where Pike's other tiny vial lay.

"Apologies we got interrupted," Daemastra said. "Now, I'm sorry I had to change our deal on you, but we are living in unique times. Tales of the unique Gifting of the Spicer's Guild have traveled as far as Aprica. I must ask, and it's very important you tell the truth. What is the power of your Gift?"

Pike looked at him through narrowed eyes. "Why should I tell you a thing, you snake?"

Daemastra sighed. "Guildmaster Pike, we've been through this time and again. Resisting only wastes your time and mine. The ice wine is infallible. I ask you again. We're in a bit of a time crunch, as Captain Ambrose just informed me. The city is beginning to wake up from its delicious infused dream, and I'd like this business to be resolved before they do."

So that was what Ambrose was reporting. After the death of the baker, people were starting to get their minds back again. No wonder Daemastra was anxious to get his potion perfected—his Golden Guard formed. His own powers secured.

"What is your Gift, Guildmaster Pike?"

Pike's dark eyes flicked to Hale's, and Hale prayed that the contents of the vial had worked. He was as good as dead in Daemastra's hands, even if Daemastra learned the truth that Pike wasn't who he was looking for. But if he lied...Daemastra would think he had his final ingredient. And just maybe two doomed men could save them all.

Only in Maradis would a series of secret messages be arranged via coffee shop. When Killian had told him the secret signal to start the Falconer's Gambit, Lucas had let out a startled bark of laughter. But Killian had been dead serious.

The bell tingled as Lucas opened the door to the Bitterbird Cafe, one of his favorite coffee shops. The shop where he'd first met with Wren what felt like an eternity ago. The proprietor was in the back, stacking chairs. "We're closed," he called without looking up. He was a thick man named Ruach, the second generation of his family to own this shop. He roasted the best coffee in Maradis, importing his coffee beans from lands to the east of even the Ferwich territories.

Lucas wore a newsboy cap low on his brow, and his scruff was long enough to pass for the beginnings of a beard. No one had recognized him on the street as Lucas Imbris, the missing heir to the Alesian crown. But Ruach had known him. It was a risk, coming here. If the man was in Daemastra's thrall—if the bread infusion hadn't worn off yet—he could turn Lucas in yet. But if he *was* in Alesia's thrall, the gambit was forfeit anyway. The best way to know for sure was to see what the man did.

"Was hoping I could place a last-minute order," Lucas said, taking off his cap.

Ruach straightened, setting a chair upside down on the table before him. When he saw Lucas, his brown eyes widened. "By the Sower," he breathed. He looked around, striding past Lucas towards the door, flipping the lock. He began closing the wooden shutters on the tall shop windows. "Are you mad, coming here? Every man, woman, and child knows your face. You're a wanted man."

"I was hoping that I still had allies in the city," Lucas said, shoving his hands in his pockets, trying to exude a calm he didn't feel.

Ruach closed the last shutter and turned. He shook his head, as if he still couldn't quite believe it. Then he crossed the room and enveloped Lucas in a tight embrace, clapping him on the back.

Tension drained from Lucas, and he patted the man back, a lump growing in his throat.

"It's flaming good to see you," Ruach said. "I'm so sorry about your family. Tell me you've got a plan to boot these Aprican bastards for good."

"That depends," Lucas said. "Could you make me the largest coffee you have? Black. Extra strong. Extra hot. With a sprinkle of pepper?" It was the code Killian's men had agreed on. Nothing any normal person would order.

Ruach's furry eyebrows rose. "Aye. That I could," he said slowly. "When would you like it?"

"As soon as you can make it. Midnight if you can manage it."

He nodded, a grin spreading across his weathered face. "I better get to it then."

Ruach hurried into the back of the shop and returned with a bowler hat and cloak. He blew out the remaining lanterns before unlocking the front door, letting Lucas out before him and locking it behind them.

Lucas put his hat back on. A spitting Maradis rain had started.

Ruach offered his hand. "God speed, Lucas Imbris."

Lucas shook it. "Do this for me, and you have my eternal gratitude."

"You on the throne would be enough for me. Make those blond bastards pay."

Lucas turned left and Ruach turned right, hurrying in the direction of the next coffee shop, Black Bean, White Cream.

Lucas cut into an alley where Ansel was waiting, leaning against the brick wall. "Well?" he asked.

"He said all the right things," Lucas said. "It's looking good."

"Let's see if he meant 'em," Ansel said, shoving off the wall.

Ansel and Lucas walked onto the street, cloaks pulled tight against the rain. This part of the plan was the riskiest. If Ruach was indeed loyal to the Falconers, he would place the same order Lucas had at the next coffee shop down the line, then notify those he was in charge of to place their charges. The next coffee shop owner, if loyal, would do the same. Killian had set it up that way, so no one knew who all the other Falconers were, in case someone was compromised. But it was possible to activate the entire network of cells by a single order of the trigger phrase.

Ruach was a dim shadow ahead of them, hurrying up the street. If he went to the next coffee shop, they knew he was loyal. If he headed towards the palace to report that he had seen Lucas...if he had just been pretending...well, Ansel would take care of him. Lucas really, really hoped it didn't come to that.

Ruach reached Black Bean, White Cream and pulled open the checkerboard door, heading inside. Lucas blew out a breath, grinning at Ansel. He couldn't help himself. "He did it."

"Your man came through," Ansel said.

"Now let's just hope everyone else down the line is as loyal," Lucas replied.

CHAPTER 42

Wren sat in the corner of their cell, her back pressed to the cool walls. She wanted to sink into it, to disappear until she was no more. Maybe then these feelings, these thoughts, would be gone too. Lucas was dead. She hadn't seen a body, but she had seen the pyre that had once been the *Maradis Morning* building, greedy flames licking to the sky. Their hands and feet had been bound—there was no way they could have escaped. Lucas was dead. Lucas and Trick and Ella. The last of the Imbris line. Olivia. Poor Olivia, who had only ever been kind and as sweet as syrup. Far too sweet for this world. Ansel and Bran. The last of her Red Wraith clan, only so recently resurrected. Her mind didn't want to believe it.

Thom and Callidus seemed similarly numb with shock. Their Aprican guards had thrown them all into a cell together, little concerned that they would get up to anything. They were well and thoroughly defeated.

"Do you think they made it out alive?" Thom asked. His boyish face looked like it had aged years, tear-stained and puffy.

Wren knew she should lie for him, but she didn't have the energy. "I don't see how."

Thom buried his face in his arm, his shoulders shaking.

Callidus laid a gentle hand on his shoulder and Thom leaned into him, sobs wracking his thin frame.

Wren wondered if she had run out of tears, for though the sight of Thom crying moved her, her own eyes were dry.

She had cried so many tears in the past months. For Kasper. For Sable. Virgil. For Hale, a dear friend lost to the dark of his own grief. For their city, their freedom. She had cried for Lucas, for how things had ended between them. For the thought that he had gone to his grave hating her, feeling nothing but scorn for her. Heat flooded through her as she tried to banish the thought of the flames limning his stately profile. It had been her last glimpse of him. It seemed that she was wrung dry of sorrow. But the horrors weren't over, were they? For her and Thom and Callidus. For Pike, if he was still alive. They were just beginning. She didn't know what she wished for. A clean death? A chance to live? Perhaps it would not be so bad, to make chocolate all her life with a shackle around her ankle. Surely, it was a better life than many. But Willings's words from the carriage chilled her. What had he meant, that she would long for the days under King Imbris?

"I keep wondering if I could have done something differently," Callidus said absently.

"Me too," Wren added.

"Me three," Thom said, his words muffled through his shirt.

"Less than two months in power, and I destroyed everything two centuries of guild masters before me worked to build. I guess my father was right. I guess I really am no good at this."

Wren shook her head. "It's not you. It's these circumstances. What could any of us do against men like Hadrian Imbris or Emperor Evander? What hope could we have ever had to make a difference? If you try to stand in their way, you just get trampled."

"Maybe you're right," Callidus said. "Maybe we were on a fool's errand all along."

"What would you do if you could do it again?" Wren asked.

"That's the thing," Callidus said. "I'm not sure what else I could have done."

"We could have run. Ansel told me to run, and I didn't listen. We were free in Forgotten Bay. We could have made a life somewhere, right? Evander's reach has limits."

"I don't know that it does. He found Lucas, didn't he?"

But the thought kept echoing in her mind. They could have run—all together, they could have made new lives for themselves. They'd come back because they'd felt a sense of duty and obligation to the city that had raised them, the Guild that had been their home. But the Guild wasn't home. She was realizing that now. These people were. She'd come back to try to save a life that had changed her—given her meaning. But it hadn't been the life that had done it. It had been the people. Everyone whom she cared about had been with her in that little fleet. Except one. Hale.

Callidus leaned his head back against the wall, looking at the ceiling. "We could have run. But in a way I'm glad we didn't. At least we tried."

Wren nodded. She supposed he was right. It was a bittersweet consolation prize. "It would have been nice to try *and* win."

Thom let out a strangled laugh, raising his head and wiping his nose. "We could still win."

Callidus and Wren laughed blackly at that.

"What?" Thom said. "We're not dead."

Callidus cuffed him over the head gently.

"You are a fool optimist, aren't you, Thom?" Wren said.

"It's seen me through," Thom said defensively.

"We're so different, the three of us," Callidus said. "I would have thought we'd have no common ground other than chocolate. But..."

Wren nodded, and in that moment, a tear did brim in the corner of her eye. "There's no one else I'd rather be here with than you two."

Thom and Callidus both nodded.

"It would be nice to have Sable here too," Thom said.

"Yes. And Hale," Wren added. "The old Hale."

Callidus rolled his eyes. "Yes. Even Hale."

Wren jumped as the door swung open. Her breath caught in her throat at the tall, broad figure silhouetted in the doorway. It was like their words had summoned a vision. "Hale?" she breathed. Even though she knew he was serving the Apricans now, a part of her trilled in hope. He had come to rescue them.

He stepped into the cell, his head nearly touching the ceiling. He didn't meet her eyes. Behind him, two more Aprican legionnaires stepped in, seeming to take up all the space and air in the cell.

"That one." Hale pointed, still not looking at her. "The girl."

The Guildhall sat dark and forbidding, its white marble columns like the tiers of a macabre wedding cake. Trick and Ella flanked Olivia, their cloaks pulled up to shadow their faces. They had talked Lucas into letting them come, despite the risk of them being recognized. Trick had contacts at the Guilds too, and they needed all the help they could get.

"Are we ready for this?" Trick asked.

"No," Olivia said. "But when have we been ready for any of it?" The thought of Dash loomed in her mind. The wound of his absence—his betrayal—was raw and stinging. Olivia shoved it aside savagely. Shoved aside the guilt. It was her fault that they were in this predicament. She had insisted that Dash could be trusted. And he had turned on them, gotten Pike caught. Ruined everything. She still couldn't believe it. Couldn't reconcile the chocolate brown eyes, the devastating smile, the heat of his sure fingers as they trailed across her skin. *How could it have all been a lie?* she wondered. But hadn't the past proved that she couldn't tell a lie from the truth? That was why she hesitated now. What if Lennon and Marina and Beckett and all the rest couldn't be trusted? What if they were still under the influence of the infused bread?

She looked at Trick. "I still don't think it's a good idea for you both to come in with me. It's too much of a risk."

"You said yourself—we'll go in the back and try to find your friend," Ella said.

"We need to know," Trick added. "It's just as dangerous for us out here. Anyone could spot us."

Olivia nodded, pushing down her nerves.

"Okay. Now or never."

They hurried across Guilder's Row, circling around the back of the Guildhall. An Aprican Guard was visible on the top stair before the door, his head down. He hadn't seen them as they passed. Olivia let out a breath.

They slipped through the servant's entrance, and it was like she'd never let. Familiar wooden floors, wrought-iron sconces, bowls of chocolate nestled in alcoves along the way. Her heart seized painfully in her chest. It was like she hadn't even been missed. She'd always thought she and her grandaunt were integral to the running of the Guildhall. But perhaps she'd been wrong.

They padded up the servant's stairs to the second floor's long corridor of rooms. She knocked on Lennon's first, her body alive with adrenaline. *Please be there,* she thought, the words a mantra in her mind. *Please be alone,* she added, horror striking her at the thought of someone being there with him. Someone who wasn't friendly.

Lennon was their best chance. He had helped in the past—when they'd freed Hale, when they'd attacked the caravan holding Thom and the other Gifted. She hadn't known then why Thom had been taken. It made so much more sense now.

The door opened to reveal Lennon's earnest face.

"Lennon." She threw herself into his arms, relief overtaking her.

"Olivia, my gods, what are you doing here? I thought I'd never see you again."

"Can we come in?"

Lennon narrowed his dark eyes at the two cloaked figures behind her but nodded, stepping back to let them inside the room.

Olivia froze when she saw who else was there. Marina. Haughty as ever, wrapped in a gray sweater, her hair pulled into a bun. But the look on Marina's face...it wasn't what Olivia remembered. It was—relief? Hope?

"It's good to see you," Marina said, crossing the room and pulling her into an embrace.

Olivia patted the girl awkwardly. "You too."

"Who are your friends?" Lennon asked.

Trick and Ella were standing by the closed door.

"Before I tell you that, I must ask. What do you think of Emperor Evander?" Olivia asked.

"I'd stick a knife in his gut myself," Marina said, "if I could get close enough."

Lennon shrugged. "What she said." His voice was flat.

Trick and Ella threw back their hoods.

Lennon and Marina exchanged startled glances. "You're...Patrick Imbris?" Lennon said.

Olivia nodded. "Lennon, Marina, meet Trick and Ella Imbris. Trick's with the Vintner's Guild. Or was before all this mess started."

"There's a price on both your heads," Marina said. "What are you doing here?"

"It's a long story," Olivia said. "We'll explain everything, but first I must tell you something that you may not believe. Magic is real."

Marina waved a hand. "Yes, yes. The Gifted, the magic food."

Olivia recoiled. "You know?" She looked to Lennon. "You both know?"

He nodded.

"My father told us a few hours ago when our minds started to come back to us. We couldn't explain the things we'd been doing. The fog we've been living in. He figured it out."

"And how does he feel about it?" Olivia asked carefully. Marina's father, Grandmaster Beckett, had been no friend to them in the past. He had been the one who had betrayed Callidus, Chandler, and the other guildmasters to King Imbris.

"He's furious," Marina said. "I know my father's ways may have seemed questionable in the past, but he always did what he thought was right for Maradis and the Guild. This—" She shook her head. "It's horrific. There's a meeting between the guildmasters in half an hour to discuss what to do."

"All of them?" Hope bloomed in Olivia.

"All of them that are left," Lennon said. "The Spicer's Guild has been disbanded. But the others are meeting."

"Guildmaster Alban?" Trick asked, referring to the head of his own guild.

Marina nodded. "My father's heard very little, as everyone's only just coming back to themselves. But from what he's said, the Guilds are furious. Ready to revolt. But the Apricans are so powerful. I'm just not sure what we're going to do."

Olivia exchanged a knowing glance with Ella and Trick. "I think we can help with that."

CHAPTER 43

Lucas and Ansel waited in the dark back hallways of the Tradehall for hours, Lucas pacing the halls, Ansel lounging and sharpening his myriad knives.

Finally, the door pushed open. It was Bran.

Ansel rose, clapping hands with his second-in-command as they bumped each other on the backs. "Griff's ships are in position," Bran said. "When the explosions go off, our men will be ready to scale the outer walls and breach the palace."

"Good work," Ansel said.

"I brought two dozen men. They're in the alley. Should be quite a scramble as the guards try to figure out where the attacks are coming from."

"Excellent." Ansel grinned his cocky, chipped-tooth smile. "This should be fun."

"And your men know what to do once we get in there?" Lucas asked. "Find Wren, Thom, Pike, and Callidus? Find the emperor?"

"They know the drill. If they're in there, we'll get 'em back," Ansel replied.

Lucas tried not to focus on the other sentiment hidden in those words. If they're still alive. Wren had to be still alive. He wondered what she was going through. Was she mourning him, thinking he was dead? Thinking that their last words to each other had been furious and tense? His anger towards her seemed insignificant now, a waste of a night together. Moments they could have shared, could have reveled in each other. He'd been a damned fool. Wren had only been doing the best she could—what she'd thought was right. And he had judged her for it.

Lucas's eyes drifted to Ansel. Was Wren mourning the mercenary too? *Which loss does she feel more deeply?* the little voice in his head asked. Ansel or Lucas? He banished the thought. It was no help right now.

The door creaked open again and the men fell silent, but for the slow, slick sound of Ansel drawing his sword from its sheath.

A figure materialized in the flickering light of their lantern. Trick. Lucas breathed out and rushed forward to embrace his brother. "Everything okay?" he asked, soaking in his brother's presence. His last brother. From six, down to one. Trick and Ella were more precious than gold to him now. The only family he had left.

"Better than okay," Trick said, stepping aside. More figures began to materialize. Ella and Olivia. Trick's guildmaster, dark-haired with white at his temples. What was the man's name? That was right. Alban. And more. Chandler—the distiller's guildmaster. The one-armed wiry man who ran the Cheesemonger's Guild. The huge brute who ran the Butcher's. Bruxius? Was that his name?

More and more trailed in until they were forced to risk lighting more lanterns, moving from the hallway into one of the large meeting rooms flanked by marble columns.

There had to be at least a hundred people crowding into the room.

"There are more outside," Trick said. "All the guildmasters brought as many of their guards as they could. The infused bread has worn off, and they're angry. When we told them that there's a chance to strike back and save Callidus and Pike in the process...they were eager to help." Trick grinned.

Lucas felt a swelling of hope. With these men, and the Falconer's Gambit, and Ansel's mercenaries...maybe they could actually pull this off.

"There's more," Olivia said, pushing through, her eyes shining. Guards sporting the livery of different Guilds were depositing baskets and platters of food, jugs of ale, bottles of wine. A cornucopia of food was filling the tables, overflowing onto the ground, being set against the walls. Bran deposited two crates that bore the seal of the Confectioner's Guild.

Chandler pushed through the crowd, holding out his hand to shake Lucas's. "Guildmaster Chandler of the Distiller's Guild," he said. "Your brother and sister have told us what you hope to do. First overthrowing the emperor, and what you'd like to do after. We're with you. It's time the Gifted stop living in the shadows. Time this secret comes out."

Lucas nodded, gratitude welling in him. "You and the other guildmasters are very, very welcome in our little alliance. But what's all of this?" He pointed to the food.

"All of us emptied our larders of all the infused food we have. Few of us are warriors. If we're going into battle, we might as well be fully equipped."

"This is all infused?" Lucas's eyes widened as big as saucers.

"Indeed. Before we battle, let's eat."

Wren marched next to Hale, her head held high. The two Aprican guards trailed them through the polished marble hallways.

"This is a new low, even for you," she said, struggling to keep back tears. It made it worse, the familiarity of having him at her side. A presence that should have been comforting, that should have made her feel safe. This betrayal stung her wounds anew. She'd thought he was working with the Falconer. That he was on their side. Apparently, Killian had been wrong.

Hale said nothing.

"Did you know?" she asked. "How could you be a part of this? Lucas is dead. His brother and sister. Olivia!"

He seemed to flinch at the last name. "It's not my call anymore, Wren."

"I don't understand how you can work with him," Wren tried again. "I know why you helped them in the beginning. You were mad with grief. It wasn't right...but I don't blame you. You weren't yourself.

What's your excuse now?"

"Maybe I'm tired of being in the wrong place at the wrong time," Hale said, finally looking at her.

His comment struck her strangely, but that thought vanished as they turned the corner into a room. It was a large kitchen of sorts. Cabinets, a sink, burners, glass flasks, and jars. But the chair. Black leather, reclining. Like a dentist's chair. The chair was wrong. This wasn't a kitchen.

She looked at Hale, the need to flee this place rushing over her in a wave.

Pity was etched across his face.

A whimper escaped her.

The two guards took her hands and pulled her into the chair even as she fought them, struggling, falling backwards, her feet trying to dig into the ground. But the floor was slick tile and they overpowered her easily, lifting her into the chair. They strapped down her arms and legs and buckled a piece of leather over her torso.

"Hale," she cried, struggling against the restraints.

He stood against the counter, his back to her, his head hanging low.

"Excellent," a voice said from the door, and her stomach dropped into the floor. Daemastra strode over, wearing a white cuisinier's smock. "Miss Confectioner. So happy our paths crossed again. Sim Firena tells me you have quite a marvelous Gift."

Hale turned, his handsome face a mask.

Wren said nothing. She would give nothing to this man by choice.

"Hale, did you have a chance to finish what you were working on?" Daemastra asked.

Hale's mask slipped a little at that, his face going pale, his mouth narrowing to a thin line. In that moment, he looked like he had aged ten years. "Yes," he responded. He pushed a small glass jar filled with what looked like white powder across the counter towards Daemastra before withdrawing his hand like it had burned him.

"Is this all of it?" Daemastra frowned, holding up the jar.

"The rest is still being...processed," Hale said haltingly. "I thought you'd want this bit."

Daemastra nodded, satisfied with the explanation.

There was a label on the jar. Wren squinted to make it out. *Maximus Pike.* Wren drew in a sharp breath, her mouth going dry, her body numb.

"What did you do to him?" she whispered, looking to Daemastra.

He wore a self-satisfied smirk on his face. "Guildmaster Pike has generously volunteered to help our cause," Daemastra said. "As will you."

"And what cause is that?"

"Ensuring the might of Aprica, of course. And securing my rule."

"Don't you mean the emperor's rule?" Wren asked.

Daemastra smirked. "Unfortunately, the emperor is quite ill. I fear he won't last the month. You can imagine how many people would be lost if the Empire fell to civil war after he passes. It is critical that someone strong step in behind him, for the good of the empire."

"Let me guess. You're that someone."

"I've been at the emperor's side for the better part of two decades. I know better than anyone how this Empire runs. And I understand better than anyone its best asset. The Gifted."

"You want me to work for you," Wren said. At this point, strapped to this chair, staring at a jar with Pike's name on it and Hale's sweaty, pale face, working for Daemastra sounded just fine.

"I'm afraid I have something different in mind for your special talents. I have spent years searching for particular Gifted with particular Gifts. Strength. Healing. Physical Beauty. Intellect. Magnetism and Virility. Most of them I found in Aprica. A few in Tamros. But I knew there was a trove of you in Alesia. I've been searching for you for years, Wren. The power of good luck. To turn each day into a series of delightful surprises. For everything to go your way."

"It hasn't worked out so well for me," Wren said.

"That is the strange irony of you Gifted, isn't it? The more you use it, the less you have it for yourself. You must have been cooking quite a bit, for me to find you."

Actually, she hadn't made any confections in a few days. She should have had some luck saved up. But it never seemed to be there when she needed it. She said nothing.

"Well, I want you to know," Daemastra went on. "You will be part of something special. Something completely new, something yet untried. By combining the best of the Gifting with the power of your friend,

Guildmaster Pike, I will become the best of all of you. Me and a select few men, my Golden Guard. Together, we will usher the Aprican Empire into a new era of prosperity."

Wren's stomach flipped. The way he'd said *Guildmaster Pike.* The way his eyes had flipped to that jar. What was in that jar? She looked at Hale, willing him to meet her eyes, but his gaze was fixed on the floor, the muscles of his jaw working furiously.

She had to think of a way out of this. *Think, Wren.* She'd gotten out of worse spots before. "I'll cook for you," Wren said, struggling against her bonds. "Whatever you want. You can have all my Gift, all my magic. Infused confections for as long as you want them. Please."

"I'm afraid that's not enough. I need the essence of your Gift."

"Then take it. I'll give it to you freely. How?"

"It's in your bones, Wren," Daemastra said. "I'm afraid you can't give it to me. At least not while you live."

Wren's eyes flew to the jar. The jar of white powder. Bones. Ground bones.

She was going to be sick. She strained at the bonds, twisting enough to throw up over the side of chair, rather than onto herself. Her vomit splattered on the ground, onto Daemastra's black shoes.

His mouth twisted in distaste. "It's all right, dear. You don't end up in my line of work without being willing to get a little dirty."

Wren panted, her stomach heaving. She thought more might come up.

Pike was dead. Ground into dust. And that was her fate.

Daemastra walked over to the cabinet, pulling out a syringe and a jar of clear fluid. He turned. "I'm not a monster, Wren. I'd like to assure you that this won't hurt a bit. It's just a body. You won't even miss it once you're gone."

Wren let out a keening sound, shying away from Daemastra. Why had she come back here to Maradis? She should have run, should have fled, like Ansel had offered. Now he was dead. Lucas was dead. Olivia was dead. Hale was worse than dead. Hale. Her eyes focused on him. "Hale!" she cried. "Stop him! Don't let him do this!"

Daemastra looked back at the frozen figure of Hale and gave a little chuckle. "I'm afraid he won't be able to help you. If he did, he'd be dead in less than a day."

Wren looked between the two men.

"See, even now, the black poison creeps through his veins." Daemastra pointed at black lines that crisscrossed Hale's hands, which were wrapped tightly around each elbow, his arms before him. "Only the antidote I give him each morning saves him. So I assure you, Hale is well and truly bought. He will follow me in all things."

Was it true? Was Hale only helping Daemastra because the man was holding his life hostage? Did it excuse what he was doing? Standing here, complicit to these horrors? If it was her, wouldn't she rather die than be a part of this? She didn't know. Self-preservation was a powerful force. Whatever the truth, in some way, it comforted her. To know that her Hale was in there somewhere. That he wasn't totally lost to her. That he hadn't become this monster entirely by choice.

Daemastra was filling the syringe from the vial now, and Wren felt herself come unmoored. She didn't care anymore about being strong or unflappable. She couldn't rescue Thom and Callidus, or Hale. She had tried to be clever, tried to be brave. Tried to play the game with kings and emperors. She had been desperately outmatched. There was no plan, no surprise ending. No allies to pull her out of this fire. She was going to die.

CHAPTER 44

Hale had seen his share of death. He had watched his brother die, his life slipping away before Hale's eyes as his blood had leaked into the dry Aprican soil. He had watched his beautiful mother go from a vibrant vintner to a sickly husk of herself as the Red Plague had eaten her from the inside out. And he had watched Sable, the light of his life, breathe her last breath. Felt his soul die with hers.

He had even chopped Guildmaster Pike's arm off at the elbow—cut through the muscle and flesh and sinew to reach the bone that Daemastra needed. He had taken that gruesome task on himself in the mad hope that he could save the rest of the man, who was recuperating in a deserted storeroom until Hale figured out a way to smuggle him out of the palace. Hale still had red under his fingernails, even after washing his hands a dozen times. Maybe he would always have that man's blood on his hands.

Hale had thought there was nothing left in him that could mourn—that could feel horror or sadness or anything at all. But watching Wren set her jaw and stand up to Daemastra, even hopeless, strapped to a chair...gods. Watching her crumple in on herself...watching the realization pass through her eyes, the realization that she was going to die... It broke him. He thought he was as broken as a man could be, yet in that moment, he fractured further.

He didn't care if the black poison took him. Let it pulse through his veins and still his heart. He wouldn't stand here and do nothing while that monster killed her.

He knew Daemastra took all sorts of infusions daily—healing, strength, reflexes. But the man wasn't a god yet, and he didn't think even an infusion could heal a knife to the heart. So as Daemastra sucked the poison into the needle he would inject Wren with, Hale slowly pulled a knife out of the knife block. And raised his hand to strike.

A deafening boom rang out, reverberating through Hale's chest and rocking him against the counter. He set the knife down hastily as Daemastra turned to him. "What was that?"

Another concussive boom sounded and dust rained down from the stone ceiling.

"I think we're being attacked," Hale offered.

"Curses." Daemastra set down the syringe on the counter, next to the knife Hale had just deposited. *Please don't wonder why that's sitting there,* Hale prayed.

"Hale, with me. We need to find Mister Willings and the Golden Guard. If we are truly being attacked, we're moving up the administration of the formula. We can do it without Wren's luck. Guards!" Daemastra called, and the two legionnaires stationed outside ran in.

"Take this girl back to her cell. Guard it with your life."

Hale silently cursed as he followed Daemastra out of the room, throwing a final glance at Wren. There had to be a way to get them out of this mess.

Lucas's belly was full as he snuck through the alleys of Maradis, the head of a silent horde approaching the palace. There was no way this number of people could stay secret for more than a few minutes. Already, citizens had spotted them moving through the dark, and if any were allies of Aprica, they'd be reporting them to the emperor.

But it didn't matter anymore. The first explosion had sounded, shaking the ground beneath his feet and sending him into the stone wall beside him. The Falconer's Gambit had worked. It had begun.

Lucas's blood sang within him as he surged forward with the rest. He felt like a knight in a tale. He felt like he could fly—energy and magic zinging through him. He felt invincible. He could see as if it were daytime; he could hear a rat scuttle three streets away. He swore he could hear whispers of the thoughts of men next to him, surges of excitement and adrenaline. It was a heady feeling. They had eaten and drank, giving little heed to what powers they infused themselves with. Men laughed out loud as they had jumped as high as the ceiling, as another had become as handsome as a god from a tale.

Ansel moved quickly through the dark streets of the city at his side, his muscles even larger and more defined than they normally were, as if that were possible. Lucas felt some comfort at the man's presence, at the bloodthirsty grin on his face.

"This is good stuff," Ansel whispered to Lucas, his blue eyes gleaming like beacons in the dark.

"Agreed."

They paused to press against the smooth stone wall of a mercantile. Ansel peeked out. The palace gates were a hundred yards in front of them. Aprican troops milled in confusion as others rushed into the city to contain the explosion. Black smoke was just visible against the dark sky, billowing from the Lyceum Quarter to the east.

Another explosion rang out, reverberating through his body. This one was close—the back of the palace. The soldiers shouted and pointed as red flames bubbled into the sky above the rooftops.

"When we get in there," Ansel said, "I want you and Bran to go for the emperor. You should be the one to subdue him."

"I need to find Wren," Lucas protested.

"Ya need to secure your rule. The security and future of this city depends on ya defeatin' the emperor. Many will recognize your claim, but if ya end 'im, it'll quiet the rest—make 'em fall in line."

Lucas frowned. Though his heart tugged him towards Wren, he saw Ansel's point. Many more would die if he didn't deal with the emperor once and for all. Unless he was certain Maradis and the rest of Alesia would accept his rule, however short-lived he hoped it would be. He wanted to be selfish. He had never wanted this crown, never wanted this responsibility. He had never wanted more than a normal life, a job to go to every day, a woman to come home to. Yet he needed to do this. He owed it to his country.

Lucas nodded reluctantly. "Swear to me on your life you will do everything in your power to get her out. To save her."

"I swear it," Ansel said solemnly. "She was my life, once," he added softly. "I won't let anythin' happen to her."

Lucas didn't get a chance to answer. A third explosion knocked him to the ground. The copper tang of blood filled his mouth.

He pushed himself to shaky feet, peering out, coughing in the dust. An explosion had taken a section of the palace wall right next to the gates. Dangerously close.

Men were down—crying, bleeding. Others stumbled, holding hands to ears, probably trying to stop the ringing that sounded in Lucas's own head. He was grateful for the extra power and healing the infused meal had given him.

"That's our cue," Ansel said, down on one knee. He pushed to his feet, pulling out his sword. "Badgers! Men of the Guilds! With me!" Ansel dashed forward into the open, like a berserker from a storybook, crashing into the first man who had the misfortune to be in his way.

Lucas darted out behind him, his own sword out, excitement coursing through him. He had never before understood his father's or older brothers' bloodthirst, their desire for battle and conquest. But today, he thought he did. A primal rage came over him, filling him with a desire for vengeance against these men, these invaders who had murdered his family and stolen his home.

An Aprican in a torn blue coat stumbled before him and Lucas didn't hesitate before running him through with his sword. The sword stuck, stopping Lucas's forward momentum, and so he put a booted foot to the man's chest and shoved him back, freeing his blade.

The soldier fell to the cobblestones, blood leaking from him. It was the first man Lucas had ever killed, some dim voice in the recesses of his mind noted. It wouldn't be the last. Not tonight.

Ansel's Red Badgers fought like demons from hell. They took the front of the assault, and though the Apricans were good fighters, the onslaught left them confused and disorganized. Ansel smashed through the front doors of the palace, sending a mass of men stumbling back. The mercenaries streamed past Lucas, and the battle for the palace began in earnest.

The palace felt like unfamiliar ground, though he'd grown up here, had run through these walls laughing and playing tag in his youth. The faces of the Aprican soldiers blurred together, the tanned skin and blond hair, the sky-blue uniforms and silver swinging swords.

Ansel had instructed two of his men to act as bodyguards to Lucas, and they did their work with grim determination, cutting down anyone who dared get close. Farther behind, away from the front line, were his siblings under similar guard, and their other Guild allies.

The group inched forward slowly, in fits and starts, rounding corners and pushing against new forces of fresh men. In one tall hallway lined with balconies they met a force of Apricans with crossbows, who rained down death upon them as they fought their way through. One of Lucas's bodyguards fell to a crossbow bolt through his throat, and Lucas stumbled behind a pillar, only to find a legionnaire waiting with bared teeth.

Lucas barely got his blade up in time to counter the other man's strike, which surged down upon him with tremendous force. Lucas frantically parried two more blows as the man facing him grinned in triumph, knowing as well as Lucas did that the prince was outmatched. Panic surged in him as Lucas found himself out of space to move, backed against a pillar.

The man raised his sword in a triumphant strike when a blade emerged from his chest. The Aprican's eyes went wide with shock as blood bubbled from his lips like a fountain. He slid to the ground, revealing Lucas's other bodyguard.

The man didn't even blink, instead turning and plunging back into the battle.

Ansel was gesturing from behind another pillar to one of his men. They were pinned down by the men above with the crossbows. Gaining any further ground would be costly—bloody.

But then one of the crossbowmen tumbled over the balcony, landing with a crunch in the middle of the hallway. A cheer went up from Ansel's men as other crossbowmen fell or were felled. More of Ansel's men were on the balconies. Where had they come from?

Ansel motioned and they surged forward, spilling through the hallway into a circular intersection of several hallways. Griff strode across, a sword in one hand, dagger wet with blood in the other. Her curly, red hair spilled around her shoulder, and her eyes shone with the heat of battle.

"You're over the wall, I see," Ansel said with a grin.

"Quite a rush." Griff let out a breathless laugh. "Your fellows can move, for musclebound brutes."

"Is that a compliment?" Ansel said with mock surprise. "Captain, I never—"

"Let's move." Lucas interrupted their banter impatiently. "Foreign army to subdue? Emperor to capture? Confectioners to rescue? Remember?"

"Ah. To business," Ansel said. "Which way, Imbris?"

Lucas looked around quickly. The rest of their group was catching up now and he scanned the faces, looking for his siblings. Relief filled Lucas as he spotted Trick and Ella. Olivia.

Bran trotted up, two bloody swords in hand.

"King's chambers were that way." Lucas pointed to the right. "Likely to find the emperor there. Not sure about Wren."

"She's probably in the west wing," Ansel said, nodding towards the left. "It's where we found the baker. Seems to be where Daemastra likes to keep his playthings."

Lucas suppressed a shudder.

"We'll find her, Imbris," Ansel said.

"We splitting up?" Trick asked, joining the group.

Ansel nodded. "Griff, Bran, ya and half my men go with Lucas. Capture the emperor. Or kill 'im. I'll take the rest."

The floor started to vibrate and Lucas looked about, throwing his hands out for support.

"I thought the explosions were through," Griff said.

"They're supposed to be," Lucas said.

"Then what's that?" Ansel asked.

It was getting stronger. Louder. It sounded...like the pounding of boots. The thunder of footsteps.

"Uh, guys?" Trick said, his gray eyes wild. He pointed down the hallway straight ahead.

In the distance was a sight Lucas's mind could hardly comprehend. Soldiers running towards them. But not soldiers—they could only be described as…gods. Their teeth and blades were bared.

"New plan," Ansel said, backing up. "Run!"

CHAPTER 45

Wren stumbled into the cell, falling to her knees as the door slammed shut behind her.

"Wren!" Thom ran to her side, trying to help her to her feet. It was useless. Her legs didn't want to work. Her body was numb—out of her control.

"Wren?" He brushed her hair back and the tears began to flow. She sprang at him, burying her face against his shoulder. She knew this was a temporary reprieve, that any moment Daemastra's men could throw open the cell door and drag her back to that place, to kill her and grind her bones into dust. But for this moment, she would take the comfort. Soak it in as if it might be the last bit she'd ever know. Because in truth, it probably was.

"Wren." Callidus's voice was gentle. He crouched down next to her and Thom, his elbow on one knee. "I know it's hard, but you must tell us. What did you see? What do they want with us?"

She let out a wracking sob. She didn't think she could tell them. It was too horrible even to admit to herself.

Callidus didn't ask her again, and for a time they sat there in silence but for the sound of Wren's sobs.

Another explosion punctured the stillness, seeming closer this time, shaking the room about them.

Wren pulled back, wiping her eyes with the back of her hand.

"What's going on?" Thom asked.

"They think someone is attacking. They don't know who."

"Could it be friendly?" Callidus asked hopefully.

"I don't know who," Wren said. "Everyone's dead."

"What did you see, Wren?" Callidus asked.

Wren looked at them with pity in her eyes. She didn't want to be the one to have to tell them. But maybe if Daemastra took her, he wouldn't need Thom or Callidus. That could be some small mercy.

"He's a monster," Wren said. "Completely insane. He's figured out how to take magic from us. To turn it into something he can take. Something he can give soldiers. To make an inhuman army for him."

"How?" Callidus asked, recoiling.

Wren shook her head, closing her eyes. "I don't even want to think about it."

"Wren, come on," Thom said. "Please."

"Bones." She whispered the word. "It's in our bones. When they take me back, they're going to kill me and chop me up and grind up my bones." Her voice hitched, growing high and hysterical.

Silence hung in the air. She opened her eyes to look at Thom and Callidus. They wore twin expressions of shock and revulsion.

"We have to get out of here," Thom said.

"Hale," Callidus said. "Hale came in here. How could he be a part of this? I don't like the man, but he never struck me as a madman!"

"I think he's helping against his will. Daemastra's poisoned him and is holding the antidote over his head to get him to cooperate."

"So maybe he can help us," Thom said eagerly. "Get out of here."

"I don't know," Wren said. "I think...if I could have gotten him alone, I might have been able to get through to him. But now Daemastra is going to infuse his soldiers with some sort of formula with all of the Gifts. To make them supernatural. Then he's going to take it himself. He's found a way to make it permanent. When that happens...it won't matter even if we have Hale's help. Daemastra will be able to have his way with all of us. The whole world."

"What about Pike?" Callidus asked, clearly trying to account for all possible allies. "Did you see him? Is he all right?"

She shook her head, eyes on the floor, a lump growing in her throat.

"What—?" Thom began, but he trailed off when he likely realized. When he took in her meaning.

"Sweet caramel," Callidus breathed, leaning back, running a shaking hand through his hair. "These really are the end of days."

A shout sounded outside their door, followed by muffled curses and a clash of blades.

They all stood in a blink, shying away from the door.

"What's going on?" Thom asked.

Wren didn't think she could handle whatever horror was bound to come through that door. Whatever fresh hell had been dreamed up for them.

A thunk made Wren jump.

Thom twined his fingers through hers, squeezing tightly.

Keys jangled outside, and then the door swung open, a huge form darkening the opening. Ansel stepped through.

Wren's knees went weak beneath her. Thom grabbed her, holding her up, blowing out a breath with a shaky laugh.

"Turns out badgers have nine lives, too," Ansel said, sheathing his sword, flashing his chipped-tooth grin.

Wren ran to him and threw herself against him with as much force as she could muster, crushing herself to his chest. "There has never been a more welcome sight," she said, her words muffled in the leather of his armor.

Ansel squeezed her back, putting her down gently. "And I ain't even told ya your boyfriend's alive yet."

Wren's hands flew to her mouth, her heart stuttering back to life. "Lucas..."

"We all made it out. Took some doin,' but everyone's okay."

"Trick?" Thom asked eagerly.

"All of us means all of us," Ansel said with a wry smile. "But if we wanna keep it that way, we should get ya the hell outta here."

"Where?" Wren said.

"We're rendezvousing at the Tradehall. Seems the Guilds have found their senses again and ain't too pleased about what's been goin' on the last few weeks."

Wren breathed out a sigh of relief. The bread had worn off. Liam's sacrifice wasn't in vain.

"And where's Lucas?"

He hesitated. "We…got separated. Hopefully on his way to subdue the emperor. There were some…circumstances we didn't expect. Now come on," Ansel said, and they hurried out into the hallway, where a group of Ansel's men were standing guard, swords out. They started down the hallway, but Wren's feet slowed, stopping.

Ansel, who held her hand, stopped before her, turning. "What's wrong? We gotta go."

Wren shook her head. This was madness. All she wanted was to run, to flee from this place. From Daemastra's chair, from that jar with Pike's name on it. Lucas was with Ansel's men, and Hale…Hale had made his bed. But still, her feet felt like weights beneath her. Could she really leave?

"Wren, we've done what we came here to do."

"But we haven't," she said. "We came back to Maradis to free the city from the Apricans. If we let Daemastra do this…it won't be safe anywhere. For anyone."

"Daemastra, the cuisinier? You're not talkin' sense. I came here to get ya. And I'm gonna get ya out. Now come on." Ansel grabbed her wrist, pulling her forward.

She took two steps before digging in her heels. "I can't go. You said you were helping us defeat the Apricans. You can't leave now."

"There's no way. There're men here—I've never seen anythin' like 'em. They'll kill everyone in their path. I don't plan to be there."

Wren shook her head. "But what about Lucas? Did others breach the palace with you?"

"Forget 'em, Wren. We've got once chance to get outta here alive, and this is it. I don't plan on leavin' without ya. I ain't losin' ya again." He pulled her towards him, and before she realized what was happening, his arms were around her, his lips were on hers.

Ansel tasted of salt and mint, his mouth firm against hers, steady in its resolve, his tongue parting her lips with a deft flick. Ansel's hands pulled her tightly against the expanse of him. Surprise warred with something deeper and older within her, something that had longed for just this in the dark recesses of her heart, so many years ago.

Wren pushed him from her with sheer force of will, gasping for breath, for space between them to let her spinning thoughts settle to earth. "What are you doing?"

"Ya, Wren. It's always been ya," Ansel said. He crushed her hand in his against his chest, where the tattoo of the wren lay in stark black ink beneath the leather of his armor. "Your world is falling apart. This city. There ain't nothin' for ya here anymore. It was a valiant effort the Guilds put together. A worthy last hurrah. But the Apricans'll regroup and crush ya. They're comin' even now. Ya and me—we can build a life together. A new life. Nothin' but the wind in our hair, the sun at our backs. Free, Wren. I can protect ya. Provide for ya. You'll want for nothin.'" He was pressing his lips to her hands now, and Wren felt the floor tilting beneath her.

His eager words rang harshly in her ears. Everything was wrong. Once, she would have wanted nothing more than this offer. To hear Ansel profess his love, to promise to take her from this place and take care of her all the days of her life. But something had changed.

"I can't," she said with a shuddering sob, pulling back from him. "I can't leave Lucas. I can't leave Hale. The other guild members..."

"You're losin,' Wren. If ya don't come with me right now, it'll be all over," Ansel said, his fingers digging into the flesh of her arm.

He was right. If she ran back into the fray, back towards that chair, she might not make it out of this palace alive. She had thought she was going to die before. When Killian was going to execute her. And she had been saved. Callidus, Hale, even Pike. Just moments ago, she had faced her death again—Daemastra's needle, that chair with its leather straps. And again, her friends—the Guilds, they had gone to impossible lengths to save her. To save her and Thom and Callidus.

"No one expects ya to die for them. No one is asking ya to," Ansel insisted.

Wren pulled in a breath, straightening. "They don't have to. I'd rather die beside my friends than live a life where I only care about myself."

"Wren—" Ansel's face darkened.

"I have always cared for you, Ansel, and I always will." She put her hand to his cheek. "But my place is here. Whatever comes."

"You're choosin' them. Him?" Ansel asked, hurt etched across his handsome face.

Yes. The Guild. Her friends. Lucas. This city. She was choosing all of it. This life. She wasn't ready to give it up. Not without a fight. "Yes. And I'm choosing to not be afraid anymore."

Ansel's face twisted, becoming an ugly thing. "Then you're already gone."

"You said you wouldn't leave me. That you'd never betray me again."

"This is your choice, Wren, not mine. If ya want to sail off a cliff for your ideals, I can't stop ya. But don't expect me to come with." He turned from her and whistled, a sharp sound that reverberated through the hall. In the distance, a whistle answered back. "What is that?" she asked.

"Retreat," Ansel said. And then without another word, he turned and jogged down the hallway, leaving Wren standing openmouthed in his wake.

CHAPTER 46

Hale was done following orders. He was done serving Daemastra. You'd think seeing a dozen men transformed into god-like monsters from a storybook would have done it, but that wasn't what had broken him. It had been Wren. He needed to get her out of here.

Daemastra had ordered him and Willings to rally the legion and defend the palace with the Golden Guard, and though Willings had protested, he had obeyed. Hale knew the sniveling man would take the earliest moment to circle back to the workshop where Daemastra was perfecting his formula. There was no way Willings would risk being left out in the cold when Daemastra sampled the perfected version.

Hale had slipped through the chaos at the intersection of corridors, men and swords filling his vision. The fighting hadn't reached through the west wing yet, and so the way to Wren's cell was clear.

A huge man with red hair and leather armor came into view as Hale rounded the corner into the hallway that held Wren's cell. He stilled, pressing himself into a doorway. Who was this man? Who did he work for? The guards before the cell door challenged him, and he made quick work of them, felling both in rapid succession with powerful blows from his sword. He kicked one of the men over, reaching down and retrieving the keyring from his belt. So a new friend?

He watched as Thom and Callidus hurried out and as Wren slowed, stopping the man, their hands intertwined. He couldn't hear the words exchanged, but from their gestures, he could tell that Wren didn't want to leave, didn't want to go with him. Hale weighed his options. Should he approach?

Then the man kissed Wren, and Hale's eyebrows raised. She pushed him away, but not as quickly as Hale might have imagined. What happened to Imbris? Was he out of the picture?

The man grew angry and stormed off, and Wren, after pausing a moment, turned and hurried down the hallway towards him. So intent was she on her destination that she didn't see him. He snaked out a hand and grabbed her arm.

She screamed, jumping halfway across the hallway.

"Shh!" he said. "It's just me!"

She let out a shuddering breath, a hand to her heart. Then their eyes met, hers filled with wariness, and something else he recognized. A sliver of hope.

"I wouldn't have let him do it, Wren," Hale said. "I wasn't going to let him kill you."

With those words, she sprang at him, throwing her arms around him.

He closed his eyes, wrapping his arms gently around her fragile body, burying his nose in her hair, breathing in the sugar scent of her. Of Wren. "Gods, I'm so sorry," he said. "I'm so sorry for everything."

"Me too," she said, her toes dangling in the air.

And in that moment, the madness around them slowed, pausing for an inhale of breath, allowing him to revel in the feel of having his friend back again. Because for all the heartbreak Sable's death had caused, he hadn't recognized that another part of him had been missing. This part right here.

He set her down, finally breaking off their embrace. "Where to?" he asked.

"We need to help Lucas," she said. "Ansel is withdrawing his men. They'll be undefended."

"Ansel..." Hale nodded in the direction the redhaired warrior had gone. Thom and Callidus were reemerging around the corner, arguing in hushed voices.

Wren nodded. "Please. I know we should go for Daemastra, but Lucas could be undefended."

"Lead the way," Hale said.

"You're not going anywhere," a voice sneered behind them. Hale swore. Willings and two Golden Guard blocked their path, swords drawn.

Lucas ran through the hallways of the palace towards his father's old room. He didn't know what he would find there, but he knew what was on their heels. Supernatural men who fought like the hounds of the Huntress herself. And a whole host of regular ones. Trick, Bran, and a few of Bran's men followed close on his heels as he skidded around a corner. He didn't know where the rest of them were, where Ansel and Ella and the others had gone. All their careful planning had descended into chaos the moment the huge warriors had appeared.

They were close to his father's old chamber. In the back of his mind, Lucas noticed the familiar hallways, saw the faded squares where portraits of his family had been taken down by the invaders, where a statute beloved by his mother had been replaced. But none of that mattered—he needed to focus on the task at hand.

There were only two doors between him and the Aprican Emperor. Two doors between him and Alesia's future.

A sharp whistle sounded in the distance, and beside Lucas, Bran looked up sharply. "What is that?" Lucas panted.

"Retreat," Bran said apologetically.

"Retreat?" Lucas exploded. "We're almost there!"

"I take my orders from Ansel," Bran said. "We all do."

"The hell with Ansel," Lucas said. "We're here, Bran. You're here with us. I respect you, man. You helped us start this. Help us finish it."

Bran's eyes flicked from the door in front of them to the hallway from which they had come.

"You'll have to fight your way back through those monsters," Lucas said, trying to summon the man's sense of self-preservation. There were likely several guards in the emperor's antechamber, and then the emperor himself. Lucas didn't know if he and Trick could take them. And even if they got in, even if they...finished the emperor...they still needed to get out of here alive. And if Ansel's men were retreating...

"Please," Lucas said, his voice low. "We're not soldiers. Don't leave us here alone."

"Come with us now and we'll cover your retreat," Bran said. "I follow orders. But I'll get you all out of here."

Lucas bit his lip, looking from Bran to his brother, a gash over one eye, an Aprican sword drooping in his hand.

Another whistle sounded.

"Retreat!" Bran called in a booming voice, and his men turned on a dime, streaming past them back towards the hallway they had just fought and died to pass through.

"You coming?" Bran asked as the last man jogged past.

He and Trick looked at each other. "If we don't finish it now," Trick said, "we'll never be safe. We'll never have a life."

Lucas nodded. "We're staying." He straightened.

Bran nodded. "God speed," he said before turning, his bulk moving rapidly down the hallway.

Lucas turned back to the door, suddenly feeling unsure. Exposed. He hadn't wanted this. Had done everything to run from this all his life. Yet still here he found himself. Blood on his hands, about to murder another ruler. In the world of court politics, it was kill or be killed.

Trick seemed to sense his thoughts. "If we do this—maybe we can make a better world. A better way."

"Or die trying," Lucas said.

"Then we'll see Mother and Virgil again soon," Trick said.

Lucas blew out a breath and with a prayer to the Sower, lifted up a booted foot and crashed it against the door, kicking it open, breaking the hinges. With a cry, they poured through the shattered frame into the king's antechamber. His father's old rooms. Lucas stumbled, coming up short at the sight that greeted him.

The sitting room looked much like Lucas remembered it from his youth. He hadn't been here in perhaps five years, since he had moved out of the palace. The emperor was sitting in a chair by the fire, a book in his hand. At their entrance, he picked up a bookmark and carefully marked his page, setting the book down on the table.

"Young Imbris, if I'm not mistaken," he said with a grandfatherly air about him. Lucas's sword tip drooped slightly. "I'm sorry for all this business."

"You're...sorry?" Lucas said. "For murdering my family and seizing our country?"

The emperor offered an apologetic smile. "I'm afraid to report that we've both been playing parts in a drama that was set in motion long ago. My role, as I suspect you will realize very soon, was a bit part. Perhaps yours as well."

"What are you talking about?" Trick asked, his eyes narrowing.

"Kill me, capture me," said the emperor. "I am at your mercy."

"But you're the ruler of the Aprican empire," Lucas protested. This was not going at all how he expected.

"Not for long, Mr. Imbris. Not for long. I suspect he's using your attack as the perfect cover for his takeover. I suspect that even as we speak, he is consolidating to him power more horrible than this continent has ever known."

"Who?" Lucas asked.

"Daemastra," the emperor said, a spark of anger lacing his tone.

"The cuisinier?" Trick asked.

"He's so much more than a cuisinier. He is as brilliant as he is power-hungry. As he is mad. He outwitted me, and you may not see it yet, but he outwitted you. He outwitted all of us in the end."

Lucas and Trick looked at each other in alarm as the emperor's words sank in.

Lucas ran to the door, peering out into the hallway. His breath caught in his throat as he caught sight of two huge men headed towards them.

"Son of a spicer," Lucas swore, slamming the door shut behind him, pulling down the crossbeam to bar the door.

He turned back to the emperor. "Does the takeover you referenced have anything to do with huge men the size of statutes? Who happen to be headed our way?"

The emperor's wizened face was grave. "Daemastra has been experimenting for years with Gifted potions. I have no doubt the men you speak of are his doing—some perversion of magic. If they're headed our way, I fear there's little hope for any of us."

CHAPTER 47

Olivia's hands were slick with sweat, her hair wild and tangled. Swords clashed around her, the screams of dying men and women echoing in her ears. The smell of blood threatened to gag her. She'd never smelled so much blood. The short sword she held felt strange and heavy in her hand, but she was profoundly grateful for the comfort it brought her.

Princess Ellarose clung to her side, a dagger grasped in one palm as they backed through the hallways the way they had come in, over the bodies of fallen allies and enemies alike. There was blood on the blade from the man Ella had stabbed in the neck when he'd tried to come for her. The girl may be frightened, but she wasn't going down without a fight.

Ansel's men fought savagely, holding the front line against the Aprican brutes who stood as tall as two men. She had never seen men like that before—impossibly strong and fast, their faces shining like the sun. They hardly seemed human.

Some of the guild members were in the fray too—dark-haired

spicers, brawny Guildmaster Bruxius, even Captain Griff slashed and parried with fierce skill and determination. But they were falling. Olivia watched, horrorstricken as her allies were picked off one by one. They couldn't keep on like this. None of them would survive.

An Aprican legionnaire slashed at Guildmaster Chandler, whose white hair was flying wildly with every swing of his sword. Another man approached from behind and Olivia heard herself scream his name, not sure if it would make a difference over the cacophony of ringing metal.

But Chandler dropped down just in time and the legionnaire's blade missed him.

Then she heard the scream of *her* name and Olivia's attention was yanked back to herself. She barely had time to register the tall brute in a sky-blue uniform coming for her before he fell, impaled on Lennon's sword.

Her mouth went dry as her stomach heaved within her. That was close.

A shrill whistle sounded in the distance and one of Ansel's men in the melee gave an answering whistle.

"What is that?" Ella asked, but it became clear when one of the mercenaries shouted, "Retreat!"

But they had been *trying* to retreat, when it was clear they wouldn't be able to make it to Wren and Thom and Callidus. It was damn near impossible with the press of the monstrous men upon them, their huge swords and axes mowing down mercenaries and guild members with each wicked strike.

"Fall back!" Griff shouted, and the momentum changed as guild members scrambled back towards the exit. Olivia was towed along in a tide of bodies and frantic faces as they began to retreat in earnest.

When they rounded the next corner, the open front doors of the palace gaping wide in the distance, the sight that greeted them was not one of freedom. It was a force of men in Aprican sky-blue uniforms jogging through the doors straight towards them.

"Oh gods." Marina moaned at the sight.

"In here!" Ella cried and yanked Olivia towards a side door. Olivia grasped out and her hand connected with Marina's wrist, pulling the woman with her. And then they were all piling inside the room—Griff and Beckett and Guildmaster McArt and Chandler and sailors she didn't recognize and even a few of Ansel's men.

Ella threw the lock as a force like a battering ram slammed against the door. The lock held.

"Lennon?" Olivia spun around and sagged in relief as she saw him, blood dripping from a shallow cut across his chest.

"Bar the door!" Griff cried and they scattered, dragging ornate furniture from the corners of the sitting room. Four men, including Guildmaster Bruxius, heaved a huge carved wooden bookshelf in front of the door, and then they piled more furniture before it—wedging chairs and a desk and velvet divan.

When every piece of furniture in the room was piled in a heap before the door, Olivia and the others stepped back into a semi-circle, subconsciously pulling themselves away from the door. From the pounding that shuddered against it.

Olivia surveyed those around her, taking in each heaving chest, each sweaty and bloodied face. She tried to memorize each one, to remember what was good and brave about each of these people. But it was impossible to focus with the attackers pounding on the door like a heartbeat, making her jump with every deafening crash.

Olivia felt fingers twine through hers and looked down to find they belonged to Marina. The confectioner stood with her shoulders squared, her head high. Olivia knew what that stance meant. For Olivia was certain the thought running through her head played in Marina's mind as well. In the mind of every person in this room.

That door wouldn't hold for long.

Wren's skin crawled as she stumbled back into the workshop, a sword point pricking at her back.

"Look who we found in the hallway, trying to flee," Willings said with a sneer.

Daemastra clucked his tongue. "Hale, Hale. A noble sacrifice, to give your own life to try to help get your friend out alive. A misguided one, however."

"I won't help you anymore," Hale said. "I don't care what you do to me. But I won't help you kill her. Or anyone else."

Daemastra nodded, his hands clasped behind his back. "I understand. You've had a resurgence of conscience. Luckily, I don't require your assistance anymore. I would have these soldiers dispose of you, but I think the poison will do that just fine."

Hale growled, but a soldier laid his naked sword on the side of Hale's neck and Hale stilled, growing quiet as the grave.

Daemastra walked to the icebox and removed a jar of clear fluid. He brought it to the counter and set it next to the jar of white powder. The one labelled *Pike*.

"You're here to witness a most auspicious day, young confectioners," Daemastra said. "The culmination of two decades of research."

"You mean two decades of exploitation and slaughter," Wren said.

"You can't make an omelet without breaking a few eggs," Daemastra said. "That expression always made perfect sense to me as a cuisinier."

He unscrewed the jars and took a tablespoon of powder from the one, stirring it into the other.

Wren looked at Hale, her eyes wild. They had to stop him somehow! If Daemastra took that powder...he'd be as powerful as a god. And Willings would be as well. She shuddered at the thought. No one would be able to challenge them. Wren could dart forward...smash the jar of formula onto the ground. Daemastra might be able to make more...but he wouldn't be able to use it now. She might be able to buy Lucas enough time to kill the emperor. Then, even if they had to flee...perhaps... Her thoughts were jumbled. Every avenue they ran down, obstacles as big as boulders seemed set in their path. This had been their last play. And with Ansel and his men retreating, getting out alive seemed impossible enough.

Hale met her gaze sideways and gave his head a minuscule shake. He was saying to wait. To hold. Not to go for the jar.

Her brow furrowed. Why? Her resolve faltered. What if Hale coming to find her had been a plot? What if he was working for Daemastra? If he played upon her sympathies to get her back here? He had almost killed her once. She had watched him behead King Imbris, had watched him kill Virgil in cold blood. She knew what he was capable of...

But no. She had refused to go with Ansel because some part of her, deep within, had wanted to believe that this was *her* Hale. The Hale who'd called her chickadee and slung an easy arm over her shoulder and spun her around with abandon under the flashing lights of a dance hall. Who had loved Sable and their Guild as much as she did. More.

Wren straightened, her decision made. For better or worse, she had staked her life on this friendship. On trusting another person. And if that was the decision that took her to her grave, she could live with it. Better to die with friends than live always alone.

Hale reached out a hand and twined his fingers through hers, squeezing. Wren bit back a sob at the comfort of the gesture. Warm and real and *Hale*. Though she had lost one brother, life had brought her another. And she wasn't about to lose him now.

Daemastra had mixed the final ingredient in his formula and had retrieved an eyedropper full of the clear liquid. The formula that would make him near invincible. The formula concocted from the broken lives and broken bodies of so many Gifted vintners and cuisiniers and confectioners. Faces and stories she would never know. She honored them anyway—said a silent apology.

Daemastra tilted his head back and emptied the eyedropper full of liquid into his mouth.

The man passed the jar and eyedropper to Willings next, who took his dose eagerly. She saw all of this out of the corner of her eye, but her focus was fixed with growing horror on Daemastra himself. The man hunched over, holding his stomach, steadying himself with one veiny hand on the countertop. A laugh escaped him, rattling Wren's bones. Then he straightened, and she saw that he had already begun to change. His shirt ripped as he grew taller. Broader. His features morphed to become more youthful, his hair darkening into a rich auburn, growing thicker. The strange tightness of his skin left him as it grew more supple and youthful. When the transformation was complete, an entirely different man stood before her. He was devastatingly handsome and fit, glowing with vitality and health. The man looked every inch a ruler—a warrior—a king—from the storybooks. No hint of Daemastra remained, except the eyes. Sharp and dark, glittering with triumph.

By the counter, Willings was clutching a silver tray, examining his reflection. His crooked teeth and pockmarked skin were gone—now he rivaled Hale's good looks, his hair as red as Ansel's.

Wren thought of the thin form of the emperor on the balcony during the coronation, his hand clutching the railing. It all became horribly clear. This was their new ruler. And his trusted right hand. There had been no need for them to overthrow the emperor, for Lucas to defeat or kill him. Because they were just doing this man a favor. Daemastra was their new emperor.

CHAPTER 48

When the sound of the battering ram against the door had ceased, a tiny glimmer of hope had bloomed in Olivia's chest. Were the attackers leaving? Retreating?

Thunk.

A different sound reached her ears—not the shuddering of a body against the door, but something more concentrated.

Olivia looked at Lennon and he shrugged, wiping the sweat from his forehead with a blood-streaked hand.

Thunk.

What was that sound?

The glinting blade of an axe appeared through the wood of the bookshelf, answering the question in each of their minds. The monstrous men outside were chopping down the door.

"Anyone have a bow and arrows?" Griff asked, looking around the room

They all shook their heads.

"Flaming too bad," Griff said, her shoulders deflating. Though the captain looked exhausted, she still held herself at the ready for whatever might come through that door.

Olivia tried to channel that resolute confidence, but terror's icy fingers pulled at her thoughts with a tenacious grip. Tears slid down her cheeks. In a few minutes she would be gone. Impaled on a sword. She wondered if it would hurt. Yes, it probably would. Badly.

The axe blade had formed a gaping hole now, and the face of a preternaturally handsome Aprican was visible on the other side, his straight, white teeth bared in challenge.

"Really wish I had a bow right now," Griff muttered.

Olivia backed up as the hole grew larger and splinters of wood flew at them with every strike of the wicked axe.

Marina's fingers gripped Olivia's painfully, but Olivia relished the feeling even as she clutched the slick short sword in her other hand. At least she wouldn't die alone. That was better than some people got.

The axe strikes stopped, the room falling strangely quiet but for the ragged breathing of the guild members.

And then the door exploded in towards them in a shower of wood and furniture.

Olivia cried out as a chair smashed into her legs, sending her sprawling onto her side. The sword clattered to the ground as it slipped from her hand.

A man was silhouetted in the doorway, dwarfing it with his huge bulk. He stepped inside, sword in one hand, axe in the other.

Olivia heard a whimper escape her lips.

The man strode forward towards Lennon, who held his sword before him in shaking hands.

Olivia squeezed her eyes closed. She couldn't watch as her friend died.

The ground shook with a thud and Olivia's eyes flew open. She struggled to comprehend what she saw. The huge brute of an Aprican soldier had tumbled forward, bowled into by a man in plain clothes. A bearded man—Dash.

"By the Beekeeper," Olivia breathed as Aprican soldiers flooded the room, falling into position behind Dash. But they weren't attacking the guild members or Ansel's mercenaries or Griff's sailors. They were attacking the huge soldier. Dash and the soldiers...were on their side!

Olivia scrambled back as the legionnaires swarmed the god-like soldier like ants at a picnic. Blood appeared from a dozen cuts as the soldier roared, moving with impossible speed, trying to take down his attackers. But they were too many.

He fell with a thunderous crash, and it was Dash himself who made the killing blow, surging forward and sliding his blade through the man's throat all the way to the hilt.

Dash pulled back as the soldier fell. He whirled about, his green eyes wild, his handsome face blood-speckled. "Olivia?" he called. "Has anyone seen Olivia?"

Olivia pushed to her feet, her heart spasming back to life within her. "Here I am," she said, her voice blessedly sure.

Dash's head whipped her way and a hand flew to his heart as he breathed out. "I thought...I thought I was too late."

She shook her head and then he was before her, his arms wrapping around her and lifting her off her feet, spinning her around with a whoop.

A disbelieving laugh escaped from her as she buried her face in his neck, reveling in the very real, very welcome presence of Dash.

Shouts sounded outside the door, and the muffled clash of metal sounded.

"What is that?" Trick asked, his eyes wild.

"If I knew, I would tell you," Lucas said, running a shaky hand through his hair. What the hell was he supposed to do now? Bran and his men had abandoned them, they were about to be skewered by two giants, and the emperor wasn't even the real threat. His spirits sank. It was over. They were done.

He shook his head at Trick. "It's over. Even with the emperor...there's no way we can beat Daemastra. All along, we were targeting the wrong man."

"I wouldn't be too hard on yourselves," the emperor said. "He outwitted me, and I had many more resources than you."

"What does he want?" Trick asked. "Can we bargain with him?"

The sounds of fighting were intensifying outside the door. Lucas strayed towards the door, straining his ears as the emperor answered. "He wants ultimate power. To be a god. To be invincible—and immortal."

"Is that all?" Trick snorted.

"I'm afraid there's no reasoning with him," the emperor finished.

The room shook as a crash sounded outside.

Trick crept up to the other side of the door, and they both placed their ears against the walls, listening. Faint voices were audible, but not the words.

The door handle jiggled and Trick met Lucas's gray eyes, his own wild. His breath caught, his inhale sharp. Who was trying to get in?

They both backed away, Trick pulling his bloodied sword from its sheath.

"I love you, little brother," Lucas said, widening his stance, bracing himself for what would come through that door.

"You too. I hope...Ella made it."

Lucas nodded. "She's a survivor. She'll be all right."

Lucas braced himself when a knock sounded on the door. Three polite raps. He straightened, letting his sword droop.

"Uh, who is it?" Lucas called.

"Thom!" a muffled voice said. Trick's eyes went wide, and his sword clanged to the floor as he reached for the crossbar to throw it back.

"Wait!" Lucas cried. "It could be a trap—"

But it was too late. Trick was pulling the door open.

Thom ran into the room, barreling into Trick with the force of a hurricane. They clung to each other, tears and muffled words mingled as they rocked back and forth.

Callidus walked in next, his pale face twisted in distaste as he wiped a knife blade on the sleeve of his black jacket.

Lucas shook his head in disbelief. "You—you were not who I expected."

Callidus sniffed, straightening his waistcoat. "Yes, well... I'm frequently underestimated."

Hale's fingers tightened painfully around Wren's as they beheld the monsters that the formula had wrought. Wren didn't care; the pain was the only thing keeping her grounded, keeping her fear from bearing her away on its rising tide.

"Willings, take these two back to the holding cell. We'll deal with them when the rest of the palace is secure."

"And you?" Willings asked.

"I'm off to visit my old friend, the emperor. I think it's time I help him lay down his heavy burdens."

Willings grinned and motioned to Wren and Hale, nodding towards the hallway. "Move."

Wren couldn't feel her body, couldn't seem to make it cooperate. Her breath came in ragged bursts.

"Come on, move!" Willings said, but then he coughed, grasping his chest with a hand. He seemed to steady himself, as whatever he had felt passed. He stood up straight again. And then his face...rippled.

Wren's eyes went wide. She looked at Daemastra, who was watching Willings with alarm.

"What is it?" Daemastra asked.

"I don't know," Willings said. "You tell me! It's your—" He coughed again, stumbling against the countertop.

Wren and Hale backed up, away from the man.

A groan of pain escaped Willings's mouth as his face rippled again. The high cheekbones, the thick hair and dewy skin—it all began to morph. A cry of agony escaped his lips and he fell to his knees, one hand to the ground, the other to his chest. When he pushed his head back, Wren gasped. He was getting older, his skin growing lined, sallow, sagging. His hair turned gray, his muscles shriveled, atrophying before their eyes. "What's happening?" Willings cried, but Daemastra launched into action, throwing open the icebox door, pulling out another two, three jars, cradling them to his chest.

"Hale," Wren breathed as Daemastra turned, because his face was rippling as well, the features undulating and morphing like a bubbling river.

Hale launched into action, running towards Daemastra, cracking the man across the jaw with a powerful punch.

Daemastra reeled back against the counter, the jars in his hands falling to the floor, shattering in an explosion of glass and liquid and dust.

Daemastra snarled and threw a punch of his own, sending Hale stumbling back towards her.

Wren shrank into the corner, not sure which scene was more appalling: Willings—writhing on the ground now, his limbs shriveled and weak, the skin of his face sunken like a corpse, or Hale and Daemastra grappling in a breathless contest of brute strength and violence.

Hale shoved Daemastra off him with a boot to the man's chest, and Daemastra fell back against the counter, slipping into the mess of broken glass and formula. The change was coming on quickly now and he let out the keening cry of an animal as the muscle and vitality and magic drained from him, taking his life essence with it.

Hale, his chest heaving like a stallion, backed up next to Wren. Her hands shook before her mouth. She was unable to look away from the unnatural magic ripping through the man before them.

Willings had stilled—his body skeletal—hardly human.

He was dead.

Daemastra fell to the floor, his hands scrabbling through the liquid and glass, leaving bloody streaks behind. "I don't understand," he said through twisted lips, through teeth rotting and falling.

Hale pushed forward, walking to just beyond Daemastra's reach. He crouched down, looking at the pitiful wreck the man had become. "Compliments of the Spicer's Guild. A gift from Guildmaster Pike himself. The magic of time. Fast-forwarded."

Daemastra let out a garbled wail of fury. The keen grew quiet, then snuffed out.

The man's shriveled head thunked to the tile floor.

A sob escaped Wren's lips, and she closed her eyes, relief flooding her with such strength that her knees went weak.

Hale was at her side in two strides, and he wrapped his arms around her. "It's all right chickadee," he soothed, stroking her hair, which only made her cry more.

Joy and sorrow, relief and regret mingled together with the scent of Hale in the sweetest combination of all.

"Wren!" a voice cried from the doorway, and Wren looked up to find

Lucas and Trick, flanked by Thom and Callidus, looking aghast at the desiccated bodies on the ground.

"Lucas!" she cried and ran to him, crashing against him, crushing him in a hug as tight as she could make it. It didn't matter that he might still hate her. It only mattered that he was alive.

"Gods, Wren, I thought..." Lucas breathed out, burying his face in her hair, cradling her head, stroking her back. "When we learned what Daemastra was doing...gods. I thought I was going to be too late."

"You almost were," she said, releasing him. "But Hale saved me. He saved all of us."

Hale and Lucas looked at each other across the room, a whirlwind of emotions between them.

They had been on opposite sides. Hale had helped the Apricans murder the rest of Lucas's family. He had killed Virgil himself. She didn't know if Lucas could set that aside. Could ever see him as anything but an enemy.

Lucas untwined his arms from around her and walked stiffly to stand before Hale. He looked down, blowing out a breath.

Hale regarded him with wariness.

"I used to think I knew what was right and what was wrong, that everything was black and white. I don't have those compunctions anymore. I've learned there're only people you can count on, no matter how dark it gets, how bad it looks. And everyone else. If what Wren says is true, then you have my thanks."

Hale nodded.

Wren fought back the tears that were threatening to pour from her. And then a thought struck her like a bolt of lightning. "The poison," she said. "Hale, Daemastra said without his antidote taken each day, you'll die."

Hale nodded but walked across the room, stepping over Daemastra's body to open one of the cabinets. He retrieved a vial, and then pulled another vial out of his pocket. He poured a few drops of the one from his pocket into the other. "Another gift from Guildmaster Pike. The real infusion Daemastra was looking for. The one that slows time to a crawl. The one that makes something permanent." He threw back the antidote, drinking it down.

The black lines in his hands began to recede and disappear, leaving healthy tanned flesh in their wake. It was a miracle. The Spicer's Guild potion had made the antidote permanent.

"Don't worry about me, Wren," Hale said with a tired wink. "I have a way of getting lucky."

CHAPTER 49

They walked through the palace slowly, stepping past limp and shriveled bodies that had once been Daemastra's supernatural soldiers. Lucas had his arm slung around Wren's shoulders, refusing to break contact. That was just fine with her. She didn't think she ever wanted to leave his side.

"I thought you were dead twice over," she murmured into his shirt. "I can't believe you're really here. That it's really over."

"Callidus saved me," Lucas said. "And Thom."

"What?" she asked, turning to Callidus in disbelief.

He nodded sagely, a smile tugging the corner of his thin lips. "The Confectioner's Guild doesn't leave any behind."

Wren looked from Callidus to Hale as gratitude flooded through her like a shot of powerful whiskey. "No. It doesn't."

Callidus looked at Hale for an inscrutable second before nodding, clapping Hale on the shoulder. "No one's insulted my suits in at least a week. Welcome back, Mr. Firena."

Hale just grinned.

With each step, they gathered more allies.

"Where did all these legionnaires come from?" Wren asked, marveling at the uniformed men who fell into step behind them.

"It seems Dash didn't betray us after all. He stayed behind to rally some friends to our cause," Thom said, his hand intertwined with Trick's.

The emperor met them in the junction of the hallways.

"Will you honor your promise?" Lucas asked, one hand tightening on his sword, the other wrapped protectively around Wren. "Will you surrender?"

"You've rid us of my troublesome cuisinier?" the emperor asked, raising one furry eyebrow.

"He rid us of himself," Hale responded. "With his lust for power."

The emperor nodded, straightening. "Then I don't have long before that wretched poison takes me. Yes, Lucas Imbris. I surrender to you. Alesia is yours, and Tamros, if you can take it. The Apricans are a troublesome bunch, so I wouldn't suggest trying to extend your influence so far."

"All I want is Alesia," Lucas said. "So I can give it back to the people."

"Very well," the emperor said. He raised his voice. "Let it be known that on this day, I cede my claim to the country of Alesia to King Lucas Imbris."

"Thank you," Lucas said.

Wren squeezed his hand, fighting back tears.

They walked together towards the palace gates, past the bodies of fallen Aprican and guild guards alike. "I don't have much time," the emperor said. "I need to get my affairs in order."

"You know," Hale said as he stepped forward, "I think I might have a remedy for what ails you."

"Do tell," the emperor said, drawing nearer.

But a group of people running through the front doors drew Wren's attention. Olivia and Dash and Ella. And so many more, people she hadn't seen in weeks—Lennon and Marina and Chandler and Bruxius and all the rest. Guildmaster Pike, with one arm around Griff's shoulders, the other in a sling. His legs were shaky and his face pinched in pain, but he was alive.

Wren ran to him and wrapped careful arms around him, pulling him tight.

"I heard a commotion and I thought I'd take a peek," Pike said. "I found this one looking like a wild banshee."

Griff laughed before her eyes went wide. "Excuse me," she said. "I think I just saw a ghost."

Wren looked back as she watched Griff stride up to Hale, punching him in the arm with all her might.

Wren turned back to Pike, smoothing his hair back from his slick brow. She saw that the arm strapped to his chest was missing from the elbow down. The little jar in the workshop... When she spoke her words were quiet. Reverent. "What you did...what you sacrificed...you saved us all. Every last one of us."

"I just did what she would have done," Pike said, his voice hoarse.

Wren pulled him back into a hug, kissing him on the cheek. "It's the best any of us can do," she whispered.

She turned back from Pike, the scene glittering through refracted tears. Hugs and tears and kisses were being passed around, and Wren was surprised to find herself in Ella's arms next, the princess squeezing her soundly. "Thank you. For Maradis," she said, then she turned away, no doubt before she was caught with her icy demeanor down.

"Lucas," Ella called.

Lucas strode over from where he was shaking hands with a bloodied-but-whole Guildmaster Chandler.

"Look what I found." Ella pulled an emerald cloth out from under her arm. "Would you like to do the honors?"

Wren peered around Lucas's shoulder trying to decipher what the siblings had exchanged.

"You know, I always resented this thing," Lucas said. "But I think I never understood the cost. Come on."

Lucas pulled her through the gaping front doors of the palace into the courtyard, where the first glimpse of morning sun was peeking over the eastern horizon, highlighting the snowcapped crags of the Cascadian mountains. Into the courtyard. To the flagpole that flew a sky-blue flag stitched with a golden sunburst.

"Hold this?" Lucas handed the green cloth to her. He untied the rope, and hand over hand, pulled the Aprican flag down.

Wren handed back the bundle and watched with tears in her eyes as Lucas replaced the flag with the emerald green banner of Alesia.

Lucas hoisted it up to cheers and clapping from the people gathered below, finally tying off the rope as the flag reached the top of the pole. He wrapped his arm back around Wren's shoulders, kissing her temple. She hadn't realized the cost either. Until now. This was her home. These were her people. And there wasn't anything she wouldn't give for them.

The flag cracked in the breeze, billowing open to display a silver Imbris falcon in flight emblazoned across the middle. Wren felt her heart soar with it—into the dawn of a new day.

EPILOGUE

"A little higher," Wren said, squinting into the morning sun, eying the banner. "The left side's a little low. Just an inch..."

"Good?" Lucas asked.

"My arms are getting tired," Thom complained.

"Perfect!" Wren cried.

Thom and Lucas stood on two chairs, tying off the ropes that held a bright pink banner fluttering over the door of the shop. *Grand Opening*, it announced boldly.

Lucas hopped down, striding over, snaking his arms around Wren's waist from behind as he surveyed his and Thom's handiwork over her head. She leaned back into him, admiring the view as Thom joined them too, dusting off his hands. "Cake & Cone." Thom read the wooden sign emblazoned above the banner. "Infused and Artisanal Ice Cream and Confections. I still think we should have gone with Cone & Cake."

Wren rolled her eyes. "We flipped a coin! My suggestion won."

"About that. How do I know you weren't...influencing the coin?" Thom raised an eyebrow.

Wren opened her mouth in mock affront. "Are you suggesting I would use my luck to influence something so important as the name of our shop? I am outraged at the suggestion."

Lucas chuckled, his chest rumbling pleasantly against her.

"Maradis's first shop for infused goods. It's a new era," Lucas said, tactfully changing the subject.

"And we're so pleased to have the king's personal endorsement." Thom inclined his head.

Lucas groaned. "Please don't call me that. It's bad enough to have the entire Guild and Nobles' Councils lurking around every corner, trying to ingratiate themselves with me! I keep telling them that I'm only standing in until the election, and then I'll have zero power over anything."

"I don't know," Wren said, turning in Lucas's arms and kissing him on the cheek. "You have some sort of power over me."

He grinned. "A power I must only use for good."

"I don't know." A sly smile curved across her lips. "Maybe you could use it for bad."

Lucas's response was lost as a new voice joined them. "Ew," Trick said, walking up, a brown paper package under one arm. "There's nothing more tacky than a public display of affection," he said before wrapping his arms around Thom and dipping him back, giving him a thorough kiss.

Thom's cheeks were red as Trick let him back up for air—his smile ear-to-ear.

"Thanks for coming," Wren said.

Trick handed her the package. "A christening present for your new baby," he said, nodding towards the shop.

"Aww. Should I open it now?" Wren asked.

He nodded, and Lucas unwound his arms from her as she pulled the brown paper off of the gift. She opened the box and lifted out a crisp white linen apron embroidered in silver thread with the diamond logo of her and Thom's new shop, a stylized ice cream cone on the bottom, a swirl of cupcake frosting on the top.

Wren pressed her hand to her heart. "I love it, Trick."

Thom and Trick wore matching grins. "He already gave me mine," Thom said. "Aren't they cool?"

Wren pulled the apron over her head, tying it over her lavender dress.

"You know, I have a present for you too," Lucas said, taking one of her hands, the other reaching in his pocket to pull out a little blue velvet box.

"You helped so much with the shop, even with all your other duties," Wren said, touched but wary about the size of that box. Though the past few peaceful months with Lucas had felt like a dream, she didn't think she was ready for what kind of step came in boxes of that size—that shape.

"I wanted to." He handed it to her.

Wren took in a breath as she opened the lid, the hinge creaking. A silver key lay inside.

She looked at him with surprise. "What's this?"

Thom and Trick were trying to act nonchalant and give them a moment, but she could tell out of the corner of her eye that they were watching with keen interest.

"I got a new apartment," Lucas said. "I don't like living in the palace, and I won't after the election. This new place is bigger than my old one. Big enough for two. I thought...maybe you'd like to live there with me."

Wren's mouth formed a little O as relief welled in her. "You're asking me to move in with you?" she asked, delight swirling within her like molten chocolate.

"Would you?" Lucas asked, nerves written across his face.

"Of course!" she cried, throwing her arms around him. "I'd love to!"

Lucas swung her around once before putting her down and giving her a kiss.

Wren shoved an auburn curl out of her face. "I thought...well, never mind. I'd love to move in."

Thom let out a barking laugh. "My god, man! I thought you were proposing!"

"Proposing?" Lucas looked at Thom with horror, then back to Wren. "Did you think...? Did you want...?"

She shook her head. "I think moving in is the perfect first step."

"Next time don't go for the ring box, brother." Trick clapped Lucas on his shoulder.

Wren just laughed, holding the box to her chest.

"Should we go in?" Lucas asked, running a hand through his salt-and-pepper hair. "Please, something to put me out of my misery."

Wren nodded and with a smile pushed her way into the shop. The silver bell tinkled as the door opened. She looked over the inside with a swell of pride. She and Thom had designed the entire shop themselves, from the whitewashed brick wall to the funky iron chandeliers that hung from the soaring rafters to the tables crafted from gnarled wood from the Cascadian foothills. A chalkboard behind the counter announced their day's offerings: Thom's newly dreamed-up flavors of ice cream on the left, her cupcakes and confections on the right. A sleek silver espresso machine nestled against the back counter, offering whatever else a Maradis native might need.

The bell tinkled again and Wren turned to find Callidus and Olivia stepping through the door. Despite the unseasonably warm February day, Callidus was swathed in a black pinstripe suit, his ebony hair in a perfect coif. Olivia wore a bright coral dress cinched with a leather belt, her blonde curls bouncing. She gave Wren a tight embrace. "Are we your first customers?"

"Very first," Wren said.

"Dash is sorry he couldn't make it," Olivia said. "He's buried with a new crop of recruits." Dash had been promoted to captain of the Cedar Guard and was busy trying to replenish the ranks the invasion had decimated.

Wren waved a hand. "He'll have plenty of chances to come by. Tell him we missed him. What can we get you?"

"I want a scoop of the lemon basil sorbet Thom has refused to shut up about," Olivia said.

"Right this way, ma'am," Thom joked as he walked around the counter, brandishing a silver ice cream scoop.

"And what can I get for you?" Wren asked Callidus with only a touch of hesitation. Things had been strange between them since Wren and Thom had announced they were leaving the Guildhall. Not bad, but...there were words unsaid.

"A cupcake, I think," Callidus said. "Maybe one of those rose ones." He nodded towards cupcakes frosted like blushing roses crowning the three-tiered display on the counter.

She looked back at him and let out a disbelieving laugh. "Really?"

A smile broke across his face. It was so uncommon, it touched her. "I hear they're to die for."

Wren smacked her hand against her forehead, groaning. "That's terrible."

A laugh escaped him. "I couldn't resist. I was sad, you know, when you said you were leaving. But now... This suits you, Wren. I'm happy for you."

"Thank you," she whispered, overcome with emotion. How far they'd come together. What they'd been through. She'd never really thought she'd end up here. Happy.

"The Guild's door is always open, you know. For both of you."

"Will you be all right?" Wren asked.

"Oh yes." Callidus waved a hand. "Olivia and Marina could run the place in their sleep. Though with the gold we sent to the Red Badger, we'll have to tighten our belt for a year or so."

Wren snorted. "I still don't think we should have paid Ansel anything."

"I debated. But he did help us get into the palace. Him and Griff and the men and women who follow them. We couldn't have done it without them. So I sent him half."

Wren had received a letter from Ansel a month ago, admitting he'd been wrong to doubt her, and wishing her happiness. She found she hoped for the same, for him.

Callidus continued. "But don't you worry about us. We'll be fine. Though things certainly are less exciting without you and Thom and Hale around."

The mention of Hale brought another wistful smile to her face. "Have you heard from him?" she asked. She had stood on the docks just two days ago, waving goodbye as Hale had stood on the deck of the Sea Witch, Griff's flagship, waving back at her. It turned out he and Griff had known each other back when they'd been young. Hale had decided he needed some time away from the Guild to find himself again. Away from Maradis and the memories it held.

"Not yet, but they shouldn't get to Centa Kana for another day. He promised to write from there," Callidus said. "At least we know Griff will keep him in line."

"She said she was going to make him work to pay his way. Can you imagine?" Wren laughed. "Hale doing hard labor?"

"It'll be good for him," Callidus said.

"Agreed." Wren nodded. She understood Hale needing to get away.

And she knew, she felt it in her bones, that when he was ready, he would come back to them. When he put himself back together again.

The bell tinkled and a family walked in—a blonde woman with two young boys. "Are you open?" the woman asked.

"Absolutely," Wren said.

"I'll let you get to your customers," Callidus whispered, and Wren nodded, hurrying behind the counter.

"What can I get you?" Wren asked as the two boys moved forward, grubby fingers pressed against the cool glass of the ice cream case. The mother smiled, her hand lingering on one of the boy's tawny heads.

"Is it really magic?" One of the boys looked up at her, his green eyes as wide as saucers.

"It is." Wren nodded. "The magic flavors are marked with the little magic wand."

"I want to be magic when I grow up," the other boy said.

"It's all he talks about." The mother offered an apologetic smile.

"Well," Wren said, leaning down, "I think that's a perfect plan. Because in Alesia, you can be an inspector, or a priest, or a pirate. Or if you believe hard enough, you can be a magic confectioner. In Alesia, you can be anything you want."

THE END

FROM THE AUTHOR

Thank you so much for taking the time to read *The Confectioner's Truth!* I hope you've enjoyed reading about Wren's adventures as much as I enjoyed writing them!

Reader reviews are incredibly important to indie authors like me, and so it would mean the world to me if you took a few minutes to leave an honest review wherever you buy books online. It doesn't have to be much; a few words can make the difference in helping a future reader give the book a chance.

If you're interested in receiving updates, giveaways, and advanced copies of upcoming books, sign up for my mailing list at

www.claireluana.com.

As a thank you for signing up, you will receive a free ebook!

ABOUT THE AUTHOR

Claire Luana grew up reading everything she could get her hands on and writing every chance she could. Eventually, adulthood won out, and she turned her writing talents to more scholarly pursuits, going to work as a commercial litigation attorney. While continuing to practice law, Claire decided to return to her roots and try her hand once again at creative writing. She has written and published the Moonburner Cycle and the Confectioner Chronicles and is currently working on several new fantasy series. She lives in Seattle, Washington with her husband and two dogs. In her (little) remaining spare time, she loves to hike, travel, binge-watch CW shows, and of course, fall into a good book.

Connect with Claire Luana online at:

Website & Blog: www.claireluana.com

Facebook: www.facebook.com/claireluana

Twitter: www.twitter.com/clairedeluana

Goodreads:
www.goodreads.com/author/show/15207082.Claire_Luana

Amazon: www.amazon.com/Claire-Luana/e/B01F28F3W4

Instagram: www.instagram.com/claireluana

Check out these other reads by CLAIRE LUANA

The Moonburner Cycle
Moonburner, Book One
Sunburner, Book Two
Starburner, Book Three
Burning Fate, Prequel

The Confectioner Chronicles
The Confectioner's Guild, Book One
The Confectioner's Coup, Book Two
The Confectioner's Truth, Book Three
The Confectioner's Exile, Prequel

The Knights of Caerleon Trilogy
The Fifth Knight, Book One
The Third Curse, Book Two
The First Gwenevere, Book Three

54150573R00187

Made in the USA
Columbia, SC
26 March 2019